Action at Aquila

By Hervey Allen

NATAL PUBLISHING LLC
ARS LONGA, VITA BREVIS

CHARACTERS OF THE STORY

COLONEL NATHANIEL T. FRANKLIN, commanding 6th Pennsylvania Cavalry

LIEUTENANT-COLONEL JOHN COLSON, second in command 6th Pennsylvania Cavalry

THEOPHILUS CARTER, merchant of Kennett Square

GENERAL JOHN FITHIAN, officer of State Militia and veteran of Mexican War

LIEUTENANT JONATHAN MOLTAN, of the State Fencibles

ARTHUR BIDDLE, gentleman, member of Philadelphia Union League Club

DR. DAVID CRAIG, an old Philadelphia physician

MAJOR DOUGLAS CHARLES CRITTENDON, C.S.A., formerly U. S. A., a Virginian of General Early's staff

MRS. MARTHA CRITTENDON, Major Crittendon's mother

MRS. ELIZABETH CRITTENDON, Major Crittendon's wife, an Englishwoman

MARGARET CRITTENDON, Major Crittendon's daughter

GENERAL PHILIP HENRY SHERIDAN, U. S. A., commanding Department of the Middle

BLACK GIRL, Colonel Franklin's black mare

JAMES BUCHANAN, ex-President of the United States

WILLIAM CRAWFORD, his white servant

URIAH H. MYERS, printer to the state of Pennsylvania

MRS. HELEN MYERS, his wife

MRS. ANNA GILL, blind woman, mother-in-law of U. H. Myers

CLAUDIUS, or "CLOUD," a contraband servant to the Myerses

MR. AND MRS. BLACK, of Harrisburg, Pa.

"JUDGE" TENER BRISTLINE, a Pennsylvania politician and lawyer

MRS. RUSSEL, a Fulton Valley, Pa., farmer's wife

MRS. MACNAUGHTON, a Fulton Valley, Pa., farmer's wife

HELEN MCNAIR, a Fulton Valley, Pa., farmer's daughter

MRS. MCLANE, a Fulton Valley, Pa., farmer's wife

SERGEANT SMITH, of Kanawha Zouaves (guerrillas)

SERGEANT KILLYKELLY, non-com in Kanawha Zouaves

JOHNSON, a Kanawha Zouave

MERRYWEATHER DUANE, proprietor of Morgan Springs, a West Virginia spa

AGATHA DUANE, his daughter

MARY DUANE, Agatha's sister

WILLIAM FARFAR, a mountain boy

JUDGE WASHINGTON, a principal inhabitant of Morgan Springs

LIEUTENANT DONALD SWEENEY, of 23rd Illinois Infantry

SERGEANT COLFAX, Q.M.C., U. S. A.

MADAM O'RILEY, a patriotic whore

MR. PERKINS, her patriotic pimp

CAPTAIN FETTER KERR, adjutant 6th Pennsylvania Cavalry

PAUL CRITTENDON, Major Crittendon's nephew

MARY CRITTENDON; TIM CRITTENDON, young children, sister and brother to Paul Crittendon

REVEREND JAMES KISKADDEN, a Cumberland Presbyterian mountain preacher

FLOSSIE KISKADDEN, his daughter

FELIX MANN, sutler to 6th Pennsylvania Cavalry

DUDLEY, Colonel Franklin's orderly

MIDGE, Margaret Crittendon's pony

MAJOR MATHIS LATOUCHE, C.S.A.

LIEUTENANT LYMAN DE WOLF DORR, of "Star Battery" of Providence, R. I.

DR. HUGER WILSON, surgeon of Confederate Army Culpepper, a contraband negro servant

CHARACTERS, MINOR OR REFERRED TO

GOVERNOR ANDREW G. CURTIN, war governor of Pennsylvania

JOHN MARSHALL

GENERAL JUBAL A. EARLY, C.S.A., commanding Confederate forces in the Valley of Virginia

COLONEL LUDWIG REINOHLFENNIG, cavalry leader of Pennsylvania Dutch "bummers"

W. H. THOMPSON, manager United States Hotel in Harrisburg

MRS. PATTERSON, old lady on the Old York Road

JOHN PATTERSON, her son

MRS. TUBB, a milliner

THADDEUS STEVENS, a Member of Congress from Pennsylvania

TELFARE, a young Confederate soldier from Ninety-Six, S. C.

SERGEANT JIM RUSSELL, 6th Pennsylvania Cavalry

ALICE CARY, a former sweetheart of Colonel Franklin

WILLIAM E. BURTON, actor and theatre manager

COLONEL JIM MULLIGAN, commanding officer 23rd Illinois Infantry

GENERAL ALFRED THOMAS TORBERT, a federal cavalry leader

JAMES CRITTENDON, Major Crittendon's brother

ANN CRITTENDON, his wife

UNCLE FREER, of Melton Mowbray, England

CAPTAIN THATCHER, "D" troop, 6th Pennsylvania Cavalry

REVEREND JOHN MCCUTCHEON, of Standing Stone, Pa.

ABRAHAM LINCOLN

GENERAL ULYSSES S. GRANT

ANDREW JOHNSON

IAN MACINTOSH, drummer

MAJOR JEPSON, on governor's staff, a newspaper editor

Note: "THE VALLEY" *is the Valley of Virginia, also known as the Shenandoah Valley. Other valleys are either referred to by name or spelled with a small letter.*

Owing to the way in which the Shenandoah River flows, directions in the Valley of Virginia are reversed from the normal order of "down South" *and* "up North." *In the Valley* "up" *means south, and* "down" *north.*

CHAPTER I

THE CITY OF BROTHERLY LOVE

Southward, two mighty ranges of the Appalachians shouldered their way into the blue distance like tremendous caravans marching across eternity. Between those parallel ridges the Valley of the Shenandoah lay, apparently, as serene and beautiful as the interior of the Isle of Aves.

From a high shoulder of the Blue Ridge, where Colonel Nathaniel Franklin of the 6th Pennsylvania Cavalry had stopped for a moment to breathe his horse, he could see almost into North Carolina. "Rebel country," for the Confederates still held the upper part of the Valley and the horizons beyond.

Not that the colonel thought of it as rebel country, exactly. The sight of that magnificent landscape--despite its great beauty, perhaps because of it--brought to his eyes a mist of sorrow that threatened momentarily to overcast the countryside which rolled away southward before him. He brushed that mist indignantly away--and swore softly. He regarded all the country he was looking at as still a part of the United States, some of the inhabitants of which needed to be reconverted to the faith of their fathers--by apostolic blows and knocks if necessary. But there was nothing personal about the process to the colonel. The problem posed by the horizons rolling before him was, he liked to think, purely a military one. And in the old days he had had too many true friends on the yon side of the Potomac to lump them all under the one indignant epithet of "rebels," even now, after several years of desperate fighting.

There were not many Americans left, however, who still felt as the colonel did. He was naturally possessed of that state of being which in the eighteenth century would have been described as an amiable soul. There was nothing weak about his amiability, but it did make hate and blind bitterness about anything hard to bear. Now, in the early autumn of 1864, he sat looking down into the peaceful, because devastated, theatre of civil war with a dull ache about his heart.

He was too far up on the mountain for much of the particular devastation in the Valley to be noticeable. Here and there a gaunt chimney rising houseless and steeple-like amid the distant fields and woods showed where a farm or manor house had been burned. But the fields had not been out of cultivation long enough to make much difference in the general view. Over the enormous checkerboard of meadow and forest below him the drifting shadows of lofty cumulonimbus clouds conferred upon the Valley a kind of dream-life of its own, as though it mirrored the visions passing in some almighty brain. Five miles down and away he could see the white tents of his own command conspicuously dotted along the border of Aquila Creek.[1]

[1] Pronounced: *Ah-wy'-la.*

Nearer yet, from a great meadow laid like a green table-cloth in the midst of tiny hills, came the flash of weapons and accoutrements, a kind of sinister blink that followed small, black lines of mounted men manœuvring in a cavalry drill. Colson, his second in command, was putting the regiment through its paces down there. He watched the squadron flash into a charge. The sound of the mass yell, which was meant to be furious and to frighten an enemy, drifted up to him. At that height it sounded innocuous and childish, like the yells of boys playing Indians. Then the sudden voice of a bugle sounding recall died away into shivering echoes that lost themselves eventually in a thousand folds of the mountain walls.

Someone might have been sounding taps over the Valley, the colonel thought. The silence that followed was ominous.

It was accentuated rather than broken by the rushing lament of a mountain stream only a short distance down the road at the ford below. For a while the man on the black horse sat like a statue at gaze over the Valley, unable to rouse himself from a melancholy--perhaps an unsoldierly--but under the circumstances a natural enough reverie. Thought is swifter than lightning. Perhaps its fluid nature is essentially the same. In a flash, as it were, while he sat breathing his horse and looking down from that giant height at his men manœuvring below in the Valley, the scenes of the past few weeks--the faces and places, the houses, the roads, and the very sound of voices--flowed through his mind . . .

In half an hour the colonel would be back with his men again. What that implied he knew only too well; relentless vigilance, and the constant anxiety of commanding in the face of the enemy. He was just returning from a long leave of absence. This pause on the crest of the ridge was not only a breathing space for his horse. It was also his last opportunity to let his mind range back freely over the memories of home and the immediate past. That is not to say he was being sentimental. To tell the truth he was troubled, even perplexed, by some of the happenings of the past few weeks. Home as found had not been home exactly as he had expected to find it. The sight of the camp below had brought the end of his leave forcibly to mind. It was only natural that his thoughts should flash back along the trail behind him to linger for a few moments upon what had been for him a memorable experience.

It had been his first leave since 1861. He had been looking forward to it for years, he remembered. Twice it had been revoked just on the eve of a great battle. Finally, he had given up any hope of getting home at all. War and the life of the army had at last eclipsed the memory and even the desire for another kind of existence. He had learned to live with the past and future cancelled. And in three unforgettable years he had seen a deal of active service and rapid promotion.

He had been shot off his horse at Antietam and had a horse shot under him at Gettysburg. A sharpshooter had drilled a hole through the top of his campaign hat during a skirmish at Winchester only two months before. The graves of his friends and those of his men were scattered all over eastern Virginia, clear up into Pennsylvania. Even the infantry admitted that Colonel Nat Franklin was one cavalryman who was a genuine fighting man.

For its fine service in the Valley of Virginia his regiment had lately been nicknamed "Sheridan's Eyes." It was composed largely of woodsmen and scouts and was in almost constant touch with the enemy whenever any movement was afoot. It was during a lull in the fighting at the end of the summer of 1864, while his regiment was camping in the Valley, for once peacefully, that he had again applied for a furlough. He had hardly hoped that it would be granted. He had simply taken a chance. And then, quite unexpectedly, the furlough had come back promptly, approved by General Sheridan himself.

Three days later Colonel Franklin was back home again, not far from Philadelphia, in the old Pennsylvania village of Kennett Square.

His was the quietest home-coming possible. He could not even expect a family welcome. He was a bachelor. Most of his relatives lived elsewhere, and he had been an only child. Both father and mother had died some years before; his mother when he was still a boy, and his father while the colonel had been prospecting in the Far West and doing some unavoidable Indian fighting on the side. There had been six years of that before he had returned to take over the old place at Kennett Square and tried to drop back into the quiet ways of profitable Pennsylvania farming in a large and gentlemanly way. Then the call to arms had come when Sumter was fired on. He had been among the first to go.

So he was prepared to find the big stone farmhouse at Kennett Square lonely. It was inevitable that it should be. He still looked forward to changing that as soon as the war was over. Circumstances, he reflected, had prevented him thus far. His life had been too adventurous, too full of shifting incident to undertake the greatest adventure of all. But he was young yet. The prime of life still lay before him, he felt. And there might be several who would be glad to share in what, at worst, could be considered a prosperous life partnership. He hated to think of it in just that way. There had been Alice Gary, for instance. He might have been happy with her. He had almost reached an understanding with her just before Sumter was fired on.

Then the war had gone on and on. Alice had finally married a well-to-do neighbour, a very respectable fellow. He couldn't blame her. After all, what the colonel hadn't been able to do was simply to make a good bargain out of life, even the best of bargains. That was why he had hesitated. And yet it might come to that yet. Here he was in the fourth year of conflict returning to his regiment, and the war still seemed interminable.

That was one reason why the old house had seemed even lonelier than he had expected. There was no longer much to look forward to there. Its future did appear doubtful. Only the past had drawn him back to it. He knew that now. And yet that was not sufficient to explain why he had actually been glad to leave home again after only a week's stay.

What he hadn't expected to find, what had caused him to leave Kennett Square so soon, was a certain covert hostility on the part of some of his neighbours. Probably it was partly political. His father had been a great Democrat, a close friend and staunch supporter of President Buchanan. He had constantly opposed and deprecated the agitation of abolition, regarding it as the cause of inevitable conflict. In the Quaker community about Kennett Square that might still be remembered against his father's son. That there was nothing immediately personal about this "hostility," the colonel felt morally certain. People generally liked him. He had a warm heart combined with a decided strength of character. He was genially social. That made for popularity. Nevertheless, somehow, somewhere the colonel felt a gulf had opened between him and his neighbours.

Perhaps he had been out West and in the army too long to drop back into a settled way of civil life, with all of its emphasis upon property and petty local prejudices, without feeling a certain lack of air. At any rate, he soon had the sensation of being stifled. He tended to regard men now for what they were rather than for what they had. Probably some of his fellow townsmen resented it. War, battle, is a very special experience, and like a good many other soldiers back on leave, the colonel found that he was no longer quite able to explain himself even to old family friends. Above all he missed the easy tolerance of the spacious days before the war. Everybody seemed to have made up his mind now about everything--and to have closed it.

But if his Quaker acquaintances were inclined to look at his politics and even his army service somewhat askance, he was even less prepared for the virulent and white-hot hatred of the enemy made vocal by the sacred patriots and angry taxpayers of his once kindly native community. Frequent ferocious proposals for the disposal of Southern leaders, the grim personal hatred expressed for all rebels, for example, both surprised and annoyed him.

"I've only been fighting them," he would say in a half-deprecatory way when his lack of enthusiasm over a proposal "to hang the rebel cabinet in chains," or some similar suggestion, caused a lifting of fervent eyebrows to which he did not respond. "Come help us catch them," finally became his favourite rejoinder when too hard pressed. Few of his friends seemed to relish the twinkle in his eye at such times.

"Sir," said one of them, a particularly pompous and healthy merchant of his own town, when this invitation was extended to him, "I am already represented in the army by three bounty men and I feel I have more than done my duty. I might have bought government bonds, you know, instead of just sending out the last two men."

"Why, so you might," said the colonel, "so you might! And think of the interest you're losing. Why, Carter, it's damned noble of you! Let me shake you by the hand. No, no, the other one--the one that's losing the interest. I don't suppose you let the right hand know what the left hand is doing under such circumstances. Do you, Mr. Carter?" And he had left that respectable gentleman not a little confused, with both hands sticking out--and unshaken.

Suddenly all this had become quite intolerable to the colonel.

He had intended to spend most of his leave at home, but he could no longer, under the circumstances, think of wasting the precious month of it that still remained trying to explain himself to sullen neighbours and doubtful friends. What he needed above all was change and relaxation. To tell the truth, a little conviviality. So quite suddenly he wound up his affairs at Kennett Square, rented the farm, sold some of the animals--and without saying anything or good-bye to anybody, he had the bays hitched to the trap before sunrise one morning and set out for Philadelphia.

It was then nearly the end of September and for the first time that autumn there was the hint of frost to come in the early morning air. Also, for the first time since the colonel had been home on leave, he felt happy and carefree, almost boyish. He would even have liked to sing. But he knew too many sedate people along the Philadelphia road to permit himself to break out into a rich baritone at that hour of the morning--and just on the outskirts of Media! It might cause comment. He was in uniform and conspicuous enough already. A striking figure, in fact, in his campaign hat with its tarnished gold cord and acorns, with his large humorous mouth, sun-puckered eyes to match, and full black burnsides carefully cultivated to conceal a youthful expression that might not be quite impressive enough for a colonel of cavalry. It would never do for the colonel of the 6th Pennsylvania to look as young as he felt. Just as it would never do to break into song at that hour of the morning. Someone would certainly look out of the window and say, "There goes Nathaniel Franklin, and he's been drinking." "Drinking again," is the way they would say it. He knew them, those noses flattened against the pane, sniffing. Well, he would soon be shut of them all and fighting in the open again. Just then, however, he compromised by whistling instead of singing--and driving like the devil.

The morning road over the hills led from one cheerful vista to another. The brisk dawn air in the vicinity of Sharon Hill was exhilarating. He let the team have their heads and tore down the old Pike in the direction of Philadelphia with the sunrise glittering on the spokes of his wheels. As the roofs and flashing windows of the city came in sight--with Kennett Square and all that miles behind him--he felt relieved, convinced he was doing wisely, at home in the once-familiar, civilian world again. In short, his own old self, as he put it.

He didn't know exactly how or where he was going to spend the rest of his leave. He was just going to let it happen. First he intended to dispose of the team of bays. They had been eating their heads off at home. Then he had some errands to do. He wanted to get himself the finest saddle horse available, for he had been riding nothing but sorry nags since his old horse had been shot under him at Gettsyburg. Also, for a quite important but purely private reason, he wanted to get a haversackful of toys.

That reason was a pleasant secret, one which caused him to smile as he watched the servant-girls flooding the sidewalks from hydrants and scrubbing the white marble steps while he rattled over the cobbles along Chestnut Street. It was still early. He ought to have plenty of time to get things done before the heat of the day began.

He soon disposed of his team and the trap for a fair price at a livery stable, and light-heartedly set out to get the toys and look up his old friends. In the City of Brotherly Love, among other things he hoped to find that the patriotic rhetoric, with which nearly everyone now seemed to address a veteran on furlough, would at least be a little less bloodthirsty than in his own formerly peaceful neighbourhood. But in this mild hope he was disappointed. For whom should he encounter at the corner of Broad and Chestnut streets but his father's friend, old General John Fithian, a hearty veteran of the late Mexican War, and as fire-eating a commander of home-guard militia as ever ruined a white marble doorstep with broad yellow stains.

"A sight for sore eyes," roared the general, shifting his quid and bushy eyebrows in genuine and cordial excitement. "Why, what brings you back from the front, you young Hector? We've been hearing great things about you. What can I do for you? Where are you bound for?"

"I'm looking for a toy-store," said the colonel almost inadvertently, and somewhat annoyed. For the old general was a picturesque figure; the colonel was in uniform himself, and a crowd of idlers sensing the unusual had begun to surround them.

"Toy-store?" bellowed the older man, looking shocked. "Oh!" said he, suddenly grinning, "I see. Congratulations! I hadn't heard."

"No, no," replied the colonel hastily, "not that! Just for a young relative of mine--nice little girl." He felt it unnecessary to lie any further and turned rather red.

"Well, then, toy-store nothin'!" rumbled the general. "Come into the club and have a drink. The whole town will be there to give you a welcome. Why, man, you haven't seen any of your old friends for years." With that he linked his arm in the colonel's, and scattering the idlers before him with a broad fan of amber liquid, led his half-willing victim along Chestnut Street into the old Union League Club.

Now I'm in for it, reflected the colonel somewhat ruefully--and he was.

"Here's Nat Franklin back from the front," roared General Fithian, preceding him as herald and ringing a cuspidor like a gong after each glad announcement. "Here's Nat Franklin," *bong!* . . .

The devil! thought the colonel, but he was too human not to enjoy the cheery and cordial triumph they gave him. His own and his family friends surrounded him. Others joined rapidly, for the general was not to be denied--and it was by more than an average-sized crowd that he was finally swept into the bar. They drank up his news, and other things, and they continued to do so all afternoon.

Perhaps that was partly the trouble. Perhaps the afternoon and the other things had been a little too long. About four o'clock the colonel began to feel weary and to remember things which those about him could not see. He began to feel aloof from them, a bit irritable. He began to answer their innumerable questions honestly, even literally. Many of them, he could see, were shocked at this and didn't like it. Ferocious proposals no longer seemed funny even to those who made them. The room became slightly hushed. He began to tell them what he really thought of the war.

"A victory for any side is a defeat for every side now," the colonel heard himself saying. "It has all gone on so long . . ." His voice trailed away.

Above the eagles on his shoulders his face looked out not a little haggard after so many campaigns. To several there seemed to be a strange contradiction there. Again there was an awkward silence.

"Copperhead!" said someone suddenly.

A young fellow by the name of Moltan, who had just received a commission from Governor Curtin in the lately reorganized State Fencibles, put his hand to his mouth and turned a brick-red. He had not really meant to insult the colonel. He was proud of his new uniform. The epithet had slipped out because he felt and wanted to be conspicuous. But the colonel had not seen his gesture of embarrassment. He looked about him, bewildered. He mistook the embarrassment he saw in the other faces for hostility.

"No, no," he cried in indignant denial. "No, I'm a strong Union man. Why, that's all I've been fighting for! Can't you see that?"

It was now that young Moltan surpassed himself. "I can't say that I do, sir," he said.

The colonel stepped forward, his eyes blazing.

"Gentlemen, gentlemen," cried Mr. Arthur Biddle, hurrying to them across the room. "This must go no further!"

"Young man, you're an ass," rumbled old General Fithian indignantly. "You've insulted a brave warrior and your superior officer in a club where you're not a member. You'll apologize to him now."

"Or get out," added Mr. Biddle.

But to do him justice, young Moltan did apologize, and quite contritely, while the colonel tried to be as decent about it as he could. Nevertheless, he was greatly shaken. That anybody--that even a tipsy young fool should have called him a Copperhead seemed incredible.

The crowd finally broke up uneasily, trying to make the best of the matter. Most of them shook hands and departed. But some of them didn't. There would be considerable talk about the incident, the colonel was sure. Feeling distinctly miserable, he went into a corner with General Fithian and old Dr. David Craig and sat down.

"I can't understand it," he said.

"Well, it's natural enough," rumbled the general, who was always willing to precede the angels. "You see, the trouble with you, my boy, is that you haven't been home for years and you think people still feel the same as they did when you left us in 'sixty-one. Why, as a matter of fact, you talk more like the summer of 'fifty-nine!"

"Yes," agreed the doctor, "Fithian is right. The feeling now is more intense than you can imagine, after just serving in the army. If you think the men are bitter, you ought to hear the women. You're not a married man, you know, so you don't catch what's really going on. What the feeling is. Thousands of people have lost husbands, brothers, or sons. There's Andersonville and Libby. This city is full of wounded and crippled from a hundred battles. Our ships are destroyed. If anybody in Pennsylvania cherished a secret warmth for old Virginia friends, believe me, after Lee's invasion and Gettysburg they were cured of it. The feeling is more intense now in this state than it is in New England. To put it mildly, Nathaniel, you can't expect folks here to understand your sympathy for the suffering of the Southern people. They are too much preoccupied and exasperated by their own terrible losses and anxiety not to hurrah for the sternest kind of suggestions for reprisal. It's natural. It's human nature. Can't you see?"

"That's right," said the old general, nodding vigorously.

"But I still maintain we're all *one* people," replied the colonel quietly after a moment's silence. "That's the reason I'm a Union man."

"It's too fine a point to be understood now, I'm afraid," said the doctor sadly. "Cherish your idea, Nat. I rather admire you for it. But don't 'maintain' it, as you say."

"No, no," chimed in the general, "don't think of maintaining it. Just let your military record speak for you. Nobody can argue about that."

"Well, then," said the colonel, "I suppose the rest is silence, and I'll try to shift by your advice. But let me tell you both something before we leave. I want you to understand how *I* feel about this matter. You know we're not just fighting one war. We're fighting many. That is, the war is different to everyone who takes part in it. There's a general feeling, but there's a particular feeling too. Let me try to give you mine."

Unconsciously the colonel had lowered his voice as though what he was about to impart was of secret import--and in fact it was. He was going to reveal some things that haunted him. The heads of the three drew a little closer, where they sat alone in a corner of the Union League Club. The big room was deserted. It was about five o'clock of a desperately hot afternoon. Outside on Chestnut Street an occasional dray rumbled home somnolently over the cobbles. Voices passing on the sidewalk below the deep windows sounded tired and subdued.

"Let me tell you some of the things I've seen," continued the colonel even more confidentially than before. "It's all very well to speak of reprisals and punishment and military necessity, but it's quite another thing to have to carry them out personally. You know Sheridan has been destroying the Valley--everything--and the Pennsylvania cavalry has had quite a lot of house burnings on its hands. Did you ever burn a house while the family watched? You feel brave and noble, of course. Well, near a little cross-corners called Aquila--there's nothing left there but a stone springhouse now--there was a fellow named Crittendon had a nice big house. White pillars and all that. Nothing fancy either. Just a fine, comfortable American home. Now, I got specific orders to burn it and clean out the whole plantation. Crittendon, it seems, was a major in the rebel army on Early's staff and a damned troublesome fellow to the United States government. So we started off on a swift ride one night, hoping to catch him at home. We got there an hour after dawn, thanks to a burned bridge, and he'd gone. But Mrs. Crittendon was there. She was sitting on the front porch in a long white bedgown. She's an Englishwoman. She looked like a Greek statue when she stood up to meet us, and she said, 'Good morning, gentlemen!'"

"That was sort of taking advantage of you, wasn't it?" mused the doctor almost inaudibly.

"Exactly," said the colonel. "If she had screamed or gone into hysterics like most of 'em do, you know, or cursed us out lock, stock, and barrel! But she didn't. She just trembled a little like a fine straight tree--and looked down at us squirrels."

"Well, what did *you* say?" demanded old General Fithian, shifting his cud intensely.

"What does a gentleman say when he comes to burn a lady's house down? I distinguished myself, of course. I began by saying it was very early."

"Splendid!" said the doctor. "That must have made everything all right."

"--And that I was under the unfortunate necessity of burning the house down," continued the colonel. He lit a cigar the doctor offered him, and went on.

"She didn't try to argue. 'I presume you will first permit me to remove the people within, colonel,--and our clothes?' was all she asked. I gave her half an hour. She thanked me, without being sarcastic, and went in. I heard her give a dry sob at the door.

"My, there were a lot of people in that house! Some of them started to scream and carry on, but I could hear Mrs. Crittendon put an end to that. The first person that came out was an old lady, Major Crittendon's mother. She was carried on a mattress by some of the servants. It seems she's paralysed from the waist down. But she isn't paralysed from the chin up, let me say. She simply curled my hair. The troop was lined up before the porch, just as we'd ridden in, and they all heard her."

"What'd *she* say?" demanded the irrepressible general.

"She introduced herself. She began by saying she was a great-grandniece of Madam Washington, and that even Yankee pedlars might understand that. Then she saw or heard we were Pennsylvanians and she apologized for having called us Yankees. 'But you're only one peg up from the mud sills at that,' she said, and mentioned that the Pennsylvania farmers had let General Washington and his men starve at Valley Forge because the British gave them better prices for supplies at Philadelphia in 'seventy-eight. And that we hadn't changed any since, because she knew that when Robert Lee had gone into Pennsylvania the same farmers sold well water on hot days to his men. 'But, sir,' said she, 'they charged their own men more even on cool days. Honesty is the best policy, Colonel Franklin. You remember? Policy is all you know of honesty. How much are you going to charge us for burning the house down?' The rest was just pure, amber-coloured invective straight from the soul with a few old-fashioned oaths embedded in it like extinct flies. At last she had herself carried off to a knoll where she could watch the house burn down.

"By that time the babies were coming out crying, with their broken dolls, and toy horses, and things--which, of course, made us all feel like big, brave soldiers. Mrs. Crittendon lined them up some way back on the lawn with the blacks, who were trying to start hymns that she kept hushing. Finally they all seemed to be out. In fact, she nodded to me. So I took a couple of non-coms into the house with me and we got out our locofocos. We set fire to the curtains in the parlour. They were of some heavy English stuff. Mrs. Crittendon's wedding gifts, I imagine. Anyway, they flared up suddenly and then smouldered on with a kind of blinding smudge. It looked as though the whole house were on fire, although really nothing else had caught, when I heard Mrs. Crittendon calling frantically:

"'Margaret, Margaret, where's Margaret?'

"We ran out, of course. Mrs. Crittendon wasn't calm any longer. 'It's my daughter,' she said. 'She must have stayed in the house. I thought we were all out.' She tried to go back herself, but just then Margaret ran out of the smoking doorway and stood on the porch. She must have delayed to put on her best things to save them, for she was dressed in the most elegant finery I ever saw: hoop-skirt, bonnet, lace dress, and ruffled pantalettes; she even had a little parasol. Another bright silk dress was thrown over one arm. She's about fifteen and one of the loveliest little girls you can well imagine. She took in everything at a glance and threw her extra dress out on the lawn for one of the blacks to pick up. Then she stamped her foot like a little empress and just yelled at us:

"'If there's one gentleman left in the Old Army he'll come in and help me put that fire out.' And with that she dived back into the smoke and started to pull down the burning curtains.

"Her mother screamed at her that she'd catch afire in her lace dress. And she certainly would have. But half the troop was out of the saddle and we were all stamping out the fire and carrying the girl out to her mother before Mrs. Crittendon could get to her. The young minx had the gall to thank us, too. Afterwards, out on the lawn.

"It's very difficult for me to tell you in so many words just how intense the excitement was on the lawn after young Margaret's rescue. The slaves burst out singing. You know how darkies can put into song what we only feel. And they were certainly doing it that morning. Mrs. Crittendon couldn't stop them. She tried at first to hush that dirgelike singing. But I think it's to her credit to say that she finally broke down herself, and coming over to me, put her hands on my saddle and begged me as a Christian and a gentleman not to set fire to the house again. Now can you really imagine what it actually is like to have a charming and noble woman looking up into your face with tears in her eyes, asking you please not to make her and the children homeless, when you know she is helpless?

Orders are orders, of course, but there was Mrs. Crittendon!" The colonel paused a moment as if the memory of that morning were overpowering.

"Oh, yes," said Dr. Craig, "I can imagine it all right!" The general cleared his throat uncomfortably. The colonel plunged on.

"It was perfectly plain the men were sick of that kind of soldiering too," he said. "They kept watching me and Mrs. Crittendon. By that time Margaret had come over to help her mother. The tension grew until even the horses got restless. The men let them have their heads, I suppose. Everyone wanted to be up and away and done with the mess. I couldn't blame them. Well, the lady begged me, and so did the young girl, and . . ."

"And so, of course, as a gallant man, you went right in and set the house afire again," suggested the doctor in a low tone.

There was a pause.

"Yes," said the colonel, looking miserable, "I did."

"What! what! Do you mean to tell me, Nat Franklin, you had the devilish crust to? The devil you did! Your father would never--no, sir," said the old general, pounding the floor with his cane, "never, sir!"

"Oh, it wasn't quite so bad as you think," continued the colonel. "No, we didn't just go in and start the fire up again. You know I couldn't! I advised Mrs. Crittendon to clear out as soon as she could with her stuff and her people, 'because,' said I, 'the next time, you know.'

"'Yes,' said she, 'I know,' and she broke down again.

"Then one of the babies with nothing on but a short night-shirt toddled up with a rag doll. He wanted to give it to 'the nice man.' That was me!

"'Come on, sergeant, we're licked,' was all I could say. 'Ride 'em off.'

"So we just rode away without looking back and went into camp a few miles higher up the Valley near a village called Aquila. We burned Aquila out. There wasn't anybody there. Everything went but a springhouse a little detached from the town. Springhouses don't catch well, you know."

"It's the dampness, I suppose," suggested the doctor dryly. "But look here, Franklin, murder will out. What happened to the Crittendons?"

"Well, we were just settled for supper, vedettes out up the Valley, and the rest of us gathered about the fires. The boys were frying their hard-tack in bacon grease, which is against medical orders, of course--when in rides General Phil Sheridan and his hard-bitten staff.

"There'd been a devil of a ruction over at Cross Keys that day. A couple of wagon trains had been cut out and looted and burned by Early, and the general was tearing mad. It meant some weeks' delay in operations in the upper Valley. He didn't say much, which is a bad sign. He's usually good enough company. But he did order the men to dump their greasy bread on the fires and turn in on dry tack and water. There was a good deal of muffled swearing under the blankets as a consequence. And I think the general felt quite uncomfortable about that. Anyway, he borrowed some of my whisky and finished it all off himself, looking into a fire as moody as you please. Then he ordered me to turn out ten troopers and to accompany him and his staff. He was riding back to Winchester that night, he said. It looked as though he might be relieving me of command. We started. After a few miles the word was passed for me to join the general. We rode in the darkness for some time.

"'Look here, Colonel Nat,' said he suddenly, 'didn't you get orders to burn out the Crittendon people today?'

"'I did, general!' I had to say that, of course. 'I set fire to the Crittendon house at six-fifteen o'clock this morning.'

"'And put it out at six-twenty-five same date.'

"I couldn't deny it.

"'Now look here, Franklin,' he went on after a little, 'I'm an Irishman, even if I was born in old York State, and I never borrow whisky from an officer I'm goin' to court-martial. But orders are orders. I know this is a specially hard case: fine people! You've made it even harder now. But we can't go into that kind of thing. As a matter of fact, I've been easy on you. We both saw some Indian fighting in the West, so I've put you on reconnaissance almost entirely and relieved you so far of most of the dirty work. I've used your regiment for scouting and turned the harrying, and horse and house thieving over to Reinohlfennig and his bummers. Those Pennsylvania Dutch can only ride farm horses anyway. They're locusts; you're cavalry. When you get an order after this, no flinching. Begad, man, do you think I like it any better than you do?

"'Burn the house tonight without touching anything,' he finally said. 'Without touching anything,' he repeated. 'Is that plain? That's all.'

"I saluted and fell back with my own men. To tell the truth I was pretty angry myself. He might have court-martialled me for disobedience of orders that morning, but to bring me back to burn the house and insinuate that we weren't to carry anything away! Just like saying, 'Don't carry off any cuckoo clocks or jewellery,' you know. That had me boiling, even if he is half an Irishman.

"When we got to the Crittendon house again there was a squadron of regulars bivouacked on the lawn, and the lamps in the house were lit.

Sheridan gave a brief order and the squadron broke camp instantly and assembled mounted and at attention before the veranda.

"'Colonel, send your own men to the woodpiles. Have them get pine knots, light them, and fall in by the porch here.'

"Then he had the officers assemble, and all of us, with his staff, went into the house.

"I was terribly relieved to find that no one was there. Mrs. Crittendon must have taken my advice and left that morning with her people. We went into the big parlour, where there was a portrait of a Continental officer over the fireplace, and a lot of candles burning. It was some moments before I noticed that on a couch in one of the alcoves there was a body covered by a tattered Confederate battle-flag.

"'Gentlemen,' said General Sheridan, 'I am asking your assistance here in a personal matter.'

"He took a candlestick, went into the dark alcove, and pulled the flag down from the face of the form lying there. The strong, bearded countenance of a handsome man, whose hair was prematurely grey, was revealed in the yellow candlelight. He looked peculiarly waxen. His eyes were wide open and the collar of his grey uniform with tarnished gold leaves on it supported his chin.

"'This was Major Douglas Charles Crittendon of the Confederate Army,' said General Sheridan. 'He was killed in the attack at Cross Keys this afternoon. Before he died I had time for a too-brief talk with him. He was an intimate classmate of mine at West Point. For many years he was an officer in the Old Army. He once commanded the squadron of U. S. Cavalry now lined up before his door. What I'm doing here is by his own dying request made this afternoon. He was most particular, and I gave him my word "to bury him in the ashes of his home." I realize now that he must have thought this house had already been burned. If there is anything in this proceeding which offends the principles of anyone present he is at liberty to withdraw.'

"No one made a move. In fact, we all stood completely awe-struck; some of us were overcome. General Sheridan paused for a moment, then laid the flag back on his friend's face.

"'Will the new officers of the major's old regiment lend me a hand?' he said.

"The general and some of the young lieutenants from the troop outside then lifted the couch, upon which the major lay, out into the middle of the room, under the eyes of the portrait. They piled fire-wood about it. We all helped in that.

"'I would like to have the guidon of the troop,' said the general.

"After a moment it was brought in to him.

"'This is my own idea,' he said. 'I think Douglas . . . er--Major Crittendon will approve.' His voice was a little husky. He put the silk guidon on the breast of the flag-draped man on the couch. Upon that he laid the major's sword.

"'I am sorry there is no priest here,' he said. 'Major Crittendon was the soul of honour, a true friend. A *very* gallant gentleman lies here . . .' He was unable to go on. 'God receive his stricken soul,' he managed to add finally. We said 'Amen' and trooped out of the room awkwardly enough. The empty house echoed with our heavy boots and the jingle of spurs.

"Outside the glare of the pine torches beat the darkness back for a space, wavering over the men and horses before the door.

"Sheridan stopped me for a moment on the porch and said, 'Franklin, you will be in charge in this neighbourhood for some time. Mrs. Crittendon must be in hiding hereabouts. We heard she left early this morning with her family and some wagons. Find her if you can. Do what you can for her. And give her this.' He gave me a small sealed package. 'And,' he said as he laid his hand on my arm, 'tell her that Phil Sheridan burned her house by a special order from Washington signed by the Secretary of War. If you can't find Mrs. Crittendon, see that the package is returned to me. These are bad times to live through. It's hard even for a soldier to tell what his duty is. Don't you find it so sometimes?' He smiled sadly and extended his hand.

"'Yes, sir, I do,' I said, and we shook hands warmly. That was all.

"He mounted his horse in the glare of the torches and brought the troop to present.

"'Colonel,' he said, 'carry out your orders.' Then they moved off at a rapid trot down the drive.

"That was a great burning. For miles the whole Valley leaped with light. The house was of pitch pine a century old. It made a great column of golden fire. Behind it the gloomy wall of the Blue Ridge towered up into heaven, watching the sparks drift out among the stars."

The spell of the colonel's deep but pleasant voice seemed to his rapt listeners to have been withdrawn too abruptly. Outside the street window, by which they sat, the head and shoulders of a lamplighter appeared suddenly and with startling clearness on his ladder as he cupped the white spurt of a match in his glowing hands.

"Lord," said the colonel, "is it as late as that? I apologize profoundly. Keeping you fellows from supper! It's not to be forgiven."

"Nonsense, nobody's going to be late for supper," said Dr. Craig, jumping up and brushing the cigar ashes off his vest and long coat; "you're coming home with me. I'm a widower, and I have meals when I want them. I keep a cook from the Eastern Shore. There'll be pepper pot and reed birds in butter. A very famous patient of mine has sent me some of the port that he's famous for. Nat, I'll bet you haven't had a meal like that in months."

"Not for years," said the colonel. "It sounds like--like eighteen-fifty-nine."

General Fithian groaned, however, and began to roll his eyes. "Craig," said he, "this is a damned outrage." He pounded his cane on the floor. "Ten days ago you put me on a diet of vegetables and milk toast. Am I supposed to go and just watch you two eat reed birds and things?"

"Tonight," said the doctor, "I'll permit you to relapse. You can take an extra five grains of calomel before going to bed."

"By God, I'm going to that homoeopath in Camden," bumbled the general.

They went out and caught an accommodation stage for Spring Garden Street. On the way up Dr. Craig kept his two military friends and the much-amused civilian passengers, all gentlemen in plug hats and paper collars, in a constant gale of laughter by dictating to an imaginary druggist prescriptions in dog Latin for the cure of delicate complaints.

The memory of that evening's dinner at Dr. Craig's "perfect little residence" remained long in the colonel's mind as the outstanding evening of his furlough. It was a return in spirit to the urbanity and security of the time before the war. For, once ensconced in the doctor's old wainscoted dining-room under the new gas chandelier, with cool airs drifting in through the wide casement,--breezes from the doctor's back garden and the valley of the Wissahickon, laden with the remote odour of new-mown hay-fields and the domestic scent of house geraniums,--once ensconced there, with the present walled out, as it were, the clock on the stairs seemed by some magic of reversal to be ticking its way again through the serene hours of its grandfather past.

Gone were the high-keyed expectancy, the waiting for news, the nervous talk, and the taut, secret apprehensions of wartime. Out of the ken of the colonel's consciousness, into a kind oblivion, drifted involuntary visions of three years of angry battles; glimpses of red cannon lighting the clouds of midnight; half-heard cries of nervous sentinels and eerie night-birds along the dark shores of the embattled Potomac; the sinister glow in the sky of rebel camp-fires beyond the mountains, and the scene at twilight of the huddled wave of dead splashed along the stone wall of Marye's Heights.

Instead, there was the doctor, leaning back in his chair with one thumb easing the tension of his vest, and talking--relating wise, kindly, and humorous anecdotes of nearly half a century of practice. The healing quality of his healing personality seemed to pervade the room with a kind of merciful ribaldry of comment and his irrepressible hope and amusement at the vagaries of man.

And there, too, was General Jack Fithian, the best purveyor of self-appreciative laughter in Philadelphia, ruddy with port and good-nature; delighted to have an audience for his tales of the Mexican War.

It was curious how *that* war no longer seemed to be a war at all. No one had died in it. The very names of its battles were now a simple poetry without bloodshed: Palo Alto, Buena Vista, Cerro Gordo, and Chapultepec; from the wine-red lips of the old general they fell like single notes chimed on a carillon of romance. It was as though he had just taken his silver knife and struck lightly the half-filled glasses before him.

Was it possible, mused the colonel, was it possible that the grim annals of the battles in Virginia, along the Potomac, and in the Shenandoah could also become by future telling a mere mellifluous tale like that?

Yes, it was possible.

Perhaps it was a quality of prophetic insight imbibed with the doctor's port that murmured to him, "That, too, shall come to pass": Manassas, Malvern Hill, Antietam, and Fredericksburg--New Market, Winchester, and Monocacy--how they would sound, tinkling in the pages of history, after the necessary scar-tissue of forgetfulness had closed the wounds of time.

Suddenly the sullen and angry face of the boy who had called him Copperhead that afternoon seemed to be looking at the colonel again. He watched the passionate young features fade slowly into the cigar smoke.

How men felt--that was what would be forgotten!

He stirred uneasily; the room and its pleasant atmosphere resumed again. But he was no longer lost in the past. While Dr. Craig and the general talked, he had come to a sudden decision. It was something so impulsive that it seemed to have been decided for him. Now he knew how he was going to spend the remaining weeks of his leave. And it was because of that decision that he turned the talk to horses.

He wanted a new horse. The finest horse there was to be had in Philadelphia. His pockets were bursting with greenbacks from his unspent back pay--and good horses in Philadelphia were still to be had. Weren't they?

"Yes, indeed." Dr. Craig knew of a wonderful horse that belonged to a patient of his who had just died.

"He's probably had his eye on that horse all along," suggested Fithian. "Now, I have a fine animal myself. Do you know, Craig, I think I'll omit that extra calomel tonight. Listening to you and Nat horse-trading in your deceased patient's chattels makes me nervous. There, there, I'm sure you can get that horse cheap, colonel, as the doctor says. And he ought to know. He's probably taking it for his bill for the man's death. But I'd look at that horse's teeth closely."

"Confound you!" roared the doctor. "It's a magnificent animal, I say! And it's time for you to go to bed--and take your calomel."

"I won't," said the general, but he did.

The old-fashioned host saw both his guests to the doors of their bedrooms, with a candle. He struggled with the general over his calomel, and he lingered for some moments at the colonel's door in a kind of benevolent good-night chat.

". . . I didn't want to remind you of it in the dining-room tonight," said he, "but if you don't mind I'm still curious about something you told us this afternoon. Did you by any chance ever deliver that package Sheridan gave you to Mrs. Crittendon?"

"No," said the colonel, who was seated on the bed trying to draw off his boots. "No, I didn't. We made a thorough search of all that part of the Valley, but Mrs. Crittendon and her family seemed to have vanished into thin air. I can't even pick up a rumour of where they went. I was going to return the package to Sheridan at headquarters. In fact, I had it with me when I left, but a curious thing happened on the way up. You remember that springhouse at Aquila that I said wouldn't burn?"

The doctor nodded.

"Well, I stopped in there to give the nag a good drink just after I left camp and the Crittendon children had evidently been playing in it. It was full of a few toys they'd saved and dolls made out of corncobs, some broken dishes on an old stone set for a sort of elfin feast with wild cherry seeds and chinquapins. You know how children, little girls, furnish a dolls' house--pretty pitiable, too. The war seemed to have lost most of their toys for them--and it was so furtive and secret in that half-dark place. It's a shame the infants can't even play house, you know!"

"Yes, but how did you know it was the Crittendons?"

"Oh," said the colonel, "I felt sure I recognized the rag doll the child brought me the morning we tried to burn the house--it had only one eye."

"Ah, I remember; 'nice man,' eh?" said the doctor, smiling. He paused a moment, peering at the colonel as though he liked to see him in the room. "Well, nice man, good-night to you," said Dr. Craig a little ironically, and went off down the hall with his candle, leaving the colonel with one boot on, still sitting on the bed.

In his room Dr. Craig undressed rapidly, from long habit laying his clothes out in a precise manner on an old green chair. He could find them in the dark that way and dress instantly if he were called. He put on a long, almost unearthly, night-shirt that fell from neck to heel, and, although it was a warm night, a stocking-shaped, flannel night-cap. Thus attired, he sat on the big bed looking somewhat like a dunce. After a while from under the pillow he drew a photograph and sat staring at it. It was the picture of a young man in his early twenties and first moustache, in the uniform of a surgeon of the Union Army. Beads of moisture stood out on the doctor's forehead. Probably it was the nightcap. Presently they coursed down the furrows of his wise and foolish old face. "Murdered," said he, "murdered," and drew his sleeve rapidly across his eyes. He put the picture of his only son back under the pillow and blew out the candle.

CHAPTER II

"HURRAH! BOYS, HURRAH!"

Next morning, Dr. Craig and the colonel drove out the Doylestown Road a way and bought the horse. It was a beauty, a black mare with three white socks and a fine, small head. Her neck arched like an Arab's and she stepped high. They returned to Spring Garden Street, and the colonel spent an hour trying out his new mount's paces, and breaking her in to the army bit and saddle before the doctor's door.

It was a spirited moment of good horsemanship.

Under the tracery of maple boughs that met over the old-fashioned street, the colonel raced back and forth, turning and wheeling, a golden stir of autumn leaves whirling about his horse's legs. The neighbours came out to see. One of them, a young boy from North Seventh Street, never forgot that morning nor the figure of the tall, dark man with flowing burnsides who rode by him with creaking leather and slapping sword. The campaign hat with bright golden cord and acorns, the long blue coat and glittering buttons, the man motionless in the saddle of the galloping black horse, were photographed on the boy's memory. Thirty-four years later he was still, secretly, "being like Colonel Franklin" when he rode forth at the head of his own regiment for the Spanish War.

But no one on Spring Garden Street was tall enough that morning to peep onto the knees of the gods. The colonel bade his friends good-bye. That is to say, he jumped down and clasped to his breast old Dr. Craig, who had brought him into this world, and he nearly had his right hand crippled by old General Jack, who "blubbed" then and there.

"I'll see you both after it's over," cried the colonel cheerily. "And when I come back, there's to be a dinner at Kennett Square. Will you come?" he shouted.

"Aye!" they called, half speechless.

But they never came. Peace has its casualties as well as war--and two old men standing on a white Philadelphia doorstep, their faces mottled by the leafy sunlight, made the last glimpse Colonel Franklin ever had of Dr. Craig and General Fithian.

"Go and see Buchanan at 'Wheatland,'" roared the doctor as the colonel wheeled to wave the last time. "He's lonely as I am."

"By Jove, I will," said the colonel to himself. "I suppose everybody's forgotten Buchanan"--and he trotted off down Walnut Street, bound on the most peaceful of errands. For it was before a toy-shop six blocks below Broad Street that he finally tethered his war horse. "Now," said he, "I'll get 'em." And he did.

No colonel in the United States Army, perhaps, had ever filled his haversack quite like that. When Colonel Franklin emerged from the shop and slung it over his saddle, besides some spare clothes now used for safe packing only, the haversack contained no less than six dolls most *elegantly* attired, a small, a very small, suite of doll furniture, and a set of dainty china dishes that might have been used at a banquet for the Queen of Mice. Thus armed to the teeth, the colonel turned his horse back towards Broad Street and prepared, with secret amusement, to swagger his way out of Philadelphia with pardonable military pride.

But he was not to get out of the city so easily as that. Drums began to beat.

The white man's beating of drums is not to be approached by that of any other race. Compared with it, the much-vaunted negro tom-tom and hand-jar sound a mere nervous irritant, a kind of fumbling hypnosis. Two-four time is a suggestion for a man to walk; for many men to walk together to a given end. Beat a drum in march time and it becomes the voice of a god roaring, "go and do." Like real thunder, the thunder of drums becomes the voice of lightning, but it rolls before. It is a warning that something is about to be riven from leaf to root.

Thunder like that, such an enormous music, was loose in Philadelphia the morning that Colonel Franklin was riding up Walnut Street. He had gone only a couple of blocks from the toy-shop when his horse began to dance, fret, and jiggle to the pulsation of drums. He worked Black Girl into a blind archway so that people might keep clear of her dancing heels. In that way he had quite a space to himself, and he could look clear over the heads of the crowd. Four blocks away, around the corner from Broad Street, wheeled the cause of tumult, the drums at the head of a regiment marching out to war.

Philadelphia is a contented town. It is situated on a river flat and most of the time breathes heavy, valley air a little more than tranquilly. But occasionally, especially in the fall, the keen atmosphere from the mountains slips into the village of William Penn. Then everything is preternaturally clear and suddenly electric. There is a positively Vichy-like quality to the air, and to a Philadelphian that is intoxicating. On such autumn mornings, Quaker housewives from a sense of inner, and perhaps spiritual, excitement have even been known, inadvertently, to scrub their doorsteps twice.

It was such a morning in late September when the State Fencibles left for the South. Grant had called for them. The iron machine that was slowly contracting about Richmond needed spare parts. And the weather being electric, Philadelphia muttered with thunder.

They came marching down Walnut Street toward the ferry, preceded by *drums, drums, drums.* It was a national election year, and a great banner was stretched across Walnut Street. At one end of it there was a portrait of a bearded man, "Lincoln"; at the other, a picture apparently of the same man without a beard, "Johnson."

OUR CANDIDATES
REPUBLICAN
Vote National Union
THAT GOVERNMENT OF THE PEOPLE BY THE PEOPLE
FOR THE PEOPLE SHALL NOT PERISH FROM THE EARTH

Under this "arch" suddenly appeared flags, taut in the breeze, a hedge of flashing bayonets, and wide lines of marching men in blue, rolling the dust before them.

The crowd formed like magic. Buses and drays drew hastily to one side. Out of a thousand shops and houses poured the sober population of Philadelphia, exalted with excitement. As the drums passed along between the teeming sidewalks, they peeled off the last intellectual queries, the petty personal reservations even from cold doubters, like a strip of thin hide. The mind darkened to let the heart burn more furiously. The deep substratum of common feeling by which a nation lives was revealed and laid bare to the quick, quivering. Bugles and screaming fifes joined in with the drums:

"The Union forever,
Hurrah! boys, Hurrah!"

The people knew those words; they knew what the words meant. An eerie folk-singing ran down the street. A high-tension current streaked down the sidewalks, welding the crowd into one thing, jumping the gaps from block to block.

> "Down with the traitor,
> Up with the star . . ."

At Ninth Street, an old gentleman in archaically tight trousers who had once seen Washington drive to the State House, fell down and died in a fit. There was no waving of dainty handkerchiefs to "departing cavaliers." There were oaths, screams, the violent weeping of hysterical women in black bombazine, roars--and that high-pitched patriotic singing that gradually mounted in intensity:

> "While we rally 'round the flag, boys,
> Rally once again,
> Shouting the battle-cry of Freedom!"

And how they shouted. For once the whole vast, patient city uttered itself with one voice.

About the colonel the excitement was peculiarly intense and enhanced by a constant flurry in the crowd. This was partly due to the dangerous dancing of the colonel's mare, and the fact that, by a natural mistake, most of the spectators thought that the colonel was stationed there to review the departing regiment. Many kept trying to press in upon him. They could see by his weathered uniform that he was a veteran, and of high rank.

Personally, the colonel would rather not have been there. He towered conspicuously above the crowd, which was uncomfortable to a man of his temperament, and to him the sight of a regiment going to the front was bound to be painful. He knew only too well what their final destination was. But as the column of marching men drew rapidly nearer, he forget all that. That is to say, he forgot himself.

He was swept by the overpowering feeling that surged down the street. His horse suddenly stood still and trembled. As though from the current of a battery, that trembling was transmitted to the body of the man. As the drums passed before him, the baton of the drum-major flashed high out of the shadow of the houses, twinkled in the upper sunlight, and streaked back to the drum-major's hand again. Black Girl neighed and shook the foam from her bridle. A hot blast of bugles tossed the air. Just in front of him a servant-girl with red arms and a dirty apron started to whinny. A large, dignified woman, who soared up out of her vast, flounced hoop-skirt like a centaur looking out of a tent, threw her little sunshade into the air and sobbed like a child at its mother's funeral. The colonel's dark face flushed even darker. He sat as though cast in bronze.

He exchanged salutes with the colonel of the passing troops, a young man whom he didn't know. The faces of the men who followed looked drawn and chalk-white above their dusty blue coats. Most of them were older schoolboys. The tension of the scene they were passing through was as great as that of battle. They seemed to be drawn down the street in the current that followed the maelstrom of drums. They were being rushed off. Some of them missed step to catch up. A sort of gasp from the crowd closed in behind them. There were few dry eyes on the sidewalks. Then the flag passed, with all the stars still there, and the crowd went crazy.

The tension was eased by the major of the last battalion. He was a dusty, determined-looking little man on a rather sorry horse. He wore his hat over his eyes and he was smoking a cigar. He didn't know it, but he looked like a caricature of General Grant. The crowd roared at him good-naturedly and laughed all the more that the little major took the plaudits for himself.

Smoking on parade, major! thought the colonel. Dear, dear, what *will* the regular army say? It's only the state militia, only the damned militia that's won all the wars the United States has always nearly lost. "You'll fill up the ditches for the generals from West Point on both sides, my lads," he said half-aloud. He felt overpowered by a desire for a cigar himself. "The damned generals!" As a soldier of the Army of the Potomac he felt bitter about generals. He rose in his saddle to roar at the last company--and sank back again. For leading it, in a pathetically new lieutenant's uniform, was the boy who had called him a Copperhead only yesterday. For some reason he was in command of the company.

Young Moltan looked up and saw the colonel. His whole face flushed a painful red. My God! he thought. Even in this short march from the armoury to the ferry, he was learning the difference between wearing a uniform and being a soldier. For the veteran on the horse he now had nothing but adoration. In his confusion he forgot to salute. He took off his hat instead.

The colonel choked. Tears ran down his face. "God bless you, Moltan, my boy," he called. "Come back, son!" He took off his own hat and held it to his breast. He waved it benignly and helplessly after him. With a look of relief and surprised exaltation, the young man passed on . . .

"You young fool, you, you'll get yourself killed," the colonel kept muttering to himself long after the last files had gone by and the urchins had linked arms and closed in at the end of the column to follow the music. An old coloured man from the Navy Yard, vending hot pepper pot, still kept bowing and taking off his straw hat again and again and saying, "Good-bye to you, Mars' Lincoln's boys. Good-bye!" A few women in black, who seemed equally dazed, lingered here and there, touching their handkerchiefs to their eyes, till a little whirlwind began to blow dirty newspaper down the empty street.

Black Girl shied violently at the papers and brought the colonel to himself. For he, too, had been, he considered, shamefully overcome. Somehow that last glimpse of Lieutenant Moltan had been peculiarly searing. Into the instant of his passing by had flowed and overflowed all the terrific emotion of the day. The mind tends to personify its griefs, and in the person of young Moltan the colonel had relived all the exaltation and glory, the proud hopes, and the unexpected agony and regret of a youth marching off to war. It was like beholding a vision. The vision remained. And it was for that reason that he had no recollection whatever of the aftermath of the procession.

When his horse shied he was still sitting her in a daze in the blind archway, and the street was all but empty. Down at the State House he could hear distant cheering where the speechmaking would now be going on. Remembering the speeches of three years ago, he smiled grimly. He was just about to move off when someone began to pound at his leg.

He looked down, annoyed and surprised, into the flushed countenance of a most curious little man.

"An indestructible union of indestructible states," cried the little man in a strange, rapt voice. He ceased pounding the colonel's leg to emphasize his proposition, and removed his plug hat. A shiny and flushed bald head appeared like a dome in the sunlight. He gave his large beaver a tremendous flourish and retired a couple of paces like a dancer, turned, faced the colonel again, and declaimed, "Destined to endure for ages to come." He smacked his hat down over his brows. The dome disappeared.

"Those, sir," resumed the little orator, apparently becoming aware of the colonel for the first time, "are my irrevocable sentiments. You will recollect the source, eh? John Marshall, a Virginian, but . . ."

"My sentiments, too," said the colonel, suddenly reaching down and shaking the little man's hand.

"Then, sir, I can see there is no point at issue between us," cried the little man, drawing himself up under his hat. He looked considerably disappointed. "Good day to you, sir," he rapped out, and marched up a pair of steps to an office door.

CHARLES R. ROSS
Attorney-at-Law

blazed from the brass shingle. The door banged.

Suddenly it opened again.

"And I might add," roared the little lawyer, once again hatless, "that it was a late great-aunt of my family who is alleged to have first conceived the American flag." The door closed. This time "irrevocably."

Colonel Franklin grinned, touched heels to his horse, and moved on. Black Girl needed exercise. The city began to fall away behind.

"Charles R. Ross, attorney-at-law," muttered the colonel in a kind of illogical day-dream. "Funny that--why the *at?* Why not Nathaniel T. Franklin, colonel-at-war?" His horse almost shied onto the sidewalk. He hastily resumed the reins.

Not many hours later he was riding along the old, dusty Western Pike through the fertile fields of Lancaster County. The war had never come here. The rolling landscape, cultivated like one vast garden and dotted with huge red barns and stone farmhouses, is one of the most peaceful in the world.

The afternoon wore away as the miles rolled behind.

CHAPTER III

YESTERDAY AND TOMORROW

"Wheatland" near Lancaster, the house of ex-President Buchanan, lay down a long alley of ancient maples. A prosperous farm, the main house was surrounded by a space of noble lawn. It was long after nightfall when the colonel arrived.

The house appeared half-ghostly in a light mist luminous with twinkling fireflies and the glow of window lamps. In the dull moonlight it seemed inordinately sequestered, and the *clop* of Black Girl's hoofs rang in her rider's ears like the hoof-beats of some messenger from the present vainly trying to carry news of battles into the past.

Yesterday, yesterday, yesterday--tapped the feet of the mare.

As he emerged on the drive the figure of an elderly man, apparently wrapped in a voluminous bedgown, rose from a rocking-chair on the front porch and disappeared into the darkened hallway.

Buchanan's old servant, Crawford, met the colonel at the steps.

"Oh!" said Crawford. "Why, if it isn't you, Mr. Nat! Lord, I'd never have known you, you've gotten so thin. And how's your father, sir?"

"He's been dead these two years, Crawford," said the colonel, a bit nettled despite himself. His father had been a fairly prominent man.

"No!" said Crawford. "Don't tell me!" He sounded more shocked than he need have been. "But that's the way it goes here at 'Wheatland' nowadays, you know. We don't hear, sir. I guess it's the war. The President never approved of it, you know. We just don't get the news often. There're not many people come, and when they do--" The man made a vague gesture in the dark. "I can remember when there used to be twenty horses tied at that bar, sir. Before we went to Washington." He sighed an old man's sigh in the darkness.

Black Girl pawed the gravel impatiently.

"Perhaps," began the colonel, "I had better not . . ."

"Oh, no," said the old man. "Excuse me, I didn't mean *that!*"

He came down the steps and took the bridle. "Don't think of going! The President would never forgive me. Your old . . . your father and him, sir, you remember. And he was alers right fond of you too when you was a boy. Why, that time you left for the West he . . ."

"Yes, I know," said the colonel, dismounting wearily. His sabre clashed a little strangely before the wide, peaceful doorway.

"Every night at supper," continued Crawford, mounting Black Girl stiffly by way of the horse block, "the President says, 'And who's been here today?' And do you know, Mr. Nat, I dasn't tell him nobody." The old man lowered his voice painfully. "I jes' says to him, I--"

"Yes, yes, I understand. He *must* be lonely."

A window opened upstairs.

"Who's there?" asked the rather flat voice of James Buchanan, tired but eager.

"It's me, Nat Franklin from Kennett Square."

"What, Young Franklin! Why, step out into the moonlight where I can see you," said the ex-President of the United States, leaning out of his window in a night-shirt and illogically trying to illuminate the outdoors with a candle in his hand. "It's a boon to have you drop in. How are you? Where's your father?"

"He isn't able to come, sir."

"Have you had your supper?" continued the President. "Crawford, you rascal, where's Pollock?"

"He'd be at the barn, sir, wouldn't he?"

"Call him. Have him take Mr. Franklin's horse and rub it down. Come in, Nat. Crawford, give Mr. Franklin the North Room--and something to eat. Oh, you're in uniform, aren't you? What have y' got on your straps?"

"Buzzards," said the colonel.

"'Pon my soul!" exclaimed the President. "Colonel, eh! Well, come in, come in. Damn it, there goes my candle!" The white head was withdrawn but the voice continued. "I'll see you tomorrow at breakfast. Six o'clock promptly, mind you. There's a lot to do here. Have to get up early." The window closed.

"Pollock's been dead a year now come October," whispered Crawford. "I'll take your horse down to the barn myself. Go upstairs to the big room at the end of the hall. I'll be back in a jiffy, sir, and get you some hot fixin's."

Yesterday, yesterday, yesterday--sounded the hoofs of Black Girl slowly, as she moved off down the drive with Crawford.

The colonel entered the big house alone. Except for a lamp on the landing, it was dark and silent. A wind waved the long white curtains in the moonlit library listlessly. The colonel waited till Crawford returned and showed him to his room. The North Room was tremendous, coldly still and furnished with gigantic walnut furniture. The bed was monolithic, with urns. Someone, it seemed, had been trying to make Cyclops cosy.

The colonel felt tired and slept soundly. But something woke him towards morning.

The moon was setting and drew long shadows across the room. Outside, the perpetual controversy of the katydids suddenly quickened as though at some instinctive hint of unseen dawn. It quickened but it also seemed to be tired and thinner, threatening to cease from sheer inertia like a tired war.

On an elephantine marble washstand in one corner of the room stood a colossal pitcher. There were white eagles on it. Even in the dim moonlight there could be no doubt that the pitcher was federal. Its eagles screamed silently. Down at Lancaster a locomotive in the yards kept wailing to its brakeman. The colonel knew those sounds. A troop train, no doubt. Some more of Curtin's Pennsylvania militia going to the front. He could tell when the last car was coupled. The train wailed its way eastward, humming into the night.

He turned on his pillow to resettle himself--and then he heard the sound that was, he realized, the background for all the other sounds he had been listening to, and unconsciously evaluating. It was even the background for the silence of the house, for it seemed more eternal than silence.

It was a long, sonorous, and soporific sound. It seemed at time to strike difficulties like a file in a board full of nails, but it overcame them and went on. It rumbled furiously but in meaningless syllables. Like the ghost of that endless debate in the federal Senate which forever haunts the halls of the Republic, it only threatened to cease. And it was some moments, for he was very sleepy, before the colonel realized that he had the honour of listening to the snoring of the man who had come nearer than anyone else to ruining the United States.

"Lord," said the colonel, sitting up suddenly in the moonlight. "I hope no one ever snores like that again. Let's do something about it," he added, and gave his pillow a smack. Then smiling a little grimly he dropped off again.

Next morning Colonel Franklin and the ex-President took breakfast together. A large urn of strong coffee, eggs, fried potatoes, small beefsteaks, buckwheat cakes and maple syrup, toast and muffins appeared all at once on the table, and were ably discussed by Mr. Buchanan and his guest, together with amusing anecdotes about the court of Russia thirty years before; how nearly we had gone to war with England over the Oregon boundary in Polk's administration; and how, by "every law human and divine," we should be justified in wrestling Cuba from Spain "as soon as we have the power."

"And that will be soon now," said Mr. Buchanan, "for when we emerge from this war the great fact will be that, whether we like it or not, we shall be the most powerful military nation on earth. Manifest destiny from now on will be merely a matter of a series of peaceful delays. The federal government is going to be supreme, and that will eventually mean conquest." He took a large apple as he neared the end of his discourse and began to pare it.

"Personally," said he, "I did all I could to prevent this. I now see the hand of God in it. But *personally* I regarded the nice balance of power between the states and the federal government, that has existed up until recently, as the triumph of the political genius of our race. That was what I wished to conserve. Slavery, I tell you, was a side issue. Most of the thinking men, the statesmen at both the North and the South, that I have known for two generations have always said so. We are a legal-thinking people. We and the English are the only two peoples on earth who understand that the government must be kept in leash.

"Now," he continued, walking over to the window and eating his apple in considerable excitement, "our balance in America has been destroyed. The federal government is going to be everything. Since Mr. Lincoln has enlisted the services of General U. S. Grant I can see that that is going to be so. There is a fatality about that man's initials, you know. History sometimes plays the Pythoness whimsically like that. And his is a new kind of generalship." The ex-President drummed on the window-pane. "U. S.," said he. "U. S. . . . U. S.? . . . It is only men of genuine philosophical sense who can understand that the form of government is the most important thing in the world. Everything is contained in that," he muttered. "I did my best to prevent this. I did my best!"

"Would you have let the South go?" asked the colonel, fascinated at hearing an ex-President confess himself to a window-pane.

"No, I would have prevented them but I wouldn't have conquered them. Is that too nice a distinction? Too nice, I am afraid, to exist now in the fires of passion that so much killing has kindled. But it will be the final test, I think, for Mr. Lincoln after the war. God help him!" said James Buchanan. He turned from the window, and his face worked.

"Come," said he, "let me show you about 'Wheatland.' It is the pride and comfort of my old age. Most of my life was given to the Republic. I could wish that 'Wheatland' should not be forgotten--afterwards." He sighed and ate the last of his apple pensively.

They walked down to the farm buildings together while the ex-President expatiated upon his barns and acres. And, indeed, "Wheatland" was a magnificent farm.

Time was when it was possible for a young man to bow his head naturally before an old one to receive his blessing. And this the colonel did before James Buchanan. The blessing was brief. But it was given with an old-fashioned piety and a courtesy in farewell that justly marked Mr. Buchanan as one of the great well-mannered gentlemen of his time.

Much moved by this leave-taking from his father's old friend and the hero of his own boyhood, the colonel saddled Black Girl himself and prepared to depart. But he was not so affected as to forget to press a greenback into the fervent hand of old Crawford, who walked with him a space down the lane for old time's sake and out of sheer gratitude.

"Ah, it's only local shin-plasters I get around here now," said Crawford, "and not too many of them. At the White House, I remember, the Brazilian ambassador used to give me gold. Great days, sir!" he whispered.

"Good-bye, Mr. Nat, good-bye!"

The colonel broke into a gallop. The trees on the old road rushed by him. It was a magnificent September day. "Wheatland" and its memories lay behind him. Some weeks of his furlough and the open road lay before. He drank in the cool morning air with delight and whistled shrilly. A field of late wheat rippled goldenly in a valley. It reminded him of the corn colour in Mrs. Crittendon's hair. He whistled even louder at that.

"Why, the idea!"

It *was* good to be alive. Black Girl gathered herself under him and thundered down the Pike towards Lancaster. *Tomorrow* and *tomorrow* and *tomorrow*--was the tune her hoofs now seemed to be drumming on the road away from yesterday.

CHAPTER IV

TWILIGHT AT HARRISBURG

At Lancaster the army quartermasters and the patient employés of the Pennsylvania Railroad had been up all night, and the night before, switching troop trains going east and empties going west. They were hollow-eyed and cinder-grimy. To them Colonel Franklin was just as welcome as a wasp in a bag of candy. All he wanted was a box-car on a west-bound empty for Black Girl and a flat-car or a ride on a locomotive for himself. Only as far as Harrisburg. Where, said he, looking very official, the government was in a great hurry to have him go.

But it was afternoon before he could arrange it. A great deal of coffee and doughnuts, several plugs of tobacco, and another greenback finally made up for his lack of orders. At last a quartermaster, convinced or worn out, flagged a west-bound empty headed for the arsenal at Pittsburgh.

Consequently, about one o'clock the colonel found himself somewhat ridiculously being "made comfortable" as the sole passenger of a flat-car immediately behind the tender of a diamond smoke-stacked locomotive called the "Ambassador." A defunct rocking-chair had quickly been spiked to the planks of the car and over this the wreck of an old canvas-covered crate was hastily erected to keep off the sparks. The quartermaster who had wildly assembled this squalid contraption muttered to the fireman that some people wanted to be too damn' comfortable anyway, and winked. Under his martial pavilion the colonel now sat in a semi-woebegone state, for the fireman had thoughtfully emptied a bucket of water over the canvas to prevent the sparks. It dripped--on the colonel and onto a copy of the Harrisburg *Telegraph* that the engineer had provided to keep his passenger quiet. He, too, had handled "ginerals" before. He didn't like them in the cab.

The colonel grinned patiently. Over the top of his newspaper his blue eyes twinkled at Black Girl's brown ones, where she nickered at him through the slats of the first car behind. She had basely and falsely been persuaded into her present alarming predicament by doughnuts--and she wanted more.

"Gookamo, gookamo," wheedled the Pennsylvania Dutch brakeman, making circular gestures to the engine crew as he lured the "Ambassador" slowly backward to couple onto the colonel's car.

"Look out, you're against!" he roared suddenly. But it was too late.

The "Ambassador" settled into the cars with a smashing shock that nearly catapulted the colonel from his chair. A whistle, that set Black Girl dancing, summoned the train crew. There was a volcanic eruption of sparks and clouds of steam, a sickening, earthquake lurch taken up by each car in turn; and with admonitory wails to its long line of brakemen, alert at their wheels on every other car, the long empty train rushed screaming out of Lancaster.

The colonel was delighted. He might have caught the two-o'clock express for Harrisburg. But in that case he would have had to trust to providence and the quartermaster corps to see that Black Girl got to Harrisburg too. Providence might be all right, but he had his doubts about quartermasters. Besides, like all old campaigners, he was now easily at home almost anywhere he found himself.

Flaming clinkers caromed off the roof of his "pavilion." A constant rain of cinders pattered about. Behind him the square rear of the tender leaped up and down and rocked frantically to and fro as the "Ambassador" negotiated the right of way at all of forty miles an hour. But he sat contentedly enjoying the feeling of rushing out into space which the open flat-car conveyed. His two saddle-bags, all that he needed, were beside him. Presently he placed Black Girl's saddle over the broken chair, sat on it comfortably enough, and managed in the shelter of the tender to read the Harrisburg *Telegraph.*

The jerks of the train no longer annoyed him. He had crossed the continent and fought three campaigns in that saddle. It was now the most comfortable seat he knew. The lovely fields and valleys of his native state flowed backward into the east, followed by the telegraph wires loop by loop by loop. The colonel chewed the end of a Wheeling tobie, which is one degree more stunning than a Pittsburgh stogie, and settled himself to his newspaper.

Sheridan, he was glad to see, was thoroughly reorganizing the new "Department of the Middle." Snipers were being ruthlessly wiped out in the Valley. Early was temporarily quiet beyond Port Republic. Grant was--but he turned the page.

Clement Laird Vallandigham was loose again, thumbing his nose at "King Lincoln." There was a real Copperhead for you! He skipped the item impatiently.

Representative John M. Broomall, of Pennsylvania, had "introduced a bill in the House to reimburse every officer above the rank of captain"--the colonel's attention became fixed--"for oats consumed by the said officer's horse or horses during the period of the rebellion."

Why only oats? thought the colonel. But the Democrats were opposed--the villains! The colonel grinned and continued. Here was the kind of news he doted on:

REMARKABLE OCCURRENCE AT SHAMOKIN

Our Northumberland County correspondent informs us by electric telegraph that a frog having four perfect back legs and two heads was recently taken in the mill-race at Mary Ann. Although dead when first seen by our correspondent, he was assured by its captor, a prominent member of the local bar, that it was normal in every other respect. The person transmitting this information is of such a high order of moral character that it is impossible to doubt the correctness of his views.
"What hath God wrought!"

For some reason or other this tickled the colonel enormously. Brushing occasional cinders from his eyes, he continued:

Dauphin County--a great many Rutherfords in the vicinity of Harrisburg were visiting a great many Rutherfords . . . The ladies' bazaar at the . . .

He turned the page:

URIAH H. MYERS
Printer to the
Commonwealth of Pennsylvania
will
--for a trifling emolument--
beautifully bind, trim, and decorate
Copies of *Harper's Weekly,*
The Illustrated London News
also
Leslie's Weekly and *Other Periodicals*
(Preserve your illustrated history of the
present great war)

Followed a long list of the killed, wounded, and missing of the present great war.

The train rocketed out onto a long trestle. Over the end of the tender climbed a fat soldier "to borry the loan of a chaw." The colonel extended him a tobie, upon which he began to ruminate. He was, he confided, from Doylestown. He belonged to the Pennsylvania Reserves and was returning to Camp Curtin at Harrisburg. "Mine off is all," he said. By this the colonel presently understood that the man meant his furlough had expired. Presently the tobie began to get in its good emetic work. The man arose, tottered, saluted with open fingers, and managed with some difficulty to crawl back over the tender to his friend the engineer. He wanted sympathy.

Sometime about sundown, with brakes and whistles screaming, the train pulled into the yards of Harrisburg.

The colonel enticed Black Girl out of her box-car by a final doughnut that he had saved for the occasion. She picked her way gingerly over the frogs and switches in the yards and snorted upon finding a good city road under her feet. They galloped down into town.

But Harrisburg was packed. The legislature was still in extra session. There was to be a great review by the governor at Camp Curtin next day. Politicians and soldiers, their families and relatives, swarmed. Not a decent bed was to be had. Even Mr. W. H. Thompson, the manager of the United States Hotel, could do nothing and said so. With some difficulty the colonel found a stall for Black Girl, but nothing for himself. It was already late twilight when he found himself, still supperless and shelterless, standing much perplexed in old Capitol Park looking down State Street.

There was something peculiarly inviting, genteel, and domestic about State Street. It ran for only a few blocks, with the river and an island glimmering at its end, seen down a tunnel of ancient trees. Through these and the honeysuckle vines covering the trellised porches shimmered the pale yellow of parlour lamps; sounded the voices of children going to bed and a low hum of conversation and click of supper dishes.

The colonel felt a wave of homesickness sweep over him. Behind him a few belated squirrels still frisked from tree to tree about the glimmering, white stone buildings of the old Capitol. A gig with its lamps burning like twin stars stood waiting for someone by the kerb. He walked up into the park and sat down on a bench with his haversack beside him. Twilight died slowly in the wide valley of the Susquehanna. Darkness comes softly in Harrisburg.

The colonel sat for a while in one of those half-pleasing, timeless reveries that fatigue and loneliness will bring upon the best of us. It was a quarter of an hour later when a tall man in a plug hat came down the walk from the Capitol, briskly, as though he were late for supper.

"Good evening," said the colonel suddenly out of sheer loneliness as the man passed him.

"Oh," said the gentleman, somewhat startled, for he had evidently not seen the man on the bench. "Who is it?" he asked a little doubtfully, stopping.

"I beg your pardon," replied the colonel. "I am a stranger here and had really no reason to speak to you. Except--that it seemed a bit lonely."

"Reason enough," said the gentleman, with a pleasant laugh. "Well, my name's Myers," he added, holding out a white hand in the darkness.

"Not Mr. Myers, the state printer!" said the colonel by journalistic inspiration, while he introduced himself.

"The very man," replied the figure in the plug hat and long black beard, for that was about all the colonel could see of him. "Were you looking for me?"

"Why, yes, in a way," laughed the colonel, straining circumstances a little. "I thought, since you are a person of some consequence, you might direct me to the home of a respectable family who could put me up overnight. I am unwashed, unshaven, supperless, and a stranger. You see, I need influence."

"In fact, a desperate character in desperate circumstances," said Mr. Myers, chuckling. By this time they had strolled down to the foot of the park together. "Come with me, sir. I think I know a fairly respectable family not far from here who will be happy to accommodate you. But I can't guarantee that my influence will necessarily prevail." Whereupon, much to the colonel's embarrassment, Mr. Myers insisted upon shouldering the colonel's bags and, much to his delight, turned down State Street.

"Good evening, all the Blacks," said Mr. Myers, raising his plug hat mock-loftily as he passed the side porch of a house on the corner. A chorus of familiar greeting and the giggles of girls came out of the darkness.

"Helen has been waiting supper an hour for you," said a motherly voice.

"You'd never do that for *your* mister, would you, Mrs. Black?" replied Mr. Myers.

"I'd never keep her waiting," shouted Mr. Black. At which tremendous repartee there was warm laughter from all hands.

Something about this simple neighbourly warmth, perhaps something in the umbrageous atmosphere of State Street itself with its broad brick walks and dark spreading trees laced below with the glow from bedroom windows, contrived to warm the cockles of the colonel's heart. Somehow he felt as though he were going home, and he surrendered himself gladly to the impression. Mr. Myers turned in at the house next door to Mr. Black's. "Sit down for a minute," said he, "till I speak to Mrs. Myers."

"But, my dear Mr. Myers, I had no idea of imposing myself on you!" began the colonel.

"My dear sir," replied Mr. Myers, pausing for a moment on his own threshold proudly, "no officer in the Union Army shall go without supper and shelter in Harrisburg so long as there's food and a roof at my house. Now wait just a minute," he added and went in with the colonel's bags.

"Uri, how late you are," cried a clear, womanly voice somewhere in the hall. There was the sound of a kiss, whispers, and the swish of skirts rushing upstairs. Somewhere up there a room was being rapidly put in order for him, the colonel thought; and he remembered how empty and bare the old house at Kennett Square had seemed since his mother's death. Decidedly it lacked something.

What a sensible fellow this Myers is, he began to reflect, when he noticed that he was not, as he had supposed, alone on the porch.

The porch was dark except where a dim glow came out of the front door from a room beyond the vestibule. But at the opposite end of the veranda a clear stream of lamplight escaped in a downward bar from beneath a blind to illuminate the lap of someone seated there. From the waist up the figure was invisible; a black skirt from the knees down--and a great splash of scarlet, blue, and white, smouldering and squirming in the lap under the bar of light.

In the cavernlike perspective of the porch, behind the dense vines that shielded it from the street, the trunkless figure, the living, moving mass of colour in so mysterious a lap, produced an all but occult effect. Back and forth through the beam of light flashed a pair of birdlike hands that seemed unattached and to be feeding, as it were, upon the mass of colour over which they hovered. Nothing else was to be seen, and there was nothing else to be heard but the breeze in the vines and a faint rustle of silk.

It was some instants before the colonel's eyes were able to resolve this *camera obscura* vision into the more prosaic view of a pair of woman's hands engaged in mending an American flag.

Still there was something aloof about the half-concealed figure. Although he was tired and hungry, the colonel's curiosity was aroused. Nor did it lessen when he observed that neither darkness nor light made any difference to the busy fingers sewing the flag. With a strange indifference, but an infinitely delicate touch, they sought out the rents in the fabric, whether in lamplight or shadow, and went to work upon them with the smallest of needles that flashed occasionally like a firefly as it darted in and out of the beam of light.

The silk rustled. The colonel *did* wish Mr. Myers would return. . . .

"Helen will be ready for you presently," said the woman in the corner.

The colonel started a little. The voice seemed to be coming from behind the veil. There was a queer other-world quality to it.

"I have felt your eyes upon me for some time," the woman continued. "You are a soldier, aren't you? At least I can smell your horse." She laughed a little languidly.

"Yes, madam, I am Colonel Franklin of the Sixth Pennsylvania Cavalry," answered the colonel, somewhat awe-struck.

"I am Mrs. Anna Gill, Mr. Myers's mother-in-law," replied the woman. "Uri would have introduced us if he had seen me." She sighed a little. "He is not indifferent."

"That is beautiful work you are doing, Mrs. Gill," said the colonel, at a loss what else to say.

"So they tell me," replied the voice patiently. "But perhaps they are only being kind? I can't see the work myself, you know. I have been blind now for nearly fifteen years."

Lord! thought the colonel. I might have known.

"That makes it a little difficult, you see, sometimes."

"Yes, Mrs. Gill," said the colonel.

"Uri gets me the torn flags from the adjutant-general's office when the regiments turn them in," continued Mrs. Gill. "Uri is quite a politician, you know. He knows how to get things. I repair them before they go back to the field again. Some of them are shot full of holes, and the state has to buy new ones. This one, they say, has been back twice. I repaired it, I think, just after Gettysburg. Do you know, I dream over these flags a good deal." She sighed almost inaudibly. "I have three sons in the army myself. None of them has been killed yet. I am very thankful. Ah, here comes Uri!"

Mr. and Mrs. Myers were both at the door.

The colonel was introduced, formally to Mrs. Myers and with some gaiety to Mrs. Gill, who, as she was led into the house by her daughter, enjoyed immensely the kindly banter heaped upon her for having adroitly annexed the colonel in the dark.

"But it is always dark for me, you know, colonel," laughed Mrs. Gill. "I have to do the best I can."

"You do extraordinarily well, mother," said Mr. Myers, winking at his wife. "Every morning, colonel," he continued, "Mrs. Gill holds a levee on the front porch when State Street goes to work. She is better than an extra cup of coffee. Even when the war news is terrible she sends us all to the office laughing."

"The finest stimulant in the world," said the colonel, taking Mrs. Gill's arm to lead her into the dining-room. "Madam, permit me."

The wonderful face of the blind woman, calm, invincible, with a kind of cosmic benignity caught in its lines of suffering, looked up at him and with closed eyes flashed him an unquenchable, coquettish smile. She patted his arm. It was the signal that he had been taken into the family circle. Mr. and Mrs. Myers looked at each other and smiled.

"Mother and I have had our supper," said Mrs. Myers, "but we can sit with you and Uri while you eat, if you like."

"Certainly we should like," said Mr. Myers, putting an arm around his wife--and they entered the little dining-room, elegant with coloured glassware, stuffed pieces, and whatnots. An oil lamp threw an intimate circle of light on the broad roses of the low ceiling.

By some domestic magic Mrs. Myers had not only rearranged the guest chamber, but had also set the table for a pleasant little supper for two, all, so to speak, in the twinkling of a mouse's eye. She had even managed her long jet earrings, a fresh lace collar, and her best cameo brooch.

What is important to the soul is always mysterious. Just why the supper that night in Harrisburg with the Myerses afterwards assumed an importance in the colonel's memory equal to a major and vital event was largely inexplicable. That it did, he could have no doubt.

Curiously presiding over the scene was the patient and yet determined and exalted spirit of the blind Mrs. Gill. Already past middle age, with two homely but kindly furrows extending from her nose to her mouth, she gazed seemingly into the future with unseeing and unwinking eyes. Events could no longer much affect her. Her affliction, by darkening the world, had intensified within her a secret source of blander radiance. Absent from her eyes, it seemed to shine through her lips slightly parted in a smile as calm and reassuring as lamplight under the threshold of a closely-shuttered house.

Not that she said anything in particular. She simply sat there with all the vivid awareness and all the aloofness of those who for some reason are at one within; whom nothing can overcome. And while Mrs. Myers poured the coffee and spoke of the difficulties of raising tame blackbirds and children,--both of them died easily, it seemed, in Harrisburg,--Mrs. Gill continued to look into the future blindly and to provide the human atmosphere that surrounded them all; in which the four of them gathered under the misty arch of lamplight reflected from the ceiling were as one.

They were not particularly aware of this. No one spoke of it. It was a mutual and understood feeling. Suddenly, quite suddenly to the colonel, who was fatigued and somewhat hazy for lack of sleep, it seemed that Mrs. Gill had become--was--in herself the essence of the town, the state, the nation that lay all about them in the night without.

The blackbirds that died were embalmed, that is--The colonel started a little.

Mrs. Myers was still speaking of blackbirds.

They were under a glass dome on the mantelpiece, poised coyly on an obviously artificial branch and supposed to be about to peck at a berry that was--that looked uncommonly like a shoe button lost in the painted leaves of yester-year at the bottom of the dome. They seemed to have attained a complete domesticity, a timeless existence in a vacuum under the glass. The colonel, a bit weary, envied them for the time being. Marriage had its compensations. After the war he would like to crawl under a glass dome like that, with someone. That precious pair of birds, how they looked at the shoe button--while he forever smirked, she poised in air--elegantly.

And above them was Mrs. Myers's child, who had passed with the blackbirds, so she was saying. He also was embalmed, but in paint.

It was a startling portrait in a tremendous gilt frame. A little boy with wide clear brows, dressed in a virulent red dress. ABC blocks were heaped over his chubby legs, and behind him were two tremendous painted curtains with tassels, and a light that seemed to be beating up from the Sea of Glass. Nothing else could be reflecting it.

"Poor Henry," Mrs. Myers was saying.

By a curious telepathy or sleepy propinquity, for the room was very silent except for the soughing sigh of the lamp, and Mrs. Myers's soft voice, the colonel suddenly saw the picture through her eyes. *Her* baby sitting in paradise bathed in eternal light. For an instant the long shadow made by one little foot across the golden sands assumed the importance of the shade cast by the gnomon of Cleopatra's Needle. It led fortuitously to "Alf Wall, pinxit, Pittsburg, Pa." The artist had somehow contrived to bathe his name in not a little of the eternal light.

With a start the colonel just prevented himself from nodding and chuckling at the same time. It would never have done, never!

"For when he died," said Mrs. Myers, her eyes hanging on the portrait softly, "mother said she thought she heard music in the room. Harps," she whispered. Under her lace cap Mrs. Gill smiled like a sibyl and said nothing.

Perhaps this was too much for the credulity of Mr. Myers, or perhaps he did not care to have so intimate a family miracle confessed to a stranger.

"Mother does hear things," he said. "She heard Gettysburg before the news came. The morning of the first day she made us bring her chair down to Front Street and she sat there on the river bank talking about the guns. No one else could hear them."

"I *felt* them," corrected Mrs. Gill. "It was like distant bells in the air. A great tolling."

"Quite a crowd gathered about," said Mr. Myers. "She kept saying a great battle was going on. Some of them laughed. Well, afterwards they got the papers. Then some of them said *they* could hear the guns." Mr. Myers laughed at that himself.

"She sat there for three days. We took her down every morning. People kept asking her what was going on. You'd think she was an oracle the way they acted."

"On the third day something died," said Mrs. Gill. "I told them! I said it was over. I knew I was right. What do they still go on fighting for?" she asked with a little quaver.

"Heaven only knows, madam!" said the colonel.

"Uri, don't talk about the war," said Mrs. Myers. "I'm sure that the colonel, that all of us, hear enough of it. I can't bear it. Sing us a little something. Mr. Myers plays the zither, you know," she added proudly.

Somewhat shamefacedly, yet evidently pleased, Mr. Myers brought his zither from the next room and laid it on the table. He sat down and in a moment lost himself as he ran his hands over the low-toned wires. He sang a few old German songs a little sleepily, like echoes from the past. When he finished, Mrs. Myers filled four tiny blue glasses with parsnip wine. They drank to one another and retired. Next day was a Thursday and a bright shining morning in Harrisburg.

The colonel rose early. But not so early that Mrs. Myers and Mrs. Gill had not already been to market and returned laden. Their "plunder was toted by a contraband." That is to say, their purchases were carried home for them by a coloured boy whose master in Virginia, owing to Mr. Lincoln's proclamations, no longer enjoyed his services. Harrisburg was already full of "contrabands." They poured across the narrow neck of Maryland into Pennsylvania and in the southern towns and counties of that state already constituted a problem which was not being solved.

Mrs. Myers's contraband had, for an old pair of Mr. Myers's shoes, virtually become a family retainer, who expected to be retained. He followed the two ladies every morning to market, taking a peculiar personal pleasure in watching the blind woman buy melons. Her touch told her whether they were ripe or green. The rejection by Mrs. Gill of a fine-looking but unripe fruit offered by some wily Dutch farmer caused the contraband Claudius, or "Cloud" as he was known, to whoop loudly, and to do a cart-wheel or two in front of the farmer's stall. This negative advertisement and Mrs. Gill's uncanny touch gave the market-men the feeling of being "hexed." As a consequence Mrs. Myers's basket was supplied with nothing but the super-best.

Upon such delicacies Cloud dined contentedly in Mrs. Myers's kitchen, dressed in an old mail-sack from which the iron collar, like a badge of slavery, had been removed. A pair of frayed scarlet suspenders, an ancient, moth-eaten beaver hat crushed beyond hope, Mr. Myers's boots, and the large black *U. S. Mail* staggering over his breast gave Cloud the appearance of an Ethiopian uhlan, and an importance that sustained his soul.

It was he who brought Black Girl, beautifully groomed and shining, from her stable and watched the colonel depart for "ole Virginny" with homesick eyes.

Poor Cloud, thought the colonel, your shadow lies black across the land.

Noon was booming out from the old Capitol clock when he at last rode down State Street, after a fond farewell to his hosts. Trotting along Front Street, he finally merged himself in the half-darkness of the long covered bridge across the Susquehanna--headed south.

CHAPTER V

A BAREFOOTED RECITAL

The pattern of alternate light and shade from the ports of the old bridge through which the head of his horse seemed to proceed like some animal in a weird legend, the hollow boom of Black Girl's hoofs in the long wooden cavern, marked in the colonel's mind the crossing of the river that flowed between the lands of peace and the realms of war.

As he came out in the sunlight on the other side, the familiar sight of a long line of army wagons climbing up from the river on the Carlisle Pike, bound south for Sheridan, confirmed his fancy. For a rough interchange of greetings and the whole-souled profanity of the drivers and escort as he passed along the train welcomed him with authentic vocabulary into the regions of Mars.

And it must be confessed that the smell of leather and horses, the squealing of wheels, the familiar odour from bags of coffee, beans, and bacon brought back memories of field and camp-fires that seemed, with a strange contradiction, also to be welcoming him home. For many years now the stars had been his roof and the trees his canopy; the ever-changing fields of war the landscape of his home--in the saddle. A horse was now almost like a part of his own body.

As he rode rapidly past the wagons he took the opportunity by light blows of his gauntlet about the tender ears of Black Girl to break her of the dangerous habit of neighing at every horse she met. It was a bad, it might be a fatal, habit for a soldier's mount. Black Girl, being female, laid her ears back and neighed the more. She could not, however, avoid the spurs. Her punishment was light, but she tore down the dusty highway towards Carlisle. He let her have her head half the way.

There was just a touch of autumn in the air. Here and there a maple burned gloriously before him. Constellations of golden pumpkins lay scattered amongst the cornstalks. The wheat sheaves were piled high. It was a bountiful harvest, but it was being taken in late. Only a year earlier Lee's invasion had swept over these border counties. Most of the mules and horses were gone and nearly all the wagons. And there had been subsequent raids for more horses and fodder. Many people, even lawyers and ministers in the smaller towns, still went hatless, barefoot, or in the flimsiest of pumps and slippers. From Chambersburg to York,

Pennsylvania had been swept clean of hats and shoes, and had not yet reshod itself. Many women's shoes had gone South too, for the Army of Northern Virginia had wives--even babies, it appeared.

At Carlisle the colonel stayed the night. Part of the town was still in ruins from the bombardment of the year before. How Lee had massed his troops there, and the various adventures of people in the vicinity: that and the rebel raid of two months previous were the common talk of the neighbourhood. The colonel left early next morning and again overtook his friends of the wagon train encountered the day before. They were plodding steadily ahead, having camped outside the town overnight. Through the afternoon the long, wavering ranges of the Alleghenies began to climb above the horizon until the ridge of Tuscarora Mountain towered like a fortress against the western sky.

The distant sight of the green Appalachians never failed to make his heart leap up and to increase his fund of spirits. He regarded the calm, fertile, and magnificent valleys that lay between their wavelike, forested heights as the most characteristically native of any scenery in America-- and he had seen a great deal of the United States both East and West. This Appalachian country was not huge, barren, and monotonous like so much of the West. There was nothing here to suggest that perhaps one had always better be moving. On the contrary, there was a kind of overtone from the countryside that whispered, "Tarry, traveller, tarry. Here is comfort for the soul of man. Here are verdancy and peace."

For two hundred years, under the King's Peace and the Federal Union, the benign promise of these valleys had been fostered and matured. In them European bones had grown longer, old ways of life had been forgotten and new habits formed. These kindly, rolling mountains had rocked the cradle of a new, perhaps a better, race--the North Americans. And the hope of that race was peace.

For if there was anything "new and better" about America it was the hope of peace--of peace on a more secure, vaster, continental scale than had ever been tried or attempted before. Oceans to the east and west of her, arid wilderness to the south, and the self-same friendly people to the north- -the nation could not be seriously threatened by anything but disturbance from within.

And now that had come. If Lee and his gallant rebels succeeded, if the South successfully asserted her independence, a great armed barrier would stretch across the land from the Atlantic to the Pacific. There would be wars, endless Gettysburgs, raids, burnings, implacable anger and growing hatred, reprisals for generations to come.

Already the ancient, grim, and merry game of "Harry the Border" had begun.

The Valley of Virginia was laid waste from end to end. Neutral Maryland and the teeming southern counties of Pennsylvania with their shady towns, long the abodes of decency and peace, were ablaze with alarm lest the same fate should befall them.

In three years two blood-letting invasions and a constant series of raids had wrought incalculable havoc all along the Mason and Dixon line. The country on both sides of it was already full of new cemeteries and smoking villages. And as yet the bonds of federal union were only loosened. How when they were gone?--when every state was sovereign to do wrong! Or would it end even there?

Virginia had already divided in two and was fighting herself internally. Sinister accounts of villages "occupied" and ravaged by guerrillas who cared nothing for either cause, but a great deal for other people's property, were rife. In those hills to the south the dreadful revelries of chaos were already going on. Those hills the colonel regarded as rightfully the castles of a peace destined to endure for ages to come. His love for his nation was still somewhat English and was closely connected with the land. Those hills were to him the symbols of his country and, when he looked at them, he knew what he was fighting for.

For arguments about slavery and the negro, he cared little. They might be the ancient cause of this war. He could do nothing now about causes, but he could help to prevent the *effects;* save the future from continual chaos.

About four o'clock that afternoon he rode into Chambersburg, where the "effects" were abundantly evident. The town was mostly in ruins. Two hundred and fifty houses had been burned by Early's men seeking horses, shoes, fodder, and a half-million in cash--and other sundries scarce in Virginia. This had been only a few weeks before. A village of temporary shacks and shebangs had already sprung up amid the ashes. In the business section of the town, shops and stores were gallantly making shift as best they could to carry on with "business as usual" signs and a new stock of goods. The lower story of the old hotel had been made habitable, and the combined dining-room and bar, in particular, was doing a roaring, boom-time business, with the added excitement of the approaching election in full swing.

Chambersburg was one American town where the presence of the army was now genuinely desired and appreciated. The colonel found his uniform an easy passport to more hospitality and conviviality than he was able to enjoy. In some of its aspects the scene at the bar reminded him of his early Western days. All that was needed was the presence of a few drunken Indians to complete the illusion that Chambersburg was a frontier town. A number of rough-and-ready brethren as well as respectable citizens, farmers, sutlers, wagoners, soldiers, and politicians filled the room with a roar of talk and eddying tobacco smoke. One "Judge" Bristline, the henchman of Thaddeus Stevens "over to Lancaster," was busy turning out the regular Republican vote. He proved to be not only affable, but breezy. He stood against the bar with a glass of whisky before him, smoking a large El Sol cigar and welcoming every new-comer like a long-lost son. It was the colonel who made the initial mistake of starting a conversation that threatened to have no earthly end. . . .

"Bad as it is, it ain't as though the guerrillas had come here," said a young militia officer, interrupting Judge Bristline, but only temporarily. "The rebels were in a hurry because Averell's men were hard on their heels, but there was no one murdered, and I didn't hear of none of the girls being molested. That crowd that rode into Chambersburg last July looked like brigands, all right, but they had discipline. You will have to admit that."

"Yep," said Judge Bristline, who was more or less the oracle of the tavern, "you'll have to admit that." As the judge spoke he settled comfortably over the brass rail one high arch of a pair of fine new boots he had recently purchased in Philadelphia, and squinted reflectively into a tall glass of raw rye whisky.

"When the rebels came there was no promiscuous looting. They were in too much of a hurry for that. Yet when they burned this town, they burned it methodically. The half-million dollars they levied on us was taken in a positively cavalier manner. That is, what they could get of it. No promissory notes were accepted. Some of our citizens paid cash promptly for the first time in their lives. When they saw the money going off in boxes in a wagon they could scarcely believe it. It was just like a minstrel show taking all the small change out of town. Not much worse, either. They might have gotten all they demanded but they didn't know how to go about it. They don't know how rich these towns are, and cavaliers, you know, have always been poor financiers.

"The shoe business, however, was more annoying. That was an individual affair. They just stopped you in the street or went into your house or office and took the shoes off your feet or out of the closet. It was most humiliatin'. And it was a mistake, because they took both Democratic and Republican shoes. And I have observed that ever since then a barefooted Copperhead is as ardent a Union man as a black Republican. Yes, sir, it was evident that the Union meant shoes."

"Among other things, I hope," laughed the colonel.

"Admittedly, but *below* all--shoes," continued the judge, taking a deep swallow and fixing the flames of two bar lights in line in the remaining amber of his glass.

"You see, I'm a reflecting man. I look deep into things," said he, twirling his glass about, "after they happen, maybe. But like most people along the border, I've thought a good deal about what they call 'Lee's invasion,' and it occurs to me that, if Jeff Davis was responsible for it, phrenologically speaking he must have a hollow instead of a bump of sagacity under that shock of statesman's hair he sports. After all, he's an American and he used to be a good politician. So he must know that in America, next to love the most important thing is state politics. They say he sent Lee up North to force foreign recognition for the Confederacy-- England, I suppose. What a damn-fool stunt that was! Trying to make friends with England, sir, he thoroughly antagonized Pennsylvania!"

The judge brought his fist down on the bar so that a dozen bottles jumped and everyone in the place looked at him.

"You can laugh if you like," he continued almost grimly; "you can say that I talk like a cider-barrel statesman or call me a barroom patriot." He refilled his glass, again held it up, and looked through the clear whisky at the lights.

"Never mind if I seem to be taking a strange view of things. Remember that I am now looking at affairs through one of the finest focusing mediums known to the mind of man. And what I say is that when Lee invaded Pennsylvania he sealed the fate of the South."

At this point the judge felt impelled to swallow his view of things.

"Gentlemen," said he, inspired now and no longer addressing the colonel in particular but everybody in the room, and an unseen audience besides, "--gentlemen of the bar, did you ever pause to consider the grand old Keystone Commonwealth? There are forty-five thousand square miles of her. She rolls superbly through mountain, valley, and plain from the Delaware to the Ohio. She teems with millions of hardy and prosperous citizens. In the East she deals with the seven seas. In the West she makes what all the world must have. Her farms are fabulously fertile and her mines pour forth the wealth of Golconda. Her many cities are beehives of ingenious artisans. Her philosophy is always the one that eventually prevails. Alone, and by herself, she constitutes one of the powerful nations of the earth. And it was this mighty commonwealth, a nigh and good neighbour to Virginia, that an armed rabble led by plantation owners mounted on hunting horses fell upon with fire, sword, and bloody slaughter. What for? To gain the possible recognition of England three thousand miles away! Was that strategy, was that statesmanship?"

"No!" the whole room roared back at him.

There was a great thumping of glasses and bottles, a stamping of feet--and not a little laughter.

"Make us another speech, judge," someone called.

"Where's your uniform?" yelled a soldier near the door, and dodged out.

The judge was instantly much embarrassed. He had not meant to make a speech. He had simply been a little overinspired by his "view of things," as he hastily explained to the colonel while leading him firmly by the arm to a table in the corner. There was no escaping him.

On this furlough the colonel seemed to be doomed to listen to other people's views on the war. Well, it was natural enough, he supposed. Civilians seemed to think that every soldier, every veteran in particular, was more interested in the war than in anything else. The colonel made up his mind then and there that as soon as the judge got through speaking his piece he would go out and saddle Black Girl, no matter what hour it was, and ride--ride away--over the mountains if necessary, to some valley that was peaceful.

"No," insisted the judge, "I should not have made a speech, although it was a good one about Lee's invasion, but I could write a book about it."

"I am sure you could," admitted the colonel hastily.

"But I won't," said the judge, "I'll just give you a few random impressions of it that will tend to confirm the point which I recently made, *ahem,* before the bar, as it were."

The colonel settled himself resignedly, but with an air of polite attention.

"Well, sir, when the rebels first poured into this town I couldn't believe it. I was surprised. What surprised me? Why, they seemed to have come out of the past. It wasn't that they were in Pennsylvania that was so astonishing. It was that they were in the present. Talk, clothes, manners, the way they acted was, well, it was colonial! Damn me, I can't quite explain it, maybe, but it seemed like hearing echoes and watching ghosts of something I thought I'd forgotten. They seemed like so many yesterdays trying to palm themselves off as the heirs of tomorrow. And that's what made us all feel that for certain they'd have to clear out. Time itself seemed to be against them. I believe they felt uneasy about it themselves. They acted that way. Taking old hats and shoes too!

"Old Mrs. Patterson who lives down the Old York Road--she's nearly eighty--told me the same thing. 'Land sakes,' she says, 'I'd forgotten folks could look that way. They come tearin' down the road like somethin' out of an old, bad story of hard times. Them officers with long, droopy capes ridin' loose on rangy horses, with a curl in their hats, so bearded and proud. It's like what English Uncle Ned used to tell us about fightin' Boney. And the cannon comin' tearin' and bumpin' after 'em. That's what they wanted our good wagon wheels fer! And if you think the riders went by fast, you ought to've saw their foot soldiers. They don't march like our boys, all regular and together. They come stormin' along, bare feet and tattered trousers; cursin', whistlin', lettin' out yowls. It was the yowlin' made us all so mad. You could tell that people what whoop like that ain't fer law an' order, even at their own homes. No, sir, they don't march together. Each one fer himself with long strides kind o' wolfin' it along, and long rifles straight back over their shoulders. I never seen so many lean faces under broad felt hats all et round the brim. Land! Folks ain't wore hats like that around here sence the stumps was took out. Swan ef I know where they got 'em. 'Course they was hungry! They just et us out o' house and home. That's all they took in the house 'cept shoes. A general and his staff come in the yard and I give 'em a bakin' o' blackberry pie. There they set eatin' wedges of pie and tryin' to keep the juice from runnin' down onto their dusty breasts by wipin' their mouths with their gloves. I give the general a bottle of elderberry wine too. He stuck it in his holster like a pistol and thanked me like a gentleman. I guess maybe he was one. Our little Billy was a-settin' by the pump watchin', and he speaks up sudden-like and says "Hurrah for Abe Lincoln!" "That's right, son," says the general, "stick up fer your own side." And they all galloped off laughin', latherin' down the road with the dust rollin'. My, there was a sight of 'em. All day they kept comin' down the hill. You'd see a bunch of old flags against the sky and hear 'em yowlin', and then another hull colyum ud go by. After a while we jes' closed the shutters and set in the parlour like it was a funeral. When we come out the horses was gone and most o' the hay, and wagon wheels. That's what we're tryin' to get the government to pay fer now--the United

States government! They ought to pay or keep people like that where they belong. It was like somethin' let out. Next day our John jes' went off and jined the militia. "I ain't a-goin' to stand fer it," he says. Next thing we heard was about Gettysburg. Served 'em right!'"

The judge was an excellent mimic. In the rôle of old Mrs. Patterson he had again contrived to get the attention of the entire room. The colonel was amused despite himself.

"Laugh if you want," said the judge, "but that's history. You see, the point I'm making is that the personal appearance of the rebels in Pennsylvania was a mistake. After we saw 'em we knew they couldn't win. You'll always read about Gettysburg in the books after this, but what you won't read, and what I know, is that it wouldn't have made much difference if they'd won. They'd have been awful tired even after a victory. They might even have got into Baltimore, or Washington or Philadelphia--and there they'd have been waiting for English help. They wouldn't ever have gotten North. Do you remember how the farmers turned out and shot the British off around Lexington? Well, it would have been like that only on a big, big scale. It's a long walk up three hundred miles of the Susquehanna, with fine shooting from every hill, and then you come to the border of New York. What Lee's invasion did was to turn out the *posse comitatus* of the nation to put his people down. Up to that time the war had been fought by Abe Lincoln's government from Washington with the U. S. Army. Lee turned out the militia of the big powerful states against him. What Lincoln's and Governor Curtin's proclamations and bounties and the draft couldn't do, the invasion of Pennsylvania did. It got swarms of men for the Army of the Potomac. That's the finest army the world has ever seen. The more you beat it the better it gets. And now it has a great man for its general. Let's drink to him," cried the judge. "It's on me. This nonsense about two governments in one country is soon going to be over."

"To the last battle then," said the colonel.

"The only one that finally counts," said the judge. They drank.

The judge seized the colonel's sleeve. "I want to tell you one thing more," said he earnestly.

"Good Lord, man," said the colonel, "I won't run off with your best audience, even if it's me. But a bargain! Only one thing--not two. I've got to go--sometime!"

"I know it," replied the judge, looking rueful nevertheless. "It's too bad. But did you see the rebels in Pennsylvania?"

"No, sir, I was in Virginia at the time," laughed the colonel.

"It would have encouraged you to have seen them in Pennsylvania."

"I can scarcely conceive that it would," said the colonel.

"But it would have. You see, they came all excited and full of enthusiasm as though they'd won a victory just by invading. They came 'yowlin'' along the roads, as old Mrs. Patterson said. And after a while the yowls kind of died away. I talked to some of them here before they burned the town. They were surprised and discouraged already. There were more men about than they'd ever seen before, even in peacetimes. And white men. No signs of war. The most prosperous towns most of 'em had ever seen, and farms like they hadn't dreamed of.

"'You didn't know theh was a wah till we-all come No'th, did you?' a young feller from Mississippi says to me.

"'No,' I says, 'not unless we read about it in the papers.'

"'How fah across is it, strangeh?'

"'How far across what?'

"'How fah across Yankee-land till ye git to Canada?' he jerks out, kind o' firin' up as though I ought to be able to read his mind.

"'Oh, about seven hundred miles, stranger-r-r,' I growls. 'And swarmin' with militia!'

"'Shucks,' he says, looking kind o' sody-biscuit green. 'They told us you was all tuckered out at the No'th. 'Tain't so, is it?'

"'Nope,' say I, 'it ain't.'

"'Well, if it's that fah across Yankee-land,' he adds kind o' soft, 'I'll jes' esk fer yer shoes.'

"So I got down on the kerb and unlaced 'em.

"'You can keep yoh co-at,' he says, 'it would make my par look like an abolitionist. Er *you* one?'

"'No, my pa owned niggers right here once and not so long ago.'

"'Do tell,' says he. 'Well, then, ah reckon ah'll take the co-at!'

"Now that's one thing I want to tell you, but there's another thing I want to ask you."

The long-suffering colonel nodded and took a restorative drink. The judge joined him.

"It's this. That same day as I walked, rather I should say, sir, as I *limped* barefooted down Main Street, there was a couple of young rebels looking in Mrs. Tubb's window. She's our milliner. And one says to the other, 'Lookee, Telfare, thar's moh poke bonnets in that thar window than *you'll* ever see in fohty Easters at Ninety-Six.'

"Now what do you think he meant by that?"

"Ninety-Six is a town in one of the Carolinas, I believe," replied the colonel.

"No! You don't say so! *Ninety-Six!* Why, that proves the point I've been making all along," cried the judge, his face brightening irrationally. "If you want to talk *that* kind of arithmetic I'd put it this way: They have as much chance of beating us as Ninety-Six is to Philadelphia. Do you get my point?" He looked a little confused. "You will," he insisted, "if you take my point of view."

He raised the glass in the air and looked at the light again. He seemed to be having some difficulty with his eyes. And the glass was empty. The finger which had been detaining the colonel by the sleeve all evening now relaxed. The colonel carefully detached himself and rose, leaving the judge sitting there looking through his glass. He almost tiptoed over to the bar.

"What do I owe?" said he.

"Are you payin' for the judge too?" whispered the barkeep thoughtfully.

"Yes," said the colonel, "rather than disturb him now, I'd . . ."

The man nodded.

"Well, the judge came in about three o'clock this afternoon."

"Old Thad Stevens over to Lancaster says he's going to make 'em pay for all the trouble they put us to," began the judge.

"Lord!" said the colonel, looking frantically at the barkeep.

"Seven-fifty," said the barkeep.

The colonel paid and ran.

Judge Bristline continued to sit in the corner looking through his empty glass. He had lost his point of view. One eye had set up a Confederacy of its own and insisted upon deviating from the true line of sight. Where there should have been one light, the judge saw two.

The colonel looked up and saw ten thousand. He was standing outside once more, breathing freely, and looking up at the stars.

All about him rose the blackened chimneys and fire-scarred walls of the burnt town. Here and there amid the ruins a light twinkled from the window of a house where the inhabitants had returned and set about repairs. There was already quite a number of these cheerful beacons of returning peace, but the place still smelled of charred, damp wood and had about it the indescribable, owlish air of ruin and a great burning. The memories thus aroused were for the colonel, momentarily at least, unbearable. It smelled like the Valley of Virginia.

He must get away from this. Only about three weeks of his precious leave remained. For each one of these weeks he had already spent a year in the midst of war, and that part of his furlough which lay behind him had, it seemed, been devoted to the same thing--nothing but talk about the war. If he could only get a few days', even a few hours' change! Perhaps in the remote Fulton County Valley just to the west, where there were no railroads and where few raids had come, he might find--oh, well, just a brief respite. That was all he was looking for. Black Girl would be tired, but she was now a soldier's horse and in any event she must get used to being frequently roused at night.

He borrowed a lantern, and going to the stables, which were as yet only half-roofed-in, he roused the mare, gave her an extra feed and a good rubdown. She stood patiently while he saddled her. She made no effort to refuse the bit. . . . He was glad to see that already she trusted him. "Poor beast," he murmured, "this is not your quarrel, but you will probably be killed in it--bearing your master." He rode out, quietly keeping to the turf.

Some hours later he was ascending the long winding road that leads over a high ridge of Tuscarora Mountain to the Fulton Valley beyond. It was well after midnight when he reached the crest and one of the great views of the Eastern United States burst upon him.

The remnant of a late moon rode high, pouring a solemn glory into the giant furrow between the straight lines of mountains. Farm and hamlet, orchard, wood and meadow lay preternaturally clear in a metallic light. Southward as far as the eye could see a little river of quicksilver glittered in S-shaped curves. There was not the slightest suggestion of movement anywhere. It was like a glimpse into the hidden Garden of the Hesperides.

Here, if anywhere--thought the colonel.

He removed his hat and let the cool night breeze run through his hair. Black Girl stood, her feet apart, breathing slowly. Miles below, a few lamps in the valley marked the village of McConnellsburg.

CHAPTER VI

THE VALLEY OF DELIGHT

To act on impulse alone is frequently dangerous and usually disappointing. As a military man, the colonel had long ago discovered that. Yet this midnight ride over the mountain into the remote Fulton County Valley had been scarcely more than a whim. But it was a whim which he never regretted. The week that he spent in the golden autumn weather between the flaming mountain walls of that Pennsylvania valley, remained ever afterwards in his memory as a brief classic of heartsease and happiness. It was a kind of timeless and halcyon tarrying between battles in a vale of peace.

He rode into McConnellsburg, the quaint green metropolis of the Fulton Valley, about dawn on a Saturday morning and put up at the Waggoners and Drovers Hotel which, though fallen upon somnolent days, still welcomed him bountifully. The colonel had a feather-bed, and Black Girl a stall of clover. He slept all day, rose, ate his supper alone in a dream, tried to read a volume of General Albert Pike's *Hymns to the Gods*--and naturally enough, slept again.

It was the rumble of the organ in the church on the green near by that wakened him late Sunday morning.

Rapidly he made the best toilet he could with a razor, a comb, and a small whiskbroom, and strolled over to the church. A bald-headed and sunburnt farmer, obviously a pillar of the community, welcomed him in whispers, but warmly, to "our house of God."

The colonel had not been inside a church for many years. The Western frontiers and the war had seen to that. But his mother had been a Presbyterian, and from childhood associations he felt like a boy in church again. The presence of many children, who often peeked back at the "soldier-man" in uniform, kept the feeling of the place from being grim. Yet the service was austere, its simplicity impressive.

This was the tabernacle of the valley. It was full of Scotch-Irish Presbyterians in the presence of their Lord of Hosts. The Scotch God who had come into Ireland before Oliver Cromwell had migrated with them to Pennsylvania. There was many a "Mac" in the colonel's regiment, some from this very valley, and the colonel sat among them now at prayers with a certain deep and intuitive understanding with which his more rational philosophy did not interfere. In a sense they were his people. Stonewall Jackson, he reflected uncomfortably, must also have been of the same persuasion, it reports could be believed. And he wondered whether the God invoked in Mr. Lincoln's more recent proclamations were not also a familiar in this place.

Nowhere in that chapel was the Christian symbol of salvation and mercy to be seen.

The uncompromising mountain sunshine flooded through the clear, white window-panes, slightly distorting the trees outside that seemed to be moving and making vague gestures from another world. The light rushed like cold, blue lake water over the whorled woodwork of the pews, so that the weather-tanned heads of the men, the poke-bonnets of the women, and the icy-faced elders with spade beards, sitting aloft on the platform by the pulpit, were revealed in a state of super-reality. The mere static vigour of their presence was overpowering. They seemed to exist unalterable, sitting there in some distant reflection from the incandescent lamp of Justice burning between the cherubim--praising it through their noses. For there was a twang, not of harps, and only a far, quaint echo of the litany in:

> "Behemoth must salute his God;
> The mighty whale doth spout;
> Up from the deep wee codlins peep
> And wave their tails about."

That was the last verse of the last hymn. It was therefore repeated. The colonel was so delighted with it that he released the full fervour of a hearty baritone into the lines and thus succeeded, inadvertently, in turning many a sweet face in a poke-bonnet towards the back of the church.

Outside in the calm autumn sunshine every hint of spiritual grimness in these people disappeared in the world of nature, as though Pennsylvania and Calvin could not mix. Dourness seemed to drop from them as their healthy and smiling faces passed out the church door. A Mrs. Russell, the mother of a sergeant in his regiment, recognized him. Instantly, he found himself surrounded by friends and fellow patriots; overwhelmed with invitations from Russells, Pattersons, MacNaughtons, McLanes, and McNairs.

To these simple people it seemed the most natural thing in the world that Colonel Franklin should have chosen their beautiful valley in which to spend the precious days of his leave. And best of all, from having received back into their hearts many a lad on furlough, they seemed to have attained a keen sense of just how precious those days must be. Of deserters they said nothing, nor did the colonel. And that, too, was part of his passport to hospitality.

"Land of Nation!" said Mrs. Russell, as they drove off with a surfeit of Russells great and small in the Russell surrey, with a youthful Russell following proudly mounted on Black Girl. "To think that you went to a hotel, and every letter from our Jim has been full of news of you."

The colonel was forced carefully to explain the unholy hour of his arrival in McConnellsburg. But that was the only embarrassment of his stay in the county. That, and his inability to eat more than half his own weight at a sitting.

For the demise of corpulent calves and the silencing of voluble turkeys marked his course southward as he rode down the valley, stopping off at the various Macs'. He took part in the harvest in regimental trousers and shirt-sleeves, and swung a scythe with the best. He swam in the deep holes of the quicksilver river while Black Girl rolled in bracken on the banks. Heavily-laced peach cobblers, pumpkin pies, creamy cider, and sombre, potent perry became merely a daily ration. The art of whisky-making lingered surreptitiously in those regions, he was forced to conclude, not regretfully.

Oldsters took down their fiddles to while away the evenings. At the McNairs', after the dishes were done one evening, Helen, the dark-haired blue-eyed daughter of the house, brought out a battered foot-organ and sang to it:

> "So over the heather we'll dance together
> All in the mornin' airlie,
> With heart and hand we'll take our stand,
> For who'll be King but Charlie?"

She did not know who Charlie was any more or why he was to be king, except that his story had something to do with an old claymore over the mantelpiece. So the colonel spent an enviable evening on the front porch explaining it to her--along with other things not entirely historical--and rode on next day to the McLanes'. But not before Helen had "unbeknownst" pressed a package of her best veal sausage into one of his saddle holsters.

Aside from a few naturally anxious questions by relatives about some of the boys in his own command, there had been few, if any, references to the war. Of the raid of the previous July they said little. The rebels had just come--and gone.

Yet the draft had come into this valley too, plucking boys from the school-desk and the plough, and there were sad faces here and there and women in black. But they had not obtruded their sorrow upon him. Either their natural reticence and hospitality were above it, or they had learned how to renew the heart in a soldier on leave.

Maybe it is because there are no newspapers here to refresh daily that haunting sense of crisis that forever weighs down the heart in these days, mused the colonel. There were newspapers, but they were mostly old ones.

"And what so ridiculous as the scarehead of yesterday," he pondered half-aloud, tossing an old sheet about the "appalling defeat at Fredericksburg" back into the bin, where it was being saved, along with other fatal defeats and victories, to wrap elderberry jam pots for Mrs. McLane's well-lined shelves. In all this valley there was not even one nervously clicking telegraph. There was nothing more disturbing than the giant rumours of the changing seasons forever raised by the winds as they ranged down the endless mountain walls. Here he had found peace again for a little, and he was thankful for it.

He was grateful to the people of the valley who had taken him into their homes. Their emotions about the war were private ones, mostly sorrowful, and therefore not to be communicated. They seemed to regard war in the light of a natural and unavoidable calamity. Like childbed fever, it was a form of fatality that frequently went along with life and birth. It was one of God's feeders of cemeteries that was not to be discussed. For those who had gone there was silent honour, and no more.

Towards the end of his stay, as he stood one afternoon part way up the mountain looking out over the clustered roofs of a little place called Big Cove Tannery into the peaceful and solitary fields beyond, he was suddenly and forcibly reminded of some lines by E. A. Poe:

> ". . . They had gone unto the wars,
> Trusting to the mild-eyed stars,
> Nightly, from their azure towers,
> To keep watch above the flowers,
> In the midst of which all day
> The red sunlight lazily lay . . ."

So it had been with the people of this valley, he thought.

Even now the red sunlight lay lazily across the fields below as he descended the path to Big Cove Tannery, where he was to pass the night.

This was to be his last evening in the valley. It was time to go. His own desire and the calendar said so. His thoughts now wandered, with an eagerness and a bright anticipation that surprised him, to his own regiment camped in the Valley of Virginia a hundred miles away. He wondered if Dudley, his orderly, had kept the flaps of his tent tied and the rain out; if he had found that last cherished bottle of nappy old English ale which Bayard Taylor had sent him. Suddenly, and quite anxiously, his hand went to his inner breastpocket to see if Mrs. Crittendon's packet was still safe.

It was still there.

At the thought of her a certain apprehensive, yet strangely pleasing melancholy overtook him as he rode through the sunset along the mill-race path into Big Cove Tannery. It was very green and cool along the mill-race. There was a constant sound of deep-rushing waters.

"Roll, O Shenandoah, roll," he trolled, his mind still in Virginia.

But there was nothing melancholy about the evening at Big Cove. The ample upper floor of the tannery had been cleared for a barn dance given for the entire neighbourhood. They had been making shoes there for the army out of the new tanned leather, and the half-hundred employés as well as the owners of the place were flush with a wartime, paper-money prosperity.

Lights shone from all the windows of the long stone buildings and were reflected softly in the big mill-pond. A notable battery of fiddlers had been assembled, and there was plenty of hard cider and whisky.

The colonel danced, and danced late. He enjoyed it hugely. Most of the families he had visited were present. He danced with them all, mothers and daughters, and saw them off home in the big carts deep with hay provided by the "Management." A thousand farewells and a hundred messages to the boys at the front with the 6th Pennsylvania rang in his ears. The exhilaration of scraping fiddles and the stamping of feet seemed to bubble in his blood. Just before the last dance was over, on sheer impulse, he mounted Black Girl and galloped off down the valley with the sound of music and summer laughter behind him.

Hard cider rides well. The moon was rising. The trees rushed by him in the cool night. Black Girl's hoofs devoured the road. His sabre banged his hip, reminding him of battles to come. Frantic dogs overtook him, and fell behind. The neighbours spoke next morning of a crazy man on a foam-flecked black horse, that passed like a tipsy angel in the night, singing and shouting:

"We are coming, Father Abraham, three hundred thousand more . . ."

"You never can tell what a soldier will do next--unless he's a Union general," said the colonel, as he whirled over the Pennsylvania border early next morning and found himself in Maryland.

CHAPTER VII

A MAD DOG INTERLUDE

There was no doubt that he was in Maryland. If his frayed map hadn't told him, his ears and eyes would have. That subtle something that makes it unnecessary to pick things up for a long time, if ever, that permits the chickens to wander and the dogs to become legion, had even here, in the far western and mountainous portions of the "Old Line State," cast a certain oblique and faintly visible reflection of Ethiopian decrepitude and slavery over the countryside.

One could see it if one looked sidewise at it, so to speak. Not all the buildings were upright. The talk was a little softer and of a mode more ancient. The emphasis by tongue and gesture was just easy enough not to be tired. And in the small town of Bellegrove only a mile or so over the line, where he stopped for breakfast, the colonel noticed the universal tag that marked every Southerner, except the opulent planter class--an air of concealing a great secret about which nobody must ever talk.

It had taken the colonel several years to guess the secret. There wasn't any. Yet, in a way, it felt comfortable to be back over the line and "taken into the secret" again. For that reason he merely nodded at the dowdy matron who waited upon him at the little hotel.

"Hog meat an' coffee's all used up. It's been took by the armies," she said by way of explanation, as she placed his eggs, hot biscuits, and molasses before him. "There's melk."

The colonel nodded.

"I ain't used to waitin' myself," she continued, giggling a little uneasily as she slopped some of the milk. "The niggers hev lit out."

"All of 'em?"

"Well, most o' the young'uns," she said, sitting down in a rocking-chair and beginning to do her hair, "an' them that stayed, even the old'uns, are askin' for wages. Did you ever hear the like?"

"Never," said the colonel. "It must be terrible!"

A large strand of hair held firmly in her mouth while she combed the other side of her head kept the lady from replying immediately.

"*Mo*'lasses?" she said at last inquiringly, although still muffled.

"No, there's plenty, thank you," replied the colonel, and choked a little. "I should think the border patrol would stop the contraband."

"They do git some of 'em. But laws! Ye cain't stop 'em. They creep up through the woods from Virginny at night just like fleas through a dog's har. And they take our niggers along with 'em. The gals, ye know, go off with the boys. They say they treat 'em like white folks in Pennsy."

"That's an exaggeration, I can assure you, madam," replied the colonel. "They only do something for them, the best they can."

"That's about all any of us can do these days with a passel o' Republican scum in Washin'ton," sighed his hostess. "Sometimes I've thought o' movin' up Chambersburg way myself, but I ain't got no kin there. I'd jes' be among strangehs. Do you think you-all will be stayin' with us now or will Lee chase you out agin an' come back, rampagin' up out of Virginny?"

"This time I *think* we've come to stay."

She shook her head a little dubiously at his reply.

"Well," she said at last, "I wish to Gord you'd both get yer fightin' done with and leave us alone here in Maryland. Ain't that reasonable?"

"It's very reasonable, madam," said the colonel, laughing heartily. "That's the trouble with it and Maryland, I'm afraid."

"Oh, you men!" said the woman. "If you don't stop all your bang-bangin' and your raidin' and burnin', your yowlin' and toot-tootlin', and stealin', there won't be no use hereafter of even startin' a settin' hen." She swept all the empty dishes into her apron indignantly, took up his half-dollar bill with a sniff, and departed into the kitchen. The colonel waited for the crash of dishes.

It came.

He rose and went out onto the shady side porch. An old coloured man with a grey, woolly head sat on the steps in the sun, leaning over his cane.

"You the last one left, uncle?" said the colonel.

The old man lifted his head, brushing the flies away weakly.

"Yas, sah. All dem wid sound limbs done gone No'th. Please, Mars' Gineral, do gib me dime fer snack. Dey ain't feed us no moh. Jes' slops!"

"Go look after my horse," replied the colonel, giving him a paper quarter.

"Yas, sah, I'll let her into de clovah paddock behin' de hoose. You'll find yoh saddle lef' in de bahn." He went off folding the note and muttering thanks.

Neither colour nor politics kept anyone from admiring the federal currency, the colonel noted. The enthusiasm for it was universal.

He threw himself down on an old couch through which the stuffing exuded in wads and, despite the flies and the chickens, slept on the porch well into the morning. In the paddock behind the house Black Girl rolled, four feet in the air. The sunlight most "lazily lay."

He slept much longer than he had intended. He wakened to the sound of cackling. One of the chickens had laid an egg on the porch. But the shadows were not yet lengthening, he noticed. It was just about noon. He saddled Black Girl hastily and rode out of the town.

Maryland is only a few miles wide where he was crossing it. Rather to his own surprise, for he had forgotten the exact lay of the land, within less than an hour he clattered across the canal bridge, found himself trotting down a sharp declivity with the Potomac River before him. It was the border of the new state. He urged Black Girl into the water, spattered through the shallow ford of the muddy stream, up the other bank and was suddenly brought to a stand.

"Ha-awlt," said an unpleasant voice with an impudent drawl. "Who be ya, and whar do yer think yer goin'?"

Despite the fact that the man who challenged him was fingering a pistol, the colonel could hardly keep from laughing at him. He had on a pair of what had obviously been red woollen underdrawers, with white tape sewed down the sides for stripes, toeless boots, and a blue uniform coat with buckeye buttons. He peered at the colonel out of such thick, blond whiskers that his eyes seemed to be lost in taffy that needed pulling.

The colonel felt inclined to do some pulling. But, instead, he stated his rank and destination. The man might be an authorized sentry even if he had only red underdrawers on.

"Kunnel, ee?" said the sentry. "You don' say? Well, yer cain't go to Morgan Springs."

"Why not?" said the colonel.

"Oh, jes' 'cause yer cain't. It's Sergeant Smith's orders."

"Is Sergeant Smith in charge at Morgan Springs?" asked the colonel in a surprised and delighted tone.

"He ain't egzactly in charge, he's our 'lected leader," replied the man, now almost friendly with so much conversation. "Why? Do yer know 'im?"

"I've met him in the army again and again," said the colonel.

"Now thar's whar I caught ya lyin'," said the fellow suspiciously. "He ain't in the army. He's Kanawher militiar."

"Kanawha militia! What's that?" demanded the colonel.

"West Virginny; West Virginny, I should hev said. That's what they're a-goin' to call the State, I hear. They wuz goin' to call it Kanawher fustest.

That's the reason we're still called Kanawher Zoo-aves. But yer cain't go to Morgan Springs, no how."

Oh, can't I? thought the colonel.

"Well, I suppose I can't," he said in a resigned manner, and took a bite from what seemed to be a large plug of tobacco but was really a small brown copy of the cavalry drill regulation which he drew from his pocket. He pulled it slowly through his teeth.

"Have a chaw?" said he.

"Don' care ef I do," said the man; "but pitch that ar plug to me, and I don' say I'll pitch it back neither," he added, and pointed his pistol at the colonel with a cunning grin.

"Catch," said the colonel. He pitched the book easily.

The man put out his hand to snatch it. About a foot from his face the "plug of tobacco" suddenly seemed to burst as the book opened and fluttered.

"Jesus!" said the Kanawha Zouave. His pistol went off in the air.

Almost at the same instant the colonel and his horse collided full tilt with the gentleman in military underdrawers, catapulting him into a patch of briers . . . .

"'. . . and scratched them in again,'" quoted the colonel quite unconsciously, as he bent low in the saddle and came up out of the river bottom like a flying fish out of a wave.

"Go it, old girl!"

A short distance down the road the rest of the picket, lolling about a blanket with cards and a large jug on it, flashed into view. The colonel switched to the bank of hard turf on the side of the road.

Someone shouted.

There was a drumming of hoofs on the turf, and Black Girl and her rider passed right through and over the prostrate forms of the picket rolling or leaping to one side. A sharp *clink* as one of the mare's iron shoes caught the jug marked her passing. A rolling volley of oaths was the only ammunition expended.

Faced by the irretrievable disaster of the shattered jug and the agonized howls of their comrade, the Kanawha Zouave in the briers, it was several minutes before the gallant outpost could even agree on what had happened. It was finally argued, plausibly, that someone had passed. A new deal of full-deck poker ensued, after the scattered cards were picked up.

Meanwhile, the colonel had long ago disappeared in a cloud of red dust around a curve in the road.

Before him, over the pleasant rolling hills the white steeples and red hotel roofs of Morgan Springs were already coming into view as he topped the crests. It was five or six years since Nathaniel Franklin, then but newly returned from the Oregon country, had last visited the little resort. Doubtless the "Springs" would now be almost deserted. But he remembered the proprietor, Mr. Duane, pleasantly, and all that he wanted now was a room overnight and a decent meal or two before he finally turned back east into the Valley of Virginia to rejoin his command.

After tonight, campaigning, field rations, and the hard ground would again be his lot--perhaps forever. This was to be a sort of last respite and harmless indulgence coupled with pleasant recollections. For, although he would scarcely have conceded it, there were certain sentimental memories of moonlight on the broad verandas, of dancing, and the cherished recollection of vanished, boyhood vacations that had drawn him with the ghosts of satin ribbons to the spot. Of course, he would never admit it. But the scenery *was* getting painfully-pleasantly familiar.

"My, my!" If that wasn't the little "Pagoda-cottage" where the Cary girls had stayed!

The swing--that was gone. Only a frayed rope dangling. How Alice's skirts used to rustle in the breeze of swinging, and flap loose, and how she would tilt them under her hoops! Black Girl pointed her ears down the vacant path where he had unwittingly let her stop.

The place was high with weeds, wasps in the porch, and all the paint scaled off. The little house looked eyeless and hopelessly dilapidated. Some one had taken all the fence palings. And it had once been so charming!

A wave of anger and disappointment swept over him as he turned Black Girl up the road again. The village was just beyond around a short bend. Ahead of him a rifle-shot rang out. The sound of hoarse laughter and loud, loose talk came through the trees. Another rifle-shot--a distant tinkle of glass. The village street opened before him. Moving warily, he took to the turf again. Yet it was all so familiar.

The great trees with horizontal arms across the double road with the green down the middle, Judge Washington's house with the cupola, the long façade of the old hotel, all lay before him. But heavens, in what decrepitude! There were the starshaped bathhouses, and gay-latticed privies, scattered about among the trees to the left, but deserted--literally only skeletons of themselves. Someone had been stealing lumber. And all the beautiful scroll-saw gates and fences, once the pride of the street, where the girls had leaned to watch the gentlemen riding around the green under the trees were gone. Cows wandered over the lawns. Even the village houses looked deserted. Or were people peeping at him through shuttered windows? Not a rose or a geranium anywhere. Rubbish scattered everywhere, tangles of weeds and honey-suckle, and--a rifle-shot rang out again.

He could see what was doing now. At the far end of the green under the trees there was a large group of men. They looked like more Kanawha Zouaves. Someone was having a little unofficial rifle practice. The flash of a round and wisps of powder smoke caught in the trees showed where. But there were only two men shooting. The rest, a dozen or so, were pitching horseshoes. Scattered all about them on the grass were some large black-and-brown animals stretched out asleep in the sun.

Hogs, thought the colonel. Lord, I might have known it! Fit company--and right where the covered chairs used to wait for the ladies. It made him mad clear through. To see "soldiers" there disguised, as it were, in blue Union coats made him madder yet. Soldiers!

He started up the turf at the side of the road at a rapid trot just as a quarrel and loud shouting broke out among the horseshoe pitchers. The two men with rifles paid no attention even when a fight started. As the colonel rode up, one of them leaned back against a tree and took aim at a window in the hotel. The shot rang out and a light tinkled out of a window in which only one pane now remained. Most of the other windows in that wing were gone.

The colonel walked Black Girl very quietly from under the trees onto the lawn in front of the hotel. He came up behind the earnest marksmen unnoticed. The din of the fight over the horseshoes a little farther down the green was hearty and ferocious. Somebody was being gouged.

"You take the next shot, Jeb, and that'll finish that winder fer to-day," said the man with the rifle.

"Never mind doing that," said the colonel.

The two men leaped to their feet. One of them shouted with surprise. Somewhere a hound with a voice like a buoy bell began to bay. He came out from under the hotel porch.

"What the hell . . .?" exclaimed the man with the rifle. "Hi!"

The fight stopped. A complete silence fell on the green. The men stood gawking at him. And it was then that the colonel saw them coming. Not hogs--but dogs!

They weren't razor-backs as he had thought. They were big, massive curs like wolves that gathered themselves in a pack as though they understood their business. They gathered first. That was what saved him. Someone whistled shrilly. He noted that man, big full lips and spread nose. Then the pack was after him, sounding like a night hunt let out of hell.

All this had happened in the space of a few heart-beats. His mind raced. It would never do to try to meet them. They would drag him down. His only hope was to string them out.

He spurred Black Girl madly down the left street of the green. The double road was like an oval race track with the deserted verandas of the old cottages staring at it up and down both sides. Many a time he had ridden around that oval with the other gentlemen at the Springs, raising hats to the ladies on the porches. How fashionable then!--Now he was being hunted around it by dogs! Black Girl's hoofs hummed on the road. She was bolting. That would never do. He held her in, and drew from his right holster.

A big cur leaped suddenly at him from the right side. It knew its business. It was running like a deer, yet it soared up straight from the ground in one clean leap for the mare's nose.

"Got him!"

Maddened by the shot that had just gone off by her ear, Black Girl seemed to settle nearer the ground and to skim.

He flipped around suddenly in the saddle and began to ride backward. It was an old Indian trick. He had five shots left. He began to shoot dogs.

He shot five of them--deliberately.

He reached back in his left holster for his other Colt and pulled hard-- pulled out a package of sausage! The one Helen McNair had put there out of kindness. He flung it down, and pivoting on his hands, turned forward again. Oh, fatal kindness of Helen McNair!

He had his other revolver by now but he was almost at the lower end of the drive where it made the turn and went up the right side of the green. There was no exit there. The cottages went right around the curve. He would have to make the turn. Someone had piled all the old park benches at the end of the green. If the remaining pack got among those he could never get them. But if he could string them out across the green! That would give him clear space to shoot. He might make it.

He swung across the green before the benches and started coming back up the right side.

The dogs used their noses rather than their eyes. They overran their trail. They were confused for a moment or two. In those few instants he gained many precious yards on the back track. Then one of the men whistled to them--the same whistle. The dogs saw him and came tearing across the green. There were still four of them there, the bigger and heavier beasts that had fallen behind. He checked Black Girl. She reared. The eager whining was close. He began to shoot.

Black Girl shied. He missed--twice. The group of men began to roar. Then he got them.

The colonel was literally blind with rage. For an instant the scene before him darkened and glinted with red sparks. Black Girl pawed the ground and neighed. When the view cleared for the colonel he saw the group of men at the other end of the green silently staring at him. They had drawn together now. Trotting towards them quite calmly across the grass was the sole survivor of the pack, the biggest brute of them all, with that package of Helen McNair's sausage dangling from his jaws. The calm absurdity of this, the impudent indifference of the animal to everything but the loot retrieved, released a spring in the colonel's brain. Indeed, it would be more accurate to say "exploded a small mine." For the next ten minutes things continued to happen with explosive rapidity at Morgan Springs. Sausage, in a manner of speaking, was the cause of it.

The colonel had now emptied his pistols and there was no time to reload. One glimpse of the dog, trotting nonchalantly through the calm afternoon sunshine with the meat in his mouth for his amiable masters at the far end of the green, brought the colonel into instant action! His sabre flashed and Black Girl sprang forward, her hoofs drumming frantically.

The dog saw him coming; broke into a trot, then into a rapid lope. As his pursuer gained, he made a dash for it.

Black Girl caught up with him almost opposite the group of men. They stood fascinated. The dog dropped the meat and turned; crouched. The horseman thundered down on him. The dog sprang. A blinding flash of sunlight struck him where he might have worn a collar.

The colonel reined Black Girl in violently. He brought her around on her hind legs, her forelegs striking out, and came to a halt before the gang on the green. His sabre clanged home in the scabbard. They eyed each other.

"Mah Gode!" said someone. "'At's the fust time ah ever did see a dohg cut ra-ight in two!"

It was the man with the thick lips.

The colonel drew a revolver. He forgot that it was not loaded. The laugh that had started died away.

"Come here," said the colonel to the man with the thick lips. He was undoubtedly the clown of the company. Everything depended on getting him. He stepped forward, still grinning.

"You whistled the dogs on me, eh!"

The man stopped grinning.

"Didn't you?" roared the colonel.

"Yes, suh, but . . ." A look of cunning came into his face. His eyes shifted to the side.

The colonel flipped his revolver about in his hand. The butt of it came down like a hammer on the man's head. He dropped. The revolver flipped about again. Each one of the group before the colonel thought its little O-shaped mouth was now looking at him.

"Fall in!" roared the colonel.

It worked.

Afterwards the colonel thought they would certainly have murdered him that day if they had not at some time or other had some drill. But they had. At the voice of authority the Kanawha Zouaves began to fall in line. They even had a sergeant, it appeared. Naturally, even in this remote spa of West Virginia, he was an Irishman.

"Guides on the loin. Centre dress. Hump, ye damned spalpeens! Front!"

At the sound of this cheerful Irish voice the colonel put his revolver back in its holster. He was no longer dealing with individuals. A company, a disgraceful, a ragged, dirty, and a sullen company--but a company--had assembled itself before him. The little Irishman finished dressing the line and actually came out and saluted.

"Keep your men at attention, sergeant," said the colonel. "Face about and see that nobody moves."

A short silence of rigid attention ensued. The figure stretched on the green began to twitch.

"Johnson," said the sergeant to one of the men in ranks, "if you brush that hars-fly off yer pate, I'll kick you loose from yer arse." The horsefly remained.

Meanwhile, the colonel quietly reloaded his Colt revolvers. It gave him great satisfaction to do so while the men watched.

"You can brush that horse-fly off now, Johnson," he said when he finished. "Sergeant O'Toole."

"Killykelly, sor," replied the sergeant.

"Sergeant Killykelly," continued the colonel. "Where is Sergeant Smith?"

"He's after playin' he's king of the warld in the bridal soote at the hotel, an' . . ."

"Very good," said the colonel. "Then I won't be able to promote him. But I'm going to call on him--now."

"Yis, sor," said the sergeant.

"Whatever noises you may hear arising shortly from the bridal suite, pay no attention to them, sergeant."

"Oi will not," said the sergeant.

"I'm taking charge at Morgan Springs," said the colonel. "The troops to relieve your men will be here shortly. Where are your quarters?"

"In the west wing, sor."

"March your men off there and confine them to quarters. Mount a guard at the door." The man on the ground moved and started to groan. "Lock him in the horse stalls," said the colonel. "The caged ones in the racing stable. You know?"

"Oi do," said the sergeant, somewhat amazed. "Right face! Forward march!"

The colonel sat quietly watching while his orders were being carried out. The little column of men trooped across the green towards the west wing, carrying their stunned comrade. They seemed scarcely less stunned than he. The sergeant mounted guard at the door.

Correct, thought the colonel.

Then he suddenly swung Black Girl and forced her directly up the front steps of the hotel into the main lobby of the Morgan Springs establishment. There was no one there.

If there had been, he had intended to start a small indoor cavalry action of his own. He felt disappointed and a little foolish sitting astride a horse under the chandeliers. But he didn't intend to tether Black Girl outside for the first wandering Kanawha Zouave to appropriate, or to advertise his whereabouts. To the outside world he now seemed to have vanished.

He dismounted and threw Black Girl's bridle over the extended arm of a massive brass statue of Robin Hood. In one hand Robin Hood held a card tray and in the other an oil lamp. Thus the exact atmosphere of Sherwood Forest was nicely recalled, and the rest of the hotel lobby was--or rather had been--furnished to correspond. Someone had taken Robin Hood's sword, a real one, once the wonder and envy of all little boys at the Springs. The colonel remembered wearing it once himself in a charade.

Indeed, the Crystal Palace rusticity of the lobby had long been famed and thought elegant in four states around. But no one would have recognized the room now. Its grotesque ruin was strange even to the colonel, who was more than familiar with its erstwhile glories. The long mirrors painted with scenes of forest revelry and woodland lakes haunted by swains and swans were starred by bullets, shattered and smashed. A pair of filthy trousers hung gibbet-like from a wrecked chandelier. The safe had been blown open. The giant, calf-bound ledgers of the establishment had been dragged out and lay torn and littered about, "illustrated" with scenes of enormous dalliance by one of hell's most copious artists. The effect was a visual stink. The disembowelled stuffing of furniture and the skeletons of crippled chairs that seemed to have cried in vain for mercy spoke of a certain wicked patience or a primordial barbarian rage in their ravishers. And all this was contrasted in the colonel's mind with the politeness, the decorum, the elegance which he had last beheld in this room--before the war.

Mr. Duane, the proprietor of the place, was, the colonel recalled, an ardent secessionist. Well, secession had come! Probably Mr. Duane had not expected that one-half of his own state would secede from the other half--with such violent effects on his hotel lobby. Nevertheless, the colonel was by no means pleased. He loathed the work of guerrillas to begin with, and the fine specimen of obscene anarchy amid which he had just tethered his horse filled him with rage. It was not a blind rage this time. It was a calm one. There was something crystalline and icy about it.

The silence in the place was oppressive. He was at a loss as to just where "the bridal suite," alleged by Sergeant Killykelly to be the abode of Sergeant Smith, might be. The hotel was a large one, rambling into several wings. He dismounted and took both his revolvers from their holsters and stood listening. Outside a turkey gobbled. It reminded him of the erstwhile voluble and effusive conversation of the pompous proprietor. Where, by the way, *was* Mr. Duane? Then at some distance down one of the corridors he heard a woman laugh.

It might have been the ghost of laughter from old times supplied by his memory, he thought. But then he heard it again. There was something sinister about it. It came now quite clearly, apparently from a window in the east wing; and the lady had certainly been drinking--was drinking. The rumble of a man's voice joined in.

He walked down the corridor as quietly as he could, sticking close to the wall. One of his Colts he tucked into his belt. It was dark in the corridor.

The doors of open rooms he stepped by swiftly. They were all empty. Presently he approached a small vestibule. The light streamed into it from the side entrance, a door half-dragged off its hinges. On the other side a flight of steps led to the upper story.

Seated by a small desk formerly used by the porter was a man in a "uniform" which only a minstrel show would have regarded as military. He slept with his mouth open, tilted back in his chair against the porter's desk. At his feet lay a rifle and an empty bottle of, to judge by the odour, gin. In the regions upstairs there was a sudden outburst of lively conversation; several people seemed to be arguing. The laughter of the woman floated down again. It died away in an ugly giggle.

The colonel stepped forward and moved the rifle away gingerly with his foot. The "sentry" made no response. Finally he picked up the weapon and put it in a broom closet where it seemed to belong. Then he went over, and seizing the man by the back of his collar, led him, still sleeping, to a rear door with a key in it. He opened the door. A long flight of servants' steps with a skylight over a laundry roof near the bottom was revealed.

Splendid, the colonel decided. He had the feeling that the architect had been both clairvoyant and obliging. He poised the specimen of Kanawha Zouave just at the brink of that long flight of steps. All he had to do was to let go the man's collar. Gravity did the rest. The colonel stared entranced.

The man's head drooped to his shoes. He did a somersault. He flew straight. He bounded from a landing. He did a loop. He soared triumphantly--and disappeared with a soul-satisfying smash through the skylight. Upstairs, the lady who had been giggling screamed. The colonel locked the door and pocketed the key.

All those in the room upstairs would now be looking out the window to see what the crash was about, he thought. He took the stairs on the opposite side of the vestibule in a few strides--and found himself in a corridor of considerable length that still had its heavy carpet.

This was somewhat disconcerting as he had supposed that the room he was about to enter, judging by the voices, was just at the top of the stairs. It wasn't. It would have to be approached down the corridor. The little vestibule below had acted as a kind of sound-box that had made the voices seem much nearer than they were. He was alone. There was no telling who, or how many, might be in the room. And his success depended upon surprise. He stepped hastily behind the half-open door of a linen closet, and for the first time that day stopped to reconnoitre.

Evidently the noise he had made on the stairs had not alarmed anyone. The voices in the room continued as before. But he could hear them now quite plainly.

"Ah guess he's knocked cold, er de laundry doh's locked," said a feminine voice, the tones of which sounded muffled but like those of a coloured girl. "Anyhow, he ain't come out yet. Ah reckon he cain't." Here a hiccough received the tribute of a giggle.

"Don't tell me no more about that dern fool," replied an unpleasant and rasping man's voice in an exasperated tone. "When a sentry on juty gits so hog drunk he falls clean through a transom in the roof of the house he's gyardin', I leave him lay. Thash what I do! I leave him lay! I'll hev dishipline around here, I will! Now, you gel, you come away from that window. You quit 'sposin' you-ah pusson. Do you want the hull town to see you thataway?"

"Ah don' mind," said the girl, and giggled.

The man swore bitterly. "Great . . ."

From the crack in the door, through which the colonel had been looking while this conversation was going on, most of the stage for the dreary drama he had overheard--but not all the actors in it--was visible.

For at the end of about fifty feet of dim corridor he was looking up a couple of steps through a pillared arch into the long perspective of a brilliantly lit room. There were apparently windows along one side of it, since five long panels of sunlight fell slanting across the apartment, swarming with motes of dust. At the far end of the room, half-lost in the shadows of disarranged portières that now and then flapped in the wind, stood the full-length portrait of Eugénie, Empress of the French. At first glance, owing to the distance and the trickery of sunlight and shadow, the colonel had thought this incredibly arrayed woman was actually in the room; that the voice of the girl proceeded from her. This confused and ventriloquial association had occupied his mind only a few seconds, but it had been a peculiarly disconcerting one, and had kept him glued to his crack in the door weak with astonishment. His amusement at his own expense upon realizing that "Giggles" must be sitting in one of the windows, invisible from where he stood, was equally great.

But the "voice of a coloured girl" and the Empress Eugénie were not the only persons in the room.

Draped upon an elaborately carved and curved sofa upholstered in burning red velvet sprawled the form of a powerful, bearded man with his hands behind his head and his muddy cowhide boots cocked up on the opposite end of the couch. To punctuate his remarks, he from time to time made vicious jabs at the upholstery with his sharp heels. A ragged kepi was cocked down over his face to shield his eyes from the sunlight, and it was from under the visor of this once-military headpiece that his drawling and complaining profanity proceeded.

". . . Great Christ in the Mountains I Em boss of this yere Morgan Springs or ain't I? Em I your lawful commandin' officer, young man, or ain't I?" he demanded, sitting up suddenly and producing from behind the sofa a jug which he deftly swung over his forearm by one thumb and applied to his mouth. The musical diminuendo from the jug for a moment effectively interrupted him. The motes in the sunlight now seemed to be dancing to the tune of a gurgling flute.

"Answer me!" roared the man, putting the jug down and his hand to his throat. Under the impact of the fiery corn liquor his frame seemed visibly to expand. "Em I or ain't I?"

This last question, like those preceding it, was hurled in a bullying manner at the pathetic and yet somehow dauntless figure of a young "soldier" who stood erect, heels rigidly together, before the man on the sofa. The boyish solemnity of his fine, clear face, the mouth of which was still childish, an air of trying to do his duty while overwhelmed with chagrin, touched the colonel to the heart. Quite evidently here was the innocent and bewildered subject of much evil mirth.

The youth hitched uneasily and then, recollecting himself, came to attention again.

"You air, sir," said he.

"Air what?" roared the ruffian on the couch.

"You air my lawful, commandin' officer," replied the boy almost inaudibly.

"Say it again, and yer come to salute when yer say it," insisted his tormentor.

At this the lad drew a sword from a thong in his belt and came to the "sabre salute." He stood there rigidly, the polished blade glowing yellow in the sunlight. The colonel goggled. The sword was of brass. He recognized it. Years and years ago he had once for a proud moment of boyhood worn it himself. It was Robin Hood's sword.

The girl in the window began to titter in a peculiarly irritating way. Evidently the farce was being staged for her benefit, she thought.

"But who air you?" continued the man.

"I'm officer of the night," replied the boy, still saluting.

At this the giggles in the window became continuous and the man had to lie back on the sofa again to laugh. The colonel took advantage of this to emerge quietly from behind his door and to advance silently up the hall, pistol in hand. If only the planks didn't creak under the thick carpet! He went gingerly.

"Recite the juties of yer office," said the man, cocking his boots on the sofa again.

"Ter take charge of this town an' all of Sergeant Smith's property in view. Ter walk the streets in a military manner and report the presence of any pretty gels to Sergeant Smith . . ." The young voice died away as though its owner could not remember the rest of the rigmarole.

"And what else?" demanded Sergeant Smith, sitting up.

The colonel paused where he was, only a few paces from the arch, but still in the darkness of the corridor.

"Ter do whatever Sergeant Smith says," said the boy.

Somehow the colonel had the inspiration that his exact moment was about to come.

"All right," said Sergeant Smith, "then *do* what I say. Thar's a pretty gel a-settin' in the winder over thar. Kiss her."

"Never mind doing that," said the colonel. His voice, speaking suddenly out of the shadows of the corridor, seemed to have suspended time in the sunlit room.

The girl stopped giggling. The boy stood transfixed. Sergeant Smith sat on the sofa with his jaw open--left hanging, so to speak, in mid-air, while he stared down the steps into the dark hall. To his somewhat befuddled view, as the colonel came up the steps with a levelled weapon, the whole archway of the room contrived to turn into one large cannon of barrel like calibre, pointing exclusively at him. It was this vision rather than the obscure dictates of a troubled conscience which caused him to call upon the name of his Saviour and to reach for heaven at the same time.

"That's right," said the colonel, as he came into the room, "keep 'em up." Out of the corner of one eye he took in the apartment.

The girl was crouching back in one of the deep windows, half behind a curtain. She had nothing on but a red petticoat, and not much of that. She was almost white, he observed.

"Sit down, son," said the colonel to the "officer of the night."

With a look of surprised relief the young fellow took the place of his late commanding officer on the sofa. For a moment he sat there as though revolving in his mind the possibilities of his deliverance. He looked at the colonel. He looked up at the long, bearded figure of Sergeant Smith, whose hands were now tremblingly pointed at the ceiling, and laughed. He laughed aloud, and a little hysterically.

There *was* something subtly ludicrous about Sergeant Smith. His feet were too small for his bulk, for one thing. They were cruel little feet. He swayed on them while his eyes wandered towards a near-by table where a belt with a holster lay sprawling.

"Never mind that," said the colonel. "Keep 'em up and stand still, or I'll let the whisky out of you."

"Man, I won't move a muscle," replied the man. "But I cain't stand here forever."

"Son," said the colonel, "fetch a chair for Mr. Smith. A good stout one."

The boy on the sofa got up obediently and brought the chair.

"Put it in front of him with the back this way," said the colonel, "and stand over there."

"About face," said the colonel to his prisoner. This manœuvre started the boy laughing once more.

"Sit down, Mr. Smith, and keep your hands up," ordered the colonel. The girl in the window began to giggle again at this. Smith swore.

"Now, son," said the colonel, "go and fetch me some curtain cords. Be smart!"

At this point Mr. Smith seemed inclined to demur, and the colonel was forced to press the cold muzzle of his Colt against the back of the man's neck. It was fortunate that he did so, for as the young man approached the window to get the curtain cord the girl gave a loud scream.

"I ain't a-goin' to kiss yuh," said the boy. "I ain't partial to coloured gels, like him."

Mr. Smith wriggled.

The girl, however, was now completely panic-stricken. She modestly and drunkenly attempted to clothe herself more fully--in a curtain--and in doing so brought the heavy pole, amply weighted with brass knobs, down on her head. This, to her, mysterious attack from above routed her, and she fled like a cackling hen in red petticoats through a door at the far end of the room.

"That'll fix you," said Smith. "She'll tell 'em."

"Bring the cords," said the colonel. "Now, Mr. Smith, put your arms behind the chair.

"I'd tie him firmly, young fellow. You know you laughed at him," the colonel continued, while the lad lashed and knotted Mr. Smith's hands behind him to the slatted back of the chair.

"You can trust me for that," said the boy. "I ain't takin' no chances. He's the meanest Melungeon bastard that ever came out o' the hills."

Mr. Smith confirmed this view of his character and doubtful family antecedents by a burst of profanity that achieved lyric eloquence. That, however, did not prevent his feet from being bound firmly to the chair, while a cord was also passed about his middle.

He sat there now in a kind of "apoplexy" compounded of surprise, chagrin, whisky, consternation, and fury. Tassels from the curtain cords with which he was bound hung all over him as though a madman had adorned himself as "General of Generals." So amazing was the grotesque appearance of this piece of semi-military and bearded upholstery that the colonel motioned to his young collaborator in the masterpiece to remain seated in the window, where he had ensconced himself, while he sat down on the sofa to admire his handiwork. The profile of Mr. Smith, he observed, was not noticeably intellectual.

"Smith," said he, "how long have you been the boss at Morgan Springs?"

Mr. Smith's reply to this was to give three long and peculiar whistles that were exceedingly shrill.

Outside, there was complete silence. The sunlight continued to stream through the windows.

"We've been here three weeks, sir," said the lad by the window. The colonel waved to him to keep quiet. Mr. Smith whistled again, more shrilly.

"They're all dead, Smith," said the colonel. "I shot them all just before I came in."

"You shot them houn' dawgs! You did?" said Smith. "You, you . . .!"

"Never mind that," said the colonel.

"So that's what all the ruction was about. I thought the boys was just organizin' a nigger hunt for fun out on the common. An' now all them lovely dawgs is dade!" To the colonel's vast surprise, Mr. Smith burst into tears.

The colonel utilized this moment of noble grief to take Mr. Smith's belt and holster up from the table, where they had been thrown, and to buckle them about his waist above his own.

"God damn yer soul to hell," said Mr. Smith.

"The same to you, sir," said the colonel as he walked over to what had once been a beautifully-appointed ladies' writing desk and sat down. He beckoned to the young man to join him.

"What time do the pickets that are watching the roads come in?" he asked in a tone too low to reach the prisoner's ears.

"The 'blockaders,' you mean?" said the boy. "Why, they come in 'long about sundown fer grub. They change the guard then."

"Good! Could you get by them?" he asked. "I want you to carry a message to the Union troops stationed at Hancock."

"I kin git by, all right," replied the boy; "they know me, and I kin tell 'em I'm riding fer him, over there."

"Then I'm going to trust you," said the colonel.

"You kin do that," said the lad.

Looking at him, the colonel thought he could. He opened the drawer and rummaged for paper. There were old plume holders, steel pen stubs, odd bits of stationery, and other rubbish in the drawer from which a faint odour of ladies' scented notepaper still exhaled. He pulled out a torn sheet of paper. "Dear Mimsy--" ran a fine little copper-plate hand:

I promised to tell you how I liked being married, and should have written to you ages ago, but I have been very busy--being married. And I like it! Three months seems an age (one does not really change by being married) since we last rode out to the old "Hermitage" together and had one of our good gossips. Goodness, how I miss them and you, you dear old goosy! I suppose Richmond is full of fever and teething babes as usual. Mine will be this time next year I hope. There! You see my great news is out, so don't tell it to a soul! Oh! Mimsy!

The Springs this year is very gay. I am still dancing. Yesterday Mrs. Chestnut gave a reception in the Ladies' Parlour, now elegantly refurbished and called the Empress Eugénie Apartments. Ronnie Lee was there, the Beverleys, your friend Jack as gallant as usual. A Captain Crittendon of the U.S.T.E. and his wife, a charming Englishwoman (he married her while attaché in London), celebrated their . . . ing . . . anniversary . . . dance, . . . ice cream, champagne, and fire-works. You ask what to wear. My dear, magenta has *quite* gone out this summer. Skirts are bigger than . . . and nicest of all une chemise de nuit, batiste et dentelle . . .

and the torn letter ended in mid-air, somewhere in the summer of one of the 1850's.

She had been here--happy then!

A great longing for that happy, waltzing, music-box time came over him. He roused himself, looking around at the frightful mess in the once "elegant and genteel" ladies' parlour; at the ruffian tied in the chair; at the smooth copy of Winterhalter's Eugénie, looking at the present with disdainful, sloping shoulders and a weary smile. The combined reality and incredibility of what had happened to his world, the unlikelihood of the present moment, the complete fracture of the past in its own familiar surroundings almost stopped him . . .

It was with some difficulty that he finally brought himself to rummage through the drawer again, find a blank sheet of paper, and pen a brief description of his situation with an appeal for instant help to the commanding officer of the federal troops at Hancock, Maryland.

"Can you get a horse?" he asked finally, folding the note.

"No, sir, but I kin find me a mule," said the lad, who had been standing at strict attention all the while.

"Hurry," said the colonel. "It's only a few miles. Try to be back before sundown. And, son," he added, "if I were you I'd put back that sword where you got it."

The boy turned scarlet.

"It was *him* made me wear it," he said, angrily jerking a thumb at Smith. "I knowed better. I wanted to be a real soldier. I tried. I did!"

"I know," said the colonel. "Leave him to me, and get that message to Hancock."

The boy saluted elaborately and darted out of the room.

The sun went behind a cloud and the room suddenly seemed dark and lonely. The litter in it was more than awful. Smith and his lady must have been living in it for some time, to judge by the unemptied slop jars borrowed from other rooms, the inconceivable number of empty bottles, and a pile of valuable articles ranging from clocks to silverware, evidently fancied by Mr. Smith, who seemed to have the taste of a jackdaw for anything that shone or glittered.

The colonel got up, and walking over to him, gave an extremely expert demonstration of how to tie almost anyone permanently in a chair. The curtain cords were only covered with silk; they were good hemp underneath. Mr. Smith whined a little, cursed, and finally began to negotiate--with threats.

"I kin make it wuth you-ah while to leave me go. I'm sheriff of this county. Thar's a lot o' friends o' mine round about. They're *fer* me. Look out! Ouch! I ain't got no feelin' left in my hands. Let up!"

"What did you keep the dogs for, Smith?"

"Fer huntin' niggers mostly. I used to pick up a right sizable passel o' change thataway. Now look here, you've got my gel and my plunder, what more do . . ."

"I'm going to court-martial you, Smith. I'll send you to a Massachusetts regiment down Frederick way. The officers are all abolitionists."

A bad vista opened up before Mr. Smith.

"Now listen ter reason, kunnel, fer God's sake."

"Never mind that," said the colonel. "I'll leave you here for a while to think it over. Don't make any noise."

"I'm goin' ter be sick," said Mr. Smith. And he was, very.

The colonel went to the window and looked out. Across a wide space of lawn he could see Sergeant Killykelly and another man on guard before the door of the west wing. No one else was in sight. The village looked deserted. So far, so good.

He went down to the lobby and much to his relief found Black Girl where he had left her.

Robin Hood had his sword again.

He mounted Black Girl and, giving his old friend the statue a mock salute, with a restrained triumph in it, he rode down the steps of the hotel with great solemnity as though he always came out of hotels that way. But he was thinking hard. It might be several hours before the troops from Hancock came in, provided the boy delivered the message.

Meanwhile?

Meanwhile he was going to be czar of Morgan Springs!

He rode over to Sergeant Killykelly. He observed with great satisfaction that the arms of the Kanawha Zouaves were stacked on the road where they had last been dismissed. That was a good sign.

"Sergeant," said he, "where did you get your drill?"

"Oi served two enlistments in the U.S. regulars, sor, before the war."

"All of them?"

"Well, not all of the last enlistment, sor. You see . . ."

"I'll forget that," said the colonel.

"Yis, sor. All of the drill they ever had oi gave them. They was raised in the hills above Morgantown to jine Gineral Averell's corps in the Valley. It was that divil Smith persuaded them to stop off an' occupy Morgan

Springs en route. He's a politician, he is, and he got himself elected sergeant. It's the life of a monarch they've been leadin' ever since. Oi protested, oi did."

"I've no doubt," said the colonel. "Well, sergeant, there'll be a detachment of United States troops here very shortly, and I'm leaving you and . . ."

"Johnson, sir. He's reliable. He wouldn't brush a harse-fly off his neck, if oi told him not to."

"I remember. Well, I'm leaving you and Johnson on guard at this door and the orders are that no one is to come out. Not a man! No going to the privies. They stay in, or--"

The colonel reached down and gave Sergeant Smith's pistol, belt, and holster to Sergeant Killykelly. "Use that, if necessary," said he.

Sergeant Killykelly saluted. Colonel Franklin rode across the green, wondering whether Sergeant Killykelly would put a shot through his back. He rather thought not, and the risk had to be taken. He stopped before the well-remembered proprietor's house, where he thought he had observed signs of life.

"Mr. Duane," he called. "Mr. Duane." The door opened cautiously after a while, a few inches. "Come out, I want to see you, sir."

Evidently the entrance had been barricaded. He could hear some heavy articles of furniture being moved inside. At last the door was flung open. It was the girl he had last seen sitting nearly naked in the window and giggling at Sergeant Smith who came out.

He gawked at her in astonishment.

She was dressed in excellent, quiet taste. She might almost have been a Quaker's daughter. He had never seen anyone more sober and ladylike-- almost demure. From her very nice tortoise-shell snood over her tightly brushed and slightly curled hair to her spotless linen cuffs she radiated black alpaca gentility. And yet her features and that tell-tale olive flush in her cheeks were the same. It was admirable, he thought. He almost winked at her.

"Well, sir?" she said.

"Tell Mr. Duane I want to see him," he said.

"Mr. Duane isn't feeling so well--lately," she said hesitatingly, with only a trace of accent. "We've been having a good deal of trouble about here, and . . ."

"I've no doubt," said the colonel. "That's over now. Tell Mr. Duane it's Nat Franklin--the Pennsylvania Franklins who used to have the 'Magnolia Cottage' summers. He'll remember."

"Oh!" said she, smiling, and went in.

"Well, well, well! Well, well, well--well, well!" said the well-remembered voice of the proprietor of Morgan Springs, sounding from the hall in a kind of continuous gobble. "My, I'm glad to see you, glad to see you . . ." He stopped suddenly on the porch. "Even if you *are* in a Yankee uniform, Nat Franklin." He held out his hand.

The colonel could hardly keep from laughing, good-naturedly, at the memorable idiosyncrasies and affectations of Mr. Merryweather Duane. His pomposities were endless. A great reader of Sir Walter Scott, he was also a confirmed admirer of William E. Burton, the noted actor and comedian, whom in the old days he had scarcely ever missed seeing every theatrical season in Philadelphia or New York. A glorious visit to Mr. Burton's estate on Long Island had finally "settled" Mr. Duane. He had ended by trying to be Mr. Burton. And like all such attempts to transfuse character, the result was curiously artificial, an effect of strained caricature by poor acting. Add to this a natural but egregious self-importance on the part of the man himself, much accentuated by having been manager and owner of a fashionable resort and numerous slaves, so that everybody he knew seemed to take him seriously--and you had the inwardness of Mr. Duane. Gentility was his hobby, affability his profession, and chivalry his rôle. He had unconsciously created "Morgan Springs" as the stage for his carefully-assumed character and, as a consequence, he loved it even as his own soul.

So complete a compendium of artificiality could, indeed, scarcely have existed in nature, if Nature had not herself accidentally collaborated. Mr. Duane's physical appearance, however, enabled, even aided, him to support his part. A large, moony face ended in a double chin tending towards a dewlap. He wore habitually a bright cashmere shawl with frayed fringes that inevitably suggested bedraggled wings and plumage. A very round paunch usually encased in a flaming vest looped over with watch-chains was supported precariously by long thin legs in tight trousers. And his speech with its endless repetitions *did* resemble a gobble.

It was no accident, therefore, that he had always been known behind his back, to both servants and clientele, as "Turkey" or "Turk" Duane.

"Come in, come in, come in. Come in and sit, sir. Sir, come in and sit down. This afflicted town has been delivered by you. By you! By no one else. I saw you from the window. A noble deed, a deed of derring-do. A feat of arms to be remembered in song. Told by bards, sir. The slaughter of fierce beasts. The . . ."

There was no stopping him. No one had ever succeeded. For half an hour the colonel sat on the porch and listened to the long tale of woe of the conquest and occupation of Morgan Springs by Sergeant Smith and his gang, couched in the archaic and heraldic language of "Turk" Duane.

Meanwhile the colonel kept one eye on Sergeant Killykelly, and noted with the other, as it were, that various other houses in the village were also coming to life. People began to peep out, to come out, to begin to visit from yard to yard. Evidently a state of siege had existed. "Neither the sanctity of property nor the chastity of our noble women, descended from the Norman race, sir," said Mr. Duane, "were thought to be safe. In fact," he insisted, putting his hand up to his mouth, "I am told that even the latter has been violated." The colonel did not confirm this, as he might have.

"And what brings you to our humble native heath?" gobbled Mr. Duane, posing the same question in four different ways without waiting for an answer. The colonel's confessedly sentimental reasons for his visit touched Mr. Duane to the quick.

"You shall have the best we can do under the circumstances, the lamentable circumstances. The Springs have never closed, sir, never. They never will close. They will always be open. You shall have supper in the big dining-room. Agatha!" he called. And despite all the colonel's protestations, arrangements were made by Mr. Duane for supper and a room--as though the war had never been.

"No, sir, the Springs have never closed. They will always be open. Always!" insisted Mr. Duane.

But when he saw the interior of the hotel he sat down and wept.

The colonel went to his room, from the window of which he could keep an eye on the green below and on Black Girl tied close by his door. He sat there cold with anxiety. How long Killykelly could keep his men in hand was a question.

Outside on the green old Judge Washington could be seen standing by the gate of his front yard giving directions to his blacks. They were burying the dogs about the grape roots in his arbour. A good many people were now hurrying to and fro, apparently ignorant of how precarious was their deliverance. About six o'clock five army wagons rumbled onto the oval and disgorged as many squads of infantry in charge of a lieutenant. The conquest and occupation of Morgan Springs were complete. The colonel gave his directions, saw Black Girl stabled, and took a shave. In the hurry he forgot Sergeant Smith, temporarily.

That gentleman, seated alone in the growing shadows of the great Empress Eugénie apartment, gave a profane exclamation of relief as he saw "his gel" sneak quietly into the room. She held one hand behind her back.

"I thought you'd never come, honey," said he. "Godamighty, what kept yer so long? What you got for me there? Somethin' tasty?"

"Shut up," said the girl. "I'll show yuh."

CHAPTER VIII

THE ESCAPE OF SERGEANT SMITH

More battles have been lost by fatigue than won by forethought. The colonel was no iron man. The events of the past twenty-four hours had drawn heavily upon his reserves of energy. Since the night before last he had enjoyed small sleep. The afternoon had been one of intense excitement and anxiety, which he had had to support with complete outward calm. Hence, the arrival of Lieutenant Donald Sweeney with a platoon of the 23rd Illinois Infantry had brought him unspeakable relief.

He delivered the keys of Morgan Springs to the pleasant young Irishman from Chicago with enthusiasm, and a carte-blanche order to take over the place and run it. As it was, the trick had barely been turned. A few minutes more and he must have ceased to be the one-man garrison of a hostile town.

Perhaps, if he had been more explicit in his directions to the lieutenant, several things would not have happened later. But he wasn't. He was tired, and he went to his room, which Mr. Duane's darkies had prepared for him; washed up, and sat down in a large, stuffed rocking-chair to wait for supper.

A thousand things kept running through his mind while he rocked, and nodded, and rocked. Time lapsed. But he slept uneasily.

The death of Jim Mulligan, the brilliant colonel of the 23rd Illinois, killed only a few weeks before at Winchester, came back to haunt him. He had been very fond of Mulligan--whose men had enthusiastically loved him. The 23rd Illinois was one of the finest-drilled volunteer regiments in the service, a marvellous living machine, a perfect and keen instrument to enforce the national will. (So was the 6th Pennsylvania Cavalry.) How hard that was to achieve, he knew. Mulligan had done it. Now he was gone-- and how many others?

They seemed in the shadows of the room as he sat, half-asleep, half-dreaming, to be near him; he felt himself one of their doomed company gathered about a dark campfire. Somehow the face of the young soldier who had carried the message for him that afternoon was there too. It shone in the darkness like an illuminated cameo, delicate and fine, then horribly scarred, blotted out. What a pity that one so young should be there in the darkness among the dead! A feeling of infinite mourning, a sense of irretrievable, irreparable loss, and pity overtook his sleep and merged into a nightmare of sheer charnel horror that wakened him and brought him to his feet standing, shaken to the life. Something horrible had happened. He knew it!

It was some moments before he could shake off this inner conviction of disaster and ghostly trouble. He went to the washstand and dashed cold water over his head. He lit the fire and turned up the lamp. Lord! What time was it? It was dark. Had Duane forgotten about supper? Why, it was nearly nine o'clock!

Someone was knocking at the door.

"Come in." Out of old habit he loosed his holster flap.

It was Mr. Duane full of apologies, full of exclamations about how cheerful the room looked, of explanations why supper was so late. It was to be in the big dining-room.

Of all places! thought the colonel. He flinched from what he knew would be the grand loneliness of that saloon: he and Mr. Duane alone, draped chandeliers, and all the ghosts of the past diners in lost summers and muted music floating around. He became tremendously irritated at Mr. Duane. The man had invited himself. He would much rather have had dinner at Duane's house, or alone in his own room. But in that desolate dining-room!

Something of the depression of his dream held over and gripped him all through the strange supper that evening.

That the Springs had always been open, that they had not been closed, weren't closed now, and never would be closed, was still the constant theme of Mr. Duane. It was evident, indeed, that the Springs could not be closed without closing Mr. Duane. And he was out to prove to himself and to his guest that they *were* open. He regarded the colonel as merely the first of a host of patrons about to descend upon him--after the war was over-- soon. He had opened-up the deserted dining-room, killed the last bit of poultry secreted by his negroes, searched his sadly-ravaged bins, and had the dinner cooked by his daughter.

The scene was even worse than the colonel had anticipated. In the precise centre of the huge, morguelike dining-room, surrounded by swathed chandeliers and high, shuttered windows with catafalque drapings, was one table with a lamp on it. It alone was brilliantly set and lost in a level sea of vacant tables and empty chairs. At this festive board the colonel and his host sat face to face and tried to converse.

Mr. Duane meant to be affable, heaven knows he did. The colonel also meant to be polite. He had pleasant memories of his host, and he pitied him now. He felt that he should feel grateful for his entertainment, even though he understood the reason for so much forced cheer. But their conversation seemed doomed. Every sally ended upon some note of further irritation. True Mr. Duane did most of the talking, but the colonel's attempts to soothe him and turn the talk into pleasant memories of the past were disregarded. The voluble little proprietor of the Springs had kept close in his house during the past few weeks. Like most of the other people who resided at the Springs continuously, he had not dared to risk either his person or his household goods to the tender mercies of the guerrillas who had settled on the town like a flock of eagles and buzzards. He had simply remained barricaded indoors. Consequently, he had had no idea of the extent to which his hotel had been wrecked and damaged. A brief glimpse of the lobby had sickened and outraged him. He was a violent pro-Southerner, and, without meaning to do so, he forgot that the colonel was his rescuer. In fact, he seemed rather to pick on him as the cause of his misfortunes. For across the table was the hated blue uniform and the brass buttons with "U.S." on them. It was enough. He raved. During the intervals a scared, barefooted negress brought in the dishes and shrank back into the boundless shadows. The meal took on the aspect of a nightmare feast waited upon by a genie.

Would the United States pay Mr. Duane for his losses? He put the same question in five ways ten times over.

Perhaps, the colonel suggested. But Mr. Duane must remember that the government was aware of its immortality and sometimes took more than a mortal time in paying.

At this, despite the uniform and his guest, Mr. Duane lapsed into treasonable invective. His face became flushed and he waved his hands. He wished he might live to see that beast Abe Lincoln crucified upside down.

"Come, come," said the colonel, at once amused and shocked at this reversal of hanging Jeff Davis on a sour-apple tree. "Come, come, Mr. Duane, don't be so damned apostolic. I'm sure General Lee, for instance, would never agree with you."

"I don't know about General Lee, but you can't blame me," shouted Mr. Duane, waving his hands about at the empty sideboards and deserted tables. "Look at me! I'm finished! Me, a loyal Virginian, too!"

"West Virginian; you believe in secession, don't you?" corrected the colonel, now pretty angry himself.

"Virginian!" roared Mr. Duane, pounding the table violently.

"Everyone to his own loyalties, of course," said the colonel. "For my part, I try to deal delicately with them. Perhaps, under the circumstances, you would rather have me pay for my entertainment here tonight in Confederate notes instead of Yankee greenbacks."

"That ain't delicate of you," choked Mr. Duane. "It sounds to me like just another damned Yankee trick." He sat there choking. "A very good evening to you, Colonel Franklin," he finally rasped out, rose, and stalked out of the dining-room, the picture of hurt pride.

The colonel watched him go without saying anything. Presently he turned to finishing off his brown Betty and hard sauce alone. In the immense, empty dining-room the lamp on the colonel's table seemed a lighthouse in an ocean of gloom.

"You don't hev to pay nothin', ef you don't want ter," said a voice from somewhere.

The colonel rose and thrust his chair back uneasily. A chuckle from the deep embrasure by one of the high, draped windows followed.

"Come out of that!" said the colonel, not a little nettled. "Let's have a look at you."

The youth who had carried the message for him that afternoon emerged from the shadows and stood before him, turning a frayed straw hat around and around in his thin, nervous hands.

"Oh!" said the colonel, relenting. "The officer of the night, I believe."

"Yes, sir," said the lad, colouring violently, "but I hope you won't never tell nobody about that. I delivered your message and I told 'em to hurry. You oughtenter tell on me."

"I won't," said the colonel, "honour bright!"

"Oh, thank *you,* sir," said the boy gently.

The colonel now took careful stock of him for the first time.

He was barefoot. He wore a pair of preposterous nankeens evidently found in the hotel, a ragged military blouse with a rawhide belt. A huge and ancient horse pistol, minus its flints, had taken the place of Robin Hood's sword. Above this portable arsenal appeared, on a long thin neck, as stonily innocent, as freshly boyish, and yet as determined a young face as the colonel had ever seen.

In fact, there was something peculiarly intrepid about this youthful apparition in the lamplight. Even the scarecrow clothes could not conceal the axelike determination of the youth inside them. If there was a distinct contradiction between the clothes and their wearer, just as there was between his dreamful, grey eyes and his blunt, mountaineer's jaw, it was a conflict that had already been quite successfully resolved by the wilful young person himself. As the colonel looked at him he had no doubt of it. "Well, son," said he, "what do you propose that I should do for you?"

"You kin take me whar thar's fightin'," said the boy simply.

"What makes you think I'll do that?" asked the colonel, fencing for a little time to consider so direct and unexpected a proposal. Already he felt on the defensive.

"'Cause I kin tell," replied the lad. "I was watchin' yer this afternoon, an' I got the second sight like Mrs. Farfar."

"Mrs. Farfar?" repeated the colonel, at a loss.

"She's my mar. I'm William."

"Oh," said the colonel, "I see."

"Cain't we sit down?" asked William Farfar. "We're both white men, I reckon."

"Pardon me," said the colonel, "of course, we can. Suppose you take the late Mr. Duane's chair."

"I reckon I will," murmured William.

Across the table the colonel found himself looking into a pair of wide grey eyes that regarded him with a positively mystical solemnity. He could almost believe they did have the power of second sight. Contrasted to Mr. Duane's bloodshot little orbs that had lately been glaring at him from the same place, the difference was startling. Mr. Duane had hardly been able to see his guest through the mist of his own anger; the eyes now before him were not only able to see the colonel but seemed to be looking through him into space beyond. He stirred uneasily. Something in the all but pathetic gravity of this youthful face reminded him how he had last seen it glimmering in his disturbed dream of a short while before.

Certainly I won't take him to the front, he thought. But he said, "So you want me to take you South to get shot, eh?"

A smile lightened the boy's gravity like sunlight breaking through a cloud. The whole atmosphere of the table brightened.

"You cain't scare me, kunnel," grinned the boy. "I'm a-comin' with you. I jes' know I am. It's boun' to be so."

And, curiously enough, the colonel felt that it was. But he was not going to admit that he did--even to himself.

"No joking, son," said he, "if I did take you with me, you probably wouldn't come back, you know."

"Mrs. Farfar said I wouldn't," replied the lad, "but that'll be as may be. An' I might fool the old woman yet. Ef you're a real soldier you jes' take what comes and you don't worry about hit, or much else, fer that matter. That's no use, once you're jined up. That's the best part of fightin', ain't it?"

"It is," said the colonel, immensely sympathetic with this truly soldierly philosophy.

"Well, I could be like that," said Farfar. "I could be a real soldier ef I onst hed the chanst, ef I was really jined up in a real army."

"Yes, I believe you could," admitted the colonel almost inaudibly.

"So you *will* give me a chanst, won't you?" cried the boy eagerly. "Oh, I knowed you would! When I was a-tyin' that ar man Smith on the chair fer you this arternoon I knowed it was the last of him. 'I'm through with you,' I sez. Ain't none of the Farfars come back from big fightin' nohow. Granper was a Jackson man, and he never come back from South Car'line, and par was a Unioner and the secesh got him in Kentucky. And now thar's me."

But the colonel had not heard all of this. A word or two had just reminded him that unaccountably, quite unaccountably, he had forgotten something.

"Come," said he, rising suddenly, "I'll talk this over with you tomorrow. Run now to Lieutenant Sweeney and tell him to meet me in front of the hotel immediately with two men, and to bring lanterns. I've forgotten something."

"Was it Smith?" said young Farfar.

The colonel nodded. The lad gave a low whistle and dashed out.

Now what the devil? thought the colonel as he hurriedly threaded his way through a host of vacant tables towards the rear door. He intended to cut around to the front by the side portico and to meet the lieutenant and his men there.

Outside, it was quite dark as he stumbled down a broken step. For a moment the pain of a turned ankle drove everything from his mind. He manipulated his boot and cursed mentally. Presently it was better and he got up to go on. Through a near-by window came a dim light and the clatter of dishes.

"You gel," suddenly said a voice he seemed to recognize, "whar's that buckhawn knife?"

"Ah ain't seen him, Miss Ag-atha," replied the soft voice of a coloured woman. "'Deed ah ain't. Ah cain't fin' him when ah set de table foh suppeh. Dah's only de foke hya."

"That's pa's best silver-mounted carvin' set, the one he used for pussonal visitors, and now the knife's gone like everything else round here lately. Whar you put it?" The woman's voice rose in a scream of exasperated inquiry.

"Ah ain't never seen dat knife dis evenin', 'foh Jesus, miss, ah ain't."

The sound of a hearty slap followed.

The colonel leaned against the window-sill, partly to ease his foot and partly out of curiosity.

He was looking into the cavernous kitchen of the old hotel. A couple of guttering candles and the red light from the open grate of one stove gave the place, with its rows of idle ranges and long tables disappearing into the dark perspective, the air of a robbers' cave. Before a sink piled with dirty dishes stood the coloured woman who had lately waited on him and Mr. Duane. She was holding her arm with an expression of extreme pain and cowering before Mr. Duane's neatly-dressed daughter, who had a large butter paddle in her hand.

"I'll larn yer!" said Miss Duane, and prepared to swing at the woman again with the paddle. Someone came out of the shadows and seized her arm. It was the girl he had seen in the room with Smith that afternoon. Seeing the twin daughters of Mr. Duane thus struggling with each other for a butter paddle, the colonel wondered that he had not recognized the truth before. They were so alike--and so different.

"You leave mah nigger alone," said Smith's girl, pushing her sister Agatha into a corner and twisting the paddle out of her hand. "And leave me tell you somethin', Agatha. Jes' fergit about that ar buckhawn knife. Fergit it! See?" She seized her sister by the shoulders and thrust her face forward until their noses touched. The colonel heard them both breathing heavily. From the sink the black woman gaped at them in astonishment. In the tense silence the colonel heard his own watch ticking.

It reminded him.

He picked his path carefully and quietly away from the window and hurried along the portico, still limping a little. Even a brief glimpse into the charming sisterly relations of the Duane twins was sufficient.

The lieutenant and his two men with lanterns could be seen approaching the front of the hotel. Young Farfar was leading them. His nankeens twinkled before the party in the long shadows cast by the lanterns. The moon was not up yet. Except for a few lights in the hotel wing being used for a barracks, the village looked deserted. One lamp gleamed at the Duanes'. The hotel behind him was silent as a tomb. He listened. From the open windows of the room where Smith must be sitting bound and helpless in the darkness there was not a sound. Perhaps the man had twisted himself loose, or--?

He felt angry with himself for having forgotten him. Tired as he was, he shivered a little.

"This way, lieutenant," said he with some asperity.

"Comin', sir."

The two officers and the men with lanterns now stood looking up at the gloomy façade of the deserted hostelry. A curtain blew out of an open upstairs window and fell back into the darkness again.

"Go back to your quarters, young man," said the colonel to Farfar. "You're not needed here."

The boy looked sadly disappointed, but saluted cheerfully.

"You'll not ferget about talkin' with me tomorrow, kunnel, will ye?" he asked anxiously.

"Certainly not," said the colonel--and in the unpleasant events that followed that night forgot it forthwith. "Now, good night."

One of the men chuckled as they went up the steps into the deserted lobby. "That kid wants to stick his beak into everything," he said. "I was tellin' him only tonight, someday he'll sure get it shot off. And--"

"Hold your lantern up," snapped the lieutenant.

They were standing in the deserted and devastated lobby now. In the semi-darkness the area of wreckage seemed immense. Robin Hood rose out of it like a colossus. The trousers on the chandelier swung in the wind that sighed through the shattered windows. They stood listening. A rat leaped suddenly out of the empty safe and brought a ledger down after it. Everybody jumped. But no one laughed. There was something about the place that made them unconsciously draw a little closer to one another.

"Fine people, these Kanawha Zouaves!" remarked the lieutenant as they tramped down the hall.

"A credit to the service, undoubtedly," said the colonel. "I trussed up their leader in a chair in one of the upstairs rooms this afternoon--and forgot to mention him to you," he continued. "We're getting him now. He's responsible for all this mess. But he may not be there. He had friends, he said."

"Oh, he'll be there, all right," said the lieutenant with all the optimism of a young officer.

The colonel grunted.

"We got a Zouave out of the laundry about an hour ago. The one you a--you know," ventured the lieutenant.

"Yes, I know," said the colonel. The lieutenant glanced at him with some admiration, while trying to conceal a smile, and resumed: "The fellow was putting up an awful roar. He wasn't much hurt though. Had sort of a wig of broken glass. Said he'd fallen through the skylight."

"Er--that is correct, I believe," replied the colonel. "And you didn't hear anyone calling upstairs."

"Not a sound."

"That's strange."

They stopped now for a moment in the little vestibule.

"Smith!" roared the colonel. There was no reply. In the hallway upstairs the open door of the linen closet groaned and creaked in the wind. A cold draught came down the stairway. The colonel now led the way anxiously. In the big room ahead under the swirl of the lanterns, Eugénie seemed to curtsy ironically from the steps of her throne. He snatched a lantern, advanced, and held it up. Smith was still in the chair. But Colonel Franklin had never seen anyone so contorted. With one tremendous motion the man must have tried to burst all his bonds at once. He had thrown his left shoulder out of joint and that side of his chest stuck out as though he were presenting it for a blow. In the very centre of this knob the handle of a silver-mounted, buckhorn carving knife was thrust home to the hilt.

The colonel stood there pondering on how fatal it was to forget.

"Cover him up," he said at last. "Tear down a curtain and get the poor devil out of sight. You can attend to him tomorrow."

The men looked much relieved. Burial by night is always grisly.

"It's funny," said the lieutenant as they went downstairs. "I've slept on a battle-field with them all around me. But I wouldn't sleep in this hotel tonight for my captaincy. My God, did you see that face?"

"I did," said the colonel curtly.

"Murdered, sir?"

"Undoubtedly! Executed, you might say," he added. "Now come with me, lieutenant. I have some instructions and information to leave with you about straightening out the affairs of this unfortunate village. Lord, I came here this afternoon to renew pleasant old memories"--he shrugged his shoulders as though trying in vain to cast a weight off them--"and I'm getting out of here as fast as I can. That is, before sunrise tomorrow!"

CHAPTER IX

A VOICE IN THE WILDERNESS

So the colonel roused Black Girl next morning in the grey light of dawn. He had made up his mind to leave Morgan Springs before any further complications arose. Things were beginning to happen to him, and he was determined if possible to tie at least a temporary Gordian knot in the string of events. On the whole, the less said about yesterday's affairs in official reports, the better. He was on leave, and officers on leave were not supposed to take towns--at least not all by themselves. "We'll let young Lieutenant Sweeney and his wild Irishmen of the Twenty-third take care of 'em here from now on. Won't we, old girl?" said he, and cinched the girth of the mare so tight by way of emphasis that she stomped and blew her nose in protest. The colonel laughed. He was an advocate of tight girths for the cavalry.

Roused by the racket in the stall below, Mr. William Farfar peered down through the planks of the hayloft where he had snugly been spending the night, and watched his friend of the evening before depart.

The disappointment was bitter. Tears stung his eyes. Reckon he jes' plumb fergot me, he thought. But ain't no Farfar goin' to beg to be took. By way of morning ablutions, he drew a ragged military sleeve across his eyes, and began to whistle thoughtfully. Presently the whistle died away. The clip of Black Girl's hoofs at a brisk trot diminished in the distance--but not in the direction he had expected.

Now why's he took the North Mountain road? the boy wondered.

The colonel had his reasons. He had originally intended to return by way of Hancock, catch the B. & O. cars there for Harpers Ferry and then ride up the Shenandoah roads by way of Berryville into the Valley about Luray. That would have been the most careful procedure.

But he was not feeling particularly cautious. The events of yesterday had made him, if anything, overconfident. Lieutenant Sweeney had told him only the night before of Early's attempt to surprise Sheridan at Little North Mountain on the twelfth of October. According to the lieutenant, the news had come hot off the wires at Hancock with the report that the Union cavalry had kept the enemy on the jump as far south as Mount Jackson and the South Fork of the Shenandoah. That was miles and miles up the Valley. And if the lieutenant was right, the roads as far as Winchester and even

Strasburg would, as the colonel put it, "be in the United States again." How permanently, he thought ruefully enough, no one can say.

Nevertheless, he decided to risk it. He could avoid unnecessary explanations about affairs at Morgan Springs to the authorities at Hancock and a dirty railroad journey to boot simply by cutting across the mountains to Martinsburg and riding on to Winchester from there. It was rough mountain country over the Big North and Flint ridges; stony going, no doubt. But, to tell the truth, that was the attraction of it. He was eager to shake the ill odour of yesterday out of his hair and to enjoy a genuine stretch of wilderness, as wild country as one could meet anywhere on the continent.

The air was bright and tonic. It had been exceedingly dry all that summer and autumn. The first really heavy frost of the season, even in the mountains, had fallen only the night before. The road was silvery with it; the grasses crisp. As he breasted the first brief ascent, the tumbling ranges of Big North Mountain burned and seethed before him with all the unpaintable and untellable glories of the North American fall. He rose in his stirrups and held up his hand to salute so majestic and flaming a spectacle--and then turned for a moment to look back at Morgan Springs.

He would like to remember it as it had been in his boyhood. From a distance some of its old charm remained. The red roofs lost in the scarlet maples huddled together comfortably, it seemed. A faint haze of smoke was coming from Mr. Duane's chimney. What trouble there would be today in that house! He wondered what Sweeney would do about the girl. Try her? Well, he was glad he would not have to be there to testify--that it was not his responsibility.

He was sorry now that he had turned aside to renew old memories at the Springs. The results had been unexpected. It probably served him right for having been sentimental. But he would like to have had old Duane see him off as he did in the old days, after vacation was over, when he was a schoolboy going back to Unionville Academy near West Chester. Why, he could still hear him!

"Good day, sir, good-bye, good-bye. In a word, farewell. A pleasant journey to you. In the polite French tongue, adieu. In the noble Spanish, adiós. That is to say, God-speed. In brief, farewell."

"So long," said the colonel regretfully, pulling himself back into the present of 1864 and turning to breast the difficult slopes before him.

Years before, he had come part way up into these hills on a picnic in the family carryall. But he was soon past the old picnic grounds, "Burnt

Cabin Spring," where he had first tasted champagne, he remembered--and laughed now. Since then armies had passed this way. All the cabins in the clearings were now burnt cabins. It was bushwhacking country, but there were no more bushwhackers. Even on this, the one habitable side of the mountain, for two years the place had been literally a solitary wilderness. McClellan and Pegram, Wise, Hunter, Averell, Lee, and Garnett--and a half-dozen other generals on both sides--had seen to that. Man could no longer exist there, because it was the borderland between Virginia and West Virginia. Here, there was really a "war between the states." The cobbly, conglomerate road was worn and rutted by wagon trains and caissons. Wreck of army transport, the whitened oak of shattered wheel spokes and the bleached skeletons of mules and horses, lay at the bottom of precipitous slopes. Already the Virginia creeper, flaming in its fall colours, was straggling over them. A big gun, looking like the great helpless booby it was, smirked up at him out of a landslide two hundred feet below, silent. In a clearing which had once been a cornfield were the graves of half a hundred men from a number of states. Iowa, Mississippi, Ohio, Texas, and Rhode Island had all contributed to making the soil of West Virginia fertile.

There were only a few names on the graves. Most of the marker boards had nothing but regimental buttons tied to them. And yet this had been an unusually good burial squad job. Amateurs probably. Usually they just piled them in. One grave actually had a cross over it. And on top of it, perched like the personification of state sovereignty itself, sat a huge turkey buzzard, too gorged to pay any attention to him. It was pretty far north for buzzards, but the Valley of Virginia, he reflected, was not so far away. And then suddenly the road, as though it were tired of such things, soared clean up out of it all.

It left the devastations of mankind and became nothing but a smooth, leafy track running tunnellike under the branches of an immemorial forest of giant chestnuts. There was no underbrush. The sovereignty of nature held undisputed sway here. Everything was living and clean. The brown chestnut burs bursting with fruit lay scattered for miles over the floor of the forest. Tribes of fat grey squirrels chattered at him, raced and leaped through the sinewy branches. Cottontails dashed twinkling up the road. Half a mile farther up he came to the crest and began to descend.

Black Girl picked her way daintily for fear of leaf-filled holes in the trail. The intricate network of veins in her neck stood out as she held back against his weight on the steeper places. By this time he had become very fond of her. She was surefooted, gentle, strong, and intelligent. He communicated with her in a language of chirps and grunts and by slight pressures of knee or rein. She responded by tossing her head proudly or by blowing her nose--eloquently. Her only vice was neighing, and that was a high-spirited one. With his horse the man was content. He was sorry, almost ashamed, of what he was riding her into. For the nerves of a fine horse, he knew, were as sensitive as those of a man--and he had often heard them screaming. That was part of the service of cavalry. At Manassas, for instance . . . He hoped fervently *that* wouldn't happen to Black Girl--and to him.

No one ever seemed to have lived in the Valley between the North and Flint ranges. At least no one lived there now. There was plenty of ginseng, a sure sign of solitude. There were groves of wild pawpaws burst open by the frost, and delicious. Now and then a deer broke away, leaping through the maze of flaming sumac thickets. Rhododendron and mountain laurel gave to a certain tract an almost parklike aspect. The place was alive with quail, feasting upon wild wintergreen berries. He remembered his own lack of breakfast keenly at the sight of them. There was no hurry. He would stop.

Innate caution, for one could never tell who might be lurking in these regions, caused him to turn aside from the trail to camp, and to choose the spot carefully. It was in a mountain meadow at the bottom of the trail filled with isolated boulders and patches of dry grass. A stream widened out here and twisted about areas of high bank an acre or so in extent. These must have been islands in flood time. But they now stood up boldly, a man's height above the general level, covered with pines. He hobbled Black Girl and left her grazing out of sight of the trail at the bottom of one of these banks. Taking his blanket roll, holsters, and saddle-bags, he staggered with some difficulty to the top of the small butte-shaped "island" he had chosen. A flat, sandy area covered with drifts of brown pine needles stretched before him, dotted here and there with several boulders the size of a small house. Between two of them he made camp.

A pile of dry pine cones made an almost smokeless fire. From his blanket roll, which seemed neatly to contain nothing but itself, appeared rather miraculously some small folding utensils and some carefully packed rations; from his saddle-bag, a nubbin of the lean. In a few moments the fragrance of coffee and bacon so tickled his appetite, already razor-keen from his breakfastless ride in the frosty forest air, that he could hardly wait for the coffee to boil. Consequently, he sliced twice as much bacon as he had at first permitted himself, half a large potato--his last--and a small onion, and fried them all sizzling at once. This rasher he eventually packed firmly between two large, square hard-tacks that bore the legend "BC 1294" baked into them. That, the colonel felt sure, was the date when they had been baked, rather than the number of the alleged biscuit company. When put to the test, however, they disappeared rapidly along with a cup of coffee; and with something so substantial for contemplation to work upon, he spread his blanket in the warm morning sun against one of the boulders, and lit his pipe.

The solitude, the scenery, and the morning were magnificent. On either side of him, and a thousand feet above, two solid walls of forest clothed in pure yellow and scarlet rolled away into the blue, cloudless sky. The trail, only half-visible, came down the ridge to the west and skirting across the valley climbed over the eastern rampart through a notch. From where he sat he could overlook innumerable other "islands" like his own scattered over the broad mountain meadow through which, a few feet below him, a small river tumbled and rushed over its pebbly shallows, filling the whole valley with a constantly refreshing monotone and a sound as of muffled bells. That, a faint soughing in the pines, and the constant whistle of the bob-white, were the only voices pitched against the silence of the wilderness.

It reminded him of his camp near Snoqualmie in the Washington Territory, where he had once lived for six weeks completely alone. That had been a healing and strengthening experience. He wished he could return to it; and, half-closing his eyes, like an Indian, he let the sweet Virginia smoke drift through his nostrils and the past and the future drift with it into oblivion. For a few minutes--it would be hard to tell how long, for time had lapsed--he lived alone, completely in the body and the present. The past and future exist only in the imagination, and that had ceased to trouble him.

It was a small, grey shadow passing and repassing over the sand at his feet that first attracted him back into wakeful consciousness. Suddenly the shadow bloomed, as it were, into an intense black swirling flower, and he looked up just in time to throw up his arms and scare off a hawk that shot past him with snapping beak. He laughed, somewhat startled, and then sat listening. Far up the trail he could hear someone singing.

The sound came nearer. The old tune had the lilt of mountain fiddles in it. The glint of sunlight on a rifle came through the leaves. He hastily quenched a last hazy ember of his fire with sand and lay down, peering out between his boulders. There was a faint echo of the clear young voice now. The words of the song seemed to be coming from everywhere, clean and clipped.

"I'll take a country ship:
And to the beaches' lip
Of my own native land
I'll press my own,
And deep will draw my breathe
From meadow and from heath,
Sweet as the sand unto my tongue and teeth
That is mine own.
Between the pole and line
Is nothing good nor fine
As . . ."

But here the song broke off into a kind of perplexed whistle, and whoever was riding down the trail dismounted, for the colonel could see him vaguely through the trees, evidently searching for something--his own trail, he divined, because it was just about there he had left the road and ridden across the stream to where he was now. He grunted and drew his holster near. Then in plain profile on the open stretch of road immediately opposite him the stranger emerged.

It was young William Farfar, leading a white mule to whose famine-haunted frame only a human skeleton need have been affixed to have routed armies.

Four score and seven years ago--at least! thought the colonel.

And then, at the sight of the boy, he remembered his promise of the night before. "Oh dear"--he groaned inwardly--"I just can't take this young Sancho Panza along with me. It's wrong and it's ridiculous. And yet here he is! Lord!"

The colonel had forded the stream just below where Farfar was standing. Black Girl's hoofmarks disappeared into the river-bed there, and the boy now stood in some perplexity, his rifle nursed in the crook of one arm, while he scanned the wide meadow before him. Finally, he whistled shrilly.

The colonel didn't answer. He had decided to leave the matter to fate. If the boy found him, he would take him along. If not--so much the better, he thought, when fate answered through a shrill trumpet.

Black Girl began to neigh and the mule replied as mules do. The echoes took it up. *Hee, haw, haw--haw hee haw,* roared and mocked the valley.

"Hi!" said Farfar.

The colonel showed himself and beckoned. He was weak with laughter. "Come on over," he said at last.

Farfar mounted and forded the creek.

"Oh gosh, kunnel," said he, "oh gosh, I'm glad I found you. Ye *air* goin' ter take me with ye, ain't ye?"

"Yep," said the colonel.

The young fellow's face flushed with an intense, grave pleasure. "God," said he almost prayerfully, "I'm a-goin' to be a real soldier at last!"

The colonel said nothing for a moment--nothing that could be heard-- and then:

"Well, son, here's the first of military questions. Have you had anything to eat?"

"No, sir, I hain't," said Farfar, "'ceptin' a few rawr chestnuts. I lifted me that mule and my rifle and come after you right spry. That is, spry as that mule could chunk along. I don't think they'll miss her much. She was borned a long while back. Reckon she maunt hev fit at King's Mountain." He grinned, and threw himself down to bask in the warmth of the rock, looking up meanwhile into the depth of the blue sky.

The colonel busied himself preparing another cup of coffee.

"Thot bird up thar's a gerfalcon," said Farfar, shading his eyes. "You kin tell by the way he hivers on the wing."

"Here," said the colonel, "throw this into you. We must be getting along."

But the lad was not to be hurried. He sat crunching a hard-tack and drinking his coffee for some minutes, and the colonel let him. In the end the colonel smoked another pipe. And it was only when he knocked it out with a gesture of finality that they rose and left that pleasant spot.

Farfar's mule had the heaves, twice going up and once coming down Flint Mountain. It was well along in the late afternoon when they at last emerged on the white limestone roads of the Valley of Virginia and heard cannon far away to the south of them.

CHAPTER X

THE ARMING OF WILLIAM FARFAR

In October 1864 a strange, perhaps an undeserved, fate had overtaken the sleepy little town of Martinsburg, Virginia. Partly by design but mostly by necessity, it had eventually become the advance base of supply for the "Department of the Middle" that is, for all the Union forces operating in the Valley of the Shenandoah under Sheridan. Whether Martinsburg was to be in Virginia or in West Virginia--in the Confederacy or in the United States--no one in the town could yet be certain, for the jurisdiction changed with the swaying back and forth of armies, and it had repeatedly been occupied by both sides. Many of the "Virginians" had left. The inhabitants who remained could scarcely recognize the place where they were born.

Its cluster of leisurely, modest houses and a peaceful steeple or two huddled like a flock of scared, white sheep in the midst of the fields of war. All about the town were miles of picket lines dark with mules and horses, great stacks of fodder and piles of ammunition, acres of spare wheels laid in windrows. There were parks of artillery arranged like the squares in a checkerboard, spare caissons, and stacked cannon. There were camps for the regiments who stood guard at the base, and quartermaster and ordnance sheds with crooked stovepipes smoking merrily. Also, there was a host of perambulating tents that on closer inspection proved to be covered army wagons driving anywhere and everywhere across fields, down lanes, through the confusion of the camp, singly, or in fleets--regardless, so long as they obtained their loads. Every hour or so a convoy of wagons got under way in the main street and seemed to drift over the white ribbon of stony road that led towards Winchester. Through all of it, camp, town, and fields, puffed and bustled the belching and shrieking B. & O. engines, moving precariously over hastily-laid tracks and temporary switchbacks scattering sparks and billowing smoke across the landscape like so many small dragons.

From the hills just west of Martinsburg this animated, but to young Farfar unmeaning, scene burst upon him as he and the colonel rode for the town about four o'clock of a clear October afternoon. It was the colonel's intention to press on that night towards Winchester, for to him the scene was full of significance in each detail. On every hand he read the signs of preparations for a general advance. If nothing else, extraordinarily generous piles of coffins, presumably for officers, the massing of ambulances, and the constant loading of wagons with ammunition rather than rations told the tale. He was therefore anxious to be back with his men--even before the formal expiration of his leave--if a battle impended. Nevertheless, he was forced to spend some hours in Martinsburg. Black Girl might still have gone on, but Farfar's mule could obviously no longer be regarded, even by the blindest of optimists, as a means of transportation.

As they entered the town the colonel was in some doubt, and embarrassment, as to whether it looked as though he were bringing in a recruit, or whether it appeared he had been captured in the mountains and was being brought in on parole for payment of ransom. For even in the worst of Early's raids no wilder figure than young Farfar had ever entered Martinsburg. His long rifle, the ancient pistol in his belt, his bare feet, flowing locks, and bizarre "uniform" spoke loudly of the mountains--And secesh mountains, at that, thought the colonel.

So, much to the boy's surprise, the first place at which they stopped was a "barber-shop" run by a couple of contrabands in an old cabin on the outskirts of town. Here the colonel traded the white mule to the delighted negro proprietor for a haircut for young Farfar. And as the boy also insisted upon a shave, for no visible reason--"nuffin but fluff," said the barber,--the harmless pistol went for that. Since the mule was lying down when they emerged, and might never get up again, the colonel also contributed a dime to ease his conscience. Thus having endowed a coloured brother, as though with the touch of Midas, they made for headquarters in the tavern. There, without further ado but amid much ill-concealed laughter, young Farfar was mustered into the service of the United States as a recruit for the 6th Pennsylvania Cavalry.

"To defend the Constitution of the United States against all its enemies whomsoever . . . so help me God," repeated the grave and now bullet-headed youngster after the grinning sergeant-major. His right hand came down out of the air slowly.

"Did you ever read the Constitution, Bill?" asked the colonel.

"No, sir, I hain't, but I hear tell hit's something we cain't git along without."

"You know what you're doing though?"

"Jes' about as well as any pusson in this room," said the boy, angry at the grinning faces of the clerks.

"I've no doubt you know as well as any of us," said the colonel, and signed the papers for him. "Now, sir, you're a soldier of the United States."

The boy saluted gravely, apparently someone who was not in the room. The clerks laughed again.

"What you doin', colonel, robbin' the cradle?" asked the sergeant-major a little insolently. As a quartermaster who could delay or withhold supplies, he was used to being rather cavalier even with officers. Non-coms and privates were almost beneath his notice.

"Sergeant," said the colonel, "you seem to regard the swearing in of a recruit as a comedy staged for your personal amusement. I shall mention what a merry fellow you are at corps headquarters tomorrow. We need you humorists to cheer us up at the front."

An appalled silence fell on the room. The colonel stuffed some duplicate papers in his pocket and walked out with his recruit.

"Where's the quartermaster's store--for arms and equipment?" demanded the colonel of a dandily-arrayed New Jersey cavalryman on the street.

"Second street to the right from the cars depot," replied the man, gaping in surprise at Farfar.

"And the remounts?"

"Right across the tracks, sir."

But just as they were going into the Q.M. store they were joined by their friend the sergeant-major, still looking a little nervous.

"Speaking of corps headquarters, sir," said the sergeant, "I thought I should tell the colonel I heard yesterday from"--here the sergeant's voice trailed into a confidential whisper--"that the colonel's recommendation for brigadier-general of cavalry has gone through to Washington."

The colonel guessed that this was just the sergeant's way of smoking the pipe of peace. But he, too, felt it wise to stand in with the dispenser of supplies at the base. Colonels who quarrelled with quartermasters had ragged regiments.

"That's fine news if it goes through," he said. "But in any case I want you to continue to look after the Sixth Pennsylvania Cavalry, as you always have, sergeant. After all, you're needed here, you know."

"Yes, sir," replied the sergeant, his shoulders coming back into a broader stance. "We'll always do all we can for you, rely on it."

"Now here's a recruit for the Sixth needs everything," continued the colonel. "By the way, Mr. Farfar, I want you to meet Sergeant Colfax. He's going to outfit you personally and see that the boys issue you the best. No shoddy blankets or paper shoes. And you ought to be able to fit him well here. I'll be back shortly."

"We'll do all that," said the sergeant, and took Farfar in hand while the colonel rode on to the remount corrals.

He couldn't say much for the offerings on hand. They were all big, raw-boned beasts fitter for transport than cavalry. "General Wright's corps requisitioned a hundred and eighty only yesterday," said the trooper in charge. "What's left might do as off-horses for the artillery."

"Pshaw," said the colonel. "I wanted something small and dapper."

"Come down to number three," said the man. "There's some nags they've just gathered in from Luray and the upper part of the Valley down there. Mostly family pensioners, I guess. But you might find something."

The colonel leaned over the bars and laughed. All the family pets and fat old coach-horses from Front Royal to Port Republic were standing forlornly about. Some of them came nickering up to the bars.

"Act like they expected sugar or an apple," laughed the trooper.

"I s'pose they do," said the colonel. "There's many an empty paddock and empty heart represented here."

"Yep," said the man, "but Lee would get 'em if we didn't."

The colonel nodded. He was stroking the nose of a small roan mare that kept nuzzling at his pocket. "No sugar there, sweetheart," said he.

"She ain't much more 'n a pony," said the trooper.

"Bring her out and let me go over her," ordered the colonel.

The horse was sound and less than ten years old.

"A fine little lady. Looks as though she had English breeding," he said, looking her over. "Take some of the mud and burs out of her coat and bring her up to the Q.M. store. I'll sign off for her there. There'll be a couple of dollars involved for your own trouble."

"I won't argue about that, colonel," said the man. "We haven't been paid here at the depot for sixty days."

Meanwhile, at the quartermaster's store the bounty of the federal government had descended upon Private William Farfar with bewildering and startling effect. Socks, shirts, underwear, and blankets were all his at one time for the first time. A jaunty kepi, a blue blouse with brass buttons, a pair of trousers with bright yellow stripes, completed the outer man, except for a pair of boots with spurs. To cap the climax, "*The Ladies' Aid of Philadelphia present you*" with a canvas kit containing several toilet articles, a pair of knitted mittens, and a small Bible. Just to show he was a good fellow Sergeant Colfax chipped in with a yellow silk neckerchief bought at his own expense. And the weapons and horse furniture followed.

A sabre, and a belt with a brass eagle on the buckle. A Colt revolver with the blue metal glinting, a carbine that hung by a ring to a brand-new saddle. There seemed to be no end of it. A saddle-cloth, a bridle, and several small articles in neat leather cases--everything from a curry-comb to a nose-bag piled up on the counter before the youngster. And all he had to do was to sign for it.

"William Farfar, his mark †"

It was a carefully-made cross. The writing is in Colonel Franklin's hand, for he stepped in just in time to sign for him.

The quartermaster's department cherishes a receipt forever. Somewhere in labyrinthine archives that receipt still exists. The cross on it is the sole monument of William Farfar.

If clothes make the man the uniform creates the soldier. The lad who stepped behind a pile of clothing bales in the quartermaster's store at Martinsburg that day to shed his nankeen rags and the slim young cavalryman who stepped out again were two different persons. Farfar left his past behind the bales with his old clothes. The sergeant showed him how to knot his neck-cloth, and he stood there slim, erect, with his sabre hanging from his slim waist, a warrior received among men. The clothes were only an outer and visible sign. He had, in fact, been reborn. The little group of rough quartermasters who stood about under the dim lanterns in the old shed understood that.

"Want to take a look at yourself, young feller?" said a man from Kansas with a beard like a frozen sponge. No one would have suspected that he carried a pocket mirror.

Farfar looked. It was good.

"My God!" he said.

They all laughed. The colonel led him out to his horse and showed him how all his equipment went. The young man's hands trembled over the stiff buckles.

They rode out of the town together. No day could ever be like that day had been. Metamorphosis. The sun sank in an ocean of blood behind the mountains. Far off to the southward the cannon were still growling.

CHAPTER XI

MADAM O'RILEY FOLLOWS THE FLAG

The colonel reported at department field headquarters at Winchester about nine o'clock next morning. The atmosphere at headquarters was entirely different from what it had been at Harpers Ferry last August when General Sheridan had first taken charge. Everything was well-organized and running like a machine. Confidence in the chief and the feeling of victory were in the air. The defeat of Early at Little North Mountain only three days before had confirmed this. "In fact, you seem a little too confident," said the colonel to General Torbert, who had ridden down from Cedarville for a conference. "Early is an old fox, you know."

"There were reports of enemy activity about Fishers Hill this morning," acknowledged Torbert, "but I advised the general to disregard them. That's clear across the river from us and they haven't made any attempt to meddle with the railroad at Strasburg. We're working it now by way of Manassas Gap clear through to Washington. General Sheridan is going over to Washington today for a meeting at the War Department."

Colonel Franklin shook his head. "What you need is the old Sixth Pennsylvania out in front gathering news for you," he said. "Can't you persuade the general to move us down from around Luray and throw us out as a screen up the Woodstock side of the Valley? I'll soon find out what's doing."

"No he can't persuade me, Nat Franklin, you old Pennsylvania politician," said General Sheridan himself, just then emerging from an office near by. "How are you? And how did it go on leave? Welcome back! I'll be glad to know you're in charge of that gang of moss troopers of yours again. Come in here, I want to show you something."

They went back into the office where a big map of the Valley of the Shenandoah lay unrolled.

"Look here," said the general. "You see how the Massanuttens rise down the middle between the North and South forks of the river and cut the Valley in two? Well, the main army's here at Strasburg keeping the North Fork under observation. Now, there's no force to speak of at all up the South Fork. Just a few detachments, enough to keep the roads patrolled. Your regiment, you see, is near Aquila just north of where the river breaks through the gorge between the Blue Ridge and First Mountain. I want you to stay there and act as the cork in the neck of the bottle and send news promptly of any movements you may observe or hear of to the south of you. It won't make much difference if they do break through again up toward Luray, because two days ago we made a clean sweep of everything from Luray to Sperryville--barns, mills, distilleries, blast furnaces. We drove off about six thousand head of cattle, and over five hundred horses."

"Yes," said the colonel, "I saw some of them at Martinsburg."

"Nothing's left along the South Fork," said Sheridan, making a comprehensive sweep over the map, "but I want to keep Early in play awhile here on the North Fork as we have been. You know we've moved up and down the Valley so often from Harpers Ferry that the Richmond papers have nicknamed me 'Harper's Weekly.' I don't want to drive him clean out of the Valley yet. He'll simply retreat and reinforce Lee. That's the strategy of it, you see. I'm leaving the tactics at the upper end of the south valley to you, colonel. By the way, your recommend for brigadier has gone through. We'll see what'll happen in Washington." He clapped the colonel on the back.

Headquarters was certainly feeling fine! Colonel Franklin thanked the general and rode off for Strasburg. Secretly, he didn't want to leave his regiment. It was the cherished product of his heart and mind. Farfar kept pounding on behind.

"This ya little mare rides like she thinks she's goin' home," said the boy.

"Maybe she is," replied the colonel absent-mindedly, thinking of stars.

About two miles out of Winchester they overtook a curious caravan. There were six covered carriages, all black, positively lugubrious. And no wonder, for the colonel recognized them as a species of closed victoria used exclusively by Philadelphia undertakers of the most respectable kind. As he came abreast of the rear carriage and passed it, a window was raised and "a fair hand fluttered a white kerchief at the passing knights"--so he half-humorously put it to himself.

Nothing could have been more astonishing or more out of keeping with the restrained character of these chariots of grief.

What's up? he wondered.

At the head of the procession, in an elegant but battered little phaeton with the hood thrown back, sat a stout Irishwoman with the coarsened remains of great beauty. She had flaming hair and a turban about which an immense, moth-eaten ostrich plume climbed several times to a fountain. For at the very top the lady seemed to be bursting out into a kind of feathery spray. Madam was driving.

The colonel raised his hat and received a smile that was something more than cordial. His not to question why, however, and he trotted past and spurred up the road. A hundred yards or so farther on he was hailed by as seedy a little man as ever rode a spiritless nag with a snaffle bit.

"Say, are you in an awful hurry, colonel?" he asked, pulling up nervously and nearly jerking the jaw off his beast.

"Yes," said the colonel, "I am."

"I'm right sorry," said the man, "I need some advice right bad."

"You certainly do," replied the colonel, who could not restrain his indignation at the suffering of the man's horse. "Now get down and unhook that snaffle. You're tearing your horse's tongue out with that bit."

They stopped and the whole caravan of carriages stopped behind them.

"What's the matter now, Perkins?" demanded the lady in the phaeton with a strong twang of the owld sod.

"It's me horse."

"Horse me yer horse, and get on wid ye!" cried the woman, scowling.

"Just a minute, madam," said the colonel, looking back. The lady's scowl turned into a gleaming smile.

"Gosh," said Farfar.

"Come here, young man," said the lady to Farfar, who was all eyes. A number of handkerchiefs were now waving from the half-opened windows of the carriages behind.

"Never mind that," said the colonel sternly to Farfar.

By this time the bit was readjusted and they were soon under way again. The colonel looked with some curiosity and great amusement at the little man who was now bumping along beside him. He was dressed in a borrowed Amishman's overcoat that stretched buttonless from his neck to below his heels. He had no hat and a bad cold. At every jog a drop of moisture fell from his pale, sharp nose that sprang out of a face which had the mulish expression of a schoolmaster complicated by intelligent, cunning, and shifty eyes.

"It ain't so easy for me," said the man, sniffing.

The colonel grinned. "Pretty soft, I should say."

"Nope, nope!" asserted the man. "You're wrong. She's got thirty-two young ladies packed in them ve-hicles an' I got to see 'em all into the old Railroad Hotel at Strasburg or I get the sack. And I can't get the sack 'cause I ain't got no place to go effen I do. My wife's left me, she won't truck along with no madams. It was all right as long as we was just bein' a sutler for her at Harpers Ferry. But since madam's taken to followin' the flag and made me manager--"

"What?" said the colonel.

"Yes, sir; Madam O'Riley, she follows the flag. That's her motto. Every time the army moves up, so does her and the girls. Now she's movin' clear down into the front lines and settin' up at Strasburg, and the rebels is only jist across the river. Oh dear!" said the man, wiping his nose on his sleeve. "We'll be captured. You see!"

"It wouldn't make much difference if you were," said the colonel consolingly. "I hear they're very gallant fellows."

"Oh dear," said the man again. "Oh, yes, it would. All the take would be in Confederate money, and madam's a Union woman. She follows the flag."

"I'm sure the War Department would be touched by her confidence," said the colonel. "She must believe in General Sheridan too."

"Indeed she does, sir. Maybe you'd say a good word for us there?"

"I will," said the colonel, "depend upon it! I'll speak to the general. He'd just love to hear about this."

"The best thing about it is our rates, sir. That's my idear. The higher the rank the less we charge. That keeps the clientele in the upper circles, mostly--and the young ladies full of fun. Now for a colonel . . ."

"Never mind that," said the colonel.

"Oh, no, sir," replied the man, "of course not, but I thought you might just ride on with us to Strasburg in case the provosts don't know us."

"Sorry," said the colonel, "I'm in a hurry," and he proved it by galloping off down the road to make up for lost time.

But it wasn't lost time, either, he thought. Wait till Phil Sheridan hears about it. Madam O'Riley, she follows the flag!

They passed a mile or so of wagon trains and parked artillery at Cedar Creek. The army was camped only a few miles away on the heights above. The roads were rutted three feet deep. The clouds of dust never settled under the constant stirring of couriers and transport. Scarcely any rain had fallen for weeks and it was still hot at midday. The mountains were almost as clear of mist as in summer. It had been a strange fall. A good one for campaigning. Winter is the universal enemy of soldiers everywhere. But as the colonel rode into Strasburg he was mopping his brow, and he dismounted at the bar. It was by no means deserted.

"Thank God, they didn't burn *this* place down," a familiar voice was saying devoutly as he entered the bar. It was Captain Fetter Kerr, his adjutant, who had just ridden down, by way of Luray, the day before.

They fell on each other and pledged the occasion. Kerr was too genuinely delighted to see "the old man back again" to conceal it. And the colonel felt the same. Regimental news and several empty glasses were exchanged for full ones over the bar.

The regiment was all right. Colson was doing fine with the men. But an adjutant is an adjutant and can serve only one master. The colonel allowed for that while he listened. All was quiet about Aquila. "It's just like a sanatorium," said Kerr. "We're getting fat. I'm down for a draft of new recruits and remounts. Want to ride back with us? We're leaving right after mess."

"Sure," said the colonel. "By the way, I've got a new recruit for you myself. Go and look him over. He's holding horses outside now."

Kerr went to the door and stood grinning. Then he suddenly snapped to attention.

With a great clatter of sabres and much gay and loud talk General Phil Sheridan and his whole staff came swarming in through the swinging door.

They were on their way to take the Manassas Gap Railroad to Washington, and the official train still tarried at Strasburg for a drink.

The general was in the best of moods.

"Damned if it isn't Nat Franklin again--and his adjutant! This is a fine place to find your regimental headquarters, colonel. Don't try to explain the advantages. The drinks are on you. Here's to the gallant Sixth Cavalry, gentlemen. Pennsylvania, of course!"

They all crowded up. A roar of talk ensued. Sheridan was delighted at having pinned the drinks on an "old Indian fighter," as he described the colonel, for he was very proud of his own Western record and generally managed to bring it up somehow.

It was at this point that the colonel kept his promise and "mentioned" Madam O'Riley to the general.

"By God, I'll give you a ride on my train for that, Franklin," said he. "I know--I know, but it's an historic occasion. The first train through in three years. I want you to see the headquarters saloon car. Sure, sure, you can get off at Front Royal and ride up. Have an orderly take your horse around there and wait for you. It's a hot day. I'll give you plenty of horsyback before the winter's over. Hi," he cried, "here's a damn' cavalryman don't want to leave his horse! I'm goin' to *make* him ride on a train. He's scairt. Bring him along."

They all swept out of the bar and two minutes later were climbing into the cars. The colonel just had time to call out to Kerr to send Black Girl to Front Royal and to "look after that new recruit," when the train pulled out. The officers sat in the headquarters car, the only one without smashed windows. The colonel was really worried. He didn't want to go to Washington. But in the mood the general was in he might find himself there--and catch hell for it. That would be the joke. His anxiety was soon over, however. About five miles out of Strasburg the train stopped. The bridge over Passage Creek needed a little more attention before a general could be risked on it.

"About ten minutes' more work," the engineer said.

It took an hour. The staff produced cards.

Sheridan made no comment. He was the idol of his army, not only on account of his great personal magnetism, but because he trusted his men and understood when a genuine difficulty arose. He knew when, and when not, to be impatient. Consequently, he moved swiftly because he had learned how to wait. While his engineers were making sure he would get to Washington by finishing some extra repairs on the bridge, he sat with his feet cocked up on the opposite seat chewing a remarkably long-suffering stogie and reading a copy of the New York *Tribune* that someone had handed him. The remarks of Mr. Greeley and others evidently moved him, for the stogie took on a more and more perpendicular angle as his half-audible comments became louder and more profane.

"Listen to this, will you," he said, finally bursting out, and read a letter from an indignant subscriber. It amounted to an hysterical personal attack upon him for "his vindictive, useless, and ruthless orgy of destruction, worthy of Attila and his Huns, in the lovely and prosperous valley of Virginia." An editorial, by the editor, agreed. "Mercy, charity, honour, and forbearance are all alike equally strangers to General Phil Sheridan."

"Pretty tough on Phil Sheridan, isn't it? What do you think?"

One of the card players laughed, but paused in the deal as the general began to speak. His remarks were addressed to the world. He was evidently excited.

"They don't understand," said he. "I suppose they never will. They expect me to apply force but without any unpleasant consequences. Most people still look upon war as a kind of honourable duel between armies or a personal tiff between generals. Early defeats Sheridan; Sheridan defeats

Early. You know, that kind of thing--sort of a game. Something for your Walter Scotts to write about. A lot of my fellow citizens seem to think I've a personal grudge and hate the Johnnies; that I like to burn down their homes and hear their women and children wail. Editors can put it that way. It makes dramatic reading, and their business is to sell more newspapers. But I don't like war and I don't hate anybody. I want peace and it's my cruel task to bring it about by force. I'm out to get that result as quickly as possible. By burning out this valley, as I have orders to do, we can cut off Lee's supplies and save years more of war. It's bad, but it's better than another year of bloody battles." He threw the paper down in disgust.

By this time everybody in the car was listening. It was not often Sheridan "talked" except when he was angered. He had the reputation of being a little morose. But either Mr. Greeley's remarks or the drinks at Strasburg had excited him, for he went on in the same emphatic tone.

"I look at it this way," he said. "There has to be some kind of government in North America. A government that can be broken into fragments isn't a government. If the rule of the majority can't prevail by peace and logic, and a minority appeals to force, then you have war. That *is* a state of war when force has been invoked. If you accept that way of doing things, as Mr. Horace Greeley now advises us to do over his wise spectacles, you won't have peace, as he thinks, you'll just be in a condition of eternal war, like Mexico. It doesn't take two to make a fight between nations or inside a nation. When any one side ditches reason and peace and appeals to force, that is war. In Mexico you can do that any time and so they do it all the time. I'm for preventing that here. Now, the minority in this country has appealed to force. So it's a civil war. But Idon't think that war just means having one line of men shoot at another line of men. That's merely the duel idea over again on a larger scale. War, the use of force, means much more than that if it's going to be effective. People who rest at home in peace and plenty have no idea of the horrors of war by duel-- battles. They can put up with it, all right, and write letters to the newspapers telling the generals to be kind to everybody. But it's another matter when deprivation and suffering walk in at their own front doors. It's unfortunate but it's true: peace comes quicker that way. Reduction to poverty of the people behind the lines brings prayers for peace more surely and quickly than just letting the soldiers shoot it out. So the proper strategy consists in the first place in inflicting as telling blows as possible upon the enemy's army, and then in causing the inhabitants so much suffering that they must long for peace, and force their government to demand it. The people must be left nothing but their eyes to weep with over the war. Anything else only prolongs murder."

Everyone was very quiet. There was no reply when the general stopped talking. The officers sat woodenly smoking as they had been while he spoke. Clouds of tobacco smoke rolled out the open windows of the old car. Some of them were thinking. The general's idea seemed a new one. Was he right? they wondered.

Presently the hammering at the bridge ceased and the train went on its way. The colonel scribbled a note and had an orderly take it to the engineer. At Front Royal they slowed down, and Colonel Franklin jumped off quietly, nodding his thanks to the train crew. Sheridan passed on eastward through Manassas Gap.

Half an hour later Captain Fetter Kerr and his band of recruits and remounts passed through Front Royal. The colonel mounted Black Girl and rode off with them up the Valley.

CHAPTER XII

THE VALLEY OF SOLITUDE

It was a curious, almost a novel, experience, that ride. The evidences of man's occupation of the country were present, but the Valley itself was a solitude. Only the roads were left leading to nowhere, for not a house was standing. The cattle had been driven from the fields. Even the birds seemed to sense that something was wrong. Flocks of crows flew uneasily from one patch of woods to another, cawing, and looking for old landmarks that were gone. They were the only voices of the place. From the signal station on Meneka Peak behind them the signal flags flashed, were hoisted, and disappeared, accentuating the loneliness. The day was enormously peaceful. There was not a breath of air. Indian summer in all its calm, funereal grandeur brooded in the silent hills while the Blue Ridge and Massanuttens poured their ranges southward, surging up in great waves of flamboyant and sere-leaved forest to the crests of Mary's Rock, Mount Marshall, the Peak, and Stony Man. The afternoon grew solemn and magnificent as the long shadows began to fall.

Even on the main road through the Valley travellers passed were few and far between; an occasional cavalry patrol, once a procession of three wagons filled with refugees, hollow-eyed women with children cowering at their feet. No one spoke.

One of the recruits was weeping. He had been unable to raise $300 to save himself from the draft and had left a motherless little girl in the care of strangers. His anxiety was more than he could bear. The new men were all sorry for him, for themselves, and for one another. They were already painfully galled and chafed by the unaccustomed saddles, and mostly homesick. The colonel did not think much of this batch of recruits. The quality of the new men got worse with each new draft, he noticed. They would take a great deal of breaking-in and probably some coddling. But he could no longer permit himself the luxury of universal sympathy. Two years ago, at Fredericksburg and after, he had felt the nation dying. Since then the troubles of individual soldiers had seemed small. Besides, they might be killed in battle. What did it matter? They would all die anyway, and soon.

> And how can man die better
> Than facing fearful odds
> For the ashes of his fathers
> And the temples of his gods?

He had never liked that bit of heroic poetry--yet it seemed to be true in his day. Farfar looked at him from time to time with a bright smile, and the colonel grinned back. Christ! he hoped that infant wouldn't get mangled. He wished to heaven he'd left him at headquarters. He could send him back now--but, Lord! the boy would be outraged. He'd be back again--somehow--or find another regiment. The colonel gave it up.

They rode into Luray about evening and camped in a roofless brick store. A few of the inhabitants and some miserable freed men were still about. Even a roofless house was better than none. One could look up at the stars at any rate. Watching them, he slept.

Captain Kerr was delayed next morning. A wagon train was due. They had to bring in all their own supplies now, the devastation was so complete. The colonel decided to make the ride of about twenty miles up to Aquila by himself. He could take the shorter mountain road. The views were exalting. The risk was now negligible--and besides, he had a little mission that he wanted to perform alone. Secretly, he had looked forward to it for weeks. He hoped he would not be too late.

Black Girl splashed through the ford across Hawkshill Creek and trotted on up into the hills. Valleyburg and the farmhouses along the way were only ash-heaped mounds. The deeper woods began. There was not a human soul for miles. The road entered the primeval forest at the foot of the Blue Ridge. There it ascended sharply and turned south, plunging up and down over the great side spurs of the mountain. He had forgotten how wild and precipitous it was. The view from the crests grew grander and more sweeping.

There was one point in particular that he remembered well. It was at the top of a peculiarly long and arduous ascent. He would give Black Girl a good breathing rest up there. The road was scarcely more than a trail now. He plunged down into the green gloom of a patch of pines, started upward again, up and on up--Black Girl began to pant heavily. There was the clearing at the top of the trail! He came to the crest suddenly and rode out into the light.

Southward, two mighty ranges of the Appalachians shouldered their way into the blue distance like tremendous caravans marching across eternity. Between those parallel ridges the Valley of the Shenandoah lay, apparently, as serene and beautiful as the interior of the Isle of Aves.

Thought is swifter than lightning. Perhaps its fluid nature is essentially the same. In a flash, as it were, while he had sat breathing his horse and looking down from that giant height at his men manœuvring below in the Valley, the scenes of the past few weeks--the faces and places, the houses, the roads, and the very sound of voices--had flowed through his mind . . .

The failing echoes of the bugle in the Valley recalled him to himself; reminded him that he was returning. In a few hours he would be back with his men. The daily round of alert caution in the face of the enemy; of drill, skirmish and battle, would be under way. A metallic clink as though of an iron shoe against a stone somewhere in the ravine at his feet tightened every nerve in his body. Instantly a precautionary fear made each item in the landscape stand out as though a bright, white light had been turned upon it. Details became important and memorable. A triviality correctly seen might be saving, an error of observation fatal. That was the feeling of war, a glorious awareness as of super-vitality, of burning a little more brightly than life could long bear. That was the fascination of it. Existence was self-convincingly important.

How could he have sat there a target against the sky! He must recollect himself from now on. The Valley might be cleared, but it was still hostile country. Anything might happen. He dismounted and led Black Girl down the hill cautiously. The only sound was the wind in the pines; the constant rushing and eternal gurgling of musical waters over the ford at Aquila below. As he descended into the ravine, the noise of the little river rushing over its stones filled the air with a constant, delicate murmur.

There might be no one there. It might only have been a loosened boulder washed down the bed of the stream that he had heard. But now he was taking no chances. He stepped aside from the trail, tied Black Girl in a sheltering thicket, and concealing himself carefully, looked about him and down. The ruins of what had once been the prosperous little mountain settlement of Aquila lay just beyond. There had been several stores, a half-dozen houses, and a flour mill. The gaunt, fire-scarred walls of their recent burning, their bright but vacant windows, seemed utterly alone. It was through this ghostly little "emporium" that he would have to make his way to the camp in the Valley below. The grassy road fell away sharply from the bank where he stood, crossed the stream at a shallow, ran through the town, and disappeared, going downhill into the glimmering forest. It was a perfect arrangement for an ambush.

He got out his field-glass and examined the neighbourhood carefully. At so short a distance every detail was startlingly clear. He swept the roofless buildings house by house. A cat lay draped on a sunny door step. She was washing her face. From under the ruined mill-wheel an otter swam making a V in the placid surface of the race. Black Girl stomped in the thicket. Instantly the otter was gone. Except for himself, then, the place must be deserted. But there was one thing that puzzled him. There were fresh wheel ruts in the road as far as the ford. Then they seemed to turn up into the stream. On the other side the road was untrodden. Someone must have turned there and come back, he supposed.

On the town side of the creek, half-way up an orchard slope towards a ruined foundation, was a small stone springhouse. It was the only building in the place that still boasted a roof. He turned his glass on it. The door was on the opposite side. But he could see the mossy shingles, and a vacant window in the stone wall. A blackbird lit on the roof and flew away. Something white was sitting in the window. He brought his glass to a nice focus, and smiled into his sprouting beard. It was an old rag doll and it had only one eye.

He mounted Black Girl without further trepidation and rode down towards the town.

The tracks at the ford were puzzling. They did lead right into the stream, and disappeared.

Aquila Creek had a flat, gravelly bottom. Not over knee-deep where it widened out through the level meadows at the foot of the ruined town, it swept placidly round a curve into the hills and thickets like a silver road to Broceliande, only to vanish under an arch of leaning hemlocks into a dim forest beyond. Now and again, when the wind permitted, from far back in the hills came the distant roar of a waterfall. But that and the murmur of vocal stones at the crossing were the only sounds in the desolate little valley that seemed to be listening for the clink of cowbells and the calls of vanished berry-pickers. Everywhere else brooded silence and wide, afternoon sunlight. It was in this hushed, almost expectant, atmosphere that the colonel tied Black Girl again under an old apple tree, and taking his haversack made his way swiftly through the deserted orchard to the springhouse.

Five heavy flagstones set like the steps in a circular stair swept down into the ground under an immense beam and gave entrance to the place. He paused to listen intently. Nothing but the methodical and tuneful drip of water was to be heard from time to time. *Drip, drop, drip*--and then a peculiarly vibrant note as though a glass had been rubbed by a finger. He waited to hear it again. It was dark down there. On one of the limestone flags was the faint, muddy trace of a child's foot. He smiled--and stooping head and shoulder, lowered himself into the place.

How secret it was. And yet, once inside, it was not really so dark. From the open window at one end a diffused sunlight reflected the square of the window itself on a perfectly smooth pool. He could still see the rings of some sunken butter-pots there. As his eyes became more used to the silver twilight that was reflected into every part of the old stone room, feebly but equally, he gave a quick exclamation of pleasure. The doll sitting in the window was not the only one. At the far end of the building, where it ran back into the hill more like a cavern than a house, was a juvenile domestic establishment.

Tiny cups made out of acorns sat upon the heavy log shelves in dainty rows. There were little piles of peach kernels and horse chestnuts. These, he remembered, have a spiritual, even a monetary, value for childhood. There was a pile of glinting mica pebbles watched over by a faithful but cracked china dog. And there was also a dilapidated wagon laden with pine cones, drawn by a prancing cast-iron rabbit. Three luminous marbles with glass spirals in their magic depths, and a bit of worn moleskin upon which reposed in solitary and minuscule grandeur seven golden links of a brass watch-chain, obviously comprised the chief treasures of the trove. And the dolls?--

There were several of them.

They were made of corncobs and dressed in butternut sacking. One had a scarlet coat out of a bit of Turkey carpet slightly burned. Another had a "liberty cap" contrived from a baby's sock with a tassel sewn on. But most of them sat about on small chips of log or hassock-shaped stones with bright autumn leaves and cardinal or blue jay feathers in their "hair." There was something Indian about them. Their features were carved like a totem with painted or burnt spots for eyes. And it was evident, from their arrangement around a pile of small sticks over which a cracked tea-cup was suspended that they were met in a solemn council of the Corncob tribe.

The colonel looked at them and smiled with an almost boyish glee. Pocahontas might have played here. He hadn't enjoyed anything so much for years. He wouldn't have been discovered for the world.

But the springhouse was completely withdrawn from the world. Its subdued, watery light seemed the very atmosphere of secrecy. The hollow musical tone from the wooden pipe in which the spring rose slowly and occasionally overflowed, sounded the single muted note of a lonely instrument that celebrated solitude.

He reclined on one elbow in a deep pile of leaves which the children had gathered at one end of their little refuge and indulged himself in the luxury of unrestrained reverie. It had something to do with his own boyhood--and its melancholy aftermath.

Presently he opened his haversack, and brushing aside some of the autumn leaves, began to dispose its carefully-cherished contents in the cleared space on the stony floor.

First he unwrapped and arranged carefully, as though furnishing a room thoughtfully, the small set of furniture he had bought that day on Walnut Street in Philadelphia. There were tables, chairs, couches, and a sideboard--elegant, upholstered, miniature, and pristine. These he set with little dishes and a piece of his handkerchief for a tablecloth. He put a coffee bean at each plate and, from his ration tin, some sugar in the bowl. The effect was extremely fascinating, and he undid the coloured German paper from about the dolls with eager fingers and a deep excitement. There were six of them. A mother and father, obviously sedate and conservative. These he set at either end of the table to preside over the feast. In the four remaining chairs sat two boys, both in military uniform with epaulets, and just across from them a couple of flaxen-haired and blue-eyed girls.

This, to tell the truth, was disappointing. The children were all too much of an age. Perhaps there were a couple of sets of twins in this family? The girls did, as girls should, seem a little younger than their brothers, but--an even more ingenious solution occurred to him. Perhaps these were two military suitors calling upon a pair of simpering sisters. Mamma and papa did look severe. No wonder. Two young men from the army! *There* was trouble ahead for you. And indeed at that very moment one of the cadets fell forward and buried his face in the hypothetical soup.

So lost in Toyland had the colonel become that he caught his breath sharply.

A sigh of relief that might have followed was definitely prevented and cancelled into confusion by a ripple of amused, feminine laughter. Watching him through the window was the admirable face of Mrs. Crittendon.

The colonel was not only embarrassed, he was consternated.

"Well," said she, "for an incendiary, Colonel Franklin, you're the most domestic man I ever saw!"

CHAPTER XIII

COINER'S RETREAT

The colonel leaped to his feet in an agony of embarrassment. If one of Mosbys raiders had just poked his rifle through the window and drawn a bead on him, he could not have felt more dismayed. It was all simply dreadful--and Mrs. Crittendon still continued to look at him. But she wasn't laughing any more. In fact, she had suddenly become quite serious. He felt grateful to her for that.

Just at this point, however, to cap the climax he moved, awkwardly, of course, and upset the doll family completely with his sabre.

"There!" said she, "I knew you'd do that."

Still speechless, he foolishly stooped to retrieve the disaster and only made matters worse. Sacks seemed to have been wrapped about his hands. His fingers were positively muffled. He knew she must be laughing again, and he looked up at her helplessly. But she wasn't.

"Do you need some help?" she asked earnestly.

"Indeed, I do," he replied, almost hoarse from chagrin.

She suppressed a smile and disappeared from the window. The mirror of the spring basin, where the reflection of her head had lately fallen quite clearly, went suddenly vacant; the springhouse was lonely again. A few seconds later he heard her light step on the entrance steps.

She came down the big flagstones and paused at the door. Perhaps it was the comparative darkness inside that stopped her. She sat down on the lowest step and leaned back shading her eyes from the sunlight overhead and peering in at him. For a second or two they took stock of each other. He was no longer embarrassed. A certain sense of physical well-being and confidence brought by her presence overspread him. Somehow he felt that she shared it.

"I hope you won't tell the children about this," he began. "It was a surprise that I was planning for them. If they found out, it would spoil the magic, I'm afraid."

"Why, of course," she said. "I'd never think of tellin' them."

"No, I didn't think you would," he said gravely.

"For my part I didn't mean to come spying on you either," she continued hastily. "I saw your horse in the orchard and wondered who had come here. The children do come down to the spring-house to play sometimes. We used to have friends at Aquila. It was wonderful of you to think of bringin' them dolls. Poor lambs! They had lots of them in the old nursery at 'Whitesides'"--she hesitated a moment--"and they miss 'em," she added a little desperately.

"Oh, I'm sorry about that!" he exclaimed. "If you only knew. That whole miserable business will always haunt me. I tried to prevent it."

"I know," she said. "I'm grateful! But you can't expect a mere woman to understand the deep political reasons for burning her house down." Her voice sank ironically.

He did not attempt to reply.

A silence--the gulf of the war--fell between them. He wondered if they could cross it. Probably not. In the semi-darkness of the springhouse he felt he was sitting in complete solitude again. The musical note from the wooden pipe broke suddenly as though a weak harp string had let go. He became conscious once more of the steady drip of the spring.

"Does anyone else know the children have been playing here?" she finally asked. A new note of anxiety had altered her tone.

"I think not," he said. "I just happened to call in here some weeks ago on my way North--and saw you were about. I remembered that one-eyed doll on the window-sill was the baby's. I recollect his holding it up to me that morning."

"Oh, yes, 'nice man'!" said Mrs. Crittendon. "Yes, I remember that myself." She smiled a little sadly. "It's natural enough that I should, you know, *that* morning!" For the first time a note of genuine bitterness crept into her voice. Her foot began to tap the stone rapidly. She seemed to be trying to make some decision about which she was still in doubt.

Thank heaven she was an Englishwoman, he thought. If she had been a native Virginian, one of the women born in the Valley, she would never have spoken to him. Or she would have heaped contempt or insults on him--and he couldn't have blamed her. He looked up at her, grateful for her restraint. He wondered if she knew about her husband. And then--he remembered the little packet he was to give her. His hand went to his pocket. But she was speaking again. Her foot had stopped tapping.

"To tell the truth, colonel," she said, "it's curious, but you're the very man I was looking for. I--we are in really great trouble. I haven't heard from my husband for weeks. I shall soon, I trust. But meanwhile"--a haggard look came into her eyes--"I am forced to appeal to the enemy, I know your regiment is camped just below us here and I thought *you* might help. So it has been encouraging to find you here--doing what you were.

Because I don't know whether I could have brought myself to speak to you if I hadn't found you here. But"--suddenly growing almost eloquent in her urgency--"I think now that perhaps I can appeal to the man who burned my house--and yet brought dolls to the children. Can I?"

"Mrs. Crittendon, I have General Sheridan's order to help you."

"That man!" she cried. "Never mention him to me. He and General Hunter have the curses of every good woman in Virginia!" She stopped, breathless. "No, no, it is to you, not to him, that I appeal."

His hand dropped away from his pocket. Rather than give her the packet now he would have shot himself. It would have been like striking her in the face with a whip.

"I shall do anything--everything that I can!" he cried impulsively. "Please believe me!"

"This is not a bargain between the United States and the Confederacy, you know," she said scornfully. "Goverments always belong to men and act as though there were no women in the world. I am a woman appealing to you for children. The understanding must be only between you and me, a personal one, or not at all."

"Let it be that way then, between us two," he said.

"Very well," she said. "Then I shall ask you to come with me and promise not to reveal what I am going to show you. Will you?"

"Yes," he said.

She leaned forward and looked at him intently.

"Just a minute," she said. "Please get the horses, while I--I'll rearrange the dolls!"

She passed him, going into the springhouse now and looking up at him with a grave smile. So close to her, he was aware of the suffering and anxiety in her face. It was not altogether the sunlight that had kept her hand over her eyes all the time she had been talking, he noted. No, he could see that.

He walked down the orchard towards the horses. Mrs. Crittendon had tied hers under the same tree with Black Girl. The two beasts were touching noses softly, already the best of friends.

How, thought the colonel, am I ever going to be able to tell her that the major is dead? I can't do it now. She seems to have about all the trouble she can bear. No, it will never do to tell her now! Shall I let her think he will come back to her? One needs hope these days.

He thrust the packet into his breast-pocket again and took the bridle of the new horse gently. After he had fed her an apple and stroked her neck a little she stopped snorting at him.

In the springhouse Mrs. Crittendon quickly bathed her eyes and face in the cold spring water. There, that was much better! She gave a laugh of pure relief. She wouldn't have to ride down to the camp, after all. It was luck to have found him here. She began to arrange the dolls rapidly. Presently the trample of hoofs sounded above.

"All ready," he called.

When she came up out of the springhouse to meet him she had recovered some of the freshness and poise of an English girl going for a ride in Hyde Park. Indeed, that was exactly what her riding costume had been made for--in '47. It was sadly faded. To the colonel, nevertheless, it seemed just then the acme of style. He cupped his hands and she sprang lightly into the side-saddle of her eager little roan.

They rode briskly down through the leafless orchard and across the meadow to the bank of the stream. Then they turned right, in the stream itself, and splashing along its shallow bed as though it were only a flooded highway, disappeared under the arch of hemlocks into the quiet corridors of a forest of evergreens. The noise of the waterfall came closer now; much nearer as they rode up-stream.

Mrs. Crittendon next unexpectedly turned her horse up the bed of a small rivulet that flowed unobtrusively out of the heart of the forest into Aquila Creek. They followed that for some little distance around a bed. It was shallower than the creek had been but still smooth and gravelly. The hoofmarks disappeared under the swift current as soon as made. Then, where a great tree had fallen across the ravine, she turned aside and struck uphill into the forest along an ancient logging road. There were some wheel marks there. How old, it was hard to tell. But not so long ago several vehicles must have passed. All going in, he noticed.

The road took a violent rise, and they suddenly rode out of the forest and stood looking down from a little crest into an open glade in the hills.

"This is the secret you must keep," she said. "How do you like it? We call it 'Coiner's Retreat.' There is an old legend of a lost vein of silver somewhere about up here. Before your Revolution there is the story of an Englishman who came here and coined shillin's privately. There was more silver in them than in the king's. Nevertheless, they tried to hunt him down. When Major Crittendon and I were first married we used to wander all through these hills. This is part of our property. We came on this place quite accidentally one day. We think that the old coiner's cabin was down there. Anyway, we found some of his silver coins under the hearth." She held up a coin bracelet on one smooth arm and smiled. The thought of those times had brought a glow of pleasure to her face. "We always said we'd find the vein of silver too. That was our romance, you know. But we never did. My husband furnished the old cabin for a hunting lodge and did some other things. Sometimes we came and stayed summers. We were safe from the world here then, we thought. And now . . ." She stopped and choked a little.

"Perhaps you can still be so," said the colonel. And then, seeing that she was trying to hide her emotion, he turned away and looked out over the secret coign of the hills that lay below him.

Such were the times that it had not failed to occur to Colonel Franklin that he might be walking into a carefully baited trap. Union soldiers who wandered off into the hills in that part of Virginia might well be reported missing shortly afterwards. He was as yet only two or three miles away from his men, to be sure. But he might as well have been a hundred, for all the good they could do him. And in the "cove", of the hills that now opened before him a regiment of the enemy might easily have been concealed or a whole village of mountaineers. He had heard of such places, and the mountain people were known to be hostile to "strangers" of either side. It was therefore with some natural apprehension as well as curiosity that he examined the landscape just ahead.

He was looking down into a deep fold between two knifelike spurs of the Blue Ridge into what in the West would have been called a cañon. At this particular place the walls of the cañon widened, leaving a level floor of sunny valley a square mile or so in extent, covered with meadows and luxuriant patches of ancient oaks. Through this snug little cove, as through a miniature countryside, the stream meandered placidly, spreading out here and there into oval pools and small lakes. It was apparent that in some past epoch Aquila Creek must have been dammed by an enormous landslide and formed a lake here in the hills. In the course of subsequent ages it had cut through its obstruction to the level of its own floor and drained away-- leaving a little patch of Constable's England behind it.

That, at least, is the way Mrs. Crittendon regarded it.

She and the colonel were standing now on the rocky and forested top of the old landslide, listening to the roar of the stream where it still rushed down a hundred feet or more over its natural dam in a series of thin falls and frothy cascades. Most of its watery commotion arose from its final dash over some huge boulders into a deep black pool at the foot of its impediment. From the top of the dam this pool could be dimly glimpsed through the tips of the tall pines surrounding it like a dark plaque in the forest below.

To the colonel's wary eye, long trained correctly to judge the military possibilities and peculiarities of any given section of terrain by distance, height, cover, and approach, the natural and yet almost uncanny concealment of the pleasant little valley now lying unrolled before him like a model neighbourhood impressed itself as the result of art rather than accident. In that sense there was undoubtedly something dramatic, almost artificial, about it. And yet nothing could be more natural.

The valley lay east and west, and it simply so happened that there was no neighbouring height from which it could be overlooked, except perhaps from the very crest of the Blue Ridge itself. Five miles away that superb mountain wall, covered with tangled forests and cyclopean boulders, lifted at an acute angle directly into the sky. All about and between was a welter of broken ridges and seething foothills whose vertical inclines and dense, briery underbrush repulsed alike the hunter and the mountain farm. Unless one approached the valley up the bed of the creek--and only a wandering fisherman was likely to do that--the place was self-effacingly lost. The single, narrow trail up the ramp of the landslide would have been all but impossible to come upon if one did not know exactly how to find its entrance from the foot of the stream in the forest below.

All this was evident at first glance. Afterwards the colonel discovered that the Crittendons had improved the trail in past summers so that a wagon could be driven across the landslide--by the use of main force and a double team. And Mrs. Crittendon told him later that the place had been rediscovered by her husband only when, by mere chance and adventure, he had climbed up hand over hand by the waterfall. Major Crittendon had been a lifelong fisher after trouts, an angler whose theory it was that there might always be better pools higher up. The old coiner's lost retreat had first burst on his view from the top of the dam as unexpectedly as the South Sea to Balboa. The Crittendons cherished this secret of their mountain land as if the hills themselves had revealed to them personally a romantic episode out of the past of their deep, blue immortality, one which it would have been folly further to confide to the rest of mankind.

Black Girl extended her neck, breathing deeply, inhaling the promise in scent of the succulent meadows below. Except for a light haze of smoke rising from behind a clump of woods half-way up the cove, and a small flock of pigeons that circled over the same tree-tops, the place looked deserted. Of the cabin that Mrs. Crittendon had mentioned, he could see nothing. He ventured to look her way again, hoping that by now she had regained her self-control.

She made no attempt this time to conceal that she had been weeping. She gave him a firm little nod, and made a final dab at her eyes with a small handkerchief.

"Well, will the fly still follow me into the parlour?" she asked--and managed to smile at him. "There *is* trouble ahead. I won't deny that. But it is my trouble and not yours," she added softly.

He felt sorry now that she had so easily surmised his suspicions. But they had been too inevitable to require an apology. Also, although he hated to admit it, to look at her was enough to allay his doubts.

Their eyes met.

"I am following you, Mrs. Crittendon," he said, "wherever you're going."

She gave him a grateful glance and led the way down the inner face of the old landslide. The descent on that side was a short one. In a few moments they were galloping over a long stretch of perfectly smooth meadow in the direction of the smoke. Presently they passed into a kind of natural avenue under the broad limbs of ancient oaks. It was a comparatively open piece of woodland with the trees wide apart and no underbrush. A couple of wild razorbacks rooting in the mast fled before them. They then rode out of the wood as suddenly as they had entered it and drew up into a walk.

The colonel could see nothing ahead but a broad sweep of meadow with several clumps of woods clear to the point where the valley swept around into the hills a quarter of a mile away.

"Look behind you!" called Mrs. Crittendon. He stopped and swung about.

A long low cabin with massive boulder chimneys at either end now lay before him. It faced directly east, with its back squarely against the woodland through which he had just ridden. It seemed to have been tucked in under the oaks, some of whose branches stretched over its roof. In the summer it would be in dense shade. Doubtless the oaks had overshadowed it in the course of time. The roof was obviously rather new, and before the house was a trim picket fence of split-oak palings, surrounding a neat door-yard. The gate was open. Along the path to the broad veranda some late flowers were still in bloom. There were a number of rough outbuildings scattered about farther back amid the trees. He noticed a couple of wagons and an old carriage. And half-way up one large oak, concealed in its giant fork, was a tree house with a ladder and a porch. At the sight of Mrs. Crittendon the flock of pigeons began to come down and light about her.

The place had all the air of what the colonel called a "snuggery." Nothing more secure and secluded could be imagined. And, considering the surroundings, nothing more beautiful. But just at this point the colonel's somewhat uneasy pastoral musings were cut short by the appearance at the door of the cabin of a young man with a rifle in his hand.

"Paul!" cried Mrs. Crittendon, leaping down from her horse and running frantically towards the cabin. "Put down that gun!"

The boy was having some trouble with it. It was a long rifle and he appeared to have the use of only one hand.

"Paul!" she called, rushing through the gate and up the walk. "Stop him, somebody, stop him!" she shrieked.

The boy had raised the rifle to his shoulder with one hand. It wobbled in the general direction of the colonel, who had also dismounted rapidly and started towards the house. Margaret Crittendon and an old man with a white beard rushed out and grappled with the boy. The rifle went off and the bullet droned up the valley. Mrs. Crittendon collapsed and sat on the steps. On the porch behind her a violent struggle was going on. Margaret and the old man were trying to overpower Paul.

"I told you not to bring any Yanks here, Aunt Libby," he yelled at her. "I knew you'd gone for them. You can't fool me! What would Uncle Douglas say?" He seemed to be frantic.

Margaret had thrown her arms about him. "Paul, Paul, you silly, be quiet," she kept saying.

"O God, my arm!" The boy gave an almost girlish scream. There was anguish in it. "Quit, Meg, quit, you're killin' me." He staggered back against the wall of the porch and slumped down. The old man caught him in his arms.

"He's out of his head, poor lad," said Mrs. Crittendon, looking up at the colonel. "He didn't know what he was doing."

As long as he lived Colonel Franklin never forgot the look of agonized appeal that she gave him.

"That's right," said the old man. "He's had a terrible fever now for three days. It's God's visitation for his sins."

Mrs. Crittendon suppressed a sob. For a moment they all stood looking at one another blankly.

Young Margaret laughed.

"Maybe you'll help carry Paul back upstairs for us, colonel," she said. "We're a little weak around here. There hasn't been too much to eat lately." She laid her hand on his arm and smiled at him calmly. So much patience, understanding and loveliness was in the young girl's expression that his eyes went dim.

"I'll do that, my dear," he said.

He took the half-unconscious form of Paul from the old man and followed Margaret through the door. The boy was light. He felt like a sack of bones with a fire in it. The young body seemed to be smouldering inside. Grasping his worn butternut clothes, the colonel felt the fever beating through them into his hands. For the first time he noticed that the clothes were probably the ragged remains of a Confederate uniform. One of Virginia's boy-warriors, he thought--and remembered Farfar. It took the draft to bring out the older men. Something in the boy's face, flushed and drawn though it was, reminded him of young Margaret Crittendon. The family resemblance was palpable.

"Your brother?" he said to her as he laid the boy, whose eyes were now half-open, but seemed to be seeing nothing, on a cotton tick pallet in a small garret room under the eaves.

"No," she answered, speaking almost in a whisper, and looking down at Paul sadly. "He's my cousin, Paul Crittendon. Uncle Jim was killed two years ago at Mechanicsville. Aunt Ann died a few months later. I reckon she pined away. They all came to live with us at 'Whitesides' in the Valley then--Paul, and Mary, and the baby. And now 'Whitesides' has gone! It will be all right when father comes back. We can make a go of it here. But we need Paul. You can't blame him for hating Yankees, colonel, can you?"

"Poor child!" said the colonel.

"Why, he's all grown up!" exclaimed Margaret proudly. "He's been in three battles already with General Early. And he's got a girl too, Flossie Kiskadden. And he's wounded. I reckon you'd call it that. There's no blood, but look! Look at his poor arm. It was an old round shot did it. It was just rolling a little when he stopped it, he said."

She laid back the boy's coat, uncovering a filthy sling made of sacking. The colonel untied it carefully, revealing a frightfully swollen arm. From the wrist to the elbow it was the size of a small tree.

"I'm afraid it's a compound fracture at least. Maybe splintered," he said. "That's a job for a surgeon, of course."

"Of course it is! That's just what I kept saying. I told mother she'd have to go down to the camp and ask you. You helped me put out the fire at 'Whitesides' that day. Oh, I know you're going to help us. We do need Paul so much, colonel. My father would do as much for you." The young girl shivered and took hold of his coat.

"You don't have to beg me, my child," said the colonel. "Of course, I'm going to help you. I'll have a surgeon up here in a jiffy. I shall treat you like my own children."

"Oh!" said Margaret. "Oh, colonel, I don't care if you are a Yankee, every Crittendon will always thank you."

"Margaret, Margaret," called Mrs. Crittendon, "what are you doing up there for Paul? Talking? That won't help him."

"Yes, it will, mother. It's going to help a lot," replied her daughter. She busied herself folding an old coat under Paul's head.

The colonel walked downstairs.

"The first thing to do," he said, "is to get that swollen arm reduced. May I have a bucket with some cold water?"

"No water!" exclaimed the old man, rising white-bearded before the fireplace, and towering all six feet of him like a tall grim spectre till he seemed to dominate the room. "It is written that sinners for their transgressions shall burn."

"Never mind that," said the colonel, looking at the old man sternly. "Go and get a bucket of water."

To everyone's surprise, especially Mrs. Crittendon's, the old man's shoulders drooped, the light died out of his eyes, and he went quietly. Outside, the well-chain began to creak.

"Who is that old party?" asked the colonel not too reverently.

"A family I've given shelter to up here," replied Mrs. Crittendon. "An old, retired Cumberland Presbyterian minister and his daughter. The Reverend James Kiskadden. Here comes Flossie now."

Coming down the path with a lackadaisical, strolling air and a basket over her arm, the colonel glimpsed a red-haired girl of about fourteen.

"Oh, it's very complicated," continued Mrs. Crittendon. "Paul's mad about Flossie. That's the only word for it--mad as only a boy can be. I'm afraid things aren't as they should be. But it's wartime and I can't stop it. I can't!" she insisted, her hands closing and unclosing rapidly. "And now he's come back wounded--and to see that girl. The old man holds me responsible. I had to take them in, you know. He's a little bit--well, it's all religion now."

"And I suppose he has been ruling the roost?"

"Oh, yes. Oh, I haven't the strength to stop him, I've been so tired. You would not find me this way, tears and all that, if I weren't simply worn out. If it weren't for Margaret, I don't know what I'd do.

"Flossie, this is Colonel Franklin of the United States Army," she said to the girl who had stopped at the door astonished at sight of the colonel. "He's come here to help us."

"How do you do, Miss Kiskadden," said the colonel.

"Howdedo?" replied Flossie, apparently oblivious of everyone. She sat down and shoved her basket under the table. Tall and thin, with long legs and large adolescent hands and feet, there was, nevertheless, something wild and lovely about her. Her features were regular and delicate. Her uncombed hair escaped like red, spun gold from under her flabby sunbonnet, and her blonde lashes lay like faint gilt brush marks across the dark pits of her eyes. She sat apathetically.

"Did you get anything?" inquired Mrs. Crittendon anxiously.

"No, 'm, the niggers must have been to the patch and got all the taters last night. It's all dug. Thar's narry a marble even." She lapsed into a sullen silence.

"Oh my!" said Mrs. Crittendon, "what *are* we going to do?"

"Now, Mrs. Crittendon," said the colonel, "I'm going to ask you to sit down in this chair and stop worrying. There will be plenty of food here by tomorrow morning, and anything else you need. And I'll bring the surgeon with me for Paul. He can't set that arm till it's reduced anyway, and until then I'm going to do exactly what he would do for it. By the way, where's that water?"

"Pa's sittin' beside it out thar on the well-kerb looking at hisself in the bucket," said Flossie, "the old fool!"

"Flossie, you must *not* speak of your father that way in my house," cried Mrs. Crittendon, striking her hands together. The girl jumped. "Go out and bring the children in. Hurry!"

Meanwhile the colonel had retrieved the water and was carrying it upstairs.

"Water!" cried Margaret when he entered the room. She looked shocked. "Mr. Kiskadden said it would kill him. He said you have to dry out a fever."

"He did, did he!" replied the colonel. "How long has Paul been without water then?"

"Three days," replied the girl, looking at him terrified.

"Get me a glass, quick," said he.

She was downstairs and returned in a flash. The boy lay back on the old coat, his chin in the air, and a glimmer between his eyelids. The colonel raised his head carefully and tilted a glass to his lips. A surprised look as though the gates of paradise had safely closed behind him spread over the face of the sinner Paul as the divine coolness flowed down his parched throat.

Another glassful followed.

"That will do now for a while," said the colonel. "But give him all he wants from time to time, Margaret."

Paul opened his eyes and looked about him. The water seemed to act upon him instantly as though he had had a sustaining stimulant.

"That's more than the Crittendons would do for me. For a hundred years now I've been beggin' Meg to give me a drink. And they wouldn't even let me get one myself!"

Margaret listened to this indictment, standing tight-lipped at the foot of the bed. "It was the old man, Paul," said she. "He told us."

Paul disregarded her. "I'm sorry I tried to shoot you," he said to the colonel. "I didn't know you were a doctor. I thought you were a com-com-*bat*ant."

"All right," replied the colonel, glad to take advantage of the boy's mistake to help him. "Now you know how it is, just take it natural. I'm going to try to make that arm easier for you. Do you think," he asked Margaret, "I could get another bucket downstairs, something to let his arm rest in?"

"There's the old cider keg under the porch. You could break the head in," she whispered.

"The very thing!"

A few minutes later the keg, minus one end and filled to the brim, was standing by the head of Paul's low cot. Fortunately he seemed to sink into a torpor again. He made no resistance when the colonel and Margaret raised him, and with infinite care lowered his left arm into the cold well water till it reached high above the elbow. Once he cried out. It was only then that the colonel understood he was bearing silently the agony of having the terribly painful arm moved.

"You're a real Virginian, Paul," said the colonel.

The boy acknowledged the compliment by opening his eyes. This time he smiled at them. "Where's Flossie?" said he.

"Never mind her," said the colonel. "Margaret, I want *you* to stay here and watch Paul. Flossie can help you later, perhaps. But keep his arm in the water and give him all he needs to drink. If he gets cold and starts to shiver, take his arm out for a while. I'll see you tomorrow. I'll send you help early in the morning."

Margaret nodded, unable to speak, and smiled him bravely out of the room. She was a natural nurse. Taking off her worn apron, she dipped it in the cold water and began to sponge Paul's face and chest. The grateful coolness relaxed him. For the first time in days his arm had ceased to throb. He put his free hand up to pat Margaret's cheek.

"You're an awful nice girl, Meg! I'm sorry. Do you love me?"

"No," said she, "not the way you mean, not like Flossie. But you are my cousin, Paul," and she gave him a cool family kiss.

"That's lots better than the Battle of Little North Mountain," he said.

"Oh, Paul, I hope you won't ever go back," she cried.

"There, there, Meg. Don't you cry now. I'll do what a Crittendon ought to."

She nodded, her eyes brimming.

Downstairs the colonel found Mrs. Crittendon busy getting what she called "tea." It was a mess of coarse boiled oats and a little corn meal. She was trying to rub the lumps out of it with a big wooden spoon against the sides of a bowl.

"And it's the last meal we have," she said, showing him the bottom of the tin. "On the strength of your promises I am venturing to kill the fatted calf, you see."

They sat for a moment or two discussing young Paul's plight. He warned her not to let old Mr. Kiskadden interfere with the treatment.

"I shan't," she said. "Your coming has wakened me out of that spell. You know, when you're terribly tired, how a dominating person prevails somehow." She brushed one wisp of golden hair back from her forehead. "Paul has made all of us lose a great deal of sleep."

He could believe that. She was nearly worn out. It was evidently the excitement of leaving the valley that had buoyed her up in their meeting at the springhouse.

He took out a note-book and began to make a list of necessaries, questioning her methodically.

She laughed a little.

"I suppose army men always carry those note-books," she said. "It looks familiar. Major Crittendon was a West Pointer, you know."

He coloured. "Nevertheless, I find them helpful."

"Exactly--" she said, and went on with her list. It seemed endless. "You see, I am asking for everything. I took your advice that day and got away from the house as quickly as I could after getting grandma off in a wagon for the South Side Railroad. She insisted upon going to Richmond. She was right, I suppose. She would have died up here. We brought two wagonloads of stuff to the cabin and there were still some things that remained from our summer excursions. All the food is gone now and we're dark at night."

He closed the book. "I'll send you all I can," he said.

Flossie Kiskadden came into the room with the two children. Mary, a little girl of seven, and the baby Tim about three years old. Mary curtsied to him. Tim was inclined this time to be aloof. "I want some supper awfu' bad," he said. The old man kept coming and going, bringing in spare wood for the two fires.

"It's the only light we have," said Mrs. Crittendon, "and it does look cheerful. But I hate to burn it all before winter." She and Flossie were walking back and forth, busy about small domestic tasks. In the long room the firelight from the double chimneys beat warmly upon the giant side logs of the old cabin. They were silvery with age and at times glinted almost like metal. The two children sat eating their mush out of white bowls, gossiping about the tree house and their life there in subdued, bedtime voices. At either end of the room a yellow sheet of flame ran up the ample chimney-backs where some black pots hung. Old man Kiskadden took a rag-stick from a cracked bowl and rubbed his gums with snuff. He sat back in the warmth contentedly. On a near-by shelf an old clock ticked loudly.

The colonel closed his eyes for a moment. What time was this that was passing? It seemed to be a time he had lived long before--long prior to 1864. He was aware of Mrs. Crittendon's skirt touching him as she passed; of a faint scent of lavender. The clock whirred and struck--only twice. The children burst into a laugh.

He opened his eyes again.

"Tomorrow, then," he said, "depend upon it. I'll have to bring one or two of my people, you know."

"Yes," she said, looking a little shocked. "Yes, of course! Won't you stay for supper?" she asked half in mockery. And then gravely, "We'd be happy to have you."

"I think not." He smiled, peeping into the scanty mush bowl. "But that reminds me!" He went out, hastily unstrapped his blanket roll and stripped it of what rations it still contained. He took the last of his bacon from the haversack.

The children welcomed the sugar, hard-tack and coffee with a glad outcry. Young Timmy made a vain attack on the army bread.

"My goodness, is that what Yankees eat?" exclaimed little Mary. "No wonder then!" A general laugh went round. Even old man Kiskadden grinned.

She bade him good-bye at the door with the firelight wavering behind her.

"Our blessings go with you tonight," she said simply.

"I shall need them," said he, and held his hat to his breast. The door closed slowly. He stood for a moment lost in the outside world of a restless, scarlet sunset. In there he had found peace.

A few seconds later Mrs. Crittendon heard Black Girl gallop past and the hoofbeats diminish rapidly down the valley. She lay back in her chair. Somehow a certain feeling of security possessed her. Hot coffee, which she had not tasted for two years, ran through her like a genial elixir. I wonder what Douglas will say, she thought. She had promised her husband never to reveal the way into the valley to any stranger.

"And now," she said aloud, with her hands behind her head and looking at the fire, "I've done it!"

"Done what, mother?" demanded Margaret, who had just come downstairs for her meagre share of the meal.

"I've broken my promise to your father, and brought someone who isn't a Crittendon into Coiner's Retreat," said Mrs. Crittendon, as though confessing a sin. It sounded worse to her after she had said it aloud.

Her daughter came over, and standing behind her chair, began to stroke her mother's forehead. She leaned over and put her arms around her.

"If father were here he would have done the same. You know he would," she whispered. "And, mother, the old times are over!"

"Oh, *don't* say that, my dear," cried her mother, grasping her child's hands spasmodically. "How can you?"

"Because I know it's true," murmured Margaret.

"Yes?" replied Mrs. Crittendon after a little. "Then from now on we shall have to do the best we can here in the valley. I must hold things together till your father comes back. God knows how long this war will go on. Think of it, think of it! It's been four years now! You were a little girl when it began. Margaret, do you know sometimes I wish I hadn't married a Virginian. I would never have seen this beautiful, dreadful country then, these quarrelling states--until what a state we're in! Remember, if anything ever happens to me, you are to go back to Melton Mowbray, to your uncle Freek's home. There are no states there, only England and the Queen."

"But I wouldn't have been here if you had stayed in England. We wouldn't have known each other. Mother, I'll never leave you, never from now on."

"Hush," said her mother. "Come and sit on my knee as you used to do not so long ago. I need you, but none of us can keep the other for ever. But I need you now, little daughter, I need you as I never did before and I thank God we're still together. Since the house burned you seem to have grown up. We'll hold the fort here together and let the men's war go on. I was wild to talk as I did. Something seems to have shaken me today for the first time. It's the thought of change, I suppose."

The clock whirred and struck two again. It struck two every hour. Major Crittendon had once set the hands. One of them had caught. Mrs. Crittendon wound the clock regularly but let the hour hand point to her husband's time. It was her clock, the only marriage present she had saved from the fire. Of a fine English make, it kept on faithfully trying to make time into eternity.

"Paul is much better," whispered Margaret. "He's asleep. Flossie promised to watch him. She likes to hear what he says in his fever."

"Meow," said Mrs. Crittendon faintly in her daughter's ear.

"It's her turn, anyway," said Margaret. "I stayed up last night."

She got a blanket, and crowding her mother to one side in the big bench-chair, wedged in beside her. The two sat cheek to cheek looking into the fire. When the clock struck two again, neither of them heard it.

Flossie Kiskadden came downstairs in her bare feet and peeped at them. She seemed reassured. She tiptoed back to the garret and took a look at her old father in the far corner of the loft. He had gone to sleep on his knees, saying his prayers by an old stool. She threw a worn quilt over him and felt that she had done a good act. The children were breathing regularly in the little room right across from Paul's. She went back noiselessly and sat down beside her patient. The fever had left him. His left arm was still in the keg of water. He was shaking and shivering now.

"Paul," said she. "Paul, are you so cold?"

"'Pears like winter's at my heart," he whispered.

"Leave me warm you, Paul. Will you?"

He patted her arm. In the starlight she stood up and slipped her frock to the floor. Presently she was beside him under the blanket.

Very slowly he drew his numb arm out of the water and laid it across them both outside the covers.

"Don't you move, Flossie," he whispered. "It would just about kill me."

"I won't," she answered, smiling up into the darkness. She turned her face to his. He felt her firm young lips against his own.

"Did you miss me, Paul dearest, did you?"

"Lord," said he, "this is what I really came home for!"

She gave a sigh of content.

One--two, chimed the clock downstairs . . . one--two . . .

Hours before, Colonel Franklin had ridden into camp. The regiment received him home with a roar. "The old man's back and he still had two days of furlough left. *That* shows what he thinks of us! I'll bet you he takes Captain Thatcher out of arrest before reveille roll-call. Lieutenant-Colonel Colson's all right, but he sure has it in for troop 'D.'" Rumour and gossip spread from fire to fire. And sure enough Captain Thatcher was released. Colson was glad to find himself out of a pig-headed muddle, and "D" troop had received a lesson. At tattoo the 6th Pennsylvania Cavalry turned in, feeling itself one happy fighting family unit again.

Taps sounded.

Presently no one but the sentries, alert for miles southward, heard the Shenandoah rolling, singing mournfully along its shallows in the Valley of Desolation.

CHAPTER XIV

DOLLS IN THE SHADOWS

What the sentries saw all night long was the dark mass of mountains and forest outlined against a void shivering with frosty light. After midnight the fields and open spaces became visible, stretching mysteriously wide and vacant in the ashy pallor flowing from the face of an apparently motionless moon. The uniform impression to those who were watching was of a unity, black in the blue darkness, existing motionless and timeless, free from cause and effect, a something static.

What the sentries were looking for all night long was movement, any sign of change that would mean the presence of an enemy. But there was no sign of movement of any kind. The enemy they were looking for was not there. Changes, the signs of movement during a single night that marked the presence of the real enemy, were so gradual to the eyes of human sentries as to be like the genuine foe himself, unsuspected, and so, undiscoverable.

But if the real enemy was not to be seen, he made his presence audible. He operates by sapping and mining, and the sure, slow, inevitable, and ever-victorious measure of his progress was to be heard in the sound of the rolling Shenandoah, carrying away the Valley and everything in it, shifting Virginia out of space, out of time.

Roll, O Shenandoah, roll--and all you other rivers rolling rapidly. The real enemy hides not only in swords but in ploughshares. Beat your swords into ploughshares and still the destruction and desolation of the land is confirmed. One hundred years of careless farming had wrought more lasting and irretrievable desolation in the Valley of Virginia than General Sheridan could have conceived or his troopers have carried out. Who the real enemy was, how imperative it was to unite against him, none of the watchers on the night called by them October 16-17, 1864, had any idea. The sentries had no more idea of the constant presence and invisible operations of the real enemy than had the sleepers divided into opposing camps over and against whom they watched. Pale faces under white tents, or faces covered with dew looking up palely at the stars, a dead world filled their heaven with an ashy light as though warning them even in their dreams of what a devastated Earth might be.

There *are* signs set in heaven.

All their skill, all the intelligence of co-operation in a united state, all their mutual patience, loving-kindness--and more--would be essential just to prevent and delay--even to defeat temporarily, by exercising the utmost skill in minor human tactics--the overwhelming strategy of the natural forces operating eternally against them.

So all the sleepers in the Valley that night were like the dolls in the springhouse at Aquila. Sentries and sleepers alike, they were unconscious of what was upon them. In the springhouse one could have seen enacted in a kind of Lilliputian horror a microscopic mystery of the whole. Whimsically enough, the play was in the moonlight, a dumb show of the visitation of nature upon the droll waxen figures of man.

Mrs. Crittendon had rearranged the dolls carefully. The havoc wrought by the accidental sweep of the colonel's sabre had been set in order. They sat there, while the moon looked in past their one-eyed sentry in the window, eternally feasting as though nothing could ever disturb them. The water dripped and the feast went on. They sat smiling at one another happily.

Let us forget how small they are. So is a man. In the darkness behind them the dolls of the Corncob tribe are as invisible in the shadows as their actual prototypes in the darkness of the past. It is only the white dolls that the light now falls upon.

And there *is*--something terrible about them.

Something waxenly wolfish in their bright, merciless blue eyes and the frosty glint of moonlight on bared china teeth. Not so sinister, though, as that something else behind them by the spring.

It is a flat head that has the long, easy curve of the cowl of death over it. It rises slowly above the stone coping of the pool and out of that hood of darkness stare two moonstone eyes. The moonlight catches in them, the cold shimmer from the spring water flakes into green in those sockets and turns around.

The body of the otter emerges from the wooden pipe like a snake from the ground.

It merges itself in the shadows. It advances hour by hour with them. The scent of an enemy lies upon the dolls. As the moon sinks, darkness overtakes them. When daylight comes through the window again two of them are gone.

One would scarcely know they had been if it were not for the two small, empty chairs. It is all very tiny again. Really rather funny. The spring dripped on.

In the Valley just below Aquila the trumpets of the 6th Pennsylvania Cavalry hailed the sun with a fine brazen clamour. A great neighing and whinnying goes up from the picket lines. The mountains roll in thunder as the guard empty their rifles in a morning volley for fear the charges may be damp. Colonel Franklin stirs in his tent and remembers where he is. Dudley, his orderly, unties the flaps and lets in the sun.

In the cabin at Coiner's Retreat Mrs. Crittendon rises from the side of Margaret out of the big chair where they had been half-sitting up all night before the fire. She throws the blanket over her daughter, who is still sleeping, and picks up a comb that has fallen out of her long, golden hair. Then she puts a little lightwood on the embers and begins to boil a pot of coffee. The last of the colonel's bacon is just enough to go round. That is all there is. She wonders when the promised help will come. Flossie smells the coffee, and carefully rising from the side of Paul, slips into her dress again. Paul is sleeping peacefully. The fever has left him. The children dash half-naked out of their room and scamper down to the fire. Old man Kiskadden awakes, mortally stiff and still on his knees. He takes up the affair of Paul and Flossie with his Maker in his morning prayer precisely where he had left off the evening before. It is revealed to him that they should be married. Mrs. Crittendon, he realizes, may be more difficult to persuade than our Father. "And for myself, O Lord, I ask that thou wouldst help me to remember where I put things so thy old servant can find them again. Amen."

CHAPTER XV

THE LAST OF INDIAN SUMMER

Weather is a far more subtle topic of conversation than most people surmise. There is a profound reason why nearly everyone agrees about the weather. It sets the deep underlying mood, the constant of feeling, by which men act. It is, in a sense, both the cause and the barometer of events. Hence, to rehearse the exact state of the weather at any given time is to recall how men felt then, and, to some extent, why they acted in a certain way. For feeling largely governs thought; it is the well-spring of action. Take, for instance, the unusual weather in the Valley of Virginia during the autumn of 1864.

Indian summer seemed to have come to stay. There was no wind to speak of. At most, a few warm and feeble breezes. Trees hung listless with incredibly brilliant leaves that dropped one by one. Ethereal sunshine drenched the mountains, and the sky was softly brilliant at night. The weather had something monotonously eternal about it. A man felt calm and comfortable, lazy and a little amorous. Light frosts in the morning merely served to add zest to life. And for weeks there was no sign of change. Indian summer simply went on. That a bitter winter was presaged seemed unbelievable. Winter would never come.

The crystalline mountain atmosphere, as autumn advanced, gradually took on more and more the quality of a magnifying lens. Unconsciously, everybody's view slowly became telescopic. On every side the long blue mountains receded majestically into the clear, cobalt distance; fused at last with the sky. What was casually spoken of in the newspapers at home as the "theatre of war" at last became for the actual actors in it an amphitheatre of such vast and significant proportions that the futility of human conflict, for once, threatened to become generally apparent. It is no mere accident that diaries kept by soldiers then serving in hostile armies allude to such effects and attribute them to the same natural causes.

Also, many were tired of the war. At certain fords across the Shenandoah and in some villages in the Valley men fraternized. Federal coffee and sugar were exchanged for Virginia tobacco. Military bands playing patriotic airs were distantly cheered from both sides. "Home, Sweet Home" brought forth a wild universal acclaim.

All this was better than a Truce of God or an armistice of generals. It was the natural truce of man asserting itself, reason and necessity prevailing slowly over an irrational enthusiasm that had resorted to force. There were no more spontaneous clashes of madly enthusiastic partisans. Battles were coldly and calmly prearranged on the map by generals. But for that very reason, when they did occur, there was about them a certain desperation, an element of purely professional and efficient slaughter that had frequently been lacking before. The war had become a generals' game, with feeling reduced to a factor. In the Valley the pawns in the next move for the most part were content to live on, camping in the apparently endless Indian summer, enjoying temporarily the truce that the elements themselves seemed to have proclaimed.

At Aquila the 6th Pennsylvania Cavalry, watching the gorge through which the enemy never came, lapsed into a purely mechanical vigilance, none the less effective for that. Detached from all other commands, and camping alone in the solitary Valley, the regiment attained a complete individual importance and concentrated upon its routine of military life and activities as a separate unit much in the same way that an isolated family becomes totally absorbed in its own domestic affairs.

In the ample meadows a half-mile below the ruined village the wide camp seemed permanently to be pitched upon a field in eternity, safe between two giant mountain walls.

This effect of aloof permanence was, to any sensitive observer, striking and inescapable. Nothing broke the silence of the deserted Valley except the regiment's own bugle calls, the neighing of horses, or distant shouts of command. How lonely, yet how immovable the white tents seemed!

Colonel Franklin, owing to his long leave of absence, was perhaps more aware of this than anyone else. As he sat shaving in his tent the morning after his return, looking out over the military but peaceful scene before him, the fixed air of the camp, the lounging, conversational attitudes of the stable detail watering the horses at the near-by ford, the elaborate arch of woven evergreens before the drum-major's tent, all conveyed to him, not without a humorous connotation, that pleasant sense of security in which the 6th Pennsylvania considered itself to be rusticating.

It was not the colonel's intention to reveal his own alarm at thus finding his command fallen into such a dangerously comfortable state of mind. Rather, he intended to take advantage of the contentment of his people, the unbelievably good weather, and the excellent forage and drill grounds that the miles of meadows along the river bottom provided to bring his men and animals to the pink of condition. He intended also to polish the drill and to perfect the marksmanship with the new Enfield breech-loading carbines only recently issued. They had been captured at Vicksburg the year before and were still cased in their original blue-paper, English wrappings. He would serve them out immediately and get down to business.

To this end--while he still lingered over a breakfast to which the always foraging Dudley had miraculously contributed two fresh eggs presumably laid by himself--the colonel brought forth a small note-book regarded by the regimental sergeant-major with peculiar respect and aversion and began, as every good officer should, to set down item by item his plans for the new daily routines. His ideas came easily on so fine a morning, and in a short while he had before him as admirable a prospective regimen of drill and discipline as any regiment might be expected--not to admire.

But let them grumble, he thought. If headquarters and the enemy would only let him alone for a few weeks more, he would not only have the new recruits broken in, but his veterans, men and horses, all working together as one perfected and intelligent machine.

These, and other official matters, having been consigned to memoranda, he now glanced at the page marked "Mrs. Crittendon's Urgent Requirements," set down the evening before. He conned this for a minute or two and then sent the orderlies for the day after three individuals: Surgeon Adolf Holtzmaier, Private William Farfar, and Mr. Felix Mann. They were soon seen hurrying to the colonel's tent.

Dr. Holtzmaier had been born in Bethlehem, Pennsylvania,--twenty-seven years and some odd days before the colonel sent for him,--naked and without a sense of humour. Since then he had acquired clothes. Also some medical information of a sort at a seminary in Philadelphia. His uniform and rank were due to his having only just failed to pass a surgeon's examination given at Harrisburg by the state military medical authorities, plus the desperate necessity of the government to retain the services of anybody who knew the difference between quinine and arnica, or who could saw off a leg.

Dr. Holtzmaier had, however, some positive merits as a surgeon. His full-moon face had never changed its fixed, cheerful expression--even after Fredericksburg. He had iron muscles and strong, steady hands. And he insisted upon using chloroform.

He requisitioned chloroform in such lavish quantities as to cause official questions to be asked. These he answered truthfully, but in such a way that the papers he endorsed for return were carefully filed where no Congressional investigators or superiors would ever find them. And he got the chloroform, lethal quantities of it, to put "der mens to schleep."

Although the surgeon never could understand why anybody laughed, he could comprehend why wounded soldiers sometimes groaned. It shocked his big, boyish, sluggish nervous system. And he preferred to put the subjects of his by now fairly deft butchery to sleep rather than to listen to their screams.

The men appreciated this. They called him "Chloroform Jesus," but respected him nevertheless. Dr. Holtzmaier was shaped something like a ham. He was slow, literal, kindly, and doggedly conscientious. He persisted, however, in regarding Mr. Felix Mann, the regimental sutler, as his foe; as an agent in league with the devil, or one retained by the enemy to poison off the regiment en masse.

Mr. Mann, on the contrary, liked the doctor despite the fact that he stood in great awe of him. He simply couldn't understand the surgeon's objections to selling the men unlimited quantities of mouldy pies of his own fearful baking, or anything else presumably potable or solvent, so long as the men could and did pay for it. Mr. Mann's connection with the regiment was, luckily for him, of only a semi-military character. It tended to change with the trend of victory. He had been a pedlar before the war. Now he was simply pedlar-in-chief, that is, sutler, to the 6th Pennsylvania Cavalry, which he persistently followed with two wagons loaded with cargoes of notions, sundries, comestibles and terrific concoctions and confections.

Apparently his importance was slight. As a matter of fact, his constant and assiduous supplies of little comforts and knick-knacks frequently made life on the field of honour just bearable enough to prevent the desertion of heroes. Owing to the colonel's powerful persuasion, Mr. Mann now kept honest books. His accounts were paid out of the payroll and so he adhered to the regiment like a leech. His pertinacity in following it was equalled only by his precipitancy in leaving it when a fight impended. After a battle, though, he would always show up, and somehow invariably with a supply of those indispensable nothings which the government had seen fit to overlook.

There was no chaplain with the 6th Pennsylvania Cavalry. The reverend gentleman originally appointed had developed diarrhœa debilitating in direct proportion as he approached the front. Colonel Franklin had not see fit officially to lament his absence, and the Reverend

John McCutcheon of Standing Stone continued for three years to draw his salary on sick leave while at home. The mere thought of artillery was sufficient to reloosen his bowels of compassion into what was then known as a flux.

Consequently, Mr. Mann performed many of the absent chaplain's duties. Messages, letters, gifts, and personal affairs were confided to him by the men to be decently and carefully looked after. Both the love affairs and the death messages of the regiment frequently passed through his hands. And he did well. He was a little man with thoughtful brown eyes. He wore dirty white vests with military brass buttons, and a wisp of waxen moustache. It was his ambition to resemble Napoleon III. Actually he looked like an harassed field mouse.

Secretly, Colonel Franklin regarded the surgeon and the sutler as two of the most important members of his command. It was essential, he thought, to keep peace between them. But it was by no means an easy task. Thus, when Dr. Holtzmaier and Mr. Felix Mann both arrived at the colonel's tent at the same time, Mr. Mann was sure that the doctor had complained of a recent sale of custard pies only a little indigestible. In fact, the doctor intended to report the dire effects of some spoiled bottled beer. Mr. Mann's moustache started to bristle. The doctor looked at him with the cold eye of science, ready to begin his indictment. Just outside the tent fly in the morning sunshine Private Farfar was permitted for the good of the service and his own soul to stand at rigid attention during the entire interview.

"Dirty-tree men hit der report dish mornings mit pelly gomplaints. Pad peer, bery pad!" began the doctor, fixing his cold gaze upon Mr. Mann. "Und I say . . ."

"Never mind that," said the colonel. "We'll take up the sick report later. Have you any tea, Mr. Mann?"

"Tea!" said Mr. Mann, trying to get his mind off beer. "Why, yes, sir. But only a pound or two. Pretty old at that, I'm afraid. There isn't much call for tea from the men, you know, sir. Now the beer . . ."

"Ja, der peer," began the doctor.

"Never mind the beer!" insisted the colonel. "I'll take all the tea you have, Mr. Mann, and I want you to fill this list for me as soon as possible. What you haven't got on hand now, bring up in the next wagon from Harpers Ferry. I'm in a hurry, and it's a personal bill of goods for my own use." He passed a list over to Mann. "Load what you have of this on a pack-

horse now and have it ready in half an hour. The young trooper outside will pick it up directly. That's all. Good morning."

Mr. Mann wiped his brow in a relieved manner, gave the doctor a triumphant look, and departed. The colonel turned to his disappointed surgeon, and in a tone so low that young Farfar could not hear what was being said, talked to him for several minutes.

"Goot, goot! Ja, I vill do all I can, gunnel," promised the doctor, coming out of the tent.

"Farfar," said the colonel, "you are to go with the surgeon to help him." He gave the boy careful instructions how to reach Coiner's Retreat and cautioned him to keep a close mouth about where he went and what he did. "I'm picking you because you can find the way, since you're used to mountain country, and because you won't talk. Here is a note, doctor, for Mrs. Crittendon--with my compliments."

The two saluted solemnly and left Colonel Franklin looking after them a little regretfully. He would have liked to go himself, but a busy day lay before him.

"It's a gonfadential mission, my poy," said the doctor, regarding Farfar a little suspiciously.

"Don't talk about it then," replied Farfar.

From that moment they were friends. The doctor was, in his own estimation, a wise and silent man. His silence, at least, was indubitable.

Less than an hour later they were trotting through the deserted street at Aquila. Farfar went ahead, riding his little mount proudly, despite the fact that he was driving two pack-mules and a loaded horse before him. His skill in that difficult art soon caused the doctor, who sat an old horse uneasily, to follow him with more confidence and to respect this choice of a new recruit for his guide and assistant in a mission which the colonel had been at some pains to describe to him as an important one.

Aquila was not so deserted as it looked. Had the doctor not been so short-sighted, or Farfar so intent on his mules, they would have seen the heads of Mary and Tim Crittendon peep at them out of the springhouse window. Flossie had brought them down early that morning to play and to get away from her father. She herself saw nothing of the little cavalcade that turned up the stream at the ford. Farfar was leading now.

"Look," said the children, "look!" They pointed at Farfar and whispered together.

Flossie was unaccountably irritable with them now. Ever since Paul had come back they were afraid of her. Today they had not even dared to say anything to her when they found the new dolls. There they were! Four of them--and the new dishes and furniture! It was something too magic to try to explain to Flossie. She would certainly have laughed at them or "got mad." And now--guess what they had just seen from the window too? They withdrew into the shadowy part of the springhouse. Glancing at Flossie's bare feet that stuck through the doorway, they clutched their new dolls and whispered about them.

Flossie's toes were slowly wiggling. That was the only sign that she was alive.

She sat leaning back in the doorway, where Mrs. Crittendon had sat the day before. The warm sun drenched the lower half of her body. Her sunbonnet was pulled down over her eyes and her mouth was half-open. Behind the barred calico shade, under the blue veins of her slightly swollen eyelids, swam and eddied visions of Paul, visions of Flossie and Paul. She had waited so long for Paul. It was more than a year now. She was unappeasably hungry for him. No one, not even Paul himself, wished that his arm would get better more fervently than did Flossie Kiskadden.

First love when fully awakened, as hers had been, can become a monomania, an all-absorbing fever of body and soul. It is the concern of Nature to perpetuate life and to render her servants blind to consequences. Flossie could see nothing but Paul even with her sunbonnet over her eyes.

Two miles away on the level river meadows below Aquila, Colonel Franklin was putting his regiment through the morning drill. The turf trembled and spurted under the hoofs of the squadrons. Men and horses halted and sprang forward obedient to the voice of the trumpet. The silk guidons snapped in the wind. The colonel brought the entire regiment into line. It was a line of centaurs a quarter of a mile long. Then he swung them like a giant scythe blade devouring that meadow grass. Only a coward or a liar would have been unable to see that here was something magnificent accompanied by thunder.

The heart of Nathaniel Franklin leaped up and rejoiced. The fever of the exaltation of power clutched at his throat. For an instant he experienced ecstasy.

It is the concern of Nature to bring about death and to render her servants blind to consequences. Colonel Franklin could see nothing but his regiment. They began to fire volleys by squadrons. Great clouds of yellow smoke enveloped them and rolled away.

Just about this time Farfar and Dr. Holtzmaier turned up the small stream in the forest. At the top of the dam they could hear the crash of the volleys distinctly. Once on the other side of it, all that pother was only an indistinct mutter amid the hills. Presently there was nothing to be heard but the voice of the little river and the rustle of fallen leaves.

"Himmel!" exclaimed the doctor, looking about him as far as his short-sightedness would permit--even the distance here blurred pleasantly. "It's like a poem by Heine. Himmel!" . . .

"Here they come," shouted Margaret Crittendon a few minutes later to her mother, who was sitting upstairs with Paul. "Look out of the window, mother, here they come!"

Mrs. Crittendon breathed a prayer of relief, but she did not look out of the window or come down. She supposed the colonel would be there too. At the thought of him a quiet diffidence overcame her. Her diffidence gradually turned into a certain degree of resentment, and she sat with burning cheeks and knitted brows. Paul patted her hand.

"It's hard to take help from them, isn't it, Aunt Libby?" said he.

"Oh, Paul," said Mrs. Crittendon, "sometimes I wonder what's going to become of us. If it hadn't been for your arm . . ."

"If it hadn't been for the war, you mean, Aunt Libby," whispered Paul. She nodded. Downstairs she heard her daughter's feet trip eagerly across the porch to meet the new-comers.

Dr. Holtzmaier dismounted awkwardly and came up the garden path with a kit of instruments, splints, and bandages in his hand. He removed his hat as awkwardly as he had dismounted. "Der gunnel--" he began. But he saw that Miss Crittendon was not looking at him. Her eyes appeared to be fixed permanently upon young Farfar, who was tethering his mount to the ring-post at the gate.

Farfar leaned over the gate and looked at Margaret. He had never seen so beautiful a girl. She was wearing a Paisley shawl and a small flounced hoop-skirt. Her hair fell down over her shoulders in a cascade of golden-brown curls. To the lonely heart of the mountain boy she seemed the ultimate, unattainable vision of poetic beauty, the lady in the ballads for whom everybody suffered and died. He smiled at her unwittingly, a smile of surprised recognition. For the first time Margaret now became aware of him, and of a pair of haunting grey eyes. She actually smiled back. William Farfar caught his breath.

Dr. Holtzmaier by this time was considerably embarrassed. Apparently the young lady could not see him at all.

"Der gunnel--" he began again, clearing his throat.

Margaret put her hands together ecstatically. "Oh," she cried, "oh, it's Midge! They've brought her back!"

She danced down the path past the doctor, her feet twinkling under her petticoats faster and faster. She ran madly through the gate that Farfar held open for her--and flung her arms about the neck of the little mare.

"Midge!" she cried. "Midge, you darling, where have you been?"

The mare nuzzled her softly and put her nose in the girl's hand. She began to stamp for sugar. Nothing had ever pleased Margaret so much in her life. The little horse had been her companion since childhood, the first thing that had truly been her own. She was greatly excited. That her pony's return was a mere accident never entered her mind. She had a tremendous impulse to thank someone, anybody!

"You," said she turning to Farfar impulsively, her eyes dancing. "You brought her back, didn't you?"

He nodded, smiling.

"Why, I think you're the nicest boy in the world!" she suddenly exclaimed. And scarcely conscious of what she was doing, she threw her arms around him just as though he were Midge, and gave him a kiss on the neck.

But William Farfar was no pony. Since first seeing Margaret he was convinced that anything might come true. Now she had kissed him. It was true that he had drawn back at first in sheer surprise. Now, just as she herself fully realized what she had done, she felt his arms about her and his mouth on hers.

To Margaret that, too, was an enormous surprise.

She forgot all about horses. For a moment natural electricity fused them. They stood close and dizzy.

"*Gott-damn!*" said the doctor, looking on, bewildered but envious.

Then Margaret seized Farfar by the shoulders and sent him reeling back against the little horse.

"You--you--" said she, stuttering with vexation and astonishment-- "you kissed me!"

"You kissed *me*," said the lad.

"Oh, I didn't. I didn't," she asserted, stamping her foot. "I tell you, I didn't!" She stuck her tongue out at him. "I hate you!" She turned her back, and walked down the garden path, giving her curls a flirt.

Farfar stood appalled. "I'll take your horse away again," he cried after her at last.

That brought her around. She shook her head violently. He nodded. They repeated it. This pastime was still going on when Mrs. Crittendon emerged from the door.

"Margaret Crittendon, what's the matter with you?" called her mother. "Why don't you ask these people to come in? You look as if you'd been running to a fire."

"Oh, I *was* going to ask them in," said Margaret in a curious tone her mother had never heard her use before. "But you see I'm . . . I'm all excited . . . they've brought Midge back."

"So they have!" cried her mother. "Splendid! That certainly *is* thoughtful of Colonel Franklin." Her estimate of that gentleman immediately soared.

But just at this point Dr. Holtzmaier managed to get in his speech about "der gunnel" and summoned enough presence of mind to present the colonel's note.

Mrs. Crittendon greeted him civilly and stood on the porch to read the note. Her daughter walked past her, and going into the room, sat down in the nearest chair. She was still trembling and wanted to cry. She had danced down the garden path a little girl and had come back a woman. For the first time in her life she experienced a genuine antagonism towards her mother. She closed her eyes. The clock struck twice.

"Oh, dear heavens, mother," said she as Mrs. Crittendon and the doctor came in to go upstairs to Paul's room, "I *do* wish you'd have that clock fixed. It's just awful!"

Her mother looked at her in amazement. Then she looked at her more keenly and smiled.

"I think you had best ask the young man at the gate to come in, hadn't you? He might be lonely out there." Then she swept upstairs, followed by the doctor.

Margaret sat blushing to the roots of her hair. After a while she got up and beckoned to Farfar. He was lonely. The sky seemed to have fallen. Now it was brightening again. She stood at the head of the porch steps and bargained with him.

"If I let you come in, promise not to take Midge away again?"

"I'll promise," he said. "Honest--honest I didn't mean I really would take her away, miss. I jes' naturally couldn't, you know."

They stood for a moment looking at each other. Their eyes dropped.

"Come in, mister. Mister what?"

"Farfar," he whispered. "Billy they call me."

"I'm Margaret Crittendon," said she as they sat down at opposite ends of the hearth.

"My," he exclaimed, "ain't that a lovely name!"

Miss Crittendon agreed and finally smiled at him.

Upstairs Dr. Holtzmaier was preparing to set Paul's arm.

It was by no means a simple undertaking. Paul's arm had been shattered two weeks before at a skirmish near Woodstock. His regiment had been sent forward to create what is known as a "diversion." A federal battery of six-pounders, called the Cincinnati Board of Trade Artillery, had been considerably disturbed, and even after the diversion was over had continued to fire occasional nervous rounds in the general direction of the Confederate lines. The small round shot came crashing and ricochetting through the woods past Paul's company. Some of the spent balls rolled out onto a level glade of turf near by as though spirits were playing bowls. Someone of unsound mind and murderous humour had dared Paul "to try to stop the next one." The boy had actually attempted to do so with an iron spade.

Momentum embodied in a six-pound ball is a curious thing. The shot, which seemed to be rolling very gently, struck the blade of the steel shovel and travelled right up the handle into Paul's left hand. The result was, somehow, an arm broken in three places between wrist and elbow, and the elbow wrenched out of joint. In great agony the boy had waited patiently for a day to have it set at a field hospital. But the place was filling up with wounded, and there was only one surgeon, who was trying to tie up severed arteries and couldn't stop just to set an arm which had been broken as a joke.

The boy's home was only twenty miles away across the Valley. Despairing of relief at the field hospital, he had set out in the middle of the night. Two days later he arrived home delirious, to find his uncle's house burned. A negro poking about the ruins told him the family had fled to the hills and Paul had guessed they would be at Coiner's Retreat.

Dr. Holtzmaier considered it a miracle that blood poisoning had not set in, and he was quite right when he shook his head gravely at the sight of the arm.

Cold water had greatly reduced the swelling, but the arm was now so tender that even a light touch of the doctor's fingers dragged a stifled scream from between the boy's clenched teeth.

The doctor took his canteen, and uncorking it, poured out a glassful of chloroform. He then asked for a towel, and saturating it, would have pressed it down on his patient's face with the same technique as that used by a burglar had not Paul violently objected. Things were now at an impasse. Paul could not stand having his arm handled and would not permit the ill-smelling towel to come near his face. All reasoning with him was in vain.

Downstairs Farfar and Margaret had ceased looking shyly at each other and were listening to the sounds of distress from the sick-room, with averted faces. Paul began to call for Flossie, who had not come back yet. Margaret got up, and excusing herself, went upstairs. It was Mrs. Crittendon who finally solved the difficulty. Seeing Margaret's pale face looking in at the door, she told her to go and bring up the young Yankee to see Paul. This appeal to her nephew's pride was Mrs. Crittendon's last resource.

The appearance of young Farfar at the door of the room seemed instantly to steady Paul. The two looked at each other appraisingly but with the sympathy of youth for youth.

Dr. Holtzmaier had the grace to keep quiet.

"Hello, Yank," said Paul.

"Hello, Johnny," said Farfar. "'Pears like you're in a bad way."

Paul was all the stoic now. He bit his lower lip till it was blue before he finally replied. He would rather have had his other arm broken than be heard calling for Flossie now, or be seen in an hysterical state.

"Yep," said he at last, "got my arm shattered in a little old skirmish."

"Golly!" said Farfar, with genuine admiration that was a sedative to Paul. He now lay back looking as weak as he could.

At this moment Dr. Holtzmaier approached with the towel again. The two boys looked at each other.

"So long, Yank," said Paul, determined to make his last words to the enemy heroic. "Gimme your hand, Aunt Libby." Margaret added the only note lacking to make what Paul considered a perfect bedside scene. She sobbed.

The towel descended upon Paul's face. The fumes were terrible and terrified him. He choked. But it would never do to weaken now, never! The last thing he heard was Dr. Holtzmaier repeating almost like a ritual again and again:

"Blease preathe teep."

The boy sighed and ceased to struggle.

Ten minutes later under the expert and powerful fingers of Dr. Holtzmaier the arm was set and the elbow back in place. There had been no splintered bones. Mrs. Crittendon threw the reeking towel out the window and helped while the splints and bandages were put on. As the last tie was made, she also sighed. She sat down in a chair overcome by the fumes. The doctor had used enough chloroform to send a horse to dreamland. Paul did not waken till late that afternoon.

When Mrs. Crittendon came downstairs with the doctor at last she found everybody outside busy about the horses. Old Mr. Kiskadden was hitching her own horse to the buggy to go and get Flossie and the children at the springhouse. Farfar was unloading his pack animals and piling the supplies on the cabin floor. Margaret was at the gate fondling Midge.

"Kin I come again to see you? I could help take care of Paul," said Farfar to Margaret, as he and the doctor prepared to depart. He had no thought of taking Midge back. He had made his promise and he would keep it whatever the consequences.

"Oh, please do," said Margaret, with a tone so anxious and genuine that she coloured at not being able to conceal it better. She hated to see her new friend go.

"Try to come back this evening," she said. "There's nobody but the old man to watch over us now that Paul's so ill." Her expression was a mute appeal in itself.

"I'll come," he said.

Just then the doctor shouted to him. He rode off down the valley on the pack-horse, driving the mules before him.

Margaret watched him go with a strange foreboding and sense of loss that she had never known before. It was all she could do not to jump on Midge and follow. Instead, she led her horse to the old slab stable and unsaddled her.

When she returned to the cabin Mrs. Crittendon was sitting with a look of inexpressible relief by the ashes of last night's fire. Her daughter thought she looked young again.

Paul's arm was set and bandaged. The house was full of supplies. Hope had returned--all since yesterday afternoon. She and Margaret began to sort out the things they had so unexpectedly "inherited," with exclamations of delight. No doubt about it, Colonel Franklin had been both thoughtful and generous.

There was not only a great quantity of food, a whole muleload of army rations of all kinds, but blankets, shoes, and clothes; a number of little articles out of the sutler's store that delighted the two women and sometimes made them laugh. There was even a straw bonnet with a pink bow on it, and some candy and pretty knick-knacks for the children.

"Just the thing for Flossie," said Mrs. Crittendon, surveying the bonnet critically. "Where do you suppose he got it?"

It was Margaret's turn now to look at her mother, at the high colour in her cheeks. But the new goods *were* delightful. It was like being on a shopping tour. She and Margaret chatted away. A single bottle of real English ale caused Mrs. Crittendon to exclaim. But that was nothing to the tea. Two packages of it!--and a large bundle of old newspapers, both Northern and Southern. Mrs. Crittendon brewed herself some tea and sat down with the Richmond *Enquirer,* only about two months old, for her first moment of genuine relaxation in many weeks. No one but an Englishwoman could understand what the tea meant. Margaret sprawled out on the floor reading a Baltimore paper. They were still having dances there. She exclaimed over the names of friends. While they read, and waited for Mr. Kiskadden to return with the children, the sunlight crept slowly in the cabin door and began to retreat again.

"Oh, my dear, my dear!" suddenly exclaimed Mrs. Crittendon. "Look! Thank God for his mercies." She was pointing at a small item in her Richmond paper. Margaret scrambled to her feet and looked over her mother's shoulder.

We regret to state that during a minor but successful engagement with the federal cavalry at Cross Keys in the Valley some days ago, Major Douglas Charles Crittendon of General Early's staff was wounded and taken prisoner. It is reported that his wounds are of a trivial nature, and it is hoped he will soon be exchanged. Major Crittendon is a brilliant and gallant officer. The temporary loss of his services will be sadly missed by his able chief.

Charlottesville papers please copy.

"There!" said Mrs. Crittendon, wiping her eyes. "I knew it! Your father's safe in a Yankee prison, if he doesn't die there. Anyway, he's out of the war. He's out of the war!" she reiterated, beating her hands on the arms of her chair.

"And Midge's come back too," said Margaret after a while.

"You goose," said Mrs. Crittendon, clasping her daughter. But for the second time that day she felt profoundly grateful to Colonel Franklin.

The children returned to an ample lunch and a renewed sense of home. They caught the spirit of cheerfulness and it was hard to keep them so quiet as not to disturb Paul. Flossie watched by his bed all afternoon. About five o'clock he opened his eyes and found her watching him. He had slept off the chloroform quietly. After a while the room ceased to swim.

Just before supper the colonel and Farfar rode up to the cabin again.

"I'm accepting your invitation this evening, Mrs. Crittendon, you see," he said simply.

The look in her face of life-renewed more than rewarded him for anything he had done. He had the feeling now that he had been completely forgiven. He felt like a gentleman again. The burning had been badly on his conscience. Why she was so happy, he had no idea. He had not seen the paragraph in the Richmond paper. He seldom read newspapers--only the New York *Tribune,* because Bayard Taylor owned stock in it and wrote for it. He never read Southern papers at all. They seemed insane; their optimism idiotic.

But that Mrs. Crittendon was now very happy there could be no doubt. The packet he had brought with him again, firmly intending to deliver it, remained in his pocket. This was no time to strike her down. They sat down to a plentiful board together and would have been almost uproarious if it had not been for Paul.

They were, as Mrs. Crittendon said after supper, "discreetly hilarious." They played games till the children went to bed, clutching their new dolls. No word of explanation could be had from either Tim or Mary about the dolls. The colonel and Mrs. Crittendon laughed. The children went to bed with their new favourites. Margaret and Farfar sat by the fire together, speechlessly happy, looking into the flames. While the colonel and Mrs. Crittendon talked, Mr. Kiskadden whittled sticks in the corner. The colonel returned to camp about ten o'clock, leaving Farfar behind him.

"He's a guard you can trust, even if he is a horse thief," he remarked to Margaret as he said good night, and his eyes twinkled.

He had accepted the thanks for the return of the pony without saying anything. The colonel did not believe in explaining away fate. The packet remained in his pocket. He raised his hat again to Mrs. Crittendon and rode off. How different it was this evening from the night before.

It was an intensely quiet, for that time of year a sultry, night. The stars seemed to be hung low in canopies of black velvet. Moonlight tinged the clouds on the mountain horizons. The colonel arrived in camp and turned in. He awoke later feeling breathless, and uneasy about the pickets. He mounted Black Girl and made the rounds. All was quiet, all was ominously quiet.

Late in the night Mrs. Crittendon awoke with the same feeling. She felt as though she must get out of the house. Across the hall she could hear Paul and Farfar talking. The two friendly young voices went on in the darkness. There was an occasional tone of humour; the sound of water as Farfar kept Paul's bandages wet. The boys seemed to be the best of friends. Mrs. Crittendon dressed herself and went downstairs.

Margaret was sitting in the big room before the hearth. She was wide awake.

"I knew you'd be coming down pretty soon, mother," said she. "This is the kind of night neither of us can sleep. It feels like the war," she exclaimed. "You just know something dreadful must be happening."

"Let's go for a ride," said her mother. "We can ride down to the dam and back again. There'll be moonlight in the meadows."

The two went out and saddled the horses. In the barn it was overpoweringly warm, and there was a curious creepy feeling to both of the women--mice under the hay?

A few minutes later they were sitting together looking out over the Valley from the top of the dam. The stream below talked soothingly. But it was not that they were listening to. It was a kind of distant shuddering like organ music that seemed to be the discontented voices of the mountains themselves muttering together. Their horses stood with their ears pricked, facing westward.

Above the middle range of the Massanuttens, reflected back to them from the clouds on the other side of the Valley, came a constant infernal glow and red flashing. It was like continuous heat lightning but not so white, not so innocent. An hour later the whole Blue Ridge was echoing to a dismal and distant rumbling.

General Sheridan heard it that morning as he spurred out of Winchester and tore madly south towards Strasburg, rallying stragglers along the way. "Turn back, turn back!" Once again for a moment history pivoted on personality. The dogs of war growled on amid the mountains. The creeks ran red.

"Thank God," said Mrs. Crittendon devoutly, "thank God, your father isn't there--and Paul!"

Margaret said nothing, but to Mrs. Crittendon's list of dear ones kept safe she silently added another name and felt warm in the darkness for doing so.

It was not until next evening that they heard the regiment in the Valley below them break into thunderous cheers. The couriers from Winchester had just come in.

"Another Union victory," said Mrs. Crittendon stoically. She hoped the war would soon be over. She wanted to resume life.

Margaret went into a corner and cried. She cared much for "the cause" in her heart. She had been born in Virginia. The weather was still strangely like summer and seemed, like the time on Major Crittendon's clock, permanently to have halted. Perhaps it would have been better for everybody if the clock had always stayed that way, with the hours halted and only trivial minutes to pass.

One--two, one--two, all through the night.

Everybody at Coiner's Retreat now slept soundly except Flossie. She lay on her elbow, looking into the darkness, waiting. It seemed to her that something terrible was lying in wait in the darkness of the house. Paul cried out in his sleep.

CHAPTER XVI

THE GIANT'S NURSERY

Time, of course, continued. It was only the weather that paused. As unalterable days went on into weeks, and Indian summer still lingered, something ominous seemed to be accumulating over the smiling but lonely Valley. In the camp by the gorge Colonel Franklin was distinctly aware of it. Perhaps it was the felt, internal necessity that events should be brought to a climax and resolved by action.

Under the essential scheme of drill, drill--and no one to practise war upon--the regiment had grown a little restless. Discipline is a state of tension, and it must either be used or relaxed. If not used, it relaxes itself. Besides, the victory at Winchester had brought to all the Union troops in the Valley the sense that a final move was impending. Sheridan had only snatched that victory from defeat, but Early's army had finally been nearly annihilated. What was left of the Confederate forces now lay at the extreme upper part of the Valley, hiding in the hills and licking their wounds, definitely and at last brought to bay. They, too, were waiting, waiting to be shifted to reinforce Lee about Richmond for a last desperate stand.

Nevertheless, the colonel hoped he would not soon be moved. He would have liked nothing better than to winter at Aquila. It was an ideal spot. The whole camp was built in now, well-hutted. He had even housed over the picket lines with condemned canvas and pine boughs, and had accumulated a great store of forage. Although it was nearly November and the pastures were yet green, still winter, when it did come, would probably come with a rush. His farmers in the ranks had actually enjoyed cutting and storing hay. They had levied a rich toll upon deserted pastures.

At night the glee club sang. Headquarters had a quartette. The colonel's own baritone, he liked to think, was at least appreciated. Captain Kerr had a fine tenor. They sang all the old favourites: "Babylon is Fallen," "Wake Nicodemus," Foster's "Was My Brother in the Battle?" But when they began on Foster they always went back into old times and ended with "Old Folks at Home." Saturdays there were theatricals, and on Sundays a "sacred concert."

Felix Mann reroofed an old farm building near the river, and bringing up several fresh wagon-loads of goods from Harpers Ferry, conducted a prosperous little shop that was at once an unofficial post office and a regimental canteen.

Everybody was exceedingly snug; everybody agreed it would be a pity to leave all this to go back to midwinter mud marches on the Peninsula. And yet there was an undercurrent of restlessness. So much peace in the midst of general havoc seemed unnatural.

"Pretty soon," said Captain Fetter Kerr, "the sentries will begin to see things. This constant chorus of nightbirds is hard to bear. I never heard so many owls and whippoorwills in my life. The woods seem packed with 'em." He made up a camp song about them with innumerable *woo-woo's* for a chorus.

Besides the regiment, the colonel had the family at Coiner's Retreat much on his mind. For better or for worse he had now, so to speak, taken them under his wing. He and Dr. Holtzmaier visited Coiner's Retreat quite constantly. Farfar was there more or less all of his spare time. And there was a good deal of spare time, particularly in the afternoons and evenings. Yet so complete was the concealment of the little valley that, outside of a few members of the staff, no one in the regiment suspected that the Crittendons were near. Colonel Franklin had been more than careful to respect his promise and Mrs. Crittendon's continued desire for complete privacy.

The colonel had soon learned of her belief that her husband was still alive and safe in some Northern prison. She had even given him letters to forward to Major Crittendon and solicited his advice as to what could be done for him. He sadly promised to do all that he could, for she seemed to be building her entire hope for the future on the expectation of reunion after the war. His admiration for her indomitable hope and cheerfulness under conditions of hardship, which would have made many a man useless and miserable, continually increased. He might be wrong, in a way he was disobeying orders in not giving her her husband's packet--doubtless it contained a last message--but he could not think of having aided her only to strike her down. It was a nice point to decide. He pondered it often--and he kept putting it off.

Meanwhile, partly as a salve to his conscience, but more largely out of a deep well of natural kindness, he provided for the little establishment at Coiner's Retreat in every way that he could. Farfar and old man Kiskadden between them cut a large supply of fire-wood against the winter. The little barn was stuffed with hay. The loft of the cabin was filled with flour, bacon, potatoes, and preserved provisions. If the regiment did move, Mrs.

Crittendon could hold on for six months. That thought was a comfort to the man who had burned her house as her husband's funeral pyre. He was in a unique and difficult situation. The right way out was by no means clear.

Otherwise, Colonel Franklin had little to worry about. He lived, and enjoyed the life of a soldier probably at its best. The sun passed over his head from one mountain range to the other, marking the even flow of busy but uneventful days. There were no alarms. Indeed, he felt more secure than ever. Headquarters had at last heeded his repeated requests for a force in reserve and sent his old friends of the 23rd Illinois Infantry and a spick-and-span battery of Rhode Island Artillery to "back him up" at Luray. This force was only a few miles down the river, just far enough away to be "near" and yet to let him alone. Now he could not be cut off by a raid over the Blue Ridge in his rear. If the enemy finally came, they would have to get at him through the gorge from the south. That at least was that! He buckled his sabre on contentedly, and went out to look over the drills and target practice with the new carbines.

It was another beautiful morning.

On the porch of her cabin Mrs. Crittendon sat chin in hand, enjoying the unusual warmth. With her hair in heavy morning braids, she looked not unlike a Northern sibyl, and she was trying, as a matter of fact, to peer a few years into the future.

Most of her dreams, as the colonel had correctly surmised, centred about the return of her husband after the war. The war would almost have ruined them, but not quite. Elizabeth Crittendon had already concluded out of general information and intelligence that the Federals would prevail. She intended to accept that as a practical fact and to ease the sting by keeping her eyes fixed on the future. She had a strong, sweet English nature and could be firm without being bitter. The welfare of her daughter Margaret and of the two young children of her husband's brother, Tim and little Mary, whom she now regarded as her own, was therefore the main desire of her heart. Paul she was not so sure of. The war, she felt, had blighted his promise. An ardent and high-strung boy, he had been passed through the fire. The loss of his home, grief, terror, fatigue, and wounds had all been his lot before he was seventeen. Flossie had taken what remained: his pride in himself as a member of an honourable class.

A few years before, Mrs. Crittendon would not have permitted such a girl as Flossie to be at home on her property or even to be discussed in her presence. Now it seemed to her, as battle had succeeded battle, and the old life and the codes by which it had been lived vanished with those who had made them, that Flossie Kiskadden might be all of life that Paul would ever know.

War is a powerful solvent. Mrs. Crittendon was not only an Englishwoman, she was the wife of a Virginian. Yet now she could look on Flossie as a fellow human being and understand her. She had for Paul's sake, and for Flossie's, permitted the old minister and his daughter to share the retreat at the cabin. The old man regarded her with suspicion for having done so. The Kiskaddens were not poor whites--not quite.

Thus steering as best she could through all the vicissitudes, complications, and outrageous changes that the war had brought her, Mrs. Crittendon was still steadfast to salvage what remained of her life and to build into the future anew. She had some money of her own left in England, and excellent family connections there. Margaret, she was determined, should have the benefit of both. After the war, come what might, her daughter should go abroad.

For the rest, she and her husband would hold the fort at Coiner's Retreat until the other children grew up. They could do a little planting, hunting, and fishing. They would be together--what else mattered? There would be land and a house, love and hope.

Someday Margaret would be getting married. There might be a home for her somewhere too. Perhaps the land in the Valley could be farmed again; "Whitesides" rebuilt on a smaller scale? Perhaps old Grandmamma Crittendon who had gone to Richmond might leave them something, if she still had something to leave? Perhaps Paul, after the war was over, might prove a help, after all? Perhaps, perhaps . . . who knew?

So dreamed Mrs. Crittendon with her chin in her hand, looking out upon the little valley, while inside the cabin the clock still continued to chime Major Crittendon's eternal time. Elizabeth Crittendon took a secret and peculiar pleasure in the obstinacy of that clock. It chimed in with her dreams.

Actually the seeds of reality were planted for a harvest quite different.

In the old cellar of the burned house at "Whitesides" the ants that morning were also trying to surmount difficulties. They, too, had built a new home in the ashes and the sands beneath. But one of Major Crittendon's buttons was in the way. It was a steel button, made in Sheffield, that had once caught the inside loop of the major's coat when he buttoned dispatches next to his heart. Now it was in the way of the ants. Their engineers conferred about it extensively. Not all the might of antdom could move it. They decided to undermine it. Slowly but inevitably the button disappeared beneath the surface. Presently it was covered over, buried. It was the last palpable memento of Major Crittendon which remained, except for the packet in Colonel Franklin's coat-pocket.

And as for Margaret--

"Margaret will marry someday," Mrs. Crittendon had said, but she had no idea of the present state of her daughter's heart. It was engaged. Lips had not said so in words, but in other ways.

Now that Midge had been returned, Margaret had taken to riding up and down and around the little valley every afternoon. The three women divided the duties of the household, the children, and looking after Paul fairly between them. Mrs. Crittendon, however, seldom left the house. She rode early in the mornings and returned to get the breakfast. She had long ago come to the conclusion that the only way to retain full control of her household was to be up and about before anybody else. There was a primary wisdom in this habit, but things can also happen in the afternoon. And the afternoons were Margaret's.

Farfar generally managed to arrive about two o'clock. He was free then till evening roll-call. Margaret would meet him, seated on Midge, waiting at the foot of the dam with her eyes shining and her straw bonnet thrown back on her shoulders. This vision of her, with her curls glinting in the long sunlight, and a deep green, though faded bow tied under her chin, was burned into the boy's memory until he dreamed of it at night. If she didn't meet him, his anxiety was intense. He would ride up to the cabin then with his heart in his mouth. But she nearly always met him.

From the colonel the boy had learned the trick of raising his hat. He did so unnecessarily grandly just as he rode up to her. It had become understood between them that this was not only a salutation but a signal for a race. They would gallop off together, storming up the valley. Mrs. Crittendon would look out as the two young figures flashed by and the drumming of hoofs passed away up the meadow. Farfar rode well. The long drills were having their effect. Margaret's curls and bonnet streamed behind her in the wind. Her mother thought of many a ride with her cousins long ago across wide English downs, and smiled. It was all quite harmless, she was sure. How Midge could scamper!

Half a mile above the cabin the little valley suddenly narrowed and swung at an acute angle to the right. There was a decided ravine there with a narrow bridle path along the river. Then there was quite a rise and a waterfall, and the valley widened out again.

The children called that upper part of Coiner's Retreat "the Giant's Nursery." It was almost like a green room, roofless, but with straight, high walls of rock covered with ferns. The floor was of a particularly fine turf that flourishes in shade on leaf mould. There were a few huge trees scattered about like the survivors of some more than primeval forest. They, indeed, went back into time. The wind could scarcely get at the place. The sun always fell upon part of it. The stream curved through it, talking as though the silent earth had suddenly given tongue here, singing a wordy tune in a universal language.

Scattered widely about over the floor of this natural and branch-starred apartment was a jumble of roughly-square but grotesquely-shaped rocks. They might have fallen from heaven, or they might have been left there spilled out like huge toy blocks by the ruthless hand of some infant giant who had demolished his own play castle and gone away. So at least Major Crittendon had once told his little daughter Margaret. And "the Giant's Nursery" it had been from that day forth. Now in the light of days that no longer troubled her father's eyes Margaret Crittendon had come riding there with her first lover.

And it was all quite naïve and genuinely touching. If the wraith of the major had walked there he might have smiled. He might even have dashed a few ghostly tears from his spiritual eyes. Those, indeed, were the only kind of eyes that were entitled to peer at William Farfar and Margaret. For their walks were innocent and beautiful, very young, tender, and virginally green.

They sat upon the same rock and gazed at each other. They said almost nothing at all. They were too shy, too choked with their overwhelming affection in the presence of each other to speak. The stream spoke for them a swift and fluid language, a long exclamation of soft and liquid vowels. That, thought Margaret, is how birds feel in the spring.

"I like Indian summer," she ventured once.

"I love it," he said.

After a while they dared to look each other in the eyes, and they practised losing themselves that way. They gazed at each other, heaven only knows how long! Sometimes then she would let him take her hand. He knew she would not let him kiss her again. It was enough just to look at her. They saw each other's angels. For even the light of those autumn days was magicked. Something lay at its outer edges like the iridescence on the feathers of a wild bird's breast. When the bird dies the rainbow dies with it. Each seemed to the other to be surrounded by some such nimbus;

to live in a secret glory of light. Margaret always remembered that. In after days she never saw it again. She called it "the lost light."

So--while the horses wandered with trailing reins, cropping the choice herbage in sunny spots, Margaret and Farfar watched them and each other in the light of a happy dream. Or, they would wander down the little bridle path by the ravine to sail leaf boats, and stand hand in hand, speechless over the tragedy of shipwrecks or thrilled like the children they were at some lucky craft that shot successfully through the dark rapid below. Farfar seemed to be prophetic about them, to be casting their futures by every craft they launched.

"This one will make it," he would whisper. So few of them got through!

It was true that in wandering the woods Farfar had a peculiar fascination all his own. It was not only that young Margaret was in love with being in love with him. There was a quality of kinship in the lad himself that had been heightened by finding his love returned; exalted into a blithe happiness and feeling of well-being and fellowship with everything that lived and moved about him until, to Margaret, the best of warm-hearted, affectionate companions and her lover were one and the same. When they were near each other, especially when they were alone together, they lived brightly. By contrast, they found that they merely existed darkly when apart.

And yet scarcely anything memorable was said. It was understood. That seemed, to them both, wonderful. Farfar spoke one day of the cabin high above the river where he had been born. She was to go there with him sometime. It was inevitable.

"I shall miss my river," she said simply, "and my hills. There is a song about them.

> 'High is my mountain land
> And grand its hills and valleys,
> Tall are its sons and daughters,
> Laughing Bills and Sallys,
> O Shenandoah, roll, O Shenandoah, roll,
> O roll your lovely waters
> Through my land.'

Have you a song about your river?" she asked, tossing her curls.

"No," he answered shyly, "but I kin whistle. I kin make the birds answer me in our woods back home."

She sat listening. He didn't move his lips. The sounds came from his throat. She guessed that his tongue moved. The woods were suddenly full of bird song. Some of them she recognized. It was his triumph to lure a belated blue jay near and then to send him away scolding.

"I reckon," she said after a while, "that bird thought it was spring again."

Farfar laughed. Suddenly a thrush seemed to call. It was far away.

"Don't you feel like that, Margaret? It *is* spring again! Don't you feel it?"

"Yes," she said, only rounding the word with her lips in a silent whisper.

He laid his head in her lap and she crumbled brown leaves over him in a silent embarrassment of ecstasy.

"Now," she said after a while, "Willum, it's just Indian summer again."

They caught the two horses with some difficulty. It was great fun cornering them among the big rocks. The Giant's Nursery rang with happy human laughter. Farfar's best moment came when he helped Margaret into the saddle. Then they were very near for an instant. She let him hold her close to him once. He felt as though he had captured a young doe. Both of them trembled. Then she broke away from him, flinging herself into the saddle. Before he could overtake her she was half-way back to the cabin. That day he was absent from even roll-call.

Two days of inexorable fatigue duty followed. When he returned it seemed that a year had passed since he had last seen her. That was the only time she told him she hated the Yankee Army. But now he had permission to stay late. The nights were getting colder. They sat close together in the cabin that evening by one of the big fires. At the opposite end of the room sat Flossie and Paul. They bundled together in a corner.

Mrs. Crittendon looked troubled. It was not about her daughter, however. Margaret and Farfar were so shy with each other that she could scarcely take them seriously. And Margaret had been so happy lately that she had simply decided not to say anything to her about the young visitor from the camp below. Besides, she had grown fond of Farfar herself for his quaint and thoughtful manners. She persisted, unconsciously, in still regarding Margaret as a child. Little Mary explained it all by saying, "Margaret has a beau!"

But Mrs. Crittendon was troubled about Flossie and Paul. If there had been any place for them to go, she would have sent them out of the house. She could no longer control either of them. Paul, she decided, must have been "touched" a little by his sufferings. There was an air of abandon about him. She began now to be sorry for Flossie too, who could no longer be depended upon to remember anything. She seemed to be moving in a heavy-lidded trance. Mysteriously, old Mr. Kiskadden had ceased to be even a feeble ally. He no longer prayed openly for anybody. He simply disregarded, and rubbed his gums with snuff.

It was a terrible habit. Mrs. Crittendon loathed it. She remembered sitting in the fine old drawing-room at "Whitesides"--only a few months before. They had been reading Tennyson. She heard the sonorous voice of her husband speak as though he were in the room. The clock struck two.

"Oh, I can't bear it," cried Mrs. Crittendon, suddenly breaking into tears.

Margaret and Farfar hurried over to her. Margaret put her arms about her. Mrs. Crittendon dried her tears and tried to laugh. Farfar offered her some chestnuts he had been roasting. She went over and sat down between them by the fire. Paul and Flossie never moved. Presently old Mr. Kiskadden got up and rubbed his gums with snuff again.

That was the first time Mrs. Crittendon had broken down. The rest of the time, brave woman, she was actually merry enough.

The Reverend Mr. Kiskadden no longer cared how close Paul and his daughter Flossie sat, or lay, for that matter. Two days before he had joined them in holy, if not in lawful, wedlock. There had been no witnesses. Mr. Kiskadden had found them together in the hayloft and had married them then and there.

Flossie was greatly disappointed. Paul was sullen about it. No one had said anything to Mrs. Crittendon. Flossie felt cheated of a real wedding. She had hoped that she would have a new dress for her wedding, or that Mrs. Crittendon would give her one of Margaret's. At least, there should have been a veil. Even in wartime there had been enough bed-net to go around to make veils for brides. Anybody who was anything but a mountain girl had a veil. That was what marriage meant to Flossie: a new dress, a veil, wagons and buggies about a little church in the woods somewhere, excitement, and cake afterwards. Marriage was simply an event unconnected with anything before or after. Of course, there had to be a man.

So it was disappointing just to be stood up in the shadows of the old haymow and married by her father with a Bible in one hand and a whip in the other. And Paul with his arm in a sling. The horses kept stamping underneath. She had needed a veil. She had nothing on but an old corset and a skirt. And she had had to be quick about that. It was a mistake to take your corset off--ever.

Paul was sullen because he hadn't intended to marry Flossie at all; because he hated being found that way by the old man. It was very awkward when your arm was in a sling. You couldn't act quickly. And when you were found that way you had to be married--if you were found. Everybody said so. He ought to have had sense enough to draw the ladder up after him. Then old man Kiskadden's head would not, so unexpectedly, have come poking up through the floor, the old sneak! Why were old men so curious? They ought to know. They did! That was the trouble. So now he was married.

Both to Paul and to Mr. Kiskadden marriage meant much the same. It was magic words. After they were said and you kissed the bride, or the Bible, everything you did to a girl both before and afterwards was all right. The trouble came afterwards and was the fault of the girl. Mr. Kiskadden, after he had performed the ceremony, paid no more attention whatever to Flossie and Paul. They were married. Age in him had whittled his philosophy down to its stocks. All the fine points had been forgotten.

Mrs. Crittendon's brief breakdown, natural and forgivable as it was, was not without its dire consequences. Paul had intended to tell his aunt that evening of his marriage, although he was puzzled as to why she had, as it seemed to him, acted strangely in permitting the Kiskaddens to come to Coiner's Retreat. Yet he had always admired his aunt Libby and he was profoundly grateful to her for her affectionate care of him and his small sister and brother.

So, despite the fact that he was in a hopeless emotional whirl of alternate pain and passion, he had still felt that the honourable thing to do was to inform Mrs. Crittendon that Flossie was now a member of the family. He had no idea that his aunt would have viewed this news, if not with pleasure, at least with relief. That Mrs. Crittendon's ample and merciful view of things would permit her to take into account a changed order of circumstances never entered his boyish head. He regarded his English aunt as a kind of cast-iron Minerva to be placated if possible, to be defied if necessary.

To that end he had been composing in his imagination sundry speeches, and summoning to mind various scenes in which he, Paul, announced to his aunt the momentous news of his nuptials with Flossie. Owing to his irritability--for Flossie and his arm had scarcely permitted him any rest--in fact, he was nearly exhausted--the rôle of defiance appealed more and more to his fancy. Still, that was easier to think about than to carry out.

So he had stayed all evening in the corner with Flossie, waiting for Farfar to leave, and for the rest of them to go to bed before speaking to Mrs. Crittendon. He had just decided after all to approach her rather gently, when much to his astonishment and dismay his aunt had herself broken down and discovered to him that she, too, harboured emotions.

The effect on Paul, while he still lay quietly in the corner looking on, was momentous. He watched Margaret comforting her mother and Farfar's shy solicitude for Mrs. Crittendon with the disdain of a fevered exhaustion. As he reflected upon his own sufferings and hardships in contrast with those which seemed to have overwhelmed his aunt, even if only for a moment, he found himself overcome with disgust for existence in general and women in particular. To this feeling the close and constant, sleepy warmth of Flossie now contributed not a little. He couldn't stand much more of that either! He was feverish and his arm itched intolerably.

None of those things in the house are necessary, thought Paul. If they only knew, they could do without them all. In the army I was happy without them. It was cool in the woods and fields; in the bivouacs by night. There were fires by moonlight. Men sang songs there. There was the wonderful and fearful excitement of battle. Love is nothing but heat--and trouble. I think I should rather die than go on with it like in the cabin here. Maybe I would die. Anyway, out there I'd belong to myself again. Here I'm being all used up. What for? I'm finer and stronger than that. Oh, if they only knew how clear and happy the world is when Paul is well and strong!

When he began to call himself by his own name he was always tired and exhausted. His automatic drama went on and he couldn't stop it. The room before him took on the wide, clear, somewhat remote, and faintly-glassy appearance contributed by a low fever. It was like looking at a slightly-magnified reflection in which he might appear himself like his image in a mirror. Presently he would so appear! He lay watching. The fire flicked. His arm hurt. After a while Farfar departed.

Paul was surprised to find that he felt sorry for Margaret. She looked so sad for a moment after Farfar closed the door. Meg was a good girl! How lovely she was sitting there by her mother, so cool and calm and white! The clock ticked irritatingly. It seemed to be getting louder, louder. My God!

"Go to bed, Mrs. Crittendon," said Paul suddenly and aloud, digging Flossie in the ribs and speaking viciously.

His aunt and Margaret gaped at him in surprise.

Flossie rose and walked sleepily upstairs. She was just annoyed and hurt enough not to have heard what Paul had said. It was the dig in the ribs that had wakened her.

"Paul," said Mrs. Crittendon, "did you mean that?"

"Yes," said Paul. "Are you going to cry about that too?"

"Oh, Paul!" said Margaret.

The boy sprang up suddenly from the corner where he had been half-prone and walked swiftly to the door.

"Good-bye, Aunt Libby, good-bye, Meg. I'm going back to the army," he shouted. "Don't you-all try to stop me!" He banged the door behind him and darted frantically down the walk. By the time the two women recovered from their astonishment and dragged the heavy door open again Paul was nowhere to be seen.

Mrs. Crittendon went to the front fence and looked out across the woods and meadows helplessly, "Paul!" she cried. "Paul, come back, please!" She hoped he might hear her. Margaret, although she had no idea what direction Paul had taken, ran out into the meadow through the woods behind the house. Among the trees she caught glimpses of the moon and once she thought she saw a glimmer of a white bandage moving a long way off before her. She kept crying his name hopelessly. But there was no reply. After a while she gave it up and started back. She was breathless and weak from crying.

On the way back she met her mother who had come through the woods to meet her. "He's gone, mother," she said. "We'll never see him again. It was Flossie!"

"Hush," said Mrs. Crittendon, "let us never say that again. It is the war, not Flossie. Margaret, you and I must see things through alone. We must be equal to whatever comes." She stood holding both the girl's hands till she breathed more easily.

"Let's go back to the house now," said Margaret. "I'm ready. I'll be a help to you, mother, I will!"

They walked back to the cabin with their arms about each other. Mr. Kiskadden had come downstairs in his suspenders for another rub of snuff. This time Mrs. Crittendon said nothing at all.

Except in the hearts of those who dreamed of and grieved for him, the departure of Paul made little apparent difference in the now rather smooth current of life at Coiner's Retreat. Mrs. Crittendon was, if anything, a little firmer but none the less cheerful and gentle about the house. She and

Margaret now felt closer to each other than ever before. To the young girl her mother's constant understanding sympathy, her invariable graciousness to everybody, were a continual inspiration.

Paul's vanishing had made Margaret doubly anxious now about Farfar. In a way it had roused her from her first purely idyllic dreams about him. Now for the first time she began to understand what the absence of Major Crittendon must mean to her mother. This fear, however, she concealed, rather than trouble her mother further, and she said nothing to her about her girlish but happy dreams for the days to come. They remained, as they always remained, a golden haze in the distance.

And Flossie? Flossie had had hysterics the morning she found Paul was gone. Her one piercing scream when she understood that he had left had gone straight to Mrs. Crittendon's and Margaret's hearts. Their assurances that Paul would return made no impression upon her. She moved submissively and silently about the house, comforting herself in the affection and sympathy which surrounded her. She was now a "member of the family," and she liked that. Indeed, Flossie was a better girl for Paul's having left her. Once Mrs. Crittendon found her looking out the window, her hand pressed to her throat as though waiting for something further to befall. She called Margaret and the three sat down and had a cup of tea together.

What outside cheer and comfort they had were brought them continually and unfailingly from the camp below. For Margaret it was a secret, an almost ethereal, happiness that accompanied the presence of young Farfar. For Mrs. Crittendon it was a deep reassurance, a sense of hope and strength renewed that seemed to arrive at the cabin as soon as Colonel Franklin swung off Black Girl before the gate. That the cheer which the colonel brought them was obviously pondered, sometimes even elaborately planned, made it no less real for that.

For there was a genuine and natural geniality about the colonel, a certain delicate restraint even in the more lavish manifestations of his generosity and careful solicitude, that was disarming, that was even humorous. Mrs. Crittendon waited calmly, but expectantly and gratefully, for those evenings that would bring the reassuring tones of his voice with pastime and good company to the now warm and comfortable fireside at Coiner's Retreat. It was still rude and primitive, but thanks to the colonel it was indubitably comfortable.

No one peeping in through the window of the cabin at Coiner's Retreat on some of those nights about the middle of November 1864 could have denied it; no one, except for the uniforms of the visitors, would have been reminded of the war. Many a poor soul from the Valley whose hearth fire had grown dim or had been forever darkened would have been glad to slip in to join so pleasant, handsome, and kindly a company.

Margaret and Farfar always sat together. No one had the heart for any reason to deny them that. And when the shadows were propitious, it seemed as though sometimes Margaret's curls did rest against Farfar's shoulder. Perhaps it was only the firelight, but there was on these evenings a light in the boy's face as though someone had set a lamp burning behind partly-translucent marble.

Flossie and the children sat on the floor and played games or roasted potatoes and chestnuts. Mr. Kiskadden had his clay pipe, which he never smoked, for it always hung upside down, and a little whisky in water. His daughter was married. The past and the future had vanished for him. The snuff bowl and his cup were full to the brim. To the amazement of all, he sometimes sang now in a high, boyish voice that seemed to come from out of the far distant past a stave or two from Bobby Burns. They were even afraid that he might start a hymn.

Dr. Holtzmaier prevented that. The colonel not infrequently brought him, and the doctor, of all things, played a guitar. His success with the instrument was a curious one. The stubby hands of the surgeon clumped over the strings with a surprising skill, and there was absolutely no connection whatever between the emotions of Dr. Holtzmaier and the nerves of his face. He played everything with the same bland, cheerful expression, while his mouth sang bass. The children were at first fascinated, then puzzled--finally uproarious. Dr. Holtzmaier could never play enough for them.

There was one song in which nearly everybody joined. Farfar sang it first. He had picked it up from the Kanawha Zouaves. The doctor soon had his accompaniment, with variations, perfected.

"Sitting by the roadside on a summer day,
Chatting with my mess-mates, passing time away,
Lying in the shadow underneath the trees,
Goodness how delicious, eating goober peas.
Peas! Peas! Peas! Eating Goober peas!
Goodness how delicious, eating goober peas!

Just before the battle the General hears a row,
He says, 'The Yanks are coming, I hear their rifles now,'
He turns around in wonder, and what do you think he sees?
The Georgia militia, eating goober peas.
Peas! Peas! Peas! . . ."

In the chorus even Flossie took part, with a tuneless, flat sing-song that had something a little eerie in its sheer toneless monotony.

Most startling of all perhaps were the colonel's now more than luxuriant brown burnsides, his bushy eyebrows, and his kindly blue eyes looking out keenly alive over his rows of buttons that twinkled golden in the firelight.

He had a long face with a wide, firm mouth and finely-moulded red lips from which something memorable always seemed about to come. And when he did speak, his clear, full voice enhanced the impression. Mrs. Crittendon did not fail to note that her guests always appeared brightly furbished and as well turned out as service in the field would permit. As a soldier's wife, she understood, and returned the compliment.

Seated in a barrel chair draped with old calico, and dressed in her best hoop-skirt, upon which the white roses of 1860 appeared in still spotless festoons, Elizabeth Crittendon presided at her fireside with a certain gay dignity that was peculiarly her own. The quiet assurance of her manner was not merely the result of breeding and habit. It expressed memorably the core of her character and conveyed, like her gestures and voice, a conviction of force and ease. It was this quality in Mrs. Crittendon which had enabled her to accept the help that Colonel Franklin had brought, and never to doubt the spirit in which it was proffered. Across the firelight and dancing shadows of the old cabin room they looked at each other often and candidly, and with such a poignant sympathy for those gathered about them snatched from the coils of war that their glances never faltered.

For some time now Mrs. Crittendon had ceased to try to obtain news of her husband or to communicate with him through the colonel. No answer to her letters had come.

"Is there any answer yet?" she had asked once, breathlessly.

"None," was his quiet reply, with no explanation.

She had pondered that. The Northern prisons and hospitals were endless. Her letters might still be wandering. She knew army "channels of communication." Even in peace-times in the Old Army it had sometimes taken months to reach her husband. Now he was a prisoner of war. Or was he? She dared not permit herself to doubt too far. Hope was her staff of life. The shadows behind and under her eyes darkened. But she said nothing. She could wait. Even if hope seemed, like Indian summer, to be too dangerously prolonged. It would end finally. It must. The answer would come.

And come it did, suddenly, and in letters of fire.

They were all sitting in the cabin room one night talking quietly. The fire had been permitted to die down. The colonel and Farfar were the only visitors from camp. They had stayed for supper that evening only at Mrs. Crittendon's urgent entreaty.

Orders had arrived indicating that there would soon be a general move south. The colonel had said nothing about his orders, of course. But Mrs. Crittendon had guessed what was toward, for he had brought a further supply of necessaries to Coiner's Retreat that afternoon and now sat earnestly discussing with her the ways and means of passing the winter. Beyond that, neither of them cared or dared to think.

He would have liked to suggest that she go to his empty house in Pennsylvania. The mountains would soon be impassable with snow. The weather showed some signs of breaking at last. But Kennett Square was a little town with a great talent for gossip, and Mrs. Crittendon, he knew, would never leave Virginia while the war went on and her husband might return. There was "no news" from him, she admitted, but she still had hope in her eyes. He was now in more of a quandary than ever as to what to do with the packet. He might send it to her after the regiment left Aquila. If so, would she then have courage to carry on? Probably he should have given it to her weeks ago--and yet?

On a board laid out on the table with pencilled lines Farfar and Margaret were playing checkers. Sometimes their hands touched. Flossie was putting the children to bed upstairs. Mr. Kiskadden nodded over his whittling.

"Oh, Timmy, *go to bed,*" said the exasperated voice of Flossie from above, "I've tucked you in twice!"

"I tell you I *does* hear 'em," whined Timmy. They heard his bare feet pad to the head of the stairs. "Aunt Libby," he called downstairs in his childish treble, "I hears sumpin' and Flossie say I doesn't."

"What is it, my dear?" said Mrs. Crittendon, smiling.

"It's the soldiers shootin' each other with guns."

The blood left Mrs. Crittendon's face. "Go to bed, Timmy," said she. The colonel got up and walked to the door. An intense silence fell on the room. All stood listening, and looking at him.

"Would you mind stopping that clock for a moment, Mrs. Crittendon?" said the colonel. "I think I do hear something." Her skirt rustled, and the loud ticking suddenly ceased.

Then everyone heard it. It was the distant but unmistakable rattle of musketry.

"Come on, son!" shouted the colonel at Farfar, and made the gate in a half-dozen strides. He vaulted into the saddle and Black Girl thundered off into the night.

Elizabeth Crittendon stood with her arm stretched out along the mantel where her hand had reached out to stop the clock. The pendulum still swung a little in lessening arcs.

He had gone, and without even a word to her. The war had taken him too. She drew in her breath at last, shuddering. She looked up, startled. Someone was still at the door.

It was Margaret and Farfar. Margaret had her arms around his neck, her head was thrown back and her eyes closed. She looked like a blind girl and she held on to him like one drowning. The boy gave Mrs. Crittendon a look of agony and appeal.

She always remembered his eyes that evening.

They seemed to be looking into the distance at something intolerable.

"I'll hev to come back now," he whispered. "I'll jes' hev to!" He forced Margaret's hands apart, pressed them back against the door, and kissed her on the mouth. Then he fled into the darkness. They heard his horse go tearing down the little valley.

Margaret kept standing there. Mrs. Crittendon caught her before she fell. The whole place echoed and pulsated now. It was like a fast-approaching thunderstorm. One might expect lightning at any moment.

In the Valley below, the drums of the regiment were beating the long roll while the bugles screamed, "Stand to arms."

Elizabeth and Margaret Crittendon sat on the same bench and tried to comfort each other.

CHAPTER XVII

THE ACTION AT AQUILA

You will not find it in the books called history. There are only two old men alive who still remember it. In a war of colossally grisly battles, with staggering losses even in minor engagements, so small an affair was not worth the chronicling. Its statistics were simply lumped with a larger whole, for to the official military mind it was merely one phase of a long-drawn-out cavalry skirmish that extended up the South Fork of the Shenandoah from Luray to the Danville Railroad. It was all over in a few minutes--all but the grief and the suffering. Even the survivors, when they met afterwards, always spoke of it casually as "that action at Aquila" or "the cavalry brush south of Luray." What was that, if you had been at Manassas; at Antietam and Gettysburg?

"But do you remember?" they would sometimes say, do you remember-
-

"when Early's men who lived in the Valley tried to come back home? Some of them were what was left of Jackson's veterans. They were the backbone of that attack. They thought of their ruined farms. It was hard to stop them from coming home. The rest were just the last sweepings of the draft, boys or old clerks from the sidewalks of Richmond and Petersburg. But even they fought well. They were desperate. Much depended upon them. And they knew it."

That is what one used to hear. Actually--

General Early was preparing to move the bulk of his forces out of the Valley of Virginia. The dying Confederacy was shrinking its life-blood back to its heart. The Virginia Central was busy bringing empties west to take Early's men back towards Richmond. A raid northward into the Valley to cut, if possible, that important federal artery, the Manassas Gap Railroad, would create a diversion; screen the withdrawal to Richmond. It might even fool Sheridan long enough to put him on the defensive again. And time was precious then, even more precious than men.

For his purpose, a purely strategic one, the Confederate general picked his men carefully. Many of them were natives of the Valley, old volunteers, Stonewall's veterans who could be depended upon to fight their way back home. They were to leaven the lump of the new, drafted men and the raw, young recruits. Early was prepared to sacrifice them if necessary, and there wasn't much time to organize.

There was one regiment of Lomax's cavalry, commanded by a captain, and remounted on newly-captured federal horses. They were mostly veterans and would carry through. There were several provisional battalions of infantry sketchily organized for the occasion; doubtful, but the best available. There was no artillery, because there was none to spare. Cannon were almost as scarce as capable officers. Daring must be the substitute for both. So the command was placed in the hands of a fearless but wild, Mississippian by the name of LaTouche, Major Mathis LaTouche.

LaTouche specialized in forlorn hopes. "Christ help the foremost" was his motto, and he always led his own men. Also he told one funny story in Cajun dialect of which General Early was very, very tired. Perhaps he told it once too often? Anyway, he was given a general's responsibility with a major's rank. "Nothing matters to dead men," the general muttered, when he was once asked about it long afterwards.

LaTouche and his men, about twenty-five hundred in all, got off the cars at a little siding on the Virginia Central just west of Waynesboro. They could ride no farther. The iron bridge over the Shenandoah at Waynesboro had been destroyed some weeks before by Torbert's Union cavalry. The Confederates hurried rapidly down the Valley, the infantry in bad shoes and bare feet.

They passed through ruined Staunton and Port Republic, also lately visited by General Torbert. Consequently, they kept gathering in a good many "independents" and "volunteers" along the way; lean, bearded men who came out of hiding from the woods and ravines, rifle in hand and grim determination at heart. They had nothing to lose now but their lives.

So far LaTouche had seen nothing of the federal forces except their benign handiwork. By the time he reached Rockingham on the South Fork his column numbered over three thousand by "natural accretion," and he was greatly encouraged. It looked as though he might get far enough down the Valley by midnight to strike at the railroad next day. That would be magnificent! Early might have to make him a colonel yet.

So he kept pushing his one well-organized and veteran unit, the cavalry regiment, far ahead of his limping infantry, hoping to occupy Luray after nightfall. All was going merrily--when his scouts struck the vedettes of the 6th Pennsylvania Cavalry posted along the river south of Felix Run and in the gorge above Aquila.

Although it was now pitch dark, the Confederate cavalry still made a determined attempt to push on. The skirmish along the river road grew fast and furious. But the volume of fire from the breech-loading carbines used by the Federals convinced the Confederates that the gorge must be quite heavily occupied, and they fell back up the Valley to await the arrival of their infantry still many miles behind.

It was the last of this skirmish in the gorge that Colonel Franklin had heard from the porch at Coiner's Retreat. In less than no time he was back in camp and had the situation in hand. Farfar returned to camp a few minutes after him. The firing by then had died away. Evidently the Confederates were not going to risk a night attack before their main body came up to support them.

Colonel Franklin could have asked for nothing better than a delay. He took every precaution against a surprise, but permitted the bulk of his men to sleep under arms. Meanwhile, he summoned the force at Luray to join him, and sent couriers to Front Royal with the news of the threatened raid, to be transmitted to headquarters.

The night passed peacefully. Shortly before sunrise the 23rd Illinois Infantry and the Rhode Island Artillery marched in up the Luray road, quietly, as they had been instructed. By dawn they were posted. Before that time the colonel felt sure that his message must have been relayed by the signal corps at Front Royal to General Sheridan at Winchester.

The sun rose through a bank of fog. At the lower end of the Valley a lowering, black cloud, which extended from one mountain wall to the other, lingered like a patch of night, moving imperceptibly southward. It was the first major threat of a break in the weather for many weeks. At Aquila, of course, no one paid any attention to it. It was still miles away, and few in that vicinity on that particular morning had their heads in the clouds.

It seemed obvious to everyone that a clash would take place immediately between the opposing forces gathering about Aquila; that is, as soon as it should be light enough for effective fighting to begin. Men and officers strained, looking into the thinning fog and shadows before them, and as the visibility increased the tension grew.

It was found that during the night the Confederates had advanced through the gorge. Their infantry had worked along both sides of the river in small parties, filtering through the woods and over the "impassable" hills. Morning found them in full possession of all but the lower end of the little pass.

Colonel Franklin had expected that. He had slowly withdrawn his cavalry pickets rather than sacrifice them uselessly. Except for a sharp interchange of rifle fire just before daylight, when the massed Union outposts finally withdrew from the gorge to fall back on their main body, there had been no serious resistance.

It was during this brief outbreak of firing that the infantry and artillery from Luray had arrived on the field. As the senior officer present, Colonel Franklin then found himself in command of a combined force of about eighteen hundred splendidly-equipped veterans from the three major arms of the service, and he made his dispositions accordingly.

In spite of the efficiency of his little force, he must, until reinforcements arrived, play a waiting and defensive game. Both his orders and the situation made it imperative to do so rather than to waste his strength in a doubtful offensive. He had Sheridan's own instructions to "hold the bottle neck at Aquila" until help arrived, and to send word of any movement to the south of him. The latter he had done, and the former he determined to do if possible. But he was outnumbered by about two to one, and reports from his scouts led him to believe that the Confederates were in even greater numbers. He might, then, be forced back. Yet, if he were, it must only be after he had so crippled the Confederates that they would fall an easy prey to the federal reinforcements coming up the Valley--or, in any event, find themselves too enfeebled to reach the Manassas Gap Railroad.

Colonel Franklin's task was therefore "to dam" the Valley with the force at his disposal against twice his numbers; that of the Confederates, to overflow him and smash through. Time would be the deciding element. The "dam" necessarily consisted of a defendable line across the narrow part of the Valley just below where the river broke through the hills. Roughly, that line stretched along Aquila Creek from the ruined village itself to the river. There were dense forests and tumbled foothills on either flank.

The colonel put Aquila Creek behind him. It was fordable if he did have to fall back down the Valley, and it might offer in that case an excellent second line of defence. He posted the 23rd Illinois Infantry on the left. The extreme left battalion of that regiment occupied the thin woods and some of the heavy-walled buildings in the ruined village of Aquila. The artillery, a crack battery of six rifled, steel field-pieces, he posted in the centre, supported by sharp-shooters composed of some of his cavalrymen and the Illinois Irish, twenty-two in all. He held the right of the line with his own regiment, his right flank resting on the river, where Dr. Holtzmaier also set up his field hospital in Mr. Felix Mann's canteen. The empty camp lay a quarter of a mile behind him in charge of a few invalids and musicians. There were no reserves. It was the best he could do. The line was too long, but it was concave to the enemy and concentrated fire.

The line was crescent-shaped because it followed roughly the rim of a shallow bowl of meadows several square miles in extent. The hay on them had been cut some weeks before, so there were now perfectly-clear manœuvring for cavalry and unimpeded shooting for artillery and riflemen. The Confederates would have to advance over those clean, cropped fields for nearly a mile before they struck the Union troops. At the present they were debouching from the gorge and taking up position in a tangle of unbroken forest just opposite, woods that stretched from the Blue Ridge to the river.

Success in action frequently depends upon apparently quite minor features in the terrain. Such was the case at Aquila. Both sides were quick to take advantage of them. If the Confederates lay fully concealed in the woods along the south side of the meadows and in the river gorge itself, the Federals were equally well-protected by the little valley of Aquila Creek. It made a gradual, a scarcely noticeable, swale in the fields where it flowed down to the river. That wide-sweeping, grassy dip, nevertheless, was deep enough to conceal a mounted man so that his head would not show above the sky line.

It was within this hollow in the fields that Colonel Franklin placed the artillery and his own regiment of cavalry, massed and ready. Over the crest towards the enemy there was nothing but a thin line of skirmishers lying down in the short grass with their rifles and carbines beside them. That was all that Major LaTouche could see there when he examined the Union line with field-glasses, shortly after sunrise, while wisps of fog were still curling through the pines.

It was plain to the major that the Union left was strongly held by a regiment of Zouave infantry. He could see their red trousers and white leggings gleaming through the open woods in that direction and in the ruins of the village, which would, with its sturdy brick buildings, be a hard nut to crack. In the fields nearer the river, however, there seemed to be nothing but a thin line of dismounted cavalry. Hence, the major decided to attack there at once.

He generally felt impetuous just after breakfast and the five cups of eye-opening, black New Orleans coffee which his darky orderly brewed him every morning. The cherished coffee and nine Mexican silver dollars were all that remained of the major's estate. But even that was too much. Seeing only as clearly as he did, despite the coffee, he had no idea that in a slant of the fields, that looked level through the field-glasses, a battery of artillery and a regiment of cavalry lay concealed. There was, in fact, no immediate way of his finding this out, unless he had ordered one of his men to climb a tree and look over. It did occur to him to give such an order, but he felt that it would be thought eccentric, and he refrained.

What is described by clerkly historians as an "inexplicable delay" now took place. That is, killing on a large scale did not begin as soon as might logically be expected. The whole morning passed with only desultory firing by sharpshooters on both sides. It was nearly noon before the impetuous, and by now impatient, Major LaTouche was able to deliver his first thrust. His infantry illogically insisted upon having something to eat before they started to die. Most of them had been marching all night. They had few shoes and many sore feet. They sat down and made flapjacks and cooled their feet in the river. They picked their way slowly along the rocky gorge road, and it took several hours to get them deployed through the woods facing the Federals and reorganized for attack. The "volunteers" picked up along the route were particularly troublesome. They insisted upon sticking together in neighbourhood gangs.

Among them was a party of Valley men, veterans of many a fight, who had joined up at Waynesboro. And in that group was a peaked-looking youngster with his left arm in a sling.

Paul Crittendon had got no farther than Waynesboro when he ran away from Coiner's Retreat. There he had been ill again. His chance to get back to the army had seemed heaven-sent when LaTouche's column came through. Since he could not use a rifle, he had been given a six-shooter and assigned to a colour guard. He said he didn't care whether he was killed or not, and he thought he meant it. Flags were always carried into battle, although they were unnecessary. Paul's flag had been at Gettysburg, and all up and down the Valley with Early. It was shot full of holes and tattered by the weather until it looked like old lace. It had the fatal property of acting like a "magnet" for lead.

Colonel Franklin did not let his artillery shell the woods where he knew the Confederates were assembling. He was saving the guns as a surprise. Nor would he permit the lieutenant-colonel commanding the 23rd Illinois to attack and "clean out" the country in front of him, although the wild Irish were eager to advance and kept up a constant peppering fire. "Wait," said the colonel, "wait and save your ammunition."

So they waited, all through the morning. The colonel finally fed his men and horses. On the left, the little springhouse at Aquila was full of Zouave Irishmen from Chicago filling their canteens to a constant clinking of cans. All the dolls, even the Corncob tribe, were taken for "sowveneers." The men lay low and ate their rations. It looked like a big picnic through the woods while they munched their hard-tack and cold beans. Smoke rose from the chimney of one of the deserted houses where the staff made coffee. On the right the cavalry and artillery broke out nose-bags for the horses, ready to snatch them away. Details carried buckets of water, slung on poles, across the fields. A few skulkers sneaked back to camp.

At the end of the line near the river Surgeon Holtzmaier laid out his instruments and cleared the counters of Mr. Mann's canteen for operating tables. The stone farmhouse, where the store had been situated, offered a welcome protection from stray bullets, and extra hospital space. A dozen or so wounded from the skirmish of the night before had been treated there. Already four dead men were laid out on the river-bank behind. The tents of the deserted camp lay farther down the stream, still and gleaming, with the forgotten headquarters flag flopping idly on its staff as the wind gradually shifted from south to north.

A chill crept into the air. The cloud down the Valley began to draw perceptibly nearer. It slowly threatened to shut half the world from sunlight like a vast, sliding lid.

But on the bright pastures where men waited for battle Indian summer still lingered, gilding the meadows with a wide, empty yellow light. The slanting sunlight twinkled on weapons scattered through the woods and fields; glittered on the polished steel barrels of the six rifled cannons of the "Star Battery" from Providence, Rhode Island.

Lieutenant Lyman de Wolf Dorr, the dandy, young officer in charge, beat the dust out of his gauntlets against his saddle-bow, and wished to God the fun would begin and be got over with. He was twenty-three and this was his thirteenth battle. He listened with professional appraisal to the distant "howling" in the woods held by the Confederates. It seemed to him the enemy was trying to keep up his own courage rather than express defiance. Certainly those yells were nothing like the rebel yells of earlier in the war; not to be compared with the noise when they were closing in on McClellan on the Peninsula. He wondered idly how soon the war would be over. The annual subscription dances must be beginning at home now. To have missed three seasons! He whistled his favourite waltz of 1861, listening to invisible fiddles. A bullet droned over the crest and smacked into an apple tree on the knoll near by. A branch with a withered fruit bent and fell. There was no reply. The Union lines lay silent. Waiting, waiting. My God, that was what wore you out--waiting!

A courier with an exhausted and sobbing horse came stumbling up from the river road and asked for Colonel Franklin. The lieutenant pointed him out sitting on the little knoll on the crest among the bare apple trees, where he had been observing since ten o'clock. He watched the courier hand the colonel his dispatch. At that moment the entire Union picket line on the other side of the crest burst into a fury of fire.

The lieutenant never forgot the next few seconds. He kept his eyes on the colonel. He thought the man would never get through reading that dispatch:

Hold hard. Merritt's and Averell's cavalry divisions left Winchester at 4
a.m.
S.

That was all.

The colonel tucked the paper in his pocket, turned, looked over the field, and made a signal to Lieutenant Dorr.

Instantly, men, horses, and guns leaped forward, animated by a single will. The battery raced for the crest, opening fanwise, each gun heading for its appointed place already prepared hours before. The static tension was resolved into violent action.

To the line of Confederates some eight hundred strong, advancing across the fields through a hail of droning bullets from the Union riflemen, the heads of the artillery, men and horses, the outlines of the flying caissons and cannons appeared abruptly above the low sky line ahead, like a sinister apparition materializing out of the solid green earth of the meadows themselves.

The guns unlimbered. The horses trotted back over the crest.

There was a moment of frantic activity about the battery, and then a great wall of pallid, yellow smoke seemed to be pushed out against and to be rushing down upon the oncoming Southerners. The wall cracked and bellowed with thunder. Streaks of red light leaped out of its heart, followed by the howlings and hummings of the invisible things that fell upon that line of advancing men like bundles of whirling knives; that cut them, sliced them, filled them full of fine steel needles which pierced to the bone.

The line continued to advance. The distant yelling of men came nearer, heard faintly above the bellows of the volcano on the knoll. Somehow there were not so many in the line now. The yelling grew fainter. Then suddenly--no one could tell just exactly when--the advancing line was going the other way, turned back as if by command.

But it was no longer a line. It was lonely individuals converging upon one another, rushing into bunches and groups. They went tearing back into the woods they had left only a few minutes before, to lie down white, exhausted, and panting. To each man it seemed as though the guns should have ceased when he turned back. The terrible thing was that those cannons had continued to kill every foot of the way, coming and going.

Finally they ceased.

And now from the fields, dotted with motionless and squirming bundles, came a low wailing, and a high, tearing screaming that did not cease in that vicinity until early the following morning. Lieutenant Dorr had been firing alternate but continuous salvos of shrapnel and canister. The wind drifted the acrid powder smoke sinuously through the woods where the Confederates now lay silent. Silence hung over the Union lines. The battery was cooling its guns.

Someone out on the field kept calling for "William Anderson" in a hoarse, agonized voice and ceased not to do so. Curiously enough, several others finally took up the refrain. Then, as if in answer, the guns began again.

One of them tolled like a bell, the others barked and bellowed. Each had a different voice. It was like a monster with six heads roaring. They were plunging round shot into the Confederate woods. These whined and smashed through the trees, scattering branches and splinters as though lightning had struck. On the knoll the battery was once more enveloped in a dense cloud of yellow smoke. The explosions gradually grew more deliberate. After-while they stopped. The battery seemed to have run down like a clock. Doubtless they were winding it up again. In the woods men lifted pale, strained faces from their arms and stood upright once more.

Major LaTouche determined to have those guns. They were stopping him. It had been a mistake--he could see it now--to attack with only part of his infantry. He should have used every available man and broken through. Now he would hurl his regiment of cavalry on the battery and follow up with all his infantry. Horsemen could get across the field to the guns before they were all killed getting there. That was the gist of it. He still regarded his men as invincible, once they arrived. Also, he was a cavalryman.

Having made a terrible mistake, he determined to wipe out either his error or himself by leading the cavalry in person. He tugged his long moustache thoughtfully. That damn' Yankee battery was the best he had ever seen. "Well, suh, let's go over an' call on 'em," said he, as he put himself at the head of his cavalry massed in an open glade. He issued orders for the infantry to follow "instantly."

LaTouche may have been mad or just from Mississippi, either or both. Anyway, he rode a large cream-coloured stallion that actually tossed his mane. He also carried a fine repeater hunting watch. He now took this out of his pocket and held it up to his ear. All those sitting near him on their horses in the silent forest heard its faint chime. A slightly elfin look flitted over the major's face. "It is exactly two and a half o'clock," said he, and looked about him. No one disputed the fact. It was his last irrational action save one. He next gave the command to take the guns.

The guns were not very cool yet. "The trouble with these damned steel babies," said Lieutenant Dorr, "is that they heat up like hell over a brief affair. Look at number one there, her breeches are still hot as a hoar's!" He spat on the metal, and the saliva cracked back at him.

"Give the slut a chance, sir!" exclaimed a young gunner who was proud of number one. "*I'll* cool her off"--and before anyone could stop him he dumped a bucket of cold spring water over the breech. A torrent of oaths and a hail of kicks on his behind rewarded him. Someone started to laugh, when from an opening in the woods opposite a regiment of Confederate cavalry led by a man on a cream-coloured horse emerged at a rapid trot. It was a full half-mile away. The battery went into action immediately.

"Shrapnel!" roared the lieutenant, and started to move over to number two gun, which was slow in fire.

Just then number one burst with a crack like a tight earthquake, and the caisson behind it went up with red fire and a volcanic roar. Men, horses, wheels, and metal fragments were spewed all over the meadows, and the blast carried havoc through the rest of the battery. The man who had poured cold water over the breech was blown spread-eagled up into an apple tree to hang there with his bowels streaming out while he made noises like a sick rooster.

Lieutenant Dorr could not hear him, though, nor the rebel trumpets sounding the charge. He never heard anything again. He stood dazed, watching the battery trying to reassemble itself. There were only enough men left to man four guns. For a while they were clear out of action.

For several minutes the lieutenant was out too. All he could do was to lean against a shattered tree and watch things unroll before him in a stunned dream. Time seemed to have slowed up as if only the intervals of a dismal music were being played long drawn out. Yet he could see; he still knew what was going on.

Across the half-mile of meadow before him, one to the left and one to the right, two columns of cavalry, moving on parallel lines but in opposite directions, rode flashing into the afternoon sunlight. There was not quite a mile of perfectly smooth meadow between them. The Confederates were making for the guns. The Federals seemed to be heading for the line of woods opposite. The lieutenant saw this. It seemed to him to be happening slowly. He saw the man on the cream-coloured horse throw up his hands and slowly fall off backward. He saw the column of Union cavalry swing into line and start to sweep down the field, slowly. The Confederates had turned to meet them. The two lines would meet directly in front of the guns. The lieutenant could not move. Something was wrong with him. He knew he ought to move. He had forgotten how. The trouble was in his head. He groaned. Nightmare had become a reality.

Colonel Franklin on Black Girl had halted exactly half-way across the fields with his trumpeter beside him. A crackle of rifle fire came from the woods towards which his column was heading. The bullets tore up the turf about him. Black Girl danced as though she were in a swarm of bees. Half the column galloped past the colonel. The trumpet sounded. The troopers swung left into line, stretching well across the meadows, and halted. Here and there a man dropped from the saddle and a horse galloped away. But most of the empty saddles stayed in line.

History does not remember the name of the young officer who commanded the regiment of Confederate cavalry at Aquila after LaTouche fell--only that he was a captain from New Bern, North Carolina. Nevertheless, he was probably the best soldier on the field. The instant Major LaTouche was killed, he stopped the charge on the battery and brought his men into line to face the 6th Pennsylvania Cavalry that seemed to have sprung from the earth. And he never stopped galloping. He simply swung his squadrons like so many doors on hinges and swept on up the field.

It was now that Colonel Franklin made the mistake of his life. He had behind him a splendid machine for firing carbines. He used it as a sword. He might have kept his men sitting their horses in line, while they crashed volley after volley into the long front of the Confederate cavalry sweeping down upon him. He might have emptied half their saddles before they struck him. That would have been the calm, approved tactics of it.

But Colonel Franklin also was a cavalryman. He had been born in 1821 and brought up on Napoleon, Sir Walter Scott, and Balaclava. The clear field before him, the line of horsemen speeding towards him over the grass, his own regiment lined up spick, span, and ready behind him--that was the moment and the situation he had been dreaming of, living and drilling for, for years.

He gave the order to charge.

All fire from either side had ceased. It was as though that bowl of meadows full of sunlight was nothing more than a prepared field for the greatest of human spectacles. Infantrymen stood up in the woods and craned their necks. On the knoll the artillerymen waited. The lines of cavalry would meet directly in front of the battery. To fire would be to slaughter friend and foe alike. Lieutenant Dorr threw his arms behind him to grasp the tree. His vision was clearing now, dizzily. He heard nothing.

But a rolling storm of hoofs that sounded like subterranean thunder came faster and nearer from either side. Like the crest of two floods the lines of horses with manes curling backward in the wind swept forward. Men leaned low in the saddles with their sabres flashing before them. The sound of the desperate breathing of a thousand beasts, snorting, and the creaking of leather approached like a whirlwind. Fifty yards from each other a long blast of withering fire swept from one end to the other of either line. Powder smoke floated away like spume drift as though the two waves had broken--as they had. For to a storm of hoarse cheering and a screaming rebel yell the lines met directly before the lieutenant standing on the knoll.

Men threw up their hands and fell backward, men pitched forward. Horses reared and plunged. Frantic beasts, kicking and screaming, rolled over and over. Lieutenant Dorr could look down upon and clear across a quarter of a mile of furious slaughter. It was fortunate that he could not hear. Swords are really great knives. Men were chopping one another out of the saddle like so much meat on the block. The haze of pistol smoke grew denser. The sun dazzled on tossing crests of steel. Here and there groups broke through and wheeled back again into the mêlée. Horses shot through the lungs, with purple foam spurting from their nostrils, plunged, bucked, and rolled, bashing the brains and bowels out of their masters, trampling them flat. Dismounted men hewed and shot at each other. For something over two hundred seconds this went on.

Yet in the silent, dazed world of Lieutenant Dorr, where impressions still registered themselves slowly, the events before him seemed to be prolonged and delayed. A sabre fell deliberately upon the blue sleeve of a Union trooper who had thrown his carbine up to ward off the blow. A flash of crimson spray followed the severed arm and the carbine as they curved free through the air. Two officers rode around each other shooting. A hole appeared in the forehead of one and he closed his eyes, falling. A couple of horses reared straight upward, their riders slashing. One horse fell upon his rider backward, the other sank slowly upon his haunches, trembling, his backbone cut behind the saddle. A cascade of yellow water spurted from his tail. A swirl of maddened blue-coats led by their colonel passed over the beast's body, sweeping everything before them. The lieutenant closed his eyes. When he opened them again the fight had passed on. He was looking at what was left behind.

Immediately before him, the horse with the severed spine was struggling to rise on its forelegs. It seemed to be trying to crawl someplace where men could never come. Its head reared up strangely with staring eyes and open jaws. There was something lizardlike about it. Its long, smooth neck and body swept serpentwise back into its dead haunches. It looked like one of the horses of Pluto, emerging from the ground. The lieutenant turned away sickened, pressing his hands to his head that now throbbed in a returning tide of feeling with a ruinous, internal agony. The man on number two gun was just about to pull the lanyard. The lieutenant fell on him with cries out of nowhere only in time to prevent his firing into his own men. In an utterly silent world the young officer stood trying to hear himself groan, left entirely alone with his pain.

The furious confusion of the cavalry action swirled on up the field to the left. The Confederates had been forced back. From the woods their infantry, which had at last received its orders to advance, swept out to support them.

From the little knoll on the crest, where Lieutenant Dorr was standing by with what remained of his guns, the field presented a scene of disastrous confusion. The Confederate cavalry had finally broken and had been forced back, with the Federals pressing them hard, almost to the border of the woods. There they met the solid lines of their own infantry emerging from the underbrush and rushing impetuously forward. While some of the Confederate cavalry was received through intervals and thus found shelter behind the line of their advancing infantry, most of the mounted men, both Confederates and Federals, were now rolled back again towards the Union position, a seething swirling mass of men and animals locked in confused conflict.

As seen from the Union lines, the whole advancing, bayonet-flashing front of the Confederate infantry was now masked and curtained by this cavalry mêlée of inextricably-mixed friend and foe; by patches of squadrons that still held some semblance of formation; by riderless horses galloping aimlessly up and down; by distracted men still fighting or attempting to flee--and behind them a hedge of bayonets that advanced relentlessly.

The Union lines perforce remained silent. The advance had not yet come within effective range of the 23rd Illinois rifles on the left, and Lieutenant Dorr was now faced with the dilemma either of permitting his guns to remain idle, until his battery was overwhelmed by the approaching flood, or of firing upon the ranks of the enemy through the living bodies of his friends of the 6th Pennsylvania still scattered all along the Confederate front. There was no alternative. He must either fire--or not fire, and be captured.

The pain in his head was, he thought, driving him mad. A white-hot bar of metal seemed to be extending through the back of his skull from ear to ear. Someone else, he felt, finally forced the word "canister" through his lips and kept giving orders like an automaton. The four guns burst into a frenzy of continuous drumfire. The lieutenant could not hear them, their sound for him was transmuted into vibrations of pure pain. The brain of the young officer seemed to be catching afire internally, and he rolled on the grass holding his head and moaning.

The small affair at Aquila had now reached its crisis. But it was a senseless crisis. There was no general leadership left on either side. The main attack of the Confederates had been launched, in obedience to the command of a dead man, and was sweeping across the fields towards the Union line. The unfortunate cavalry being brushed before it was merely so much living chaff caught between two millstones about to engage each other. That was the situation when Lieutenant Dorr's guns began to vomit canister.

Gaps, aisles, and vacant intervals began to appear in that portion of the onrolling mass immediately facing the battery. A process as of the rapid melting of a solid appeared to be taking place. Some of the survivors of the Union cavalry rode in through the smoke, and throwing themselves on the ground, opened fire on the approaching enemy. The gunners serving the four pieces attained their physical maximum of speed. There was a moment when the knoll upon which the battery stood was involved in a continuum of explosion.

The Confederates facing the guns wavered, rallied, came on again--and then suddenly darted back. A small portion of them who came racing up onto the knoll were literally clubbed to death by the now frantic remnant of the Union cavalry that had gathered about the guns. There was something peculiarly terrible about this last fight about the still flashing and tolling cannons. There was no quarter. The sounds were ferocious. Suddenly the cannons stopped and the gunners were heard roaring hoarsely for ammunition.

When the smoke cleared, it was seen that the attack on the Union right had been halted. The field was piled with dead and wounded. Stragglers were melting away into the woods. Lieutenant Dorr was shrieking for someone to put a bullet through his head.

But it was not over yet.

A half-mile up the field to the left the 23rd Illinois Infantry was advancing out into the meadows and extending its intervals to cover the front of the oncoming Confederates. The Union regiment, trained to machine-like precision by Zouave tactics, moved as though on parade. It was "guide centre" on the colours, with the drums beating and the fifes squealing:

"The Union forever, hurrah, boys, hurrah."

The shrill, distant defiance of the fifes sounded pitiful, the drums ominous. The effect upon the Confederates was electric. They gave a long, defiant rebel yell, emptied their rifles at the blocks of blue-coats before them, and rushed forward with the bayonet.

The files of the 23rd Illinois closed up where men had fallen. The regiment halted. At a distance of two hundred yards it began to fire volleys by alternate platoons. Behind the ranks the lieutenants and sergeants counted. The rifles were reloaded in six counts. The effect was precise, mechanical, and inhuman. For nearly two minutes an unbroken series of volleys continued to flash along the front of the regiment from right to left. Billows of powder smoke rolled before the line, through which crashed sheets of flame. The Confederate centre, upon which this fire was concentrated, parted, seemed to dissolve in the smoky air. The slaughter at that point was the worst on the field. But the attack flowed around the flanks of the blue-coats. Groups of desperate bearded men with haggard faces began to throw themselves on the lines of the clockwork regiment from the rear. The volleys ceased. A fusillade petered out into pistol-shots. Then men rolled about with each other on the ground. The Chicago Irish clubbed muskets against the Bayonets. This was the kind of riot they best understood. The field dissolved into a swirling mass of inextricable confusion.

Scattered over it, and under the feet of those who still fought there, were the dead, the dying, and the wounded.

II

Evening approached, and with it the great cloud drifting up the Valley.

In the old brick farmhouse by the river, Surgeon Holtzmaier and his two hospital assistants were now completely and conclusively overwhelmed. Up until two o'clock that afternoon they had done heroically well. The casualties from the skirmishing of the night before and of earlier in the day had been rapidly disposed of. They had been subjected to rifle fire only, and their care was comparatively simple. As soon as the bullets were extracted and the wounds dressed, Dr. Holtzmaier had had them carried to the vacant camp where they now lay in the big mess tents, cared for by some of their least injured comrades.

Dr. Holtzmaier could see no difference between a Confederate and a Union wound. A wounded man was to him an example of suffering humanity. He took men as they came, in turn. So in the big tents in the camp the wounded of both sides lay together and tended one another as best they could. They, however, were the fortunate ones. They had been hit early. After the action was joined, Surgeon Holtzmaier could no more cope with the influx of wounded than a man could put out a forest fire with a tumbler of water.

By five o'clock in the afternoon the little farmhouse was surrounded for hundreds of feet by the wounded. They lay on the grass, gasping, pale and silent or shivering and moaning, according to the nature of their endurance or misery. The farmhouse itself, where the operating and dressing were going on, sounded like the headquarters of the Inquisition. The men were laid out on the blanket-covered counters of Mr. Mann's now defunct canteen and the surgeon performed on them. There were four counters, and the blankets on all of them were red and sopping.

They brought cases in four at a time, so the counters were always full. Surgeon Holtzmaier moved from number one to number four, and then back to number one again. He was dealing with every possible form of injury in all parts of the human frame. Men trampled by horses, with crushed faces and broken bones; men with smashed and mangled limbs; men with frightful head wounds from shrapnel; men riddled by canister and drilled with rifle bullets; men with the oozing weals and raw meat of sabre slashes; poor lost bodies shot through the stomach, lungs, and bowels, men and boys.

These had dragged themselves, crawled, or staggered, or had been brought by comrades to the little dressing station by the river, the one place in all that area of destruction where some element of mercy and intelligent reconstruction still remained. Surgeon Holtzmaier was simply doing all that he could. After a while he would send out the stretcher-bearers for the worst cases that always remained helpless on the field.

Already he had more than he could do. He moved rapidly, his instruments in a bucket, from number one to number four. His hospital apprentices tried to chloroform the men ahead of him. Sometimes they just held them down, if it didn't take. The surgeon amputated, cut, sawed, sewed, probed, and bandaged. To men shot through the entrails he gave an opiate--and had them carried out behind the house on the river-bank. There was nothing more he could do for them.

Mr. Felix Mann had remained to help. He didn't want to leave the goods on the shelves of his canteen. Later on, the doctor used two hundred beautiful white shirts for bandages, and Mr. Mann said nothing. He organized a dozen men as stretcher-carriers. They were probably skulkers. Surgeon Holtzmaier didn't give "a goot gottam."

As the doctor started on his sixteenth round of the line of counters he was joined by a slight, middle-aged man in Vandyke beard and worn Confederate coat with faded medical insignia.

"Dr. Huger Wilson of Charleston," said the newcomer quietly. There was a certain dry, crisp quality to his voice. "May I be of assistance?"

"Ja!" said Holtzmaier. "Vee all need assizztance here! Vat?"

"I think we do," replied Dr. Wilson, and went to work. They divided the tables between them. The new-comer worked with incredible speed and skill.

"Vilson? Not Vilson of der Garolina Gollege?" said Dr. Holtzmaier after a while, wiping the sweat from his eyes. "You write dat pook?"

Dr. Wilson nodded.

"All I know iss from dat pook," said Dr. Holtzmaier humbly.

"But you do well, sir," replied Dr. Wilson.

It was the great moment of Dr. Holtzmaier's life.

Dr. Wilson removed a patella hanging by shreds from a young lad, who shrieked and went grey under the knife. He squeezed a spongeful of laudanum between his lips.

"Knees seldom heal," said Wilson as they removed the man, who had fainted. "Take off his leg later."

"Ja, und der gloroform is gone und der lint und pandages will soon be all. Und dem damn vools iss schtill gillin' each odder out dere!"

Both the surgeons stopped for a moment to listen. The artillery was silent, but a constant popping of rifle fire was going on. The action by this time had degenerated into nothing but a series of scattered skirmishes, each side having retired to its own woods. Occasionally an obstinate group of Confederates, Valley men, would make another rush. They were determined "to drive the strangehs back." Such efforts were received by a violent burst of fire, and foiled.

"Der damn vools!" repeated Dr. Holtzmaier, as the crash of a volley came to him from far up the field--and went back to his work. A frightfully wounded young Confederate expired under his knife.

"Take him away," said Dr. Holtzmaier, tears of chagrin in his eyes.

Dr. Wilson shook his head, as he probed. His man shrieked.

"Ja," said Dr. Holtzmaier. "It is der gottam boliticians do dat! Ven dese fellers vas schust babies already dey mak sbeeches in der Senate. Und now, py Gott, der gloroform is all!"

"Sbeeches," said Dr. Holtzmaier, "sbeeches!"--from time to time that afternoon.

The two surgeons bent themselves to the desperate work that is necessary when oratory fails. Presently the surgeon of the 23rd Illinois and his hospital assistants joined them. The stretcher cases began to come in.

"Have you any sperm oil?" asked Dr. Wilson.

"In der lamps."

"Take some of it and get it boiling."

Dr. Holtzmaier bellowed to Felix Mann to start oil boiling.

"Gauterize, eh?"

"Yes," said Dr. Wilson. "It's too bad they have given it up. I observe that there is less gangrene when you cauterize. No pus, generally. Pus is the foam on the lips of death. It is *not* a healthy sign."

"Ve gauterize!" said Dr. Holtzmaier. "Und irons, alzo."

He hustled Mann with his preparations for boiling the oil in a big pot, and thrust the poker into the flames. Smoke began to pour out of the old farmhouse where the doctors worked. Presently the shrieks of those whose stumps were thrust into the boiling oil came out of the chimney too. Dr. Wilson used the hot poker unsparingly to sear wounds. He knew it saved lives. Dr. Holtzmaier could hardly stand it. The smell of roasted flesh sickened him.

"Go out and get a breath of air," said Dr. Wilson afterwhile. "You've been at it longer than we have. It will do you good, man. Do it so you can keep on." He pushed Dr. Holtzmaier affectionately to the door.

"Ja, I go and schump in der ribber und come pack."

He stood just outside the door, covered with gore from the knees up. A scalpel dropped out of his hand. He filled his lungs with clean air and wiped the bloody sweat out of his eyes with the underside of his sleeve. All the wounded near by began to beg him to do something for them. Piled under a window, where they had been thrown out, and extending almost to the height of the sill itself was a pile of mixed legs, arms, and other things. Near the top a stiff hand stuck out and pointed at him.

A sickening spasm of disgust, for himself, for the species he belonged to, and for the scene in which he found himself dragged downward on the doctor's bowels.

"Oh, scheet!" he exclaimed. "Du lieber Gott im Himmel!"--and began to run for the river-bank.

He tore his clothes off, plunged in, and rolled about. Presently he emerged again, puffing. The cold water had sobered him. The horrible reek of blood was gone. He actually felt clean. So sudden and so profound was his change of mood that he literally felt like another man.

Dr. Holtzmaier dressed slowly. He knew he must take this opportunity of a few minutes from his work, or he would go under. There would be no sleep for him tonight. The stretcher cases would be coming in for hours. They had not even begun to get to the wounded on the field yet, and it was only sunset. A lot of the boys would die out there in the dark. He went up the river-bank a bit and removed a coat from a dead man who had tried to crawl down to the water. It fitted him ill, but it was better than his own blood-soaked blouse. From where he stood he had a view over the fields past the camp and clear down the valley almost to Luray. The air was chill but bracing. He felt warm in the dead man's big coat. He took a drink from his flask and sat down for a moment. He wanted to get his hands steady again.

Twilight deepened. There was no firing from the field now. The lights of the farmhouse windows, where the surgeons were working, turned from pale white to yellow. The Valley was strangely silent except for a distant yelling, a kind of whispered complaint that came through the trees. It was the voices of the wounded scattered over the meadows. Suddenly, as if they had been turned on, the night-birds began. Dr. Holtzmaier shivered a little as he rose to go back, and as he climbed the river-bank he looked down the Valley again.

The great cloud was quite near now. Just before and above it was a patch of bright clean sky from the last reflected rays of the sun. It was still day up there. Darkness moved under the cloud coming southward fast. Its frontlet stretched clear across the Valley like the forehead of night. And before the advancing cloud wall, flashing up in great swooping gyres and circles into the light above, was a flock of buzzards and swifter-darting hawks, torn between their fear of the oncoming storm and darkness and the temptations of the table spread by man below.

So sinister, brooding, and threatening was the slow advance of the great storm cloud with the harpies before it that something melancholily German and primevally fearful was appealed to in the recesses of the doctor's simple soul.

Far down the Valley patches of white appeared here and there, touched by the last long rays of the sunset, and from where the cloud billowed lowest descended streaks of shining sleet and rain.

"Vinter, she comes at last!" he exclaimed, stifling an obscure suicidal impulse compounded of fatigue, disgust and the solemnly-terrifying landscape. "Maype we get rest now? Ha, dis is not so goot for der poys on der field!" He hastened back to get the stretcher-bearers busy and organized.

But he had to wait. The powers of nature were not the only things loose that evening. The United States Government was also manifesting its sovereignty in physical and visible form.

From the ford down the river road came the sharp note of the bugle. The black water turned to cream there under the feet of a squadron. Behind it as far as the eye could see were black masses of men stretching miles back towards Luray and moving swiftly up the river road, pouring themselves out unceasingly from under the winter and the darkness of the cloud. Averell's and Merritt's cavalry divisions were on the way south. The cloud and the buzzards followed them.

The doctor should have crossed the road immediately. As it was, he was just too late.

The roar and clatter of hoofs was upon him just as he got his legs over a worm fence at the roadside. He sat there watching. Squadron after squadron, regiment after regiment, and brigade by brigade, the dark masses of men moving at a fast trot streamed by him. There was never an interval to get through. As the darkness grew the squadrons seemed to become solid masses of darker darkness. Now and then a flag with its white stripes and stars glimmered by. Irons and sabres jingled. Sparks sprang from the iron shoes and cobbles. Before him there was a sharp outburst of firing, the sound of the thunder of galloping masses. The fight died away, raving down the pass. What was left of LaTouche's men streamed back southward or scattered madly into the forests at the foot of the hills. The action at Aquila was over. It was merely an incident of the cavalry movement that day. It was hardly well known enough even to be forgotten--it was scarcely remembered at all.

Dr. Holtzmaier sat for nearly an hour. Then he slipped through an interval. Averell's division had passed. Thundering down the road behind it, Merritt's was close behind.

The rifle fire died away in the distance up the Valley. Cautiously, one by one, as they became used to the stony roar of the passing of armies, the night-birds, which had been scared by the firing, resumed again. By eleven o'clock nothing was to be heard about Aquila but the desperate shouts and screams of the wounded lost in the woods and fields. Answering them out of the insane darkness came the long, babbled monosyllables of owls and the inane insistence of whippoorwill, whippoorwill. The stretcher-bearers worked frantically. The lights in the farmhouse glowed and the fire smoked under the boiling oil.

Meanwhile, hours before, Dr. Holtzmaier had returned to join his colleagues in their grim and apparently endless labours. As he approached the door, where the light seemed to flow out as from a furnace of suffering to straggle away into the darkness, he was suddenly aware of two women coming up the river path. They seemed to be carrying a clothes basket piled high with white wash between them.

It was Mrs. Crittendon and Margaret. They had torn up everything in the way of cotton or linen at Coiner's Retreat and rolled it into bandages.

"We asked for you at the camp," said Mrs. Crittendon, "and they told us to come here. We thought perhaps you could use these and that we might help. Can you? May we?" said she, entering the crowded place, and looking about her without wincing. An infinite compassion swept over her fine, mobile face.

Dr. Holtzmaier made grateful noises in his throat.

"Madam," said Dr. Wilson, "permit us to welcome angels of mercy to this demoniacal little dwelling."

The three doctors and the two women went to work as though they had always worked together. Watching them, the waiting men took courage. They stifled the groans at their lips. Margaret wept and smiled--and bandaged. The hours flew by. Mr. Mann renewed the oil in the counter lamps. And still they worked.

About midnight the stretcher-bearers brought in the colonel of the 6th Pennsylvania Cavalry and laid him out on table number one. He was still conscious and insisted on waiting his turn.

Presently Dr. Wilson, Dr. Holtzmaier, and Mrs. Crittendon were bending over him. It was necessary to take his left leg off just below the hip. The assistants approached to hold him down.

"If this little lady will give me her hand, I think I can lie still," said the colonel, and put his palm in Margaret's.

The swift movements of the surgeon's fingers began. The sound of a saw on bone filled the room.

"Never mind doing that," said the colonel suddenly, sitting up in spite of himself, "never mind . . ." and fell back fainting into the arms of Mrs. Crittendon.

III

Now that he had been struck again, Paul Crittendon was not so sure that he wanted to die.

Unfortunately he had fallen about the end of the afternoon, and far up the field near the ruins of Aquila, where the woods began. The stretcher-bearers would not be able to search those thickets effectively until daylight next morning. Now it was dark, and it did occur to Paul that he might be dying. He was so weak.

It was his crowd, the gang from farther up the Valley with the old Virginia militia flag, that had made the last attack on Aquila. They had been driven back several times. That is everybody gathered about the flag had been killed or wounded. The ruined town was full of the Union Zouaves, who, after their advance, had fallen back upon it and held it desperately.

They were good riflemen, those fellows. They picked you off before you could get at them. Paul knew! He had made three rushes on the place, the last time carrying the flag himself. Then those masses of Union cavalry had come and driven everybody away. There was no one left to gather about the colours, old neighbours and Valley men, until somebody should say, "Come on, men, let's drive 'em back"--and try it again. No, everybody was gone now, everybody but the dead.

Their faces glimmered here and there through the underbrush.

Paul was sitting on a log, nursing his arm. He had been struck in the same old arm again, this time above the elbow.

The pain was so maddening at first that he had dropped the flag and rushed off headlong through the woods, completely out of his head. How or where he went, he did not know. Loss of blood and a general numbness finally brought him to a standstill.

It was after sunset when he had sat down on the log. He took off a bootlace and made a tourniquet for his dripping arm. Because he could feel almost nothing now, he thought at first he felt better. As the night grew colder his head became clearer. He could still think, although the world seemed far away. The cries of the night-birds were strangely distant.

A long way off through the trees he could see a dim glimmering of lanterns or reflections from a camp-fire. Finally, the light blazed up and he caught a glimpse of old brick walls red against the darkness.

He knew then he must still be near Aquila. Probably the Yankees were about yet. But the fight was over. He might get medical aid from them.

They would probably parole him anyhow--and Coiner's Retreat was just beyond.

A great homesickness for Flossie, for Meg and Aunt Libby, overcame the boy. If they would only come and get him now, and speak to him with their soft voices, and put their warm arms about him. Oh, how he needed their comfort! He cried miserably. He felt like a lost little boy again. They had loved him. And he had run away--for this!

Well, he would go back again! Over there was the springhouse at Aquila. The children would come to play there tomorrow. Flossie would bring them. He would go to the springhouse and wait. Tomorrow they would find him, waiting, and they would be so sorry. Tomorrow . . .

He rose to his feet and was almost overcome with a sickening, empty dizziness. His heart pounded insufferably. He fell down. It was then that it first occurred to him that he really might die. And now he didn't want to die. He wanted to live, to get back to Coiner's Retreat. He lay over the log panting.

If he didn't try to stand upright, he discovered it wasn't so bad. No, he was "all right" again. Of course, he couldn't die when Aquila was just a little way off through the trees. Why, he could crawl there! They would find him--tomorrow. He started to crawl.

It was a long way to crawl. He pulled himself along with one arm and shoved when he could with his legs. He was terribly thirsty. The vision of the springhouse, finally, of nothing but the water there, danced before his eyes. Blackness and grey spots at times overcame him. He waited and breathed. Presently he would see the glow through the trees again, and it was always a little nearer.

He began to pass a good many dead men in the open. There were no trees ahead either. Rising to his knees for an instant, he discovered that he was in the open fields once more. He looked up but he could see no stars. A drop of cold rain splashed on his cheek. If it rained it would put the fire out, and he might lose his direction. It was an old fire left flickering in the ruins. He could see that now. Nobody seemed to be there. Indeed, the 23rd Illinois had evacuated the place two hours before. What was left of them was now in the camp by the river.

Paul pushed desperately on. He must make it! The springhouse! Tomorrow . . . or--or he would die. He, Paul, would die. It still seemed impossible. He was too weak to weep now. His thirst left him. He lay with his head on his good arm, resting. Afterwhile he would go on. It was impossible that he should die just a quarter of a mile away from the springhouse at Aquila. Flossie would be there tomorrow--tomorrow. She would find him. He went all over it. But he must rest. The rain was slowly beginning, big drops now and then. He heard someone calling.

He had heard such voices before. But they had been far away or lost in the thickets. Most of the wounded about the ruined village had been carried off by the 23rd Illinois when they left. Away out in the darkness Paul could still hear a lot of them "hollerin'." They and the night-birds seemed to be wailing together. But this chap was near, somewhere just in front of him. He stopped to listen again.

"Oh, lordy, lordy, lordy!" said the voice, with a kind of sob in it.

To Paul there was something dimly familiar in the tones. He started to crawl forward again, a little to the left towards the sound. A pitiful, shuddering crying came to him through the darkness.

"Colonel Franklin," called the voice again. "Oh, lordy! Oh, Colonel Franklin!"

"Hi, Yank?" said Paul, and listened.

The whippoorwills sang.

"Hi, Johnny," replied the voice.

"Who's there?" it said again at last, tense with hope or terror.

"It's me," said Paul fatuously. He crawled over towards the murmured cries. A bundle with a white face came in sight. He leaned over it.

"Bill, don't you know me?" cried Paul. "It's Paul, Paul Crittendon. Farfar!" He shook the dim form by the shoulder. William Farfar looked up at him.

"Paul," he said weakly. "Paul Crittendon?" He put up his hand and took hold of Paul's hair to assure himself of the reality.

"I'm dreamin' some and I can't alers tell the difference," whispered Farfar. "You're really there?"

"I'm here, but I'm awful hurt," said Paul.

"I'm sorry, I cain't help you. I'm shot in the back. I cain't move me from the belt down." He gasped a little. "Say, it's gitten cold, ain't it?" he added after a moment.

"Yes," said Paul, and shivered.

The whippoorwills sang on. The fire in the ruins flickered and died away to a dull-red glow. Aquila was infinitely far away. Paul rested. He remembered how Farfar had nursed him a few weeks before. He was muttering something, and Paul listened.

"Mom," said Farfar, whispering. "Mom, I'm cold. Kiver me up."

A vision of his own mother sitting on the balcony of the old house on Shockoe Hill, with her sewing basket beside her, flashed upon Paul with overpowering effect. Never imaginative, now he could no longer tell the difference between reality and the dream. Weakness suddenly thrust his mind and the past upon him. He was a very little boy again playing about his mother's chair, crawling. The warm Richmond sunlight glinted delightfully upon his mamma's fascinatingly-embroidered slippers; on a veritable rose of Sharon that glowed on the toe. Why, he had forgotten how terribly beautiful that beaded flower had been! And it was still there! "Mother!"--It was a complete hallucination. The glowing rose vanished in the past where it had lain hidden. Paul was back in the darkness again. Lost.

"Oh," cried Paul, "oh, my God," and threw himself despairingly upon the breast of Farfar.

"Don't die, don't go away," he cried. "Bill, Bill, they hadn't ought to have done this to us. Can you hear me, Bill? It's Paul, Paul Crittendon, I'm still here."

"Yes, I can hear you, Paul," said Farfar after a little. "Where's Margaret, Margaret Crittendon?"

"Lost," whispered Paul. "We're alone. Don't you remember?"

"Yes, I remember now." And then after a little--"Can you hear *me*, Paul?"

"I can still hear."

"Well, you won't never leave me, Paul, will you?"

"Never," said Paul, "never!"--and he never did.

Over the fields and woods came the pelting swish of rain. At first it was like the soft, swift patter of wolves' feet running over the dead leaves. The night-birds ceased, turned off. All those who were still left on the field began to cry out together. The tired stretcher-bearers, doing their best, heard them and tried desperately to hurry. And then, almost without notice, except for a brief flurry of bitter, damp wind, the rain turned to sleet. The ice storm tinkled. All the cries ceased. Later on, a light snow began to fall as quietly as feathers from the wings of Death. The fields at Aquila were finally silent. Nature, as always, had her quiet way at last.

The bodies of William Farfar and Paul Crittendon were frozen together. No one could tell which side they belonged to now. They died trying to keep each other warm. Peacefully.

Colonel Franklin was also sleeping peacefully, but he was still alive. They had carried him back to Coiner's Retreat.

CHAPTER XVIII

AN INDESTRUCTIBLE UNION

It was towards morning when, owing to the urgent solicitude of both Drs. Wilson and Holtzmaier, Mrs. Crittendon and Margaret were finally prevailed upon to return to Coiner's Retreat. An old army wagon belonging to Felix Mann was provided, and it was only after Mrs. Crittendon had been helped up into the high seat, when she leaned back to relax for the first time in many hours, that she understood how tired she was. Margaret rested her head against her mother's shoulder for a moment and went to sleep like a baby.

As Mrs. Crittendon looked down at the little farmhouse dooryard with the smoky glow of Mr. Mann's whale-oil lamps glimmering through the fanlight, and illuminating brief flurries of snow that whirled past the windows, the place had once more the simple, homelike air of a Virginia farm. It seemed impossible that such scenes as she had just witnessed could ever have taken place there.

No, it was not "the demoniacal little dwelling" lately so described by Dr. Wilson. It was, it was . . . She nodded involuntarily. The outer world seemed to pitch down a slope. She must sleep soon or--

The next thing she knew Dr. Holtzmaier was wrapping blankets about her and Margaret, and saying something. They were not to take cold. They were to "drink dis." They were to hurry home and to bed. Dr. Holtzmaier's hoarse, tired voice rumbled on, giving directions to Dr. Wilson how to reach Coiner's Retreat, larded with exhortations to a contraband by the name of Culpepper to drive carefully, and to remember he had a wounded man and two ladies--and if he didn't drive carefully "py Gott! . . ."

"I'll see to it, my friend," said Dr. Wilson finally, trying to reassure the anxious German, as they helped slide the improvised stretcher upon which Colonel Franklin was strapped into the dark, canvas cave of the old wagon. Dr. Wilson climbed in with a lantern and sat beside the unconscious colonel, who was breathing faintly under the effect of a heavy dose of laudanum Dr. Holtzmaier had administered some hours before. "Much too much," muttered the Confederate surgeon. But he had said nothing at the time, for he hardly expected the colonel to live since he had lost so much blood. "Faint but steady," he said to the other surgeon, as he felt the colonel's pulse under the blanket. "He may pull through."

"I gif you all der spare subblies I haf," continued Dr. Holtzmaier. "Py him I know you do the pest you can. Danks, goot luck, und auf wiedersehen. You get pack tru der lines already all right soon; you stay here und der damn vools but you in brison."

Dr. Wilson reached out through the canvas and shook his colleague by the hand. "Thanks, my good friend," he said.

Dr. Holtzmaier stood watching the wagon disappear into the darkness, its lantern diminishing into the swirling snow. Up to the last minute Felix Mann had kept piling things into it. He came out now, but too late, with another package, and stood with the doctor till the noise of wheels died away up the road towards Aquila.

"Has he got a chance?" asked Mann as they turned to go in.

"Maype," replied Dr. Holtzmaier dubiously. "Mit Mrs. Crittendon und *dat* doctor, maype. Anyvay I gif him der last chanst." They went in. The door banged behind them, and for the first time in many hours Dr. Holtzmaier sat down.

The arrival of additional medical help with the passing cavalry divisions had unexpectedly relieved him. There were now plenty of surgeons and medical supplies. Orders had already come to evacuate the wounded to the hospitals at Harpers Ferry. The ambulances had gone. The little house was silent again. It had even been mopped out. Nothing remained now but the wreck of Mr. Felix Mann's canteen, and the embers of the fire. The doctor heaped some more fuel on it and sat down with his feet stretched out. "I do der pest I know," he kept muttering.

He had. He had sent the colonel off to Coiner's Retreat, because he knew he would never survive the cold, rough trip of two days to Harpers Ferry. And he had managed to slip the Confederate surgeon into the wagon too, before any questions were asked. That gave him enormous satisfaction. As to what would become of himself, now that his regiment was all but wiped out, he would let the authorities settle that. Now he must sleep. He had the shakes. He coloured a glass of water with some laudanum and tossed it off. "To hell mit all der damn vools," he said, by way of a toast. Presently he began to snore heavily and mightily like the wind in a Pennsylvania Dutch chimney. The fire leaped and the room grew deliriously warm. Mr. Felix Mann dragged the doctor back so that his boots wouldn't burn, settled the logs, and taking the last remaining lantern, walked out into the night after carefully closing the door behind him. He had an appointment to keep at Aquila. It was a little matter of business strictly his own.

Meanwhile, the wagon had arrived at the foot of the natural dam below the meadow at Coiner's Retreat. The night was impenetrably dark there, the woods deathly silent, except for the lonely voice of the waterfall and a few owls. With the snow sifting down through the pine trees, the wagon stood at the foot of the steep ascent, a kind of huge shadow of itself, leaking a little light here and there. There was something secret and funereal about its vast bulk that seemed to need only a few plumes appropriately to crown it. By this and other things--they had passed several dead men lower down in the village--the negro Culpepper, who "belonged" to Mr. Felix Mann, was reduced to a gibbering caricature of himself. The deadly night-shade aspect of the world all about was more than he could abide. Dr. Wilson, indeed, had finally been forced to waken Mrs. Crittendon, to take the reins himself and drive up the stream under her calm direction. Nothing could have formed a more violent contrast than the quiet voice of Mrs. Crittendon directing the expert driving of Dr. Wilson against the hysterical background of the prayers, moans, and chatterings of Culpepper, who had now crawled under the big box seat.

With the cessation of motion Margaret awoke. She felt her mother's arms about her. By the roar of the falls she knew where they were. She put her arms about her mother's neck and whispered, "We're coming home again, aren't we?" In the darkness, with the frantic negro flopping about under their feet like a caged animal, mother and daughter exchanged a comforting embrace.

Dr. Wilson went ahead a little with the lantern to look at the ascent. It was manifestly impossible with only two mules. The colonel would have to be carried over the dam. Culpepper, he knew, would be useless. Margaret understood that immediately, and saying she would bring Mr. Kiskadden back to help, flitted up into the woods over the crest before anyone could stop her.

Dr. Wilson and Mrs. Crittendon were left alone with one lantern, Culpepper, and the owls. The doctor put his hand in the wagon and felt under the blanket again to see if the colonel were still alive. He was. Under the seat Culpepper began to conduct a prayer meeting all of his own that soon attained the frenzy of a revival. The roar of the waterfall continued, the snow drifted past the narrow circle of the lantern, and the negro appeared to be going insane. Dr. Wilson's patience came to an end.

He reached under the seat, and hauling him out by the throat, pointed a pistol between his eyes.

"Stop that," said the doctor, "or you're a dead nigger."

Culpepper gurgled, then he relaxed onto his knees. The doctor put the pistol back in his pocket again.

"Get up on the seat and take the lines," said Dr. Wilson, "and don't let me hear another word out of you, you rascal. You sit there and watch those mules! Keep your eyes right between their ears."

"Yas, sah, yas, massah," muttered the negro, climbing into the wagon. Dr. Wilson gave him a drink.

"I kin see dem mules' ears, tank Gode!" said Culpepper after a while. "Dere's two white ones."

"Watch 'em!" replied the doctor.

"I tank you, massah doctah," murmured Culpepper after a while, "yoh sho' fotched me outa hell."

The doctor and Mrs. Crittendon looked at each other and smiled. He leaned wearily against the wagon wheel, shielding the guttering lantern in a fold of his coat. Some heavy gusts of wind tore through the trees above them.

"We shall be happy to have you be with us at Coiner's Retreat, doctor," said Mrs. Crittendon, "for as long as you can stay. My husband is a major on General Early's staff. He was born here in the Valley. You will be among friends."

"Your kindness leaves no doubt that you are a true Virginian, madam," replied the doctor, who guessed that Mrs. Crittendon was a little worried as to what he might think of her for giving shelter to a Yankee. "And I shall do what I can for the gentleman in the wagon. In one way at least I think he is a fortunate man. I hear great things of him."

For the first time the full implications of bringing Colonel Franklin back with her came home to Mrs. Crittendon. Dr. Holtzmaier had simply put him into the wagon with the remark that he would certainly die if he had to send him by mule ambulance to Harpers Ferry. "Mit you I gif him der one last chanst." It had seemed inevitable. It had never occurred to Dr. Holtzmaier's simple heart that Mrs. Crittendon might demur. As a matter of fact she had not. To her, too, it had seemed inevitable. She had been terribly tired--much too exhausted to think it over, anyway. Dr. Holtzmaier had loaded the wagon. Among other things in it, bound for Coiner's Retreat, was Colonel Nathaniel Franklin. And yet now that she fell to thinking it over, "What else could I have done?" she asked herself. "I couldn't just say, 'Well, let him die,' could I?"

Would he die? she wondered. She trembled at the thought.

"Do you think--do you think Colonel Franklin will live?" she asked the doctor.

"It will be impossible to answer for some little time yet," replied Dr. Wilson. "But no, I shall be honest with you!" he exclaimed suddenly. "I don't think so. He has lost too much blood."

Mrs. Crittendon gasped. Her emotion was curiously mixed. It was a poignant and unbearable fear and grief at the thought of losing the colonel. It was a feeling of shocked surprise and indignant annoyance at herself for feeling so.

"You knew him before the war?" Dr. Wilson was saying.

"Oh, yes," she answered almost automatically. It seemed the only way out. Immediately, she was thankful Margaret had not been there to hear her.

A lantern danced on the top of the dam. Dr. Wilson signalled. Old man Kiskadden began to descend the slope. The colonel's litter came sliding slowly out of the wagon. Dr. Wilson and Mr. Kiskadden staggered up the slope with the colonel. Mrs. Crittendon went before with the light. It was all inevitable, she kept saying to herself. "Inevitable!"

Presently they were carrying him upstairs into Paul's room and making him comfortable. She brought one of her husband's night-shirts. She had kept them in case . . . Dr. Wilson took off the colonel's coat. A packet dropped out. He looked at it.

"It is addressed to you," he said simply, handing it up to her. And Mrs. Crittendon stood looking down at her husband's familiar handwriting.

She was not clairvoyant, yet she knew as certainly as though she had opened it what was in that packet. Her eyes wandered to the face of the man on the bed.

Suddenly she was down on her knees beside him, shaking him by the shoulder. "Why didn't you give it to me," she said vehemently, "why didn't you?"

"Madam," said Dr. Wilson, shocked and surprised, "can't you see? Don't you know the colonel is unconscious?"

Elizabeth Crittendon looked at the pale, calm face before her. The shadows seemed to be gathering about the mouth. She did not repeat her useless inquiry. She didn't have to. As she looked at Colonel Franklin she knew why he had not given her the packet. She could guess it all, and she put her head down on the bed and sobbed.

Dr. Wilson did not make the mistake of trying to comfort her. Ever since 1861 he had seen women weeping like that. The colonel, he felt sure, was going to die--was dying. He sat down on a chair and wrapped a blanket about himself. His head slumped down on his breast. Eventually he was dimly aware that Mrs. Crittendon had left the room. He wished to God she would get him something warm to drink. He dozed.

Mrs. Crittendon stopped at the children's door and heard them breathing quietly. The sound brought a certain sense of comfort to her heart. She went half-way down the stairs and listened. The house was very quiet below.

"Margaret," said she, "Margaret?"

There was no answer.

"Meg, Meg," she called miserably. "Come to me. Your father's dead."

But there was still no answer. Someone had started the clock again. She could hear it ticking. The fire crackled. She came down the rest of the way into the big living-room. Both fires were burning brightly. Mr. Kiskadden must have replenished them only a few minutes before. But the room was deserted. Margaret, Flossie, and old man Kiskadden had gone and taken the lanterns. There was nothing but firelight in the room.

Ordinarily she would have wondered; have worried about them. All that she knew now was that Margaret had not come to her. That she was left alone. She sat down before the fire and picked open the packet with dull fingers. A ring and a brooch fell out.

She leaned forward towards the fire and by its wavering light read the last message from her husband, written months before. There were no tears in her eyes. It was beyond that. If the writing wavered it was due to the flickering light of the flames. She sat back now dry-eyed, her hands folded in her lap.

The letter seemed to have come to her out of the remote past. Try as she would, she could not recapture it. It seemed to be someone else's past. Someone who was very dear to her and who had told her the story. It was a happy story. Happy, except that all through it now rang like the recurring lines of a dirge in a ballad three words of desolation--"Douglas is dead."

Stop! Stop! Why did they keep on saying that to her?

She put her hands over her ears and realized then that she had been saying it aloud to herself.

And now she knew, understood quietly and with all its implications--"Douglas is dead."

The clock ticked on.

For the first time in her life Elizabeth Crittendon sat looking grim. She was not thinking about the past now. She was trying to rearrange the future, and in certain ways she could see it clearly enough. She was entirely alone. She was glad now that Margaret had not been there to comfort her or to be comforted. She had been left alone, and from that nadir she could go on again through anything. When a woman once realizes that she can be left alone and still go on living, that life lies in herself and not elsewhere, something either heroic or diabolic is set free. Mrs. Crittendon was not diabolic. Time was still going on and she with it.

She was reminded of that forcibly when, with an indescribable harshness, the clock on the mantel above her whirred and struck three. Undoubtedly someone had deliberately set it going once more. It would never pause eternally on two again. That had been, after all--an accident.

Oh, dear accident! How she had tried to project that into eternity. And now she was back in time again, alone.

She picked up the letter in her lap, the ring and brooch, and wrapped them in it. Then she rose, opened the front of the clock and dropped them into its deep base. She stood there for a moment watching the hand move slowly in the firelight to the sound of the slow, somnolent ticking. Then she turned rapidly. Someone was coming downstairs.

It was Dr. Wilson.

"Madam," said he, still formally and with an Old World courtesy, although his face was grey with fatigue. "It is the custom in Charleston to have a little coffee and grits in the morning. Now I wonder . . ."

But he didn't have to wonder long.

"You are an *angel,*" said he a little later over his third steaming cup-- "and what coffee!"

"Made by a *woman,*" said Mrs. Crittendon without looking up.

The doctor paused and looked at her keenly. He accepted the correction by turning the cup about in his hands. "But it has a divine flavour," he murmured. His wise, old, grey eyes looked at her with great kindliness over the brim and they smiled at each other.

"You have had much to bear," said he. "Women do. Come, help me with the gentleman upstairs! He is in a bad way. And I am only a surgeon, you know. The time for the knife is over. It is warm blankets, whisky, and hot water--coffee--things like that that can help."

They fought together for Colonel Franklin's life all morning. They tried to keep him warm and his heart going.

He came out of the opiate afterwhile. "Oh, Elizabeth," he said, "did they send me to you?" She nodded and gave him her hand.

When the late winter dawn came through the snow-spattered panes, he was still breathing and his pulse was steadier. Dr. Wilson leaned his arm on the bed and wilted down into an exhausted sleep. Outside, it was still snowing and the girls and Mr. Kiskadden had not come back yet. Mrs. Crittendon would ordinarily have been frantic about them. But she could feel no more. She got the children their breakfast and managed to smile at them.

"Where's Meg and Flossie, Aunt Libby?" demanded little Mary.

"I know. She's gone to find her beau," sang out Timmy.

> "Far, far away
> Far, far way."

The two children chanted it together and giggled. It was a joke they had made up all by themselves to tease Margaret.

"Come here, Mary," said Mrs. Crittendon. She laid her hand on the little girl's hair. "Look at me," said she. "Now remember, Mary, *never sing that again!*"

Years afterwards Mary remembered the look in her aunt Elizabeth's eyes that morning. In it was concentrated all the agony of the years of war. She dropped her head into her aunt's lap and let her stroke her curls.

Timmy kept charging about the room on a stick, shouting "boom, boom, boom." There was no stopping him. It would take another war to do that.

II

Snow is probably the best thing that can take place on a battle-field, especially if the battle has been fought only the day before. It covers the remnants of human frailty and havoc with a pall of impersonal innocence, it restores a decent surface to the appearance of things. Probably, if there had not been snow the night after the action at Aquila, Margaret and Flossie would not have been able to search the battle-field in the darkness of the early morning hours with only a single lantern between them. The snow, of course, did not make their task any easier. It did not help them to find what they were looking for--quite the contrary. It did, however, make it just bearable--and just bearably tellable.

All during the fiery hours of the ordeal at the dressing station the evening before, young Margaret had kept looking for one face, and one only, among the wounded. She had asked Colonel Franklin if he had seen Farfar, but he had only been able to shake his head. Strangers she could not bring herself to ask, but that Farfar had not returned to camp among the survivors she had been able definitely to ascertain. When she returned to Coiner's Retreat ahead of her mother, to get the help of old Mr. Kiskadden in carrying the colonel up to the cabin, she had found Flossie obsessed with the idea that Paul had been in the battle too.

Flossie could give no reason for the conviction--did not attempt to do so. She and her father had stayed all afternoon with the children, listening to the manifold reverberations of the fight on the fields below, and with every discharge of artillery the fear that Paul might be there had been re-aroused and magnified until she knew that he *was* there, must be there, and that every gun was killing him.

Indeed, the rolling echoes of slaughter continuing for hours had brought everybody at Coiner's Retreat into an unbearable state of tension. It had been all the worse that they could not see, did not know surely, what was going on. At the height of the action the face of the hill just opposite the cabin had seemed to be speaking to them with an articulate thunder. Peal after appeal. It was that, in particular, which had finally caused Mrs. Crittendon to begin tearing up the available material in the house for bandages and to start with Margaret for the hospital in the Valley. Flossie had necessarily been left behind to look after the children--and to worry about Paul.

Mr. Kiskadden had taken as much looking after as the children. As the rumbling echoes went on hour after hour, as little Timmy continued to rush about shouting "boom, boom," while Flossie sat on the steps weeping and little Mary hugged her doll--it had gradually dawned upon the half-eclipsed consciousness of the once-fiery old preacher what was going on. His face flushed, the sweat streamed down under his wide, flopping collar, some hidden spring of energy seemed released in him, and he rose to the occasion by striding up and down the plank porch of the cabin, uttering exhortations, lamentations, and wild prayers for the dying in exalted and at times prophetic imagery.

To Flossie this sudden metamorphosis of her father was uncanny and terrifying. He looked to her once more like the father she remembered, ten years before, the man whose word was moral law, whose eloquence had stirred and seared the people of the mountains. It made her feel like a little girl again, and it made it difficult if not impossible for her to command him.

So Flossie clutched Mary, while Mary clutched her doll; and they both sat listening to the thunderous echoes of the fighting and the no less rolling periods of the now rejuvenated Reverend James Kiskadden. That, and her fears for Paul, had horribly whiled away the afternoon of the battle for Flossie.

Towards nightfall, when the children went to bed, she had finally prevailed upon her father to come inside and sup. He had become quiet then. He no longer strode up and down. But his eyes still smouldered, and there was a strange flush of youth in his cheeks.

Neither he nor Flossie could sleep. The silence now seemed tremendous. Making a sheer guess at the time, the old man started the clock ticking again. When Margaret had finally rushed in during the small hours of the morning, demanding help to carry Colonel Franklin, Mr. Kiskadden had sprung from his chair and run clear to the dam. Nor did that exhaust him. It was not until they entered the house that Dr. Wilson realized that his fellow litter-bearer was not exactly an agile young man.

Meanwhile, Flossie had poured out her fears for Paul on the breast of Margaret. Margaret stood listening as though to the words of her own heart, looking out into the shadows over the bowed head of Flossie, with wide and fearful eyes.

"And my Willum's there too," she finally whispered.

Flossie looked up at her.

"Oh, Meg," she said, "God forgive me, I'd forgot about him!"

The two girls kissed each other.

"Listen!" whispered Margaret. "We'll go look for them both tonight. Can you do that, Flossie--durst you?"

"Let's never come back till we find them," wept Flossie. "I don't care if I don't."

"Nor I," said Margaret, and they clung close again. "Now run up to the chest and get some heavy shawls. It's going to snow hard."

And so it had all been arranged before Mrs. Crittendon and Dr. Wilson got back with the colonel. While they were upstairs settling him in Paul's bedroom, Margaret and Flossie slipped out.

"Come on, pa, you're needed," said Flossie, tossing a shawl over her head, "and bring that light."

Margaret did not realize that Mr. Kiskadden was with them till they reached the top of the dam. At first she had intended to saddle Midge and her mother's horse but she had given that up in favour of the wagon that she knew must still be waiting. And Mr. Kiskadden might as well come, she supposed. He could return in the wagon after they reached Aquila.

Culpepper was so glad to see them--and the lantern--that it took both Mr. Kiskadden and Margaret to get the mules and the wagon turned about. Margaret drove. She used the whip on the mules, and threatened to use it on Culpepper. The animals felt they were returning, and waded down the pebbly bed of the icy stream without balking. But it would have made little difference if they had. For in the mind of Margaret burned a fixed resolve that was not to be balked.

Snug in the lee of a battered brick wall in the ruined village of Aquila sat Mr. Felix Mann and a pale, sharp-nosed gentleman all wrapped up in a buttonless Amishman's overcoat. A log fire was smouldering in the featureless fireplace of what had once been a living-room but was now a ruinous hole gaping open to the sky, except for a convenient portion of collapsed roof propped upon fire-scarred timbers. This, at the moment, kept the snow off.

That the nature of their business was private rather than official was best indicated by the fact that Mr. Mann had been at some pains to nail an old blanket across a small window that looked down the Valley towards the camp. On the opposite side the wall had partly collapsed, and a considerable extent of wild landscape towards the Blue Ridge was to be seen.

"I'm damn' glad the wind ain't whistlin' down from the mountings," remarked the gentleman in the long overcoat, as he heaved part of an old stump on the fire. "It's cold, and it's gettin' colder. Tomorrow you'll see it'll come on to snow in arnest. I'd like to git back to the Ferry before the roads are closed."

"You can go back tomorrow with one of the sick convoys," growled Mr. Mann.

The log, full of resin, unexpectedly blazed up into a sudden glare.

"Lord!" said Mr. Mann, "what did you do that fer, Perkins? You'll have all the provosts for miles around comin' down on us. And I'll bet you there's still plenty of rebels lurkin' about in the woods."

"I'll bet you a dead man's watch there hain't," countered Mr. Perkins, jingling in the pockets of his overcoat. "And I ought to know. Ain't I been all over this part of the field in the last two hours? Thar's no rebels, 'cause none of the dead hev been stripped. Our cavalry's made a clean sweep this time. Any skulkers left in the woods is layin' low, and there ain't no provosts either. I tell you the hull of Sheridan's army is on the move south. You'll see! They're leavin' the Valley. It'll be lonely as one shoe. I'll bet you some of them pore fellers out there don't get buried till spring."

"All the same, Perkins," said Mr. Mann, "don't throw no more wood on that fire."

"All right, all right," replied the gentleman in the overcoat. "But how about gettin' down to business?"

"Well, how many have you got?" demanded Mr. Mann.

"Not so many," said Mr. Perkins, beginning to whine a little. "This wasn't a big fight, you know. I think it's about eighteen or twenty. I lost count, you see. It ain't any fun crawlin' around out there in the dark and feelin' 'em. Whew!" A look of stark horror came into his eyes. "God, you oughta seen . . ."

"Never mind, never mind. Shell out!" exclaimed

Mr. Mann impatiently. "What d'ya expect? This is a war, ain't it?"

At which Mr. Perkins dived down into the deep pockets of his Amish overcoat and began to dribble gold watches, seals, and chains onto the old hearth before the fire. There were twenty-one.

"Not so bad," said Mr. Mann. He began to divide the watches before him into two piles after examining them carefully. "That's Sixth Pennsylvania time," said he. "I can get more returnin' 'em for reward to the boys' people than they're worth. Them are mine," he added, "and I'll give you half of what I get from the rest when I sell 'em. Ain't that our agreement?"

"Yep," said Mr. Perkins, who had learned from previous transactions that Mr. Mann kept his word. "What do you think they'll bring?"

"Dunno," mused Mr. Mann; "depends what gold's fetchin'. It's goin' up I think, and I'm goin' to wait till spring. I'm goin' to set right through the winter at the old canteen down there. It's comfortable, I've got grub, and now that the old regiment's bruk by this fight my business is gone. So I'll wait. Do you know," said he half to himself, as he tied up the watches in two large bandannas, "I kind o' think the war's gettin' near its end. I'm jes' goin' to wait and set pretty. There's bound to be good pickin' down South afterwards, if you're smart."

"May be," admitted Mr. Perkins with a certain note of admiration for Mr. Mann's perspicacity. "D'ya know I hadn't thought of that."

"Well, think it over," yawned Mr. Mann. "You might want to stay with me here till we can talk it out and fix somethin' up."

"No, no, I think I'll be gettin' back to Madam O'Riley and the girls for a while," replied Mr. Perkins. "She won't be able to follow the flag no more if the army's movin'. She'll go back to the Ferry. There's bound to be a big base and a garrison there for some time, convalescents, and the railroad. I ain't doin' so bad either," he chuckled. "What with my share of the take, an' little favours from the girls o' various kinds, an' friskin' the pore dead boys, I'm gettin' ahead. If it will only last a little longer . . ." He paused thoughtfully to transfer a large bead of moisture from the end of his nose to his sleeve.

"Gawd-amighty!" said he. "What's that?"

Cloaked in the ambiguous glow cast by a smoky lantern and seeming to glide along through the slowly-drifting snowflakes, for their feet were in the shadows, two hooded figures were passing rapidly along the road to the battlefield. As they passed they turned white faces towards the glow of the fire.

A spasm of terror contorted Mr. Perkins's face.

The figures rapidly disappeared into the snowstorm. Only the faint glow of the lantern could be traced. Sometimes it stopped. Then it would go on.

"Bhoy!" whispered Mr. Perkins, drawing his breath. "Who's them?"

Mr. Mann did not reply at once. He also had experienced some of the effects of a reminder of a world that does not deal in watches.

"It must be some of the Crittendon women," he said at last. "Now what the devil can they be doing out there?"

The two men stood staring over the top of the broken wall with some apprehension and great curiosity at the peregrinations of the mysterious lantern. They kept getting up and going over to the wall to watch it. It was scarcely more than a silver glow at times through the falling snowflakes, at others it came nearer. It went all along the border of the woods and once came so near again that they caught a distant glimpse of the two girls. An hour or so passed.

"I know," said Mr. Perkins finally, "they're lookin' for somethin'!"

"God, you're a bright light!" said Mr. Mann witheringly. "Look out, or you'll bring the morning up before it's time."

Not far away the lantern had come to a long stop. Then one of the girls emerged out of the snowy darkness, running.

"Is that you, Miss Crittendon?" called Mr. Mann.

"Oh!" said Margaret, stopping in her tracks. "Yes. Who's there?"

"She's lost her shawl," said Mr. Perkins. "Pore gal!"

"Bury them watches under that pile of leaves in the corner," growled Mr. Mann. "She's comin' over here!"

The girl emerged into the firelight. She had recognized the voice of Mr. Mann. Her face was that of a beautiful dead woman with wide-open and staring violet eyes. The snowflakes lay in little feathery pockets over her golden hair.

The two men involuntarily drew back from her.

"Don't go away," she said. "There is one thing to do yet."

"What's that, miss?" said Felix Mann contritely.

"Bury them," whispered Margaret. "Please."

There are some things so supercharged with emotion that the thin wires of human speech burn out if they attempt to convey it. Only once or twice in their lives did either Margaret or Flossie speak of their experience that night on the deserted battlefield, and only long afterwards. What they did say was brief enough, but it was remembered and set down. This remains:

The snow was what made it possible. When they walked out of the ruined village onto the fields where the fight had taken place, all that they saw was an endless extent of meadows with snow feathering down through the half-luminous winter darkness against the loom of dark woods beyond.

After they had advanced some distance beyond the village they began to come across little mounds covered by about an inch of snow. It was a fine, dry blanket.

That was where the snow made it difficult. It was necessary to brush it aside to see who and what these mounds were.

Flossie held the lantern and Margaret used the fringe of her shawl as a kind of gentle broom. She had to take it off to do that. The cold numbed her. "I was glad of that."

The girls, it appears, said almost nothing to each other the entire time they were out there. "We spoke once or twice."

Once--when Flossie saw frozen, bearded faces peering up into the lanternlight the first time Margaret used the shawl--"Meg, I'm going to faint," she said then.

"If you do," said Margaret, "I'll take the light and leave you alone."

The greater fear prevailed. They stood for a moment.

"Can you go on now?" asked Margaret.

"Go on," said Flossie. She followed.

They must have gone pretty far, for they found what was left of Black Girl, and Margaret recognized it. Colonel Franklin had been struck off his horse near the border of the southern woods by shrapnel.

At that point they turned back again. They did not dare hunt in the thickets. That was hopeless.

In the open Margaret used the shawl--how many times.

They finally had to give up. That was the worst. The lantern had become badly smoked and it was necessary to hold it close. Flossie was getting too cold, or too weak, to do that. So they gave up. Flossie moaned a little.

They started back towards the glow of the fire against the brick wall at Aquila. That had all along given them direction. It was the same fire to which Paul had been trying to crawl hours before.

Not far from the village they came across a lonely mound in the snow. They must have passed within fifty feet of it going out.

"Try it," said Flossie. It was Margaret who was failing now. Her shawl flapped.

The faces of the boys looked up out of a pile of leaves. There was snow on Farfar's lips. Someone had disturbed them to take their shoes. Paul was smiling a little.

Margaret instinctively spread her shawl over the bare feet. The two girls clung together. Flossie wrapped her shawl about Margaret. They swayed a little and trembled. Margaret shivered as though in an ague.

"Listen, Meg darling," said Flossie after a little, "you're cold as they are. Run now and get help. I'll stay here. I don't care no more. Only leave me the light!"

Margaret gave a dry sob and ran. . . .

Flossie put the light down and covered Paul with her shawl. She arranged Margaret's over Farfar. This simple act gave her unspeakable comfort. She sat by the failing lantern, waiting. "Paul," she whispered after a little. "Paul! Speak to me. I've got your baby here, and I ain't told nobody but you yet."

By this time Margaret was sitting by the fire with Mr. Mann and Mr. Perkins. Mr. Mann gave her a drink of whisky and wrapped her in the blanket he took from the window. She could feel nothing at all. Mr. Mann went to fetch Mr. Kiskadden from down the road to go with him to get Flossie. Neither Culpepper nor Mr. Perkins would go out on the field again.

Margaret sat on in a half-frozen dream. Somewhere, away off, she heard her father's watch chiming--a little golden bell ringing out of the past. How curious! It was the watch Major Crittendon had given to his nephew Paul when he was sixteen. She remembered that now. What a foul trick of memory! Maybe she was going crazy hearing a bell like that. How proud Paul had been. O God! if she could only forget everything. There had been snow in Willum's mouth. And now she was always going to be alone.

"Lost your feller?" asked Mr. Perkins, eyeing her and the pile of leaves in the corner narrowly.

"Oh, yes!" said Margaret, and wept bitterly. Mr. Mann brought Flossie to sit beside her. It was a comfort having her near again. Mr. Mann took everything in charge now. Margaret's eyes closed. The fire roared and crackled up the old chimney as Mr. Perkins piled on log after log. Morning began to show grey over the mountains.

When Felix Mann wakened the girls it was full daylight but snowing steadily. There was no wind. The snow simply drifted down in large feathery flakes a little faster, it seemed, every minute. Dr. Holtzmaier had come up from the canteen where Mr. Mann had sent Culpepper for tools. There were a couple of heavy army coats for the girls.

"Quick, blease," said the doctor, "or mit dis schnow you vill nefer get home. All iss ready."

He led them through the village and down the road towards the ford over Aquila Creek. The wagon loomed up suddenly through the snow. There was a group of men standing near by, but out in the field. They were gathered about something. The snow had changed the aspect of everything. Here and there a misty fan of light shot clean across the Valley high over their heads. The sun was just looking over the Blue Ridge. Below, you could see only for a short distance now. Margaret and Flossie seemed to be moving through a weird world, lost somewhere. For an instant as the sun topped the mountains the woods all along the crests burst into a flaming line of glory--and faded out.

They climbed an old wall and joined the group in the field. Mr. Mann, Mr. Perkins, old man Kiskadden, Culpepper, and three soldiers from the camp stood by. There was a mound of fresh earth and two figures beside it wrapped in the girls' shawls. Flossie screamed. The men moved uneasily. Margaret put her arm about Flossie to steady her.

"I'd forgot," sobbed Flossie. "I wasn't really awake yet."

"All ready," said Surgeon Holtzmaier.

There was sudden activity. Margaret thought she couldn't weep any more, but she could. Mr. Kiskadden stood on the top of the mound. It was coming on to snow much faster. She could just see him dimly, high up there in the storm. Suddenly there was silence again and then only Mr. Kiskadden's voice.

"O God of life and death, God of hosts and of the everlasting cradle, the battle has rolled down the valley. Let it pass. Stay the hand of them that trample and slay. Let those that brought confusion upon the land answer to thee. Look down from thy mercy seat upon these thy stricken servants. Overshadow them tenderly like a great tree in the spring. Remember forever thy children we leave here in the ground. Catch them up on the wings of the morning across the river of darkness. Number them among thy saints, and lost babes. Cause thy daughters here sweetly to remember and mercifully to forget. Send comfort unto thy troubled servants, O God. Have mercy upon us, and bring peace back into the land."

The old man's hat blew off and he pursued it feebly, his beard and white hair streaming in the wind. There was the sound of stones, shovelling, and Margaret and Flossie were being led to the wagon.

The snow closed around them like folds of a great curtain, swirling nearer and nearer; white, hurtling through grey darkness out of nowhere. It threatened to enter the mind.

III

Despite the fact that he was not above making a ghastly little profit upon the sale of watches whose owners had no more use for time, Felix Mann was humanly inconsistent in having a warm heart for his friends. He was one of those shady little men capable of giving away with one hand generously what he craftily extracted from strangers with the other. But not all his profits were illicit. Under compulsion he could work honestly and hard. Colonel Franklin had forced him to do that, genially, and for that reason Mr. Mann was devoted to Colonel Franklin. Dr. Holtzmaier felt the same about the colonel, but for different and better reasons. Both the surgeon and the sutler found themselves, however, in the same predicament in that their world, the regiment by which they had lived, moved, and found self-importance, was no more.

All that remained of the 6th Pennsylvania Cavalry was the deserted camp torn at by the winter winds, a few desperately wounded men, who could not be moved, and a small hospital detail left to look after them. The rest, the fit, as well as the convalescents and the evacuable wounded, had been taken away to hospitals or incorporated in other commands.

Surgeon Holtzmaier was the commanding officer of the remnant. He set up his "headquarters" in Mr. Mann's ex-canteen, where he proceeded to make himself disconsolately cosy in a semi-permanent, military style. He guessed he was "in for it" for the winter, and he was. But even he, although he was no optimist, had no idea just what and how much he was "in for."

It was the snow.

It was snow by accretion. Storms hovered inveterately over the upper part of the Valley along the Blue Ridge. It snowed every day, day after day. And generally it snowed hard.

It had been deep enough the morning they had finally taken the girls back to Coiner's Retreat. Mr. Mann had put four mules to the wagon and had dragged it, loaded as it was, by main force over the dam. He had left the wagon, Culpepper, and one team in the barn near the cabin and brought two mules back. Culpepper was to rest overnight and drive back next day. That was early in December. Culpepper did not appear again in the Valley until the following March. The stream, the only road into the place, froze that evening, and it snowed all night. Dr. Holtzmaier forced his way through for a visit the following afternoon--and just managed to get back.

That was the last of any visits between Coiner's Retreat and the Valley for many a day.

A week later even the main road north to Luray was definitely closed. Dr. Holtzmaier and Felix Mann began to reckon up their rations. They still had twenty-eight men to subsist and there would be no drawing of further supplies from passing wagon trains for a long time. The roads along the South Fork were--There no longer were any roads. Coiner's Retreat, only three miles away, might as well have been a lamasery in Tibet.

"Vot ve need is vlying machines," said Dr. Holtzmaier wryly, wondering what would happen to the colonel.

Afterwards--when she was able to think over that winter fully, calmly, and in long perspective--Elizabeth Crittendon could only marvel that those left at Coiner's Retreat had survived. There was one good thing about it, however; all other difficulties that she was afterwards called upon to surmount seemed comparatively trivial.

For the "campaign" of the winter of 1864-1865 at Coiner's Retreat was like the campaign of the same winter about Richmond. It was a siege gallantly maintained against overwhelming odds, with no reserves and diminishing supplies. It seemed hopeless and it ended in a surrender. But it was almost entirely a woman's war--the woman's side of the war--almost, but not quite.

For there was Dr. Huger Wilson. He had, of course, intended to work his way south again as soon as possible to rejoin the Confederate forces. Surgeons, he knew, were as much in demand and almost as scarce as gold about Richmond just then. He would have gone if he could. But nature would not let him. He could no more get out of Coiner's Retreat than Dr. Holtzmaier could get in. At the end of a week or so of much snowing the mountain roads and passes no longer existed. He would simply have to wait for a thaw and then try it. And that was what he did.

But that was not all that he did. He devoted himself first to caring for Colonel Franklin. He dressed the terrible wound daily. And he brought to this task not only great surgical skill tempered by a lifetime of experience, but a precious quality of indomitable gaiety which he had inherited from Huguenot ancestors. It helped sustain not the colonel alone, but everybody else in the household. That, and Elizabeth Crittendon's invincible English cheerfulness, her mental inability to admit defeat, provided the morale for the defence of the mountain cabin.

And beleaguered they certainly were, threatened constantly by overwhelming assault from without, and like all besieged garrisons, weakened by illness and the troubles of themselves within. Elizabeth Crittendon began the defence by doing quietly every day what had to be done then, and no more. That was in December. Eventually she wore time and the elements out, and only surrendered to march out with the honours of war in the early spring.

The chief enemy was darkness closely allied with cold. The main defence against both was the great fires at either end of the big log room downstairs. There were only a few candles left and a pitifully small supply of oil for the lamps and lanterns. This was kept for emergencies and for the sick-room. They lit one lamp at dinner; a candle went upstairs with the children when they went to bed.

The snow drifted into the little mountain valley until it was above the tops of the low windows. Culpepper and old man Kiskadden dug "canals" through it to let in the grey, white light through the old bottle-glass panes. Culpepper smashed one of them, of course, and the snow started to drift in, a sifting, impalpable powder that covered the floor near by with a fine spray when it melted. And through the smashed pane came also the howls of the wolfish wind.

It was really nothing. Dr. Wilson stopped the smashed window with a piece of board and carpet--but the outside seemed almost to have succeeded in forcing an entrance. At the sight of the snow cascading inward Margaret had become hysterical.

That snow! It was more than she could bear. Her mother quieted her. It was the only time save one when the name of Farfar escaped Margaret's lips, the only time any of the women broke down.

There was also a path dug from the front door to the barn and another to the woodshed. In some places the banks were higher than the heads of those who passed between them. These paths, the barn and sheds, and the house itself were all that remained of free space to move in for the little garrison of four men, three women, and two children at Coiner's Retreat. Later on, Culpepper shovelled a way to the tree house where the children would go to play for hours, wrapped in the blanket suits the girls made for them. That was a blessed relief for everybody. From their sheltered crow's-nest in the old oak Mary and Timmy could look out over the changed and snowbound mountains. Sometimes they saw the sun. No one in the house did.

Culpepper and Mr. Kiskadden tended the fires. A thousand times Elizabeth Crittendon had cause to be thankful that the long Indian summer had been used by Mr. Kiskadden and Farfar to cut wood. Nevertheless, they husbanded it. Dr. Wilson doled out the supplies from the room in the garret. It was close going, for they must be made to last. No one knew how long the snow would remain. Culpepper was an extra and unexpected mouth and his two mules ate sadly into the supply of provender. But supplies there were, and, as it proved, enough to go round. Colonel Franklin's forethought had saved not only the lives of the family at the cabin, but his own as well.

It was not long before Elizabeth Crittendon realized that Flossie was going to have a child. She forever won Flossie's abiding trust and lasting affection by simply accepting the fact and talking it over with the girl as a bright hope and comfort for the future. Flossie was inarticulate and had an innate sense of bodily guilt. That, if it had not been relieved by a sensible and comforting attitude towards her condition and circumstances, might well have made her melancholy during the dark days in the dark old cabin of that dark and dangerous winter.

But now there was hope, something to comfort her for the loss of Paul, an event and a future to look forward to. And best of all, understanding and affection.

Margaret also was told the "secret." And that for weeks was the only thing that made her smile. Indeed, the three women drew a deep draught of hope and comfort out of the well of nature in the thought of the coming of Flossie's baby. They chattered about it together. They laid plans. They made and remade what little clothes they could. To them it was the pledge and hope that the world was going on; that not even the war could stop it. Seated by the fire, smoking his pipe, and watching the three women gathered eagerly about some little problem of sewing, or knitting an infant's garment, Dr. Wilson smiled and marvelled.

Margaret's immediate salvation was much more difficult. Elizabeth Crittendon knew her own daughter well enough to understand that she would hide her horror and her loss so deep within that it would be almost impossible to reach it. To try to discuss it with her, even to mention it, would simply be to cause her to retire further into her reserve--perhaps beyond hope.

And yet it was for Margaret, for her "gay and happy Margaret," for her bonny and charming girl, that Elizabeth Crittendon cared more than for anything else. It was her daughter's future that gave any importance to the times to come for Elizabeth Crittendon, since for many months now she had entirely forgotten herself. The temptation to weaken by dreaming of the old days; to live over in reverie the rich and delightful years of her youth with her husband; to grieve for him, she had put aside. Not sternly but strongly, in order to plan for and to be able to help others--and Margaret.

And now Margaret seemed to have been removed from her to a place beyond. She seemed, despite her bodily presence and her unfaltering devotion and sweetness of manner, to be rapt into another world. How to reach her there--how to reach her!

That was what kept Elizabeth Crittendon awake at night as she sat by Colonel Franklin's bed during those first weeks when the colonel wandered between life and death, and frequently audibly in the paths of his past.

Most of the time Colonel Franklin seemed to know that she was sitting there. He would open his eyes wide, as though he were still in darkness. Then he would find her again and smile. Often they would talk together in low tones while the household slept, taking mutual comfort against the silence in the sound of their voices. Then the colonel would slip off into some corner of his mind, from sheer weakness unable to hold to the present. At first he would be telling her something about the past--then he would be alone in it again, still talking, until his voice died away in a low, busy murmur into sleep.

It was a help to him, she found, to let him do this. It reassured him, and gradually she discovered it reassured her that she, too, was not alone. As he grew stronger, they would discuss some of the immediate problems of the besieged household, or of the future, until those talks with the colonel at night became a rod and a staff to Elizabeth Crittendon.

Nothing had daunted him either. Neither pain nor the loss of his leg and the regiment. He seemed to regard them as equally calamitous--but not as defeat.

"With one leg and one mind one can still march far," he insisted, with a little whimsical touch that more than anything else always brought a lump into her throat as she watched him.

Thus she came to know him, to understand him as she could never have come to understand him otherwise, for the veils had been drawn aside, at times unconsciously, and she saw Nathaniel Franklin's inner world by occasional glimpses, and in it Nathaniel Franklin as he saw himself.

It was he who finally helped most with Margaret. Margaret and Dr. Wilson used also to go and sit with him as he lay those long winter months in Paul's lonely little room. Flossie could not bear to go there. But one day as Elizabeth Crittendon was going upstairs she heard the colonel telling Margaret how he had found Farfar. It was, she understood immediately, like a father talking to his child. She heard Margaret's choked voice saying something, and then she fled downstairs again and left them alone.

That evening Margaret came into her mother's room and put her head in her lap and cried a little. "Mummy," said she, "I've been a selfish old thing. But I heard something today that's brought me back again. I've just been away awhile. All of you were like dreams to me, even the house. Do you know I got lost in it the other day, just trying to come downstairs. It was because of something I was thinking about that I was trying to hide from and trying to keep, too, forever; to keep always real because I loved it--and it's gone away. But I know I can't lose it. I know it's with me like you still have father--and you go on in the world where we are now. I reckon we've just been left alone here together, mummy. I wish you'd give me something to do."

So Elizabeth Crittendon took her child, who was no longer a little girl, to her heart and comforted her. And they were no more alone. Margaret was not lost in the shadows, and her mother gave her something to do. She gave her the exacting task of mothering little Mary and Timmy Crittendon.

"My!" said little Mary to her aunt a bit later.

"My goodness, Meg's just the bestest girl. She's just a honey to me and Tim, and we don't never tease her at all. I 'membered about that song."

"Good," said Elizabeth Crittendon, "good!"--and her eyes filled with tears of grateful relief and sad memory.

It was wonderful, indeed, how the glow of cheer and warmth from the courageous hearts of those who were imprisoned in the cabin irradiated the whole of Coiner's Retreat like the fires that also burned constantly that winter in the old log room. Actually that room was walled in by drear silence and deathly cold. It was lit at best by a grey twilight reluctantly penetrating from the short winter day without. But that was not the light they lived by.

Everything went on in that room. The day began by Culpepper and Mr. Kiskadden dragging in logs and building up the fires from the embers of the back logs that glowed from the night before. Then the women came down and got the morning meal. Culpepper helped. He loved to fry bacon, and he waited faithfully and cheerfully upon them all, redolent of Africa and the stable. There were two tables set close to the fires that would be leaping by this time and sending flashes of light and shadow through the room, for it was still dark outside. Margaret and Flossie sat at one table with the children; Mrs. Crittendon and the doctor and Mr. Kiskadden at the other.

It was Dr. Wilson who brought gaiety into the room. He began at breakfast to beat back the darkness. He always had a surprise in his pockets for the children, a surprise in his mind for Mrs. Crittendon, a mock formality with "Miss Meg and Miss Flossie" that both impressed and amused them. Everybody had to tell him their dreams, even Culpepper, and Culpepper had to report what the mules had said last night about everybody.

This stunt proved to be enormously popular as it always included the latest news of Coiner's Retreat with personals about everybody from the critical standpoint of Culpepper's mules. Even old man Kiskadden had to laugh. And as the mornings passed one after the other, the epic grew--till even Dr. Wilson, who was secretly alarmed at the duration of the siege, smiled inwardly, having produced that result upon himself as well as others.

Then the work of the day would really begin. Snow would be melted and the water warmed for the children's bath before the fire. All the water had to be secured that way. And while Margaret was bathing the children, and Mrs. Crittendon and Flossie were busy about the household tasks, Dr. Wilson would slip upstairs to dress the colonel's wound during a fiery little half-hour of agony for himself and the colonel. Yet because of it the wound grew better. And the day came when the doctor announced, as proudly as the bearer of the first tidings of victory that the wound was beginning to heal.

The essential thing was that everybody was kept busy. Elizabeth Crittendon saw to it. The difficulties of existing, of keeping everything clean, of living in a half-light by day and dim firelight by night, of washing clothes and getting meals and living socially all in one room, albeit a large one--the very difficulties of it were made the means by which the dreary inertia, the terrible monotony of the cabin locked in by silent walls of snow in the impenetrable mountain valley were overcome.

Everyone had a task and a routine. When one lacked, it was invented. The evenings were the greatest triumphs of all. They were often positively merry, and nothing better, under the circumstances, could have been achieved. Time passed slowly and yet, as they looked back upon it, because it was a timeless kind of existence, swiftly in retrospect.

Yet there were hours and moments when Elizabeth Crittendon despaired, when even her old Church of England prayer-book brought her no comfort when she lit her candle for a few minutes to read it before going to sleep. The faces about her, she knew, were growing whiter and more haggard. The eternal twilight of the house seemed to be pressing in on her. And it was her light that they all depended upon. If that should flicker, if that should go out!

She knew she ought not to, but since she dared not mention this growing conviction of eventual failure to Margaret, she burst out with it to the colonel one evening as she was sitting in his room. He had said something to her, diffidently, about her plans for after the war.

"Sometimes," she said, "I think we shall never get away, that we are just caught here until the end--forever!"

"All of us have felt that way at times," he replied after a while. "But I am sure now that we shall be released. By the way my old leg out on the field there keeps cutting up, I think we shall have a thaw soon." He laughed. "No, nothing lasts forever. Perhaps I wish that this would last longer than you desire it to do. I am very happy here--now. Did you know that?"

"I am glad of it," she said, and could go no further.

"There is something I have long wanted to tell you," he said again after a pause. "I had a letter I carried for months that I was supposed to have given you. It was lost, I think, from my coat-pocket the day of the battle. But you should know, even if . . ."

"I know," she said. "I found it."

There was a long silence between them. He looked worn and pale, she thought; very helpless and lonely.

"And you have forgiven me?" he asked at last in an incredulous whisper.

"Oh, long ago," she said. "Long ago!" She kept repeating it. She felt the blood burning in her cheeks, and leaned forward, burying her face in the counterpane to hide it from him.

He laid his hand on her head gently, and stroked her hair. It was as golden as a young girl's in the candlelight.

"There is peace between us, isn't there, Elizabeth?" he asked.

"Yes," she whispered. "Oh, yes! We must find peace somewhere, somehow, at last.

"Think of what has happened to us!" she cried out, throwing her head back vehemently and looking at him. "Think of it!" Her comb dropped out but she paid no attention to that. "How can people like you and me keep on hating and killing each other? What is it about the States? Our lives have been ruined by them. I am going to take Margaret back to England.

There will be peace there--for her." She looked at him with a far-away look.

"And for you?" he asked.

She shook her head. Her hair came tumbling down about her face and over her shoulders. He wound his fingers in it.

"Don't go," said he, and began to plead with her. "There is another way out. There is only one way for us two to end this war. My dear, I have a proposal to make." The trace of a whimsical smile began shaping his lips. "It is a political proposition, of course. Do you want to hear it?"

"Yes," she murmured, "but please let go of my hair." Instead, he drew her face closer to him.

"Let us," said he, "form an indestructible union!"

His great longing and strong tenderness lay like a refuge before her.

"I know it is asking you to surrender," he murmured, "but will you, Elizabeth? I don't care to live if you go away. I couldn't help loving you."

Her head sank to his breast.

"I know," she whispered, and his arms stole about her.

Her hair streamed across his breast. His white, emaciated hand kept stroking it in the candlelight. The war had left little flesh on the hand, but there might have been less. Its touch could still bring comfort. Both of them knew they had found the only peace there was.

It was about three o'clock that morning when Margaret came to her mother's room. She was surprised to see a chink of light under her door. She tapped but scarcely paused before entering. Her mother was in her nightgown, but she was standing before the old cracked mirror with a shawl thrown over her shoulders in a fashionable manner. She was trying where best to pin a brooch. Her hair was done in a way Margaret had never seen her use before, and she had evidently been trying things on, for her trunk was open and there were hats and dresses on the bed.

"Mother!" gasped Margaret.

Elizabeth Crittendon was not a bit dismayed. She finished pinning the brooch to her satisfaction, threw the fringe of her best shawl over her arm, and turned to her daughter, tilting her head to one side a little. "How do I look?" she demanded.

"Beautiful," said Margaret. "Why, you look just like a bride!" And there was the note of a surprised admiration in her voice.

"Oh, I *love* you for that," cried her mother. "Meg, you always were a darling!"

"Why don't you wear your hair that way often?" asked Margaret.

"I'm going to from now on!" was the reply. "But why are you here this time of night? Not bad dreams again, I hope."

"No, no, good news! Listen, can't you hear it?" said Margaret.

They stood listening intently for a moment. One of the mules stamped out in the stable, the clock went on ticking downstairs. Then they both heard it distinctly. It was the sound of water running somewhere, and a steady drip from the eaves.

"It's thawing," said Margaret, throwing her arms about her mother wildly. "Soon it will be spring again! And we'll be free!"

"Yes," said Elizabeth Crittendon, "we're going to come through. I believe that now." She gave her daughter a kiss on the forehead. "Sit down a minute, Meg, there's something I must tell you. Up until now I've been afraid to let you know."

"If its about father, mummy, I've known about it long before you did. I overheard Dr. Holtzmaier say something to the colonel months ago that I wasn't supposed to hear, and I put two and two together. I've been afraid to say anything to you. You had so much to bear, and we both loved him so. Now I can't cry about him any more."

"It's beyond tears for me, Meg. I called for you the night I first learned of it, but you had gone. You know where."

"Yes," agreed Margaret. "It is underneath our tears. It's sorrow. He will always be there--like, like . . ." Her mother nodded, speechless. "Like Willum!" she said, and put her head in her mother's lap. "I'm sorry I wasn't in the house when you needed me," she whispered.

"Meg," said her mother, "I want to tell you something else. I might as well tell you now, and I think you will understand." She paused for a moment. "I . . . I . . ."

"Oh, don't, mother. I know why you looked so young again to-night," replied Margaret, raising her face to peer into her mother's. "Oh, yes, it's best for all of us, and if it makes you beautiful again it must be right! But just promise me one thing--you won't let it make any difference between us. Will you?"

"Never," said Elizabeth Crittendon. "It couldn't. I had you for love, Margaret. Do you see?"

Margaret patted her hand, and they sat listening to the drip from the roof. It was much faster now.

"I'd like to sleep with you tonight, mummy, just like I did when I was a little girl," said Margaret. "I was afraid. That's why I came to your room."

Mrs. Crittendon quietly took the hats and dresses off the bed and put them away while Margaret snuggled under the bed-clothes. She blew out the candle.

"Darling," said she in the darkness, "I hope sometime you'll have a daughter like you. It's the best thing I know."

"Maybe," said Margaret, and caught her breath a little. "He might be a boy though, you know."

Elizabeth Crittendon took her "little girl" in her arms again.

The colonel's lost leg proved to be a good weather prophet. Thaw it did. The rains descended and the winds blew. The snow slid off the roof with the noise of an avalanche, until Coiner's Retreat was filled with the roar of the falls and a tumult of waters as Aquila Creek rushed over the dam. Everyone in the household went about listening to noise again with the delight of a deaf man who has been cured. The deep winter silence, they all realized now, had been appalling. And there was sunlight again. One day the windows were pried open and the doors stood ajar. They walked out and shouted, and laughed at how pale and groggy they were. Spring came marching up the Valley of the Shenandoah. The snow and rains went down the river in a great flood.

There was only one unhappiness about the welcome thaw. The roads would soon be open and Dr. Wilson was going to go. Just where, he was not sure, for he had had no news from the outside world for over three months.

"Perhaps the war is over," said Margaret hopefully. They were sitting on the front steps in the sunlight.

"If it is," said the doctor, "it will mean that the North has won."

"I hope it's over," reiterated Margaret. "The South will still be there. I can still smell it in the breeze. They can't ever do without it. It's where spring comes from." She leaned back with her hands behind her head, feeling the sun. A thrush sang far off.

She felt the weight of a head in her lap and someone was saying, "It *is* spring again. Don't you feel it?"

Someone came and kissed her lightly on the forehead. She knew it was Dr. Wilson, though. She opened her eyes afterwhile to look at him, but he had gone . . .

Mrs. Crittendon "lent" him her horse.

"You will probably never see her again," Dr. Wilson had said. "And I know you love her."

"It is all I have left to give now," she said. "But it's not a sacrifice. I couldn't keep her. She reminds me of too many things. I give her to you. I hope she carries you home."

Dr. Wilson kissed her hand. That was quite natural with him.

"Lady," he said, still holding her fingers, "I wish you much happiness to come. You are a great woman. Now, I can't say good-bye to our mutual enemy the colonel"--he smiled--"but I wish you would give him my love. And I wish you would kiss all the others for me, except your daughter. You see, I kissed her myself. Good-bye."

He waved his hat and rode off down the valley--just as they had all gone, one after the other.

"Oh," said she to the colonel a little later, "my God, Nat, I hope that's the last man I ever have to see ride off to war. My God, I *hope* it!"

"It won't be long now," he replied.

"No?" she said. "Well, they can't ever take you again, anyway."

"No, that's over," he answered a little sadly, and felt for her hand.

"I know another thing," he said after a bit. "Look!" He jogged her elbow.

She looked up. A robin was perching on the window-sill. In the spring sunlight they both sat in Paul's bare little room smiling at each other. The robin had flown in and gone fluttering downstairs.

"Amen," said the colonel.

Who so happy as Surgeon Holtzmaier when he rode into Coiner's Retreat one fine spring morning and found his friend Colonel Franklin sitting on the porch smoking a pipe and enjoying the sunlight.

"Py Gott!" said he. "Ve get you out of dis yet."

He and Felix Mann began laying their heads together. They were still living in the little stone farmhouse by the river where they had passed the winter on short rations, a pack of cards, and plenty of fire-wood.

The government seemed to have forgotten them. Most of the wounded had died. The camp was a sodden wreck. Mr. Mann drove with Culpepper to Winchester where he got two wagonloads of rations by pure finesse.

Corps headquarters had moved months before, and nobody at the now nearly deserted quartermaster's bureau there had ever heard of the 6th Pennsylvania Cavalry or of survivors at Aquila.

Dr. Holtzmaier determined to move the remnant of his convalescents to Harpers Ferry on his own responsibility. "Vot if I do cotch hell," he said.

"Ve all cotch dot anyvay." The men cheered this truism feebly. Those that were able came up to see the colonel to say good-bye to him.

Everybody gathered on the porch. A corporal with one arm tried to make a speech and bawled like a baby. The colonel shook hands. He was unable to say anything at all. All the hands felt thin, but they were still warm.

"It was just dreadful," cried Margaret afterwards. "They acted as if they were sorry they had to go home. Maybe it's because they live at the North," she said, patting the colonel's hand and looking at her mother. "I reckon we'll like it though," she added breathlessly, and burst into tears.

"Margaret," cried her mother, "please!"

"I couldn't help it, could I, colonel?" she said a little later, bending over him.

"I don't see how you could, my dear," said he.

"There!" said Margaret.

She and Flossie rode down to "Whitesides" next day and transferred some English violets that grew in the garden to a spot near Aquila in the corner of an old stone wall. They took all day to it and said nothing.

Flossie and Mr. Kiskadden were going to stay on at Coiner's Retreat. Later in the summer they were to move down to "Whitesides" to try to farm the place. One of the outbuildings was still habitable. The baby was to be born there. It was Mrs. Crittendon's plan to turn the place over to Flossie and her child if they could make a go of it. What would become of the Crittendon properties in Virginia was now problematical. They would have to wait. Meanwhile, Mrs. Flossie Crittendon would have to do the best she could. She understood that. Neither she nor her father would go North, and there was no other alternative but the farm. Flossie was satisfied. Sometimes Margaret envied her.

Margaret could scarcely bear the thought of leaving Virginia. She longed to tell her mother about the old garden at "Whitesides." How it was coming into bloom again. How there was no house there. Only a black hole in the ground. But she knew her mother couldn't bear to hear about it, and forebore.

She wondered what Pennsylvania would be like. She rode Midge all over the old hills and roads she loved, filling her eyes and heart with the spring glories of the Blue Ridge and the song of the Shenandoah. She might not see them again for a long time. Perhaps never. That thought made her cry out. She rode restlessly for two weeks, "everywhere"--everywhere but into the Giant's Nursery.

And during those two weeks she never met anyone. The Valley was one vast solitude. That solitude sank into her soul; it and the lonely voice of the rolling Shenandoah remained in the young girl's heart as the song of her country's grief. And it remained there for ever.

The colonel had not been able to travel when Dr. Holtzmaier left. It had been arranged that Felix Mann was to come back for him. Meanwhile, Margaret rode the hills and Elizabeth Crittendon prepared to depart-- bravely. She was ready now. The colonel sat in the sun and grew stronger. Flossie's child began to leap in the womb. Generals Grant and Lee met in a farmhouse near Appomattox to talk things over. At Aquila, and other places, the foxes and beetles were busy in and about shallow graves. Those who still lay in the open looking up at heaven no longer had an astonished expression. The eternal sardonic grin was showing through.

At half past five o'clock of a magnificent spring evening Felix Mann drove into Coiner's Retreat with a buckboard, a big wagon, Culpepper, and a team of mules. Next morning they left early for Harpers Ferry. Like Lot's wife, Elizabeth Crittendon looked back only once.

Southward, two mighty ranges of the Appalachians shouldered their way into the blue distance like tremendous caravans marching across eternity. Between those parallel ridges the Valley of the Shenandoah lay as serene and beautiful as the interior of the Isles of Aves.

CHAPTER XIX

A CHEQUE FOR EXPENDED OATS

The bands played "There'll be a hot time in the old town tonight," and there was, for all Philadelphia turned out to see the boys off for the Spanish War. A good time was had by almost everybody. It was just another circus parade.

Colonel Franklin had come clear in from Kennett Square to see the militia start south. It wasn't quite so much fun for him. For an old man nearly eighty, with only one leg, it was an exhausting performance. He stood on the steps of the Union League Club, propped on his crutch, with other G.A.R. veterans. Their white vests and beards, their blue coats, brass buttons, and old-fashioned caps with a wreath on them made a splash of dark colour under the glare of the arc lights and red fire. Red fire, flags, and bunting were everywhere. The crowd surged and howled. The troops came marching down Broad Street towards the station and passed under a big sign hung on a net which said, "Remember the Maine."

It was the militia again, of course. They called it the National Guard now. There wasn't any regular army to speak of, and the volunteers would have to come later. Somebody had to die first. The crowd was wise to that joke, too. Most of the bands, which were made up of foreigners, came in for a good deal of "joshing." The City Troop, the Fourth Pennsylvania Regiment, the State Fencibles and other units marched past. A colonel mounted on a black horse at the head of one regiment rode well. He saluted the veterans while his horse danced. They shouted at him. Some of them had been drinking. The Union League had been hospitable. "Hi, Santa Claus," said a passing corporal to an old veteran with a white beard and red nose. The ranks laughed. They were glad they had been called out. It was an adventure. They were tired of their jobs. They were the centre of attention. No one threw anything at them or shouted "scabs." It was their occasion. "Hi, Santa Claus!"

Colonel Franklin leaned on his crutch sick in mind, body, and soul.

After the troops came the politicians, big, heavy-jowled, gloomy fellows in high hats and frock coats, looking each other brazenly in the face from the opposite seats of double victorias. They followed the flag. A roar of welcome greeted them from the Union League. Veterans and citizens knew who was worth cheering--who supported pensions and high tariffs. The funeral procession of the Republic moved on.

It seemed impossible to Colonel Franklin that he should have lived to see it. All in one lifetime, Buchanan's prophecy was coming true. After the politicians came a Kilty band. One Ian Macintosh, the bass drummer, climbed over his drum, entering along with the bagpipes into the full cattle-raiding spirit of his ancestors and the present remarkable occasion. That the raid was now on a planetary scale and comprehended in its sweep both the Atlantic and Pacific oceans made no difference to him. He was a good American Scot and the band was only hired. After the fake Highland band trundled a float with a model of the battleship *Maine* sinking. Then came a long procession of the delivery wagons of leading Philadelphia merchants, who thus delicately took the opportunity to testify to their patriotism and to tout their goods at the same time. These marched past, like Christian soldiers, "as to war." Indeed, some of the oldest names in the city thus pressed towards the front, but turned aside at Walnut Street. The wagons were followed by a band playing hymns and a large delegation of the W.C.T.U. marching robustly and inveterately. Opposition was their meat, and the crowd fed it to them raw. After them came their sons in the various boys' brigades and cadet corps from the Sunday-schools of the city. Some young lady Christian Endeavourers in American flags brought up the rear. The very last unit of the van consisted of an old open wagon with semi-oval wheels in which upon kitchen chairs sat six ladies in six pairs of spectacles and concave profiles. "Lady Readers of Emerson," proclaimed the homemade sign over their heads. One of them waved a Cuban flag, probably a form of compensation.

"There'll be a hot time in the old town tonight," sang the band at the station, where the "boys" were getting into the box-cars provided for them by the railroad.

The colonel hobbled down the club steps as soon as the crowd would let him and across the street to the old Bellevue Hotel, where he was going to spend the night. He sat down in the lobby. Culpepper, who was a white-haired old darky now, hovered over him solicitously.

"I'll get a good rest and we'll drive back to Kennett Square tomorrow," said the colonel. "Go out and enjoy yourself."

"Ah doan jes' like de way yo looks," said Culpepper.

"Now get on with you," said the colonel. "I'll be all right in the morning."

"Maybe I'd better drive you aroun' to Miss Margaret's," said Culpepper. "It's jes' a few blocks."

"Miss Margaret" was now Mrs. Moltan. Some years after the war she had married the young man who had once called the colonel a Copperhead. He had returned a captain, minus an arm.

"Now don't you dare say anything to Mrs. Moltan, Pepper!" said the colonel anxiously. "You know I don't want her to know we've come up to Philadelphia at all. She'd worry about me, and Mr. Moltan would raise Ned about our staying at the hotel. Help me into the elevator. Be ready to leave tomorrow morning at ten."

For a moment people paused in the Bellevue lobby as the old coloured man helped the colonel, whose crutch clattered on the tiles, into the elevator.

"There's a picture for you," said the night clerk to the cashier.

"Shut up," said the cashier, "I'm counting money."

A very large man in a supremely gorgeous uniform joined the colonel in the elevator. "I'm Major Jepson, on the governor's staff," said he, inflating the gingerbread on his chest slightly, "editor of the--" he named a famous old Pennsylvania newspaper.

"Colonel Franklin of the Sixth Pennsylvania Cavalry," said the colonel, straightening a little as he said it.

They shook hands. The elevator started up.

"Fine send-off they gave the boys to-night," insisted the editor-major.

"Wonderful," said the colonel. "Politics, business, reform, and idealism saw them as far as the depot." His eyes twinkled.

"Eh?" said Mr. Jepson. "Oh, say, now I'll use that! What did you say your name was?" He pulled out a pencil.

"Fifth floor," sang out the elevator man.

The colonel stumped out, and down the hall to his room. He leaned on his crutch and tried to open the door. He cussed a little. One leg wasn't so good to stand on in the dark. Whatever you said they used it in their own way, for themselves, he thought. They always had. "Free Texas," "On to Mexico City," he could even remember that. It wasn't so long ago. And as for "Free the Slaves" and "On to Richmond," that was only yesterday. Now it was "Free Cuba," "Remember the Maine." Well, he wouldn't be around probably to find out what those words would turn into. He felt relieved at the thought and sank back on the bed. Maybe the joke this time would be unusually cosmic? The troop trains pulling out whistled in the yards, and whistled. He remembered that night at "Wheatland." The two nights seemed to be the same; merged into sleep.

"Ah sware ah doan believe yo took off yoh cloes las' night, sah," said Culpepper in a shocked tone as he helped the colonel into the carriage next morning.

"Never mind that," said the colonel. "You drive straight home. I am pretty tired."

It was some days before the colonel felt well enough to sit out on the porch again at Kennett Square. It was a hot day and he still felt drowsy. The recent trip to the city had excited him; worn him out more than he cared to admit. He read the paper and nodded. Culpepper was singing one of those endless darky tunes somewhere in the back of the house.

"If the *Maine* had been sunk in an English harbour, we'd never have gone to war with England, my dear," said the colonel aloud.

There was no reply.

It was hard for him to get used to that. His wife's chair was still where it had always been on the porch. He could almost see her sitting there in the shadow of the vines. Sometimes he forgot. It was the silence that reminded him. He laid his newspaper down uncomfortably and let his glance wander out into the deep shadows under the maples on the lawn. They were huge trees now. His father and James Buchanan had planted them. He could remember the very day. It was about the first thing he could remember. That morning would be almost seventy-five years ago, come next autumn. Strange how readily the past came back to him lately! As long as Elizabeth had lived life had kept renewing itself. The past seemed to be catching up with him now, he reflected.

Down the drive the postman was coming through the gate.

There wasn't much mail that morning. A note from Margaret, saying she and the family would be down on the late afternoon train to stay over the week-end. Would he send Culpepper to the station for them at Media? They would so like the drive over. He called Culpepper and told him. The old place seemed brighter already at the prospect of Margaret and her family's being there. They were all that remained.

Mary Crittendon had married a missionary and gone to live in Hawaii. She had two daughters he had never seen. They never came home. Young Timmy had died years ago of pneumonia. He was scarcely a dream now. Flossie and her boy Paul had found hard going in Virginia. Now that Elizabeth was gone they wrote seldom.

He turned to his mail again. Letters seemed to come out of the past.

There was one from the Treasury Department. He opened it with some curiosity. It wasn't his pension. It was out of schedule. A cheque for $18.37 fluttered out. He smoothed it out over his knee and put on his spectacles, to read the communication that accompanied it.

Somebody, it seemed, had once introduced a bill into the House of Representatives, which the Senate had passed and the President signed. That was years ago. It was to reimburse certain officers above the rank of captain, etc. etc. etc., "for oats consumed by the horse or horses of the said officers during the late Rebellion." The colonel dimly remembered once having signed a claim form about oats. About a generation ago. And now the eternal wheels of the government had got around to it--just about in time. He was a pretty old man now. He picked up his cheque for expended oats with some emotion. Actually it was for the oats consumed by Black Girl in the Valley of the Shenandoah in the autumn of 1864.

The colonel folded the cheque and put it in his pocket. He hadn't thought of Black Girl for years. And those days in the Valley! The mountains! What a magnificent autumn it had been. The very thought of it made him feel young again. Really it was only a few years ago. In retrospect time passed like a flash. He put his hands behind his head and lay back, looking up at the sunlight caught in the vine leaves of the Dutchman's pipe. Presently he closed his eyes. He scarcely heard Culpepper driving off to get the Moltans at Media. Only the sound of the horses' hoofs was taken into his reverie.

Yesterday, yesterday, yesterday came the far strokes of the hoofbeats. And then suddenly the colonel was young again.

He could feel the cool breeze from the mountains in his face, and a horse under him. He was strong and he had two legs. Lord, it was good to be able to grip with his knees and feel the horse fill her lungs! They were riding down a pass with mountain walls towering on either side, all scarlet and yellow, a molten sunshine glimmering through the leaves. Somebody was trying to catch up with him. He could hear the sound of hoofs on stones. It must be Farfar. How worried he was about that boy. He must be riding on that sepulchral mule. Why, it would be a skeleton now! He touched Black Girl and they whirled down the pass, out into a valley on dusty roads. Voices called from the farmhouses that he passed galloping, and galloping faster and faster. Yesterday, yesterday yesterday, and then as Black Girl seemed to gather speed and soar, tomorrow, and tomorrow and tomorrow.

It was Philadelphia again. A long street that diminished into the perspective, but always in the same town. Behind him were small houses and open fields, but as he galloped on, the hard stones of a city pavement rang under the iron hoofs of his horse, the houses grew closer and larger, the crowds denser and hurrying swifter and more swiftly.

At last in the distance rose a Babylon of towers that scraped the sky. The whole horizon ahead was ranged with them. Everyone was hurrying in that direction. He tried to call out to them to ask where they were going. But no one would pause to reply. They seemed not to see or to hear him. They hurried on, out of the past into the future, intent upon a vast business that time had laid upon them; getting away from something, pursuing some dream that lay before. Something that was everybody's concern, that none could avoid, a universal must that made a union and an entity, a unity and a nation out of all of them that passed along that avenue of the city; out of those that he had left toiling behind and those that now rushed headlong past him to go on eagerly before.

He could see for leagues now before and behind. He could see where the avenue emerged from the dark forest of the past and where it led far beyond the towers over hills splashed with storm and sunshine into the forest again. How unfamiliar, how terrifying the long road was getting to be. How impossible it was that he should travel any more of the way. He asked to be spared. "Let me be troubled no more." And it was then that he felt a hand laid upon his bridle rein and he and the horse were turned aside.

It was into a familiar place. It was the same blind archway where he had turned aside once long ago to watch a certain regiment march past in the year 1864.

But for him the years were numbered no longer. Where he sat in the dim archway on the shadowy horse the past, present, and future were blending into one. There were no more years.

He was a young man with his hand on his father's shoulder watching the regiments moving out of the city to invade Mexico, and he was Nathaniel Franklin, colonel-at-war, sitting astride his war-horse, and calling out to young Moltan and the regiment that had disappeared into the dust with the newspapers blowing along behind it, and he was the old veteran leaning upon a crutch, seeing the boys off to Cuba. He was that one man.

And to that one man, whose single lifetime had passed every instant in the present, all the regiments that had passed before him were caught up into that present and were as one regiment. The drums of a century sounded as a single drumming in his ears. And the drums rolling in the future thundered the same step as those that had gone before. The step of men marching, marching one foot after the other under the compulsion of time, out of the past into the future, fighting their battles along the way.

"Now we are engaged in a great war to . . ." And he understood that "now" for the first time. There was no end to it. It renewed itself for each man and so for all men in the ever-living present. It was an eternal now that belonged to the ages. It meant "forever."

How long, O Lord, how long . . .

The present was all, was more than a man could bear.

How long . . .?

Someone was beating his hand against the colonel's left knee. A vanished hand against a vanished knee. The colonel looked down from his horse as though into the present again.

CHARLES R. ROSS
ATTORNEY-AT-LAW

"Let me tell you, sir, my opinion in regard to the matter," said the preposterous little man. He removed his hat with the selfsame forensic flourish that he had employed in Philadelphia in 1864.

"'An indestructible union of indestructible states' . . . You will remember the source of the opinion, of course. The mouth that gave birth to the nation.

"'. . . destined to endure for ages to come.'"

Mr. Ross bowed, clapped his hat on his head and seemed to diminish rather than to ascend up the stairs into his office. There was a wreath round the name plate on the door.

Why, it's a dream, thought the colonel. The man's dead.

"Nevertheless," said the ghost of the law, looking down at the military, "these sentiments are now irrevocable." He disappeared into the darkness beyond. The door closed behind him slowly.

Through a space in the vine leaves the afternoon sun pierced suddenly and lingered for a few minutes on the face of the dreamer. The light seemed to have undone the work of time. For the face had suddenly grown much younger, calmer. Those who had known him in the Valley in the time of the great war would have known him again.

Nathaniel Franklin, colonel-at-peace.